T0046341

"Plunket purrs right through this looney L.A. landscape ... *My Search for Warren Harding* is as easy-gliding as a fresh lathering of Coppertone. Besides, a smile is just the thing you need to go with that great tan."

—Peter C. Wyckoff, *The Houston Post*

"A classic picaresque novel in the tradition of Cervantes."

—Michael Leone, *Los Angeles Review of Books*

"In *My Search for Warren Harding* Plunket pushes his mouthpieces to such lofty and comical levels of unreliability that he may have succeeded in creating a whole new rhetorical category—the Oblivious Narrator."

—James Marcus, *The Village Voice*

"*My Search for Warren Harding* is the funniest thing to come along since Jeeves and Blandings Castle."

—Ronald Reed, *Fort Worth Star-Telegram*

"Robert Plunket's version of *The Aspern Papers* is a paranoiac Californian farce ... a marvelous literary homage."

—Roger Lewis, *The New Statesman*

"The most outrageously cynical and funny book to have appeared in a long time."

—Antony Beevor, *Literary Review*

"A very funny novel."

—*The New Yorker*

MY SEARCH FOR WARREN HARDING

Robert Plunket

MY SEARCH FOR
WARREN HARDING

foreword by Danzy Senna

A NEW DIRECTIONS PAPERBOOK

Grateful acknowledgment is made to the following for permission
to reprint from previously published material:

"That's Entertainment": words by Howard Dietz, music by Arthur Schwartz.
Copyright © 1952 (Renewed) Chappell & Co., Inc. All rights reserved.
Used by permission of Alfred Music

"Sometimes When We Touch": words by Dan Hill, music by Barry Mann.
Copyright © 1977 Anthem Entertainment A, Sony Music Publishing (US) LLC and
Mann & Weil Songs, Inc. Copyright renewed. All rights for Sony Music Publishing (US)
LLC and Mann & Weil Songs, Inc. administered by Sony Music Publishing (US) LLC,
424 Church Street, Suite 1200, Nashville, TN 37219. All rights reserved.
Used by permission. Reprinted by permission of Hal Leonard LLC

Manufactured in the United States of America
First published as a New Directions Paperbook (NDP1568) in 2023
Design by Erik Rieselbach

Library of Congress Cataloging-in-Publication Data
Names: Plunket, Robert, author.
Title: My search for Warren Harding / Robert Plunket.
Description: First edition. | New York, NY : New Directions Books, [2023]
Identifiers: LCCN 2023001715 | ISBN 9780811234696 (paperback) |
ISBN 9780811234702 (ebook)
Subjects: LCSH: Harding, Warren G. (Warren Gamaliel), 1865–1923—Fiction. |
Presidents—United States—Fiction. | Authors—Fiction. |
LCGFT: Biographical fiction. | Political fiction. | Novels.
Classification: LCC PS3566.L798 M9 2023 | DDC 813/.54—dc23/eng/20230123
LC record available at https://lccn.loc.gov/2023001715

2 4 6 8 10 9 7 5 3

New Directions Books are published for James Laughlin
by New Directions Publishing Corporation
80 Eighth Avenue, New York 10011

Contents

Foreword

I might not have read a single truly funny novel that year if my friend hadn't stopped by my Los Angeles porch one afternoon carrying an out-of-print copy of Robert Plunket's comic masterpiece, *My Search for Warren Harding*.

We were in the worst of days—the depths of the prevaccine pandemic—and our world was on fire, both literally and figuratively. The copy of the novel that my friend, the writer Victoria Patterson, handed over to me looked the way we all felt in those days: yellowing, battered, dusty from too long in storage. Tory bellowed through the muffled fabric of her N95 mask that it was one of her favorite novels—and really fucking funny.

I needed funny. I opened the book a few weeks later—and despite my allergic reaction to the mold in the edition, kept reading for the next 256 pages. When I was done, I sat in a kind of silent, focused delight. I held in my hands one of the best and most invigorating books I'd read in years, and certainly the funniest—and yet, how was it out of print? Why had I never heard of this novel before now? (Later I learned Tory had actually written an excellent piece about it for *Tin House* magazine in 2015.) Why had it disappeared so fully from the literary landscape? And what did that say about this literary landscape if it could bury a book like this? Most intriguingly: Who was Robert Plunket?

The jacket bio for Plunket's second (and, so far, last) novel, *Love Junkie*, published in 1992 and also out of print, reads:

> Robert Plunket's first novel, *My Search for Warren Harding*, immediately established him as one of America's most promising novelists.

Unfortunately, the promise soon faded, and he now lives in a trailer in Sarasota, Florida, where he ekes out an existence as a gossip columnist, covering everything from gala charity balls to KKK meetings. He has also served on the boards of Sarasota AIDS Support and the Humane Society of Sarasota County, and is currently running for election to the Mosquito Control Board, District 6.

So much for literary fame. There are few interviews with Plunket online. In one of the only I could find—from a 2015 issue of the *Los Angeles Review of Books*—he explains the inspiration for the novel to writer Michael Leone.

"Obviously, it's based on *The Aspern Papers*," Plunket explains.

The Aspern Papers, the celebrated novella published by Henry James in 1888, is set in nineteenth-century Venice, where an unnamed narrator seduces a young woman in order to gain access to her spinster aunt's trove of letters by her dead poet-lover.

Plunket goes on to say, "It was always one of my favorites, but most important, it spoke to me in a special way. I couldn't figure out why until one day it hit me. The guy's gay! Of course! Now the book made perfect sense. His relationships with all the women characters were those of a gay man. Now, not an openly gay man or even a consciously gay man. But a man who was just not heterosexual at his core. I don't think Henry James realized what he had done, or how well he had done it, which made my discovery even more exciting."

In Plunket's retelling of *The Aspern Papers*, he sets his novel in late-1970s Los Angeles. The author himself was just emerging from that era when he wrote the book. It came out in 1983: the same year the national craze for Cabbage Patch dolls reached its pinnacle. The same year Vanessa Williams was crowned, then promptly de-crowned, the first Black Miss America. The same year Ronald Reagan decreed Martin Luther King Jr.'s birthday a national holiday and Michael Jackson moonwalked for the first time on national television. The same year Reverend Jerry Falwell described AIDS as "the gay plague."

Plunket's book, in other words, emerged out of a culture of contradictions—a world of both hedging progress and conservative backlash, an America of trash and spectacle. Which is maybe why the novel, forty years later, feels so startlingly contemporary.

Sensitivity readers, be warned: the protagonist of this novel, Elliot Weiner, is cruel, racist, fat-phobic, homophobic, and deeply, deeply petty. In the novel's opening, we find Weiner standing on a scenic lookout in Los Angeles with his friend Eve Biersdorf staring through binoculars at a large dilapidated home in the distance. Whatever mischief he's up to, he says, "it was Mrs. Biersdorf's—Eve's—idea." Weiner, we soon learn, is an East Coast snob and middling historian who has come from New York to Los Angeles on a fellowship. He holds himself in high regard, but the more he brags about his academic career—"Suffice it to say that I teach at both Mercy College and the New School, and I feel that speaks for itself"—the more we sense desperation: "Some unfortunate comments have gotten back to me about my 'qualifications.'" Elliot Weiner is hoping to retrieve some lost love letters between President Harding, traditionally ranked as the worst of presidents, and his secret mistress, Rebekah Kinney, the owner of the house in the view of their binoculars. Wiener soon learns that Kinney is alive, but now a cranky octogenarian who wears rhinestone sunglasses and spends her days in her crumbling mansion shouting at her Mexican servant from a squeaky wheelchair. Weiner believes the old woman still possesses the love letters and other Harding-related papers, and is hiding her treasure somewhere in her crumbling mansion. And he will do anything to get his mitts on those letters, even "rape and pillage," as he's hoping a discovery like this can propel him to academic stardom.

As the novel unfolds, Weiner's madcap effort to obtain these papers propels the absurd, picaresque plot. He rents out Kinney's dilapidated pool house and cozies up to her granddaughter, a naive young woman named Jonica whose ample flesh disgusts him. But he's willing to grit his teeth and seduce her if it means getting to her grandmother's historical smut.

Weiner is cruel about Jonica from the beginning, describing her as "a fat girl … wearing baggy green paratrooper pants … and a lot of plastic bracelets that added to the general din … She talked like a real California girl, no inflection, lots of r's." Yes, Elliot is unabashedly cruel about innocent Jonica. He despises all she represents—fatness, the West Coast, gullibility—and yet he begins to court the poor woman, to prey on her neediness. Soon they are romantically and sexually involved—and he's that much closer to his prize and becoming a renowned historian.

The bare bones of a plot is so often just a skeleton for a novelist to hang up their observations. The more streamlined and beautifully elegant a plot—and in the case of *My Search for Warren Harding*, the plot simply boils down to a single character pursuing a single, tantalizing object—the more tangents the author can take. And the tangents in this book are everything. They let us see Plunket—with his lacerating wit—send up the entire culture of Los Angeles at the turn of the 1980s.

But with every parody of the culture around him, Weiner is the biggest joke of all. One of Elliot and Jonica's early dates is to an avant-garde feminist performance—an audience-participation play called *All My Sisters Slept in Dirt—A Choral Poem*, performed at the LA Women's Theatre. "Then, all of a sudden, people started streaming in like they'd just got off a bus. Women mostly, with severe haircuts and aviator glasses. It hit me what an important moment in feminist fashion it was when Gloria Steinem dropped by her optician's and said, 'I'll take *those*.'" The satire in this scene is perfect, and we are aware, too, that Elliot, who has a sweating problem and is wearing a silk shirt, has strapped cut-up Pampers diapers to his underarms to absorb the sweat. Whenever the author is vicious about the people around him, he humiliates Elliot a little more. After the date, Weiner expresses his repulsion toward Jonica:

> When I got back, she was still lying on the rug, looking up at me.
> What can I say? You can guess what happened next.
> As for her body, I won't go into details but will say this: she had a lot of dimples. Everywhere.

And yet the reader knows Weiner is the one with the soggy Pampers taped under his arms.

In fact, Elliot Weiner is depicted as the most deliciously awful of New York City neurotic bachelors. For one, he puts his garbage in the refrigerator so it won't stink and attract roaches, while the girlfriend he's left back in New York, Pam, is the consummate beard. "When we first met, we discovered we had a lot in common, including the fact that our brothers had attended the same basketball camp although at different times." They were clearly meant to be. Pam even indulges his true passion—which is for "Morris dancing . . . a type of old English folk dancing, always performed by men. It can get pretty wild, since it involves a lot of swinging of clubs."

What's wonderful about Plunket's first-person narrator is how far beneath the surface his dishonesty lies. His attraction to men is hinted at beautifully, hilariously, but always cagily, never consummated. He has lied so much—so profoundly—and for so long that his attraction leaks out in twisted bromances with straight, working-class men. He leers at them, ingratiates himself toward them, describes their biceps and the length of their shorts, but his desire reveals itself sideways. His defenses have been shored behind this original lie, as he looks down on everyone and on Los Angeles itself. In the gaps between his observations, the silences, the truth about Weiner's true self emerges. Behind the bluster and arrogance he's a closeted gay misanthrope, blind to his own desires. While Weiner is not a likable character, the story doesn't ask you to admire or sympathize with him. Yes, he's a superficial, arrogant, closeted homophobe who refers to the one gay man he encounters as "the faggot." He goes into long tirades, including an elaborate racist theory about the difference between Puerto Ricans in New York and Mexicans in LA. (He prefers the Mexicans.) Fat jokes abound. But it's not empathy we are here for.

In his essay "Gay Sincerity Is Scary," Paul McAdory calls out the fiction of "gay sincerity"—that contemporary, humanistic, and above all, earnest gay novel that revels in its own poignancy and tenderness. McAdory cringes in the face of such mawkish, heartfelt quasitransgressive sentimentality, and asks: "Do we not grow tired, after so many rounds of this sentimental journey to the weepy, fantastical core of human experience? Might we not celebrate instead a more horizontal outlay of sincerity, mania, irony, horror, meanness, humor, etc. . . . In lieu of crying, a writer might try laughing, cackling, madly monologuing to the pool of cum on one's tummy, coolly observing it, overanalyzing it for effect, playing in it, rejoicing in it . . ."

My Search for Warren Harding might be the insincere gay novel McAdory has been hoping for. Wiener is a low-key monster. He projects his self-loathing outward onto fat women and openly gay men. His views are problematic. His whole way of judging other people is reductive and snobby and scathing and unkind. Of course all books and works of art are in some ways a symptom of their times, and this one has the blind spots and cringeworthy moments that remind us of its 1983 pub date. But for those of us who are greedy for models of literary fiction that are actually funny, hungry for satire that stings, craving work that pricks and prods us awake—fiction that doesn't bore us—the risk of not reading these rare works outweighs the risk of being offended.

And in the end, I don't think you can read Plunket's work straight-faced. Too often we still insist on reading the fiction of so-called "marginalized" authors as thinly veiled autobiography, or worse yet, a tool of self-help. We somehow still believe the queer novelist or the writer of color must share the moral underpinnings and opinions of the characters they create on the page—and when the character says or does wrong, we convict the author. But so much of the real pleasure of fiction lies in the nonliteral, meaning told slant—in double-talk and mischief and irony, all imbedded in the elaborate lie.

First-person narrators are often best as liars. They are most interesting when they lie to the world and they lie to us and they especially lie to themselves. Weiner is no exception. And there is a particular pleasure in this novel of witnessing the cracks where Weiner's self-delusion runs up against the reality of his true self.

Weiner learns nothing from his journey. He keeps judging, keeps lying, keeps grasping, keeps being petty. Part of what's liberating about writing awful characters, grotesque characters who do grotesque things and learn nothing from their journey, particularly for those of us who are writing from the margins, is that dark satirical comedy resists the autobiographical gaze. In writing a perceptive satire—writing monstrous characters on downward spirals that never reverse course—we resist the pressure to remediate and uplift. We reclaim our right as artists to simply fuck shit up and walk away, laughing.

The first rule of improv is "Say Yes." And indeed part of the perfection of *My Search for Warren Harding* is in how committed it remains to its premise and the persona of Elliot Weiner. Plunket says "Yes" to the problematic character and he continually says "Yes" to the absurd circumstances he puts him in. The story keeps saying "Yes" to its own twisted logic and doesn't ever shy away from the ugliness or limitations of Weiner's vantage point.

In the real world we're told we should empathize and see things from other people's points of view. In a novel, the opposite is often true: the point of view is by necessity chauvinistic. It works most powerfully when limited by its own body and times and perspective. *My Search for Warren Harding* feels like freedom because of its limitations. In reading a character so blind and blindsided, so prejudiced and self-absorbed, we are freed from our own sanctity, our own arrogance. The main character is a closeted white gay man with a narcissist's insecure vapid center. In reading Plunket, we are freed from our own delusion that we are not all Weiner. That we are not all—somehow, someway—in the closet.

His novel anticipated and influenced much of what the culture would begin to find funny (and maybe what some of us are still waiting for the world to find funny). In our contemporary humble-bragging world of filtered selfies, virtue signaling and good optics, we find increasing release, and comic relief, in fictional characters we are not asked to admire or envy—in characters so awful or amoral or vapid that the joke is on them.

The novel was critical success upon its publication in the Eighties. Ann Beattie and Frank Conroy wrote glowing reviews. Plunket, however, didn't publish again for many years and instead dabbled in acting. His IMDB page says he is "best remembered as the timid gay guy" in Martin Scorsese's dark comedy thriller *After Hours*. He went on to get bit parts in other movies, then published a second novel, *Love Junkie*, in 1992; the rights were optioned by Madonna. Plunket moved to Florida and did not publish another book. Even still, *My Search for Warren Harding* continued to quietly leave its mark—passed around through some kind of comedic-literary whisper network, where it was adored by a small, select group of readers that included Amy Sedaris and Larry David.

Rumor has it that Larry David was such a fan of the novel he kept copies of it available in the *Seinfeld* writing room and told his writers to imitate the tone. It's clear reading this novel that he even lifted details from the book, such as the absurd way that *Seinfeld*'s Elaine dances—clearly based on the novel's depiction of how Weiner's girlfriend Pam dances:

> She is one of those people who "abandon" themselves to the beat, clapping their hands over their head and emitting little yelps. To make matters worse, she studied modern dance in college and thus considers herself a Movement Expert. The thing she does—I can only describe them as Martha Graham routines. Her arms fly out into space, she makes sudden turns, then she half-squats, her head flung back in ecstasy.

After its publication, this novel did what so many great novels do: it shone briefly on the new fiction scene, long enough to be pilfered and imitated, long enough to be absorbed into the culture it would influence. And then, like so much source material, it disappeared, like the author himself, who retreated to Sarasota, Florida, and involved himself in gossip and real estate writing, rhinestone and quilt collecting, and raising succulents.

"The literary marketplace is fickle, unforgiving, and often unfair, likely to reward the second-rate," writes Victoria Patterson in her essay on Plunket. "In counteraction to this depressing reality, there's also a beautiful and hopeful phenomenon, whereby a deserving book survives."

When Patterson handed me Plunket's half-forgotten novel that day on my porch, California burning and the world in decay, the out-of-print book had already been handed to her years before, pressed upon her by another writer. And I read it and pressed it upon a brilliant friend at New Directions and so here we have it, a redemption song.

In that one rare interview in the *LARB*, Plunket comes off like I'd expect: unpretentious, unfiltered, quick-witted, honest, and completely bullshit-free. He is deeply literary, loves literature perhaps too much to sully it with careerism. He talks trash about the books that are supposed to be funny but aren't: "PG Wodehouse means nothing to me. I can't get past the first page." He throws shade at Jonathan Franzen: "I find the characters so stuck in middle-class angst that we are supposed to take seriously ..." He is also transparent about the rules he tries to follow in order to write a truly funny novel. As he says, the funny novel must include a "slightly manic, deeply flawed first-person narrator"; it must "pay attention to rhythm—make the words dance," and should include a "punch line every other paragraph."

Plunket bemoans in the interview that "people don't think anything 'delightful' can be serious. Yet the delightful works of art are exactly the ones that last, while the 'profundity' of any age dates quickly."

This turns out to be true. The cosmic joke of Plunket's delightful novel is still as fresh today as it was forty years ago. It is a gift to us—devoted readers of Los Angeles literature, of comedy, of queer literature, and of the literature of self-loathing—that it is finally being reissued now. You hold in your hands the paramount example of a comic novel. To all the greedy readers and writers, enjoy the ride.

—DANZY SENNA, LOS ANGELES, 2022

Author's preface

Dear Reader,

It's hard to believe that forty years have gone by since *My Search for Warren Harding* was first published. Who would have thought that it would end up, as my mother put it shortly before her death from dementia, "a true literary classic?" Certainly not those critics who so completely misunderstood my work. The insults they hurled—"limp," "flaccid," "dysfunctional." The words still sting. And certainly not the snobbish glitterati who run the literary establishment. Everyone agrees—there seems to be a conspiracy of silence surrounding my beloved book.

So this brand new edition is for the only "critics" who really matter—my wonderful fans. The people who discover me, tattered and dusty, in the Goodwill, who track me down in the most remote corners of the Internet. People like the lonely recluse from Queens, N.Y., who sends me pictures he draws of the characters. Or the guy from Oklahoma who drove all the way to have dinner with me. Or the nice middle-aged woman in London who reads it as a special treat on her birthday, all alone in her bedsitter. Or Karen, the hospice nurse. She's my favorite. She often reads passages to her patients so they can get a comforting last laugh.

Well, I want my fans to know that I have found peace and contentment at a lovely trailer park in Florida. My career as Mr. Chatterbox, the gossip columnist at *Sarasota Magazine* is over. True, my time there was marked by scandal and litigation but that's all in the past now. Just as Warren Harding and his era are quickly receding into the past, so are me and mine.

The Pee-wee Herman affair was my first baptism by fire. By an incredible stroke of luck I was a regular customer at the adult theater where he was arrested (indeed, the staff even invited me to the annual Christmas party), so when Pee-wee was hauled in for indecent exposure, I had the inside scoop and was prepared to "tell all" if the price was right. The results caused quite a stir and have even been reprinted in college journalism textbooks in the chapter on ethics.

I stumbled onto a much larger stage in 2000 with the contested presidential election of Bush vs. Gore. Florida Secretary of State Katherine Harris—whose duty it was to certify the election—was a dear friend, and still is. She even appeared with me in a night club act I was trying out in an effort to enlarge my fan base. During the act we led the audience in a "chicken dance." At the height of the recount crisis it was somehow leaked that I had a tape of this performance and, while a real hoot, everyone who saw it agreed that it would destroy any claim Katherine might have to being a serious person. The *National Enquirer* offered me $50,000. I said no. Loyalty to those dear to me always comes first. I am proud to say, "I cannot be bought!"

I'm sure it was to thank me for paving his way to the White House that President Bush invited me to accompany him on his education tour of Florida in 2001. I even got to ride on the White House press plane! The first day in Jacksonville there were all sorts of speeches and seminars, during which I could see the President survey the crowd, undoubtedly thinking, "Is that Robert Plunket? Is *that* Robert Plunket?" Finally, late in the afternoon, his eyes met mine and I gave him a thumbs up. He grinned and gave me a big wink just as he was promising to increase spending for the nation's public schools.

The next day in Sarasota, while he was listening to the children read that book about the goat, Andrew Card ran in and whispered in his ear that another plane had hit the second tower. The blood drained from his face and his glance darted around the room. People wondered, what on earth was he looking for? Well, he was looking for me. Our eyes locked and in that moment I like to think it was my reassuring smile that gave him the courage to hold on when, to channel Celine Dion, there was nothing left except the will which says to him hold on.

But that's all in the past now. He's in happy retirement in Texas, as I am in Florida. The big Eight Oh is rapidly approaching for both of us. He has his beloved ranch, I have my treasured trailer. He has his Laura, I have my Kyle, a young man I met while he was participating in a Wet Jockey Shorts contest in a bar out on the key.

Kyle, who placed a respectable fifth, was between "gigs" so I invited him to stay with me for a couple of days. Those days have turned into years and Kyle has become a more and more important part of my life. His help has been crucial during my recent health crises — two strokes, a heart attack, quadruple bypass surgery, prostate cancer, an anal fissure, and type 3 diabetes — and now I depend on him for a myriad of things: cleaning, grocery shopping, banking, chauffeuring me to doctors' appointments and the Senior Friendship Center for a game of canasta. He has proven so helpful that I have even given him a durable power of attorney. He often jokes that he's amazed I have lasted as long as I have.

So if he sometimes seems a little cranky and impatient with me — as he has lately — I am quick to forgive him. He can still come up with wonderful surprises. This afternoon, for instance, he has a special outing planned. We're going kayaking! Yes, I recently bought him a brand new Itiwit inflatable kayak and we're going to try it out at the Moccasin Wallow Nature Preserve down by Everglades City. What a special place. Old Florida at its best — total seclusion, just the palms and mangroves, the hidden coves and impenetrable waterways — and best of all, the gators, hundreds of them.

There's the horn. And so I bid you adieu. My race is almost run, my days are nearly done. Life is an adventure, I always say. I've had mine. And now, dear reader, it's time for yours. Just take a deep breath and turn the page . . .

—R.P.,
ENGLEWOOD, FLORIDA,
SEPTEMBER 27, 2022

MY SEARCH FOR WARREN HARDING

Acknowledgments

The author wishes to express his gratitude to the Reed Foundation, which institution, in March of 1980, awarded me a grant of $7,500 in order that I might carry forward the research effort that culminates in this book. Modest as the sum was, it nevertheless proved invaluable, and I am accordingly appreciative and wish to say so. Yet it is in the light of its initial support and encouragement that I am now baffled to learn that the Reed Foundation has elected to dissociate itself from this project and the text that represents its completion, a matter I would comment on further were it not that certain events pertinent to my researches have subsequently given rise to an array of sordid litigations—and until the courts have spoken, I, regrettably, must keep silent.

Let me also hasten to thank my attorney and literary agent, Mr. Bruce Pinsky, of Beverly Hills, California. Thank you, Bruce.

Finally, a special statement of thanks goes out to my father and mother, Mr. and Mrs. D. Ballard Weiner, of Pittsburgh, Pennsylvania—thanks, Mom, thanks, Dad—not to mention Amy Robinson, Doris Baizley, and Paul Corrigan, who stored some boxes for me in the course of the time I was obliged to spend in California.

It is to all these good persons, and to my benefactors at the Reed Foundation, that this book is respectfully and earnestly dedicated.

—E.W., NEW YORK, 1983

1

I have to admit it was Mrs. Biersdorf's—Eve's—idea. Without her input, who knows how long I could have taken it? I might have wandered around Los Angeles all summer, till all my fellowship money was gone, winding up with nothing more than a good tan. We must have looked like an odd pair, standing there at the scenic lookout about fifty yards down the street from the Kinney house. It was a sweltering Southern California morning, with the temperature past 90° and still climbing. "Dry heat" they call it, but I could still feel my heavy cotton shirt stick to my back. I loosened my tie. Eve was a little better off. She at least was used to the climate and was dressed in a smart tennis outfit.

We were fiddling around with the "spy kit" we had assembled from whatever gadgets lay around Pete's den. Eve peered through the binoculars while I tried to figure out how to load the Polaroid. Exactly what I was going to take a picture of I had no idea, but Eve had insisted that I bring it along.

For the truth is that in the past three days I had driven by the house so many times I had committed the whole thing to memory. Not that there was much to see: just a long peeling stucco wall with a rusty wrought-iron gate. Next to the gate was a little building—a guest house, I imagined—but the main house was invisible through the overgrown vegetation except for an occasional glimpse of red-tiled roof.

Eve had her attention—and the binoculars—focused on the guest house.

"All the curtains are down," she reported.

I had noticed that the very first day, of course. In fact, they had been up in the morning and then when I returned after lunch for more surveillance they were gone. I didn't think much about it at the time.

"I see some cartons piled up," she continued. "And there's something in the middle of the room. A ladder, it looks like."

A car down the hill attracted my attention. It was heading up our way. God knows I had reason enough to feel paranoid after the way I had been lurking around the neighborhood. I had read somewhere that this area, which certainly looked expensive ("very hip but not very chic," Eve had told me), was patrolled by private police cars, some of which carried vicious attack dogs.

"You know what it looks like," Eve said, removing the binoculars and frowning. "It looks like someone's moving."

The car was getting closer, rounding the hairpin turns in clouds of yellow dust. I was about to suggest we move on for a spell when Eve let out a shriek and grabbed my arm with such force I was afraid it might leave a bruise. I jumped about some, fearing she had seen a rattlesnake.

"I've got it, I've got it!" she cried.

"Got what?"

She held still and looked at me, her face the picture of excitement.

"Just ask to rent the guest house. Someone's obviously moving. And you'll be the first person there!"

It was one of those brilliant ideas that seem immediately right. The perfect solution, simple and clear. It solved a million problems. Holy Christ, when I thought of some of the plans I had been considering—the long-lost relative, the tax assessor ...

We piled into my rented Mustang and drove off, hyperventilating from excitement. We rode around aimlessly, rehashing the idea and looking for flaws. Of course it might not work—there were so many variables—*but if it did* ...

Hooking up with Eve was turning out to be a wonderful omen. Not only was she full of ideas, but she had actually met the old lady! It seems that before her most recent marriage she had served as an executive assistant to some creative bigwig at Paramount. This was when they were shooting *Chinatown*. Eve spent most of her time breaking down budgets, but she kept nagging until they let her scout locations too. The biggest problem was Faye Dunaway's mansion—everything they looked at seemed too modern, too remodeled. Then someone remembered this big old Spanish house way up just underneath the Hollywood sign. Screen great Norma Talmadge built it in 1929 just before her debut in talkies (*Madame du Barry*) revealed a Brooklyn accent so beyond the aid of speech therapy that she was forced into early retirement, followed by a troubled marriage to Toastmaster General George Jessel.

Eve found some pictures of the house in an old architecture magazine and it looked perfect—"Classic Hollywood Spanish," she said. After a little legwork she found out that it belonged to an old lady named Rebekah Kinney. Eve described her thus: "Real old, real mean, and dumb—dumb like a fox." But Mrs. Kinney wanted too much money, and after several unsatisfactory meetings they found another place, out in Pasadena, that was almost as good and snapped it up.

Eve herself had been in California almost fifteen years. She was my mother's oldest and dearest friend; my mother adored her and kept up the friendship through all of Eve's marriages, jobs, face-lifts (as Eve would be the first to admit), etc. My mother thought Eve was the most glamorous person she had ever known, and she was probably right.

And now Eve had reached the summit—marriage to a movie producer, a house in Beverly Hills, a glittering life-style involving lunch dates with the stars, and so on. My mother felt vindicated now that Eve had made it and collected press clippings about all of her husband's movies. After all, she had stood by Eve through thick and thin and it had paid off.

And it did get thin. There was the time when Eve went off to Guatemala for the winter to study archaeology with a divorce settlement and became involved with a native accountant who embezzled his firm in order to buy her a Lincoln. My father, who never could stand Eve, had to wire her plane fare back to Pittsburgh, and she showed up at our house in the middle of the night, hysterical and one step ahead of Interpol. The whole incident was swept under the carpet, and after some R & R Eve went off to New York to break into publishing.

Since the only other person I knew in "the Southland" was a tedious chemistry major I had run track with at Harvard, I gave Eve a call upon my arrival and she invited me over for dinner. It was just the two of us—husband number four, the famous Pete, was "down at the Springs"—and even though we hadn't seen each other in twenty years we hit it off immediately. Over a second bottle of wine I took her into my confidence.

Any lingering disappointment I was harboring that there were no stars around the dinner table completely vanished when I found out that Eve had actually met my reason for coming to Southern California. And she for her part was astonished to learn that old Mrs. Kinney, with the rhinestone sunglasses and the squeaky wheelchair, not only had been the mistress of a president but had borne him an illegitimate child and then, to top it off, had written a best-seller about the whole thing.

Eve was quick to point out that Warren Harding was "way, way" before her time. I wasn't so sure. He died, in office, in 1923. And as for Mrs. Kinney—"My God, she must be over one hundred years old!"

"She's barely eighty," I corrected. She was, in fact, several years younger than my own grandfather, thriving happily, from all reports, in a nursing home outside of Worcester, Mass.

"But how could I not have known?" Eve moaned. It dawned on me that it was this tantalizing piece of gossip she hadn't been privy to that was the real cause of her upset. "I know where all the bodies are buried," she had pointed out more than once that evening.

Eve's ignorance about the old lady was an encouraging sign. "At least nobody else knows," she told me, and this consoled both of us. The bigger the secret, the bigger the scoop.

For the discovery that the old lady was still alive threatened to make a mess out of the book I was planning. She was the last Harding intimate left. She alone could refute all my meticulously thought-out theories. She alone knew the truth. She alone had all the answers.

And they were answers to some very important questions. What had happened to her daughter by Harding, Blanche Marie, whose financial security was the supposed motive for writing *The Price of Love*, the under-the-counter bestseller that shocked the last half of the 1920s? Was she still alive? What did she have to say about all this? After all, she was the daughter of a US president. That is, if the old lady was to be believed.

But she was believed. Better historians than I accepted her story. There were letters (not many) and a few grudging, off-the-record acknowledgments of the affair from long-dead Harding cronies. But if she once had been so vocal in demanding her daughter's birthright, why had she now turned her back on the whole thing? And what did she know of the scandals that plagued the Harding regime? Or of his bizarre last days and mysterious death?

And most of all, did she have any material, any letters, any papers? So much had been destroyed by "the Duchess," Harding's imperious wife, that his signature was by far the most valuable of any president since Lincoln.

It was my chief rival, Paterson Decker from Yale, who had tracked her down (or rather bumped into her through blind luck and no fault of his own). Harding has never been a fashionable specialization for historians; consequently Decker and I pretty much have the field to ourselves. Our relationship is cordial but competitive. He resents, I feel, my youth and my ambition. Some unfortunate comments have gotten back to me about my "qualifications." I don't wish to bore the reader with some petty argument between a couple of fusty scholars, or dwell on my educational background. Suffice it to say that I teach at both Mercy College and the New School, and I feel that speaks for itself. And I will be the first to admit that Decker's contributions to Hardingania have been tremendous, and that the charges of speciousness that are occasionally leveled against his work are largely unmerited.

Decker has written an interesting yet (I feel) poorly thought-out monograph (*Journal of Historical Research*, June 1970), in which he classifies Rebekah Kinney as a "historical intruder [who] shouted and shoved [her] way into the history books," demanding room from the "historical personages" who really belong there. His theory, if I am reading it right, is that these "intruders" obfuscate and confuse history, and that while some are important enough to merit limited study, they are at heart easy-to-dismiss nuisances. Some other historical troublemakers he identifies are Whittaker Chambers, Pope Urban III, John Wilkes Booth, and Lord Birchall, Queen Elizabeth's personal physician and confidant, whose arrest in 1601 for procuring led to the first legal definition of the term.

So I don't find it strange that it would take a freak accident for Decker to uncover Mrs. Kinney once again. To make it more embarrassing for him, she was even in the phone book! He had previously traced her to Dover, Delaware, in 1937, where she operated a small dry-cleaning establishment called Tact Cleaners. But for the next forty-odd years, nothing.

Until last year, when he was attending a conference at USC. He happened to glance through the Los Angeles phone book, searching for a colleague's number (a certain Professor Kinsey had offered him a lift to the airport), and he came across the unmistakable name of Rebekah Kinney. A hurried and, from what I hear, very expensive investigation by a "private eye" confirmed that the Rebekah Kinney residing at 6701 Casino Drive was indeed a lady well into her eighties.

I pumped Eve for more information, but she wasn't much help. She had never even gotten inside the main house. Her negotiations with the old woman had taken place on a heavily screened verandah, and all she could remember was "lots of broken porch furniture and a fan that sounded like a DC-3."

"Did Paterson Decker ever meet her?" Eve asked.

I explained the story I had heard through the grapevine: two letters unanswered and finally, after the third, a two-sentence reply saying she had no idea what he was talking about and would he please stop bothering her as she was a widow living alone.

Eve thought about this. "Maybe it's another Rebekah Kinney," she said. "I suppose that *could* be possible."

"No, it was her, all right. We have proof."

"Proof?"

I paused for dramatic effect. "Right after the last letter she got an unlisted phone number."

"Ooooh," said Eve, her face lighting up. Here was a tactic she could relate to. "But why did Decker give up?"

"What else should he do? She refused to have anything to do with him. And he's not the sort of person who could go in there and lie."

"And you are?"

"Lie? Listen, I'd rape and pillage to get my hands on those papers."

"Jesus," she said, and for a moment I thought she had taken me seriously.

My first job out of college was with a well-known zoo in the metropolitan area. Theoretically I was "Assistant to the Director," but in reality what I performed were mostly clerical tasks, plus some weekend babysitting for expensive animals who were pregnant and had to be watched constantly. Luckily my superiors took a shine to me, and soon I was the zoo's fair-haired boy. After several years of steady promotions I found myself Director of Development, with a hefty expense account and ready access to the zoo's cars. It was a pleasant enough job. Five people worked under me: another young man who ran the direct-mail campaign, an older woman who was in charge of government and foundation grants, and three secretaries. We really needed only two, but the third was the daughter of a local politico who was hired for obvious reasons even though her skills were not the best.

I oversaw the operations of the entire department, of course, but my specialty was talking to rich people, particularly heirs to large fortunes. Once I got a substantial sum from an orchestra leader, but most of the money that came in was so old it had to be dusted off before it was delivered. My biggest coup was when I was just twenty-five years old. I had lunch with a certain Mrs. X (exactly who I can't say due to fundraising ethics) and ended up with a check for $50,000 over dessert. It was earmarked toward making a portion of the lawn look more like an African savannah. For this little feat I was chosen Employee of the Year and received a plaque which I still have somewhere.

Now, as I was standing in the living room of the mansion waiting to meet Warren Harding's mistress, lunch with Mrs. X came back to me. What a piece of cake that had been. Let's face it—I was scared to death.

Eve had let me off at the gate five minutes earlier. She was full of last-minute advice about California renting practices. Then, with instructions to meet me under a large tropical shrub just visible through the smog, she drove off, her hand fluttering out the window in a final gesture of farewell until a sharp curve in the road forced her to return it to the steering wheel.

I pressed the rusty buzzer and waited. There was no intercom, although I did find a sun-bleached flyer stuffed into a crevice in the wall offering bargains in swimming pool maintenance. After a while I began to suspect the buzzer didn't work.

But then a woman appeared and my heart gave a little jump. She hurried down the driveway with her arms folded over her breasts to keep them from jiggling as she ran. She was dressed in red slacks and a red blouse. They almost matched but not quite, which made her a little hard to look at straight on. I wondered how she fitted into the household, but as she got closer her dark complexion gave her away: she must be some kind of Mexican maid.

We had an awkward conversation through the gate. Judging from her command of the English language I'd say she had got off the bus from Guadalajara about seven hours ago. But she was friendly enough and when I mentioned "Señora Kinney" her eyes lit up and she unlocked the gate. I got the impression unannounced visitors didn't drop by too often and that I was probably the high point of her day, if not her week.

I followed her to the top of the driveway and got my first good look at the property. It was different from what I'd expected. The drive veered off to the right, continuing around, I guessed, to some garage behind the house. Directly to our left, behind a low stucco wall, was a handsome pool. Or rather the remains of a handsome pool. It looked like it hadn't been filled for the last ten years. The bottom was covered with eucalyptus leaves and brown palm fronds. At the head of the pool was a big green ceramic frog. At one time water must have arched from his mouth, but now he was covered with dust and one ear was missing.

Behind us on the left was the guest house. From this side it looked charming—a tiny cottage in Granada—although a little the worse for wear. It needed a coat of paint and somebody had to get rid of the wasps' nest over the front door before I was venturing inside. But it had a lovely porch, actually a sort of terrace, overlooking the pool. On the terrace was a playpen full of toys.

Now we must reluctantly turn our attention to the main house. I happen to know a little something about design, so I think I'm on fairly safe ground when I state that this was not the gem Eve had led me to believe it would be. In fact, let me go out on a limb and say that the house was a serious misinterpretation of just about every element of Spanish architecture you can think of.

First, the shape. It was just a long shoe box with a lot of gimmicks thrown in. A pillared loggia dominated the ground floor, so ill-proportioned it blocked off all natural light. Fussy wrought-iron grilles over the windows on the second floor competed for attention with a quaint, impossibly narrow wooden balcony that ran the length of the building. I don't know what they thought they were going to do on that balcony—go for long walks single file, maybe. Rusty lanterns and what I believe are called torchères dotted the façade at regular intervals, and tacked on to one end was a screen porch designed to look like a little chapel.

The maid led me through a carved wooden door that was so massive I had to help her push it open. We were in a murky entrance hall.

A stone staircase curved up to the second floor, past an enormous amber window on which several stained-glass Mexicans were performing some kind of folk dance involving a chicken.

We crossed the hall and went down several steps into an even darker living room. Before my eyes could get accustomed to the gloom, I realized that the maid had left and I was alone.

A few chinks of light managed to squeeze in under the heavy red velvet drapes that were hung on spears. After a while I made out some pieces of furniture scattered around the room more or less at random. They were that style that was popular back in the fifties, armless couches upholstered in nubby fabric shot through with metallic thread. They never really caught on in California, probably because when you sit down on them in shorts you get a rash on the back of your thighs. Over the fireplace a bas-relief galleon sailed westwards, toward Santa Monica. A wagon-wheel chandelier hung from the beamed ceiling. And on the floor was a big Oriental rug. I could tell it was an Oriental rug because it had pictures of the Taj Mahal all over it.

There was nothing to do but stand still and listen for sounds. After a long time they came: loud clattering noises from the tile floor out in the hall. No octogenarian could be making that racket; I decided it must be the maid returning with bad news (after first changing her shoes, probably in accordance with some Mexican custom of which I was unaware).

But in a moment the mystery was solved. A pair of clogs tripped into the room and parked themselves at the top of the stairs. They were occupied by a fat girl with messy red hair. She was waving a pair of pudgy hands in the air like she was trying to dry them.

Who on earth is this, I thought. My God, that outfit. She was wearing baggy green paratrooper pants, the kind that tie at the ankle, a yellow T-shirt advertising a bar in Ensenada, a strand of pearls and some scarves hung around her neck, and on her wrists were a lot of plastic bracelets that added to the general din.

"Sorry I took so long," she said, squinting at me and revealing a prominent set of gums. "I was out in the back polyurethaning a dead cactus. Come on, I'll show you where the stuff is."

We had a short, confusing conversation. It seems she thought I was from the Bekins Moving Company, there for a storage estimate. I tried to straighten things out.

"My name is Elliot Weiner," I began and then forgot the rest of my spiel. Lunch with Mrs. X was a picnic compared with this. I grabbed at a straw.

"Your pool looks terrific."

"*That* pool? That pool's a dump."

"But it could be terrific. With a little work."

"Well, *I'm* not doing it."

I got the feeling she was trying out some sort of assertiveness training on me. I tried another tack.

"So. You're moving."

"Yes, I'm moving."

"Well ... then I was wondering if the guest house would be for rent."

This really stumped her. "The guest house? We don't have any guest house."

"The little house. Over there." I pointed.

"Oh, the *pool* house. That's a pool house, not a guest house."

"But you are moving from there?"

"Not from there. I'm moving from *here*." She pointed at the living room floor.

"But the pool house is empty? Nobody lives there?"

She looked at me like I was crazy. "Of course nobody lives there. It's a *pool* house." She rolled her eyes and shook her head, the way one does when one is forced to deal with an imbecile.

I was not doing very well and I knew it. Fortunately, at that moment, as sometimes happens in a crisis, a great calm descended over me and instead of going to pieces I became lucid, rational, and totally charming. I told her how I had just moved to town, was doing graduate work at UCLA (in *English*), happened to drive by the house, fell in love at first sight, noticed the curtains, rang the bell, and here I was. I went on: how I hated loud music, hardly ever entertained, how I needed a quiet place for writing dissertations and papers, how a male tenant would have added security benefits. I could see her little mind working. I plunged ahead shamelessly: impeccable references from a movie producer in Beverly Hills...

She nibbled a fingernail. "We've never done anything like this. Rented anything, I mean." But the possibility seemed to intrigue her. She talked like a real California girl: no inflection and lots of *r*'s.

"Neither have I!" I said. "Imagine, just ringing a doorbell!" I made a devil-may-care gesture, flapping my hands up in the air. It must have charmed her because she laughed.

"Who owns this house anyway?" I asked.

"My grandmother. But she's very old. She never goes out."

"Maybe you could ask her. You could put in a good word for me."

She looked at me. "Maybe I could."

It was agreed that I should return tomorrow at noon to hear what Grandmother had to say. With our business completed, the girl was mellowing by the minute. I asked her where she was moving.

"To a trailer in Torrance."

"Torrance? Where's that?"

"Out past the airport."

There was a moment's pause. She was really very shy.

"I hope you're not going to be too cramped." This was the wrong thing to say to a fat person. "I mean, after this big house."

"Oh, no, it's a cute trailer. Wall-to-wall carpeting and lots of built-ins. The people next door keep ducks, but you get used to that."

As we re-entered the hall on the way to the front door, a pale, rotund infant came crawling toward us across the floor. He was decked out in Pampers and dingy T-shirt that said "So Far So Good."

The girl reached down and picked him up. They cooed and gurgled together for a moment, and then she planted a kiss on his forehead, avoiding his mouth as he was drooling rather badly. The child responded by making a few jerky movements and then whacking her in the ear with his little fist.

"What a cute baby," I said, taking a step backwards. "Is it yours?" The girl said he was and patted his bottom proudly. "Oh, oh, I think he needs changing." She sniffed. "I *know* he needs changing." "What's his name?" I asked politely, hoping he was moving to the trailer in Torrance too.

She gave him another kiss.

"This is little Warren," she said.

My friends consider me an eccentric. Don't ask me why. Sometimes I think it's because they like the idea of having an eccentric friend. While I will admit that some of my habits are a little strange, there is always a logical reason behind them. For instance, I keep my garbage in the refrigerator. This is so it won't just sit under the sink and decay, and also so roaches won't get at it. Of course, I don't keep paper garbage in the refrigerator, just food garbage. Paper garbage I keep in the spare bedroom.

My biggest passion in life, though, is Morris dancing. Morris dancing, in case there are one or two of you who have never heard of it, is a type of old English folk dancing, always performed by men. It can get pretty wild, since it involves a lot of swinging of clubs. A wonderful feeling of camaraderie builds up in men who Morris dance and we generally have drinks together afterwards. Sometimes too many drinks. Alistair Cooke once called Morris dancing "rugby for the effete" but I think that's an unfair characterization.

None of the men in my Morris dancing group are particularly effete. Most are very ordinary: a dentist, two lawyers (one with Legal Aid), four or five graduate students, a slide librarian at Brooklyn College, a Korean cellist. The dances are extremely intricate. With all those clubs, a false move can mean a bloody nose or worse, so we devote many hours to rehearsing. During the season (April through October, though we are most in demand around May Day) we have been known to perform as many as three times a weekend, usually at arts festivals, block parties, folk dance competitions, and the like. We call ourselves the Stratford Morris Men and we are nonprofit, which opens up the possibility of grants. No luck so far, though.

Last year we applied to the New York State Council on the Arts and they sent a woman to "Audit" one of our performances. All she did was sit in the back and giggle at the mistakes.

Since I am both vice-president and booking agent for the SMM, I was a little reluctant to spend the summer in Los Angeles, where there isn't even a chapter of the American Morris Dancing Society. Not only that, I was forced to teach my solo, a wonderful number and a real crowd-pleaser, to the Korean, who, I feel, does not really do it justice. And on top of that I had to sublet my apartment, one of those enormous West Side "finds," to three girls from Texas who will probably never change the sheets. You should have heard them squawk when I demanded a $250 deposit for the phone. One look at them and I knew they were talkers.

And of course I would miss Pam. Pam is my girlfriend. She works at the Ford Foundation, where she oversees programs having to do with senior citizens, women's issues, and child abuse. It's a dream job but she hates it.

Pam is thirty-five, somewhat older than myself. She's terrified she's going to end up one of those women you see all the time in the Village, dressed in a black turtleneck with a lot of Navajo jewelry, hair in a bun, attending meetings about social change. And quite frankly, so am I.

Nevertheless she has many wonderful qualities. We have discussed living together but have decided against it. It's funny how it's always the little things. For instance, I can't fall asleep unless the TV is on and she can't fall asleep if it is. So we maintain separate apartments.

We met at a fundraising seminar in Niagara Falls. I was speaking on the Effective Use of Volunteers and her topic was What to Put in a Prospectus. We hated each other at first. She told somebody I reminded her of George Hamilton. Then, through a chain of circumstances, we were pressed into service co-chairing a panel on Raffles and Sweepstakes. We were so bad we went out drinking afterwards to commiserate and discovered we had a lot in common, including the fact that our brothers had attended the same basketball camp, although at different times. Her brother's name is Ira and their last name is Berger. I call him Irate Berger, a nickname he pretends drives him crazy. We don't see nearly as much of him as we should. I called Pam that night to fill her in and ask for advice. The discovery of a Harding great-grandchild was news in itself, maybe worth the whole trip. How should I handle it?

Eve certainly hadn't been too impressed. She said it was a bad sign that the whole thing wasn't settled right then and there. Mrs. Kinney would nix the whole plan, she told me, just wait and see. The part of the story that interested her the most was the Oriental rug. "It's not Oriental, it's Chinese," she said, "And I know a dealer on Melrose who would kill for it." She even suggested that maybe he could go with me in the morning. I finally told her politely to shut up.

Pam, at least, realized the importance of my discovery. "But keep it to yourself for the time being," she advised. "Remember what happened to Paterson Decker."

Fearing the size of the phone bill we said good-bye. The candy bars from the motel vending machine were doing something awful to my stomach, and I spent about three-quarters of the night lying on the bathroom floor suffering from cramps.

I suspect that nerves played a major part. The thought of meeting a living legend isn't exactly conducive to slumber. And she was so old—I worried about that a lot. What if she had trouble with her faculties? What if her hearing was impaired? So much could go wrong before I even got to first base.

I didn't have any Valium, so I washed down a couple of Sinutabs with some Pepto-Bismol. That stuff always puts me out like a light. Then I ironed a shirt on the dresser and went back to bed.

I had given a great deal of thought as to what I would wear and finally decided on my tweed sports jacket. It had cost over $250 and I was extremely proud of it; besides, it was very conservative and well bred. I feel that one cannot be too conservative or well bred as far as landlords, job interviews, and court appearances go.

Furthermore, I had read *The Price of Love* many times, so I knew how clothes-conscious Rebekah Kinney was. Whenever anything important happened she would always describe what she was wearing, where she had gotten it, and how much it cost. H. L. Mencken called it "A book about clothes." Judging from the photographs, I'd call her taste refined and expensive.

That was all in the past. Today, when the granddaughter wheeled her into the second-floor sitting room, Rebekah Kinney was dressed in white clam diggers and a red-and-white print blouse. It looked like it had been used to clean up after a bad traffic accident. On her head was a golf cap with four plastic tees—red, green, blue, and yellow—sewn into the brim.

I was a little disappointed. This was the woman I had traveled three thousand miles to see? This was the glamorous Rebekah Kinney, who was denounced from the floor of the United States Senate as a "brazen adventuress"?

"You sure look hot in that getup," she croaked.

"Oh no, I'm just fine," I said. My eyes were glued to her shins, They were milky white with blue veins and the skin was scaling off.

"You look like you're burning up."

"Gramma, leave him alone."

"Me, I dress for the heat," she babbled on proudly. "Sit down."

Feeling thoroughly humiliated, I looked around for someplace to sit. There was a daybed against one wall. I perched on the edge.

My God, she was old. I could detect no resemblance whatever between the young Rebekah Kinney's photographs—she had been something of a beauty—and the crone in the wheelchair.

First of all she was *tiny*. Skeletal. She must have shrunk over the years. Particularly her head—her ears looked enormous. Her arms and legs were like little matchsticks.

But there was something in the eyes I was able to connect with. They were still blue, bright, and sharp—and (I realized suddenly) *mean.* The poor granddaughter. Living with her must have been an ordeal.

I waited for her to speak, feeling very uncomfortable. She seemed on the verge of saying something. Each second passed like an eternity. "There's a colored family down the block," she began. I relaxed a little—at least we were discussing real estate. "They have five cars. Mr. Klotter blew his brains out. Don't ask me why. Things like that happen all the time."

"They do indeed," I agreed.

"We have mud slides . . ." She stopped and began to pick at an African violet. The granddaughter, apparently used to this sort of behavior, was thumbing through a *TV Guide.*

Well, there goes one fantasy, I thought—we're not going to be having too many lighthearted chats over tea.

"Do you drive a car?" she asked suddenly. It is indicative of my frame of mind at this point that I was afraid she was going to ask for a ride somewhere.

I said that I did.

"Put it in back. By the garage. Never park in the driveway. I don't like the way it looks."

Did this mean I had the house? I didn't dare ask. I glanced at the granddaughter for guidance. She was staring impassively at her magazine.

"I expect the rent on the first of each month," the old lady went on. "You can leave it in the mailbox or you can give it to Guadalupe."

I felt that I had missed something, that something very subtle had gone right over my head. It was too quick, too sudden. What about all those fibs I'd spent all night rehearsing? Didn't she want references? Wasn't I going to have to sell myself?

"Well," I said in the pleasantly dazed tone of someone who has just won a poker game with a pair of twos, "I guess it's all set."

"Yep," the old lady said. "It's all set."

I got to my feet for no particular reason.

"By the way, what is the rent?"

"Eight hundred dollars a month," she said, clear as a bell.

"Eight *hundred*?" I sat back down.

"That includes the electricity."

I looked around the room helplessly. Eight hundred dollars a month! Only a fool would pay that. I was prepared to go to four.

"I can't pay eight hundred dollars a month rent," I said flatly.

"Suit yourself." She put her hands in her lap. "That's what I'm charging."

"But I'm a *student*."

The old lady shrugged. "I'm not coming down."

I looked at the granddaughter. Her eyes were fixed on the back of the wheelchair.

I entered into some mathematical calculations. There was no way I could afford it. The opening of my account at the Bank of America the other day had been a sobering experience. So much of the fellowship money was already gone, spent on God knows what . . .

On the other hand, there was no way I could *not* afford it. If it got me what I wanted, it would be a bargain. Besides, how long could it take? With any luck I'd be out of here in a month.

"Okay," I said with a sigh. "Eight hundred dollars." The sound of it made me cringe.

"Just give Jonica a check for the first and last months," the old lady said, plunging me further into despair. "She'll get you settled."

The fat girl led me to my new home. She was full of apologies for her grandmother's behavior. "I told her not to ask so much money, but she said she knew what she was doing."

"She knew all right," I said grimly.

"Then why did you take it?" the girl asked, giving a worried look over her shoulder. "It's not worth it, believe me. It's a dump."

With these words ringing in my ears, we approached the pool house. Someone had swept the porch since yesterday; and in spite of myself, I was touched. Then my eye caught the wasps' nest and I started fuming again. Guess who was going to end up taking *that* down.

We walked through the front door into a room perhaps twenty feet long. It had green carpeting, spotted here and there with stains. At one end was a large window overlooking what must have been, on a smogless day, a view of Los Angeles. A fireplace stood against the west wall, its plaster mantel blackened by smoke. The east wall was covered with a homemade photomontage mural of rock and roll stars. My heart sank. I wandered around, seeing if the room looked better from other angles. It didn't.

The girl—Jonica—watched me out of the corner of her eye. She seemed terrified I was going to change my mind. "There's a lot you could do to it," she said after a while.

I stared down at the only piece of furniture in the room, a mattress.

"That mattress is cleaner than it looks."

I poked at it with my foot.

"You can use it if you want."

"No thanks," I said.

Jonica suggested we look at "the rest of the house." Two doorways led out of the big room; we took the one by the fireplace. I followed Jonica down a narrow passage to a pair of festively painted doors. Each bore a sign. One read *pepe*; the other, *maria*. Inside were dressing rooms—a row of clothes hooks, a bench, a shower, and a toilet (each in a little cubicle), and, in Pepe, a urinal. The dressing rooms were decorated in tile of the most virulent colors.

While I tried out the water pressure, Jonica discovered a dead rat floating in one of the toilets. She tactfully tried to flush it before I noticed, but the water in the toilet kept rising. We watched, mesmerized, as the rat reached the level of the toilet seat.

"This is bordering on the gross," Jonica said.

After a nervous ten seconds, the water began to decline and the rat disappeared, only to be burped up again.

"Let's look at the kitchen," Jonica said.

It was on the other side of the house. We retraced our steps through the living room. Every time Jonica put her foot down, the house shook to its very foundations.

The kitchen was long, dark, and narrow. The appliances were so old they looked like relics from an ancient civilization. I couldn't even tell what they were for.

"You can use those dishes," Jonica said, pointing out a warped set of Melmac that sat in the cupboard.

"Where are the bedrooms?" I asked.

A panic-stricken look crossed Jonica's face. "Bedrooms?" she said. "There are no bedrooms."

"So this is it, huh?"

"There's a boiler room in the basement," she said in a tiny voice.

"Boiler room?"

"For the pool heater . . ."

"How interesting."

We went back into the living room, this time with me leading the way. I examined the mural. It was polyurethaned.

Not believing what was happening to me, I wrote out a check for $1,600. A torpor began to take over as Jonica handed me the various keys. I looked at them dully, all the information about how to open the front gate going in one ear and out the other.

After she left, I slumped down on the floor. When I realized I was rocking back and forth in an orgy of self-pity, I forced myself to my feet. Then I got in the car and drove down to Standard Brands, where I bought one hundred dollars' worth of white paint and a plumber's friend. Only when I got back home did I realize I'd forgotten the rat poison.

2

Rebekah Kinney was born on 13 June, 1898, near the city of Marion, in central Ohio. The Kinney family, originally from Vermont, had resided in Ohio for several generations, long enough to be considered natives, and were of some importance locally: Franklin Kinney, a cousin, owned a bank in nearby Owensboro, and another relative, the Reverend Howard Kinney, achieved some fame with the publication of a book of sermons, *The Road He Trod*, which reputedly had a great influence on the young Billy Graham.

But every family has its poor relations, and it was into this branch that Rebekah was born. Her father, Mahlon, inherited a thriving chicken farm; but through mismanagement and indifference, it was finally sold for taxes in 1904. Thereafter, the family moved into Marion proper, where the luckless Mr. Kinney became a partner in a livestock medicine company, then a hardware salesman, and finally what Rebekah cryptically refers to as a "routing specialist" for the United States Post Office.

Mrs. Kinney, a highly intelligent farmer's daughter who thought she was marrying money, soured as the passing years brought new business reverses for her husband. She finally opened a lending library to supplement the family income; soon she added a newsstand and soda fountain and was making more than her husband. But even this success brought her no happiness. A social climber at heart, she realized the fact that she worked for a living precluded her acceptance by the Klings, the Abbotts, the Steinmullers, and the other families that made up the cream of Marion society.

Mahlon Kinney was singularly unconcerned with the Marion social scene, though, for he was a man with a passion. "My father was crazy for cats," Rebekah wrote later. Indeed a neighbor, Mrs. Naomi

Wetszal, recalled, "The only time you ever saw Mahlon Kinney under the influence was every year on the day after Thanksgiving when he returned from the big cat show in Cleveland."

Persians were the breed he preferred, though throughout his career he raised every kind of longhair. By special arrangement with the new owner of his bankrupt chicken farm, he kept a special "cat pen" on the property, as Mrs. Kinney refused to let more than six inhabit the family home at any one time. In spite of a childhood spent among chickens and cats, Rebekah developed such a loathing of animals that she once gave the grocer's boy five dollars to "get rid" of a puppy Harding had given her. She told Harding it had been run over.

Thus, the pattern of Rebekah's early life was set: an unsuccessful, eccentric father, and a bitter, severe mother. Her brother Fred did not help matters. He was in constant trouble with the police; and her other brother, Walter, contracted polio and was paralyzed from the waist down until an accident ended his life in 1919.

Understandably, Rebekah and her sister, Amelia, sought refuge in fantasy:

> We would spend hours dressing up in Mother's old clothes, pretending we were wealthy and famous. Our favorite game was called "Rich People" in which we would give lavish albeit imaginary garden parties in our backyard for European royalty and the "400" of New York Society. Amelia usually poured, and I would impersonate Mrs. Stuyvesant Fish for hours.

In spite of her less than sunny childhood, Rebekah had much in her favor. She was a good student, an excellent pianist, and after recovery from a recurring bout of ringworm, a budding beauty. At the age of twelve, she was quite well developed physically and was beginning to be noticed by the boys.

And not just the boys. During the lazy summer afternoons when school was out, many of the town youngsters would sneak out to Elm Thicket, a wooded area adjoining the Negro section of town.

Of course, it was strictly forbidden for them to play there, but this prohibition only made it more attractive. On one such hot August day, Rebekah relates, she was playing a game of hide-and-seek with her friends when she realized she had become lost in the underbush. After wandering scared and aimless through the brambles, she finally came to a path and followed it to a small clearing.

In the clearing I was most astonished to find none other than Mr. Harding, cavorting with two of his newsboys. This unusual trio seemed even more surprised than I, particularly the newsboys who had just been swimming in a nearby pond and were quite naked. They immediately disappeared into the woods, so embarrassed that I, a mere girl, should catch them in such a state. Mr. Harding, after his initial astonishment, could only laugh and laugh. Since it proved impossible to coax the distraught youths from their hiding places, he offered me a lift back to town in his automobile.

As far as we know, this was the first meeting between the two. But if Harding did not know who Rebekah was, she certainly knew all about him. Not only was he one of the town's leading citizens, but as publisher of the *Star*, Marion's daily paper, he was a figure to be reckoned with by the town's youngsters. Practically every boy had a paper route, and Harding took a personal interest in making sure that this end of his business ran with the utmost dispatch. Softball teams were organized, there were incentive awards, and the Newsboy of the Year got his picture on the front page of the special Fourth of July edition. Rumors had circulated for a while that Harding took too much of an interest in his boys. When Mrs. Harding took over as office manager after her husband suffered a nervous breakdown, this was the first area she had usurped for her own. Harding, cranky and dispirited, turned his energy to politics.

Rebekah had found her hero. During the ride into town (her first trip in an automobile), she stared at the silver-haired publisher and realized—what? Here was the man she wished her father had been? Here was an escape from the banality of her life to the rich esoterica of her dreams? Who knows? What *is* evident is that her passion, indelibly imprinted at the very beginning of her adolescent sexuality, became so strong that it would go on to change the course of history.

All this would have seemed preposterous at the time, however. Life in Marion went on. Rebekah's crush was limited to following Harding's career in the papers. His years of political spadework began to pay off. He became Ohio's governor in 1910 and its junior senator five years later. Rebekah wrote songs and verses about him and began collecting whatever memorabilia she could get her hands on, including one of his garters which he discarded after it snapped during a visit to his campaign headquarters on Main Street where she worked as the youngest volunteer. He always seemed to have an extra special greeting for her whenever their paths crossed, which was as often as she could maneuver it.

Although she was thrilled by his success, it was a bittersweet triumph; he hardly ever came to Marion any more. She began, much to the relief of her family, to devote more time to other interests, particularly dramatics. A leading role in *The Admirable Crichton* during her senior year in high school proved a sensation. A bit of scenery collapsed and fell on her during her second-act soliloquy (some old-time Marion residents say the "Accident" was rigged by an anti-Rebekah cabal of certain of her classmates), but Rebekah's presence of mind, finishing the scene though her sleeve was ripped and her wig askew, won over the audience and she received a standing ovation. An article describing her performance appeared in the *Star*; and though Rebekah was certain she would receive some sort of congratulatory note from the senator, "it must have slipped his eye."

Fired by her local success, Rebekah decided her future lay on the New York stage. Her family protested, but she could not be stopped. Clutching the $75 she had saved from her part-time job as pianist at the local movie theater, she boarded a train for Manhattan scarcely one week after her graduation from high school.

Not surprisingly, Rebekah found her talents were much less appreciated east of the Hudson. She settled in a cheap but respectable rooming house in Washington Heights and trudged from audition to audition, seeking roles. Nothing turned up, save a one-day stint modeling gloves at Saks Fifth Avenue. She blamed her lack of success on prejudice against midwesterners, though others attributed it to a slight speech defect (she clipped her consonants; this was later corrected), plus the fact that she was woefully untalented. Emily Frobisher, who knew her at the time, said years later, "Rebekah was a terrible actress. Whenever she started to act, her eyes bulged out so bad you thought they were going to pop out and land in the front row."

Discouraged, but not yet ready to give up, Rebekah realized she would have to find some source of income if she was to remain in New York. An ill-advised job in a pet store lasted one afternoon; she then accepted an offer to play the piano in a dance studio where the latest steps were taught. This led to an engagement, Emily Frobisher reports, with an all-girl orchestra at the legendary Club Bohemia, a ballroom on West 38th Street which catered to male homosexuals. The club was clandestine, admittance being through a series of locked doors; but it was considered very daring and chic for visiting celebrities to drop by and watch the young men, some from the best families, others common criminals, glide around the floor to the latest tunes.

Rebekah kept this episode from her readers for obvious reasons; consequently, we know nothing of her feelings about working in such a disreputable milieu. It must have been heady stuff for a naive eighteen-year-old from Ohio. But Emily Frobisher gives us a clue: "Rebekah had such a thirst for celebrity that she was in awe of nothing."

Important show business figures frequented the club, but after several months Rebekah realized none of them was the least bit interested in her, or in any of the other girls in the orchestra for that matter. A friend suggested she learn to type; then she could work anywhere she pleased. For some reason this thought depressed her even more and she was on the verge of chucking it all and marrying a middle-aged German journalist whom she had met on a bus when an article in the *New York Times* caught her eye: harding urges stricter jewish quotas it was headlined (referring to the current debate on the restriction of immigration), but the body of the piece concerned itself with the growing prominence of the senator.

Something in Rebekah's mind clicked. She had, for the first time in her life, a plan.

The first step was a letter.

Dear Senator Harding:

While I think it unlikely that you remember who I am, I am writing this letter to offer my support for your views on the state of world affairs, which I have been following closely in the newspapers. My name is Rebekah Kinney and my family is from Marion, Ohio. My father, Mahlon Kinney, often spoke with fondness of playing alongside your sister in the high school band.

I am particularly impressed with your admonition that nations should live by the precepts of the Bible in conducting their affairs. I, personally, am currently residing in New York City, attempting to further my career as an actress. With this end in mind I have obtained employment as a musician. But the hours are inconvenient and I find it difficult meeting my financial obligations on my current salary. However, I am sure my problems are petty compared to those the nations of Europe are facing, and I find comfort in this thought.

At any rate, my acting career progresses. I am currently appearing in a production and would be honored to arrange tickets if you or any Ohio friends should be in New York in the near future. In the meantime I rest more soundly knowing my country is in the hands of men such as yourself.

Sincerely,

Rebekah Kinney

To jog his memory, Rebekah enclosed a photograph she had recently had taken for the purposes of self-publicity. It showed her posed as a farm girl, scattering feed to an imaginary group of chickens. Perhaps because of carefully controlled lighting effects, she appeared incredibly youthful: one would have guessed her to be no more than fourteen.

Rebekah professed that the letter was a shot in the dark. But it was so craftily composed, and the photograph so oddly compelling, that within two days a handwritten reply arrived. Of course he remembered her. Her crush had been the talk of Marion for years. Mrs. Harding had more than once threatened to call the police if Rebekah did not stop hovering about the Harding home; she had even gone so far as to discuss the situation with her minister. He recommended that Rebekah join the church youth group. Mrs. Harding flung up her hands when she heard this; her husband had been chairman of the youth committee since its inception.

The senator went on to write that he would be in New York in ten days' time on business and would be delighted to attend her play and then discuss any way he might be able to help her with her prospects.

Though Harding's letter propelled her to the very heights of ecstasy, it also presented her with a problem. The "production" she alluded to was in reality a sort of recital being given by her class at Amos Foster's Academy of Music, Drama and Speech. They were performing an abridged version of *The Taming of the Shrew*, and due to the insufficient number of male students enrolled at the Academy, Rebekah had been given the role of Petruchio. She had already had fittings for an artificial beard, and Mr. Foster himself had worked with her on her "swagger." But newsboys aside, Rebekah's intuition told her it was unwise to let "the love of my life and the key to my future get his first view of my thespian talents veiled under such a role."

She fretted for days. Her worry turned to panic and she considered it the crisis of her life. Pleas to Mr. Foster did no good; he refused to redistribute the parts, and the actress playing Katharina, a young socialite named Anne Bemis, was quite content with things the way they were.

What happened next is difficult to determine with certainty but it appears that Mrs. Bemis's husband received an anonymous letter accusing her of certain indiscretions with Mr. Foster. Mr. Bemis withdrew his wife from the Academy and reviled Mr. Foster with such threats and vilifications that the poor acting teacher became despondent and feared his business might go under.

Rebekah, sensing a power vacuum, moved in and took charge. She announced that she would play the part of Katharina for the entire run and then restaged the play to bolster her role. She also organized the other students into work crews and redecorated the entire auditorium in anticipation of the senatorial visit.

The night of 17 October arrived. The performance went well, although an early evening storm was blamed for the small house and for the coughing and sneezing that punctuated the second act. Rebekah admitted to being nervous and almost missed her first entrance while trying to reattach a false eyelash that had come undone. The actress playing Petruchio, recruited, of course, at the last moment, read her part from the script. Most performers find it difficult playing opposite a fellow actor still "on book"; it threw Rebekah for a while, until she sensibly began to play her scenes directly to the audience.

But if the senator noticed any imperfections, he kept them to himself. His compliments were profuse as he met Rebekah in the lobby afterwards. He told her he had never seen a performance of such intensity in an actress so young. Then he asked her to dine.

Rebekah, who possessed total recall when it came to restaurants and clothes, reports they had a supper of oyster stew and chops at Childs and that the bill came to six dollars, "including the coatroom." As far as the conversation went, foreign affairs were dispatched early in the evening, leaving plenty of time to discuss Rebekah's acting career (Harding thought she would make a fine Joan of Arc) and merry reminiscences of the old days back in Marion. They both laughed as she brought up long-forgotten incidents, including their first meeting at Elm Thicket.

Rebekah was certain she could feel his knee pressing hers under the table.

After supper the pair strolled uptown and soon found themselves in front of the apartment Harding had borrowed from a "fellow politician." He invited her up so that they might continue their conversation.

Rebekah tells what happened next:

> The flat was a charming one, albeit rather small, and my gaze kept going to the bed, visible through a pair of glass doors. Mr. Harding seemed nervous, and under the circumstances I felt it entirely appropriate to take his hand. It was only a few moments later that my most rapturous dreams came true and I yielded to his kiss.

That's all she yielded to that night, but apparently it was exciting enough for Harding. Rebekah describes his whimpering ecstasy at some length: the labored breathing, her fears for his heart, his shrill moans of passion.

Once Harding calmed down somewhat, they shared some lemonade and discussed Rebekah's financial problems. Harding was most anxious to help. He confessed that nothing would give him greater pleasure than to have "Becky" established in New York where he could come to visit her from time to time.

Rebekah announced that it was getting late. Though he pleaded for an extra hour, she insisted: there was a curfew at her boarding house. It was so restrictive living there. How ideal it would be to have a place of one's own.

The senator tucked twenty dollars in her purse for cab fare. They bade each other good night "with very ardent kisses." Then Rebekah went home. She had a lot to think about.

For the next two months, Rebekah tells us, she wrestled with her conscience. Should she give in to the senator? The consequences could be disastrous. But on the other hand, he was the love of her life and surely he would never let her down. Certainly he was attentive: small gifts arrived (an enameled vanity-table set, a teddy bear) and he visited New York whenever he could. Once they rode around in a hansom cab for hours while he told her allegorical stories about a stubborn maiden and a powerful king, the point of which Rebekah found distressingly obvious. On another occasion, they visited the zoo I was to work at years later. The afternoon was marred when Rebekah accidentally slammed the senator's finger in a cab door. Harding, fearing publicity, wrapped it in his handkerchief rather than seek medical aid. As a result, it healed improperly and altered, he felt, the characteristic flourish of his handwriting.

But still Rebekah had no income. She had quit her job at the club and her funds were almost depleted. How long could she exist on the sporadic gifts of cash Harding presented after each meeting? Not knowing what to do, she began to complain of time on her hands.

Harding took the hint. On his next visit to New York, he escorted a puzzled Rebekah to the offices of the New York Central Railroad. The railroad's president ushered them into his private office, where they were served refreshments and presented with souvenir locomotive paperweights. The two men discussed the excellent prospects for passage of some bill or other that was up before the Senate while Rebekah eyed the paintings on the walls.

At the end of the short and pleasant visit Rebekah was slightly nonplussed to discover that she had just been hired as a "special stenographic assistant" to the company comptroller at the salary of $22 a week. Harding assured her that her ignorance of stenography would in no way hamper the execution of her duties. To celebrate, he invited her to accompany him to Scranton, Pa., where he was scheduled to make a speech. She ran home to pack her suitcase and they met at Penn Station.

There followed several days of general hilarity as the couple lolled around their suite at the Hotel Callicoon, playing checkers while the senator dodged calls from local politicians and the press. Rebekah kept running down for doughnuts.

A car had been put at their disposal, and one afternoon they ventured out onto the icy roads, where he taught her how to drive. She picked it up immediately and after that he would refer to her affectionately, and with surprising grammatical accuracy, as "my little chauffeuse."

Their holiday ended 20 December when the pair returned to New York on the evening train. Rebekah knew something was up. The senator seemed nervous. His hands shook, even his voice shook. In the privacy of their Pullman section he began a long, rambling monologue.

She was torturing him. The strain of the past several days had been unbelievable: her sleeping virginally in the next room while he paced the floor all night with only a bottle of whiskey and some old magazines to console him. He was a man, after all. And it had been years since his situation at home had been "amenable." He had gotten her a job; what more did she want? Besides, everyone already thought she was his mistress. No one would believe the real truth. How would it reflect on his manhood if they found out?

Rebekah smoothed her gingham dress, the one that she had purchased in the Girls' Department at Arnold Constable. The time had come. She was ready.

"I surrendered myself to Mr. Harding—for that night and forever—somewhere in the Delaware Valley."

Now that she was officially the mistress of a United States senator, Rebekah's life began to pick up. She moved to a furnished apartment on West 54th Street on which Harding took a year's lease. They both shuddered at the cost, but Rebekah fell in love with the décor—"French furniture done up in the finest silks and satins." And besides, Benay Bamer, the motion picture star, lived right upstairs.

Rebekah's job proved not very taxing. Her desk, on which flowers were mysteriously placed each day, faced a beautiful view of the river. She found her assignments "varied and interesting." One day she might arrange theater tickets for some top executives, the next she might go through the copy of some promotional material, checking for errors of grammar and syntax. She was conscientious about arriving on time though it hardly seemed necessary. Most of the time, there was nothing to do but chat with her co-workers or spend time on some verses she had been struggling with. In late January, she played hooky for a day to attend the white sales. If anyone noticed her absence, it wasn't mentioned. She began to spend more and more time away from the office and was surprised to find that relations with her employer not only remained satisfactory, they actually improved.

Realizing she was onto a good thing, Rebekah lost no time in obtaining jobs for the rest of her family. Her mother became chief reference librarian of the Marion Public Library System and her father received a substantial promotion at the post office. Harding balked, though, at appointing her brother Fred to West Point, particularly in view of criminal proceedings against the young man regarding the theft of a yacht on Lake Erie. Walter, however, ended up in a veterans' hospital, even though he had never been in the service—a blessing that backfired when he was electrocuted in an "Invalid's Helper," an early form of whirlpool bath.* Amelia married an osteopathic physician and moved to Indianapolis, ignoring her sister's offer of a sinecure.

Much of her time, Rebekah tells us, was spent in keeping up a voluminous correspondence with her lover. While she is annoyingly coy about divulging the contents, she does tell us that his letters were often forty pages or longer, written in pencil on "Senate Chamber" stationery and sealed in thick blue envelopes. Her own replies were much shorter and written on ruled paper.

Of the Harding prowess as a lover, we learn little except for a few gratuitous remarks like "In the history of Love, surely Warren Gamaliel Harding was a Michelangelo!" Rebekah does tell us that he was particularly aggressive in the morning, and liked nothing better than feeding her cantaloupe in bed. He complained constantly about his wife, and on one occasion "prankishly set a photograph of her on fire while humming a funeral dirge."

But on the whole, their life together was quiet. For Harding, this was a necessity. By this time (1919), he was a famous man, one of

---

* Rebekah's attempt to claim survivor's benefits after his death, and behind Harding's back, was the source of one of their major fights. She claims she merely filled out some forms that were sent her.

the leaders of the Republican Party and a possible candidate for the presidential nomination, and there was much to keep him busy in Washington.

Rebekah, on the other hand, was growing bored. She loved night life and gaiety; it was ironic that now that she could afford them, they were off limits to her. And while she never tired of making the rounds of the Fifth Avenue shops, that was not enough. Her success with Harding renewed her self-confidence—never one of her weak points anyway—and she was growing restless. Whether she knew it or not, she was looking for adventure.

She had been spending more and more time with her upstairs neighbor, Benay Bamer. Miss Bamer was at the height of her screen career. She was the prototype of the new, modern girl: spunky, free-spirited, obsessed with the latest trends and fashions; the subject of occasionally scandalous but always exciting gossip. Rebekah was thrilled with the friendship. She even offered to take Benay's dog out for a walk when his mistress was busy shooting.

So when Miss Bamer announced she was moving permanently to Hollywood, Rebekah became despondent. She wrote frenzied notes of farewell, pledging her eternal friendship. Benay, who could not have been unaware of the identity of the gentleman who visited her young friend so frequently, made an offer: Why didn't Rebekah come out west for a visit?

Rebekah tells us it was a hard decision to make. In reality, the only hard part was how to tell Harding. She journeyed to Washington for that purpose, where his reaction was worse than she feared: he feigned chest pains and threw himself against heavy pieces of furniture, begging her not to go. But she was adamant and he came around to her terms. She would be gone three months and would require train fare, spending money, and a new wardrobe.

She arrived in Hollywood early in 1919, just at the beginning of the film capital's first Golden Age. She loved it from the start. "You wouldn't believe this place," she wrote Emily Frobisher. "The biggest stars walk down the street just like you or me." She bought a secondhand roadster and settled into a guest room in Benay Bamer's lavish home in Hancock Park.

Miss Bamer arranged for her to play a partygoer in the film *Little Alice Layton*. Just one week later, she landed a much larger part on her own, that of an amnesia victim in *Doctors and Nurses*, starring Edmund Horton and Carmel Myers. Paterson Decker, who saw what is believed to be the only surviving print, in an archive in Prague, writes that Rebekah looked beautiful, but that her role was not a demanding one, as she was unconscious during most of the film.

But Rebekah was thrilled. Metro wanted her to sign a contract; Edmund Horton took her dancing—she was the new girl in town and she was making the most of it.

At first, she attributed her fainting spells to excitement and overwork. Only after she collapsed on the set and was rushed to the hospital did she find out what the real trouble was.

She was going to have a baby.

3

Somehow Eve managed to get me through the next month. It wasn't easy. She would call every day to find out how I was doing. If I sounded particularly suicidal, she'd take me out to lunch in Beverly Hills to a place called Nate and Al's. It was supposed to be like a New York delicatessen, and I guess she thought I'd feel at home. In New York I wouldn't be caught dead in a place like this, with its five-dollar sandwiches, but I pretended to be thrilled and it became our hangout.

A few words about Eve. She was a tall woman in her mid-fifties who moved with a languid grace that I later came to suspect was the result of tranquillizer addiction. One giveaway was the fact that she had no idea what was going on below her waist. She was always falling off curbs and tripping over small tables. Her shins were black and blue, but it never seemed to faze her. She'd just pick herself up and keep on smiling.

Compared to the other wealthy matrons I saw in Beverly Hills, she was a misfit. She avoided the sun like a plague and was famous for walking down Rodeo Drive with a parasol. Not that I could imagine what she was doing on Rodeo Drive—fashion interested her not a whit. As often as not, she would show up in a turtleneck that zipped up the back and a pair of plaid bell-bottom slacks, just a little too short at the ankle. Her hair was another problem. She was what is known as a suicide blonde—"dyed by her own hand."

She and Pete had been married three years and she had nothing but good things to say about him. They met on a cruise to Mexico. Eve, just "let go" by Paramount under vague circumstances, had been hired to teach bridge on an ocean liner. It was the low point of her life, and she spent most of her time planning to jump overboard.

Then Pete signed up for lessons. He had just lost his wife and was in a deep depression. He couldn't eat, sleep, or work. I don't know what happened next, but a month later they were married.

Pete became his old self again, which means he turned back into a workaholic. He was never home, always running off to develop some new project. Eve worried about him since he was near seventy and had already had one heart attack, but there was nothing she could do. Anyway, this gave her plenty of time to devote to her one great passion in life: her friends.

She had hundreds—from studio presidents and stars all the way down to hack TV writers and actors who hadn't worked in years. One thing I'll say for Eve—she certainly kept in touch. She still sent birthday cards (not just Christmas cards, but *birthday* cards) to people she had worked with thirty years ago. An afternoon spent with her always included a visit to Hallmark's to see what had just come in. Next to her bedroom was a walk-in closet just for wrapping paper, ribbons, empty boxes, etc.

The people who got all these cards and presents were a mixed bag, but they all had one thing in common. Eve had adopted them. She was willing to listen to their problems at any hour of the day or night. No problem was too small or too tedious to fascinate her.

Needless to say, she had no children.

But the big problems, like the one I was throwing her way, brought out the best in her. She was always happiest when given an opportunity to scheme and hatch plots. Let her do that and she would feed you, type for you, take you shopping—you name it.

And *still* I was getting nowhere.

It wasn't through lack of effort. There was nothing I wouldn't stoop to. A couple of weeks after I moved in, Eve called early one morning, highly excited. Had I been examining the garbage? I had not, but I added it to my list. Twice a week, under the cover of darkness, I would haul the trash bags up from the cans out by the gate and spread everything out on the kitchen floor. I had to wear Playtex gloves it was such awful work. I thought I was going to vomit when I came across the remains of Guadalupe's enchiladas.

But everything I learned was negative—there were no drinkers in the house, no one threw out embarrassing correspondence, there was no disease, no one was under medication. This is not to say I didn't pick up some interesting tidbits—somebody was a Q-tip freak, somebody threw out perfectly good heads of lettuce; and one day I was rather surprised to find a catalog of barbells and weight-lifting equipment, which I cleaned off and saved—but on the whole, the garbage was a waste.

I spent most of my time becoming acquainted with the daily routine. It moved with such precise regularity, it might have interested the Aztecs as subject matter for a calendar stone. Nothing happened except what was supposed to happen, and at the precise hour it was supposed to happen. *No one* dropped by. The first month we had exactly three visitors: two old ladies from the Jehovah's Witnesses naively wandering about the neighborhood in search of converts and a man in a salt-and-pepper toupee looking for a stray poodle who answered to the name of Queenie. *"No Queenie aquí, no Queenie aquí,"* Guadalupe said, shooing him away.

The day began early. Just how early I didn't realize, until I woke up one morning at six o'clock with a migraine headache and was flabbergasted to see Guadalupe busy hosing down the terrace. She never let up. She dashed from one chore to the next. At first, Eve said this just showed how exploited she was; she didn't dare refuse or they would ship her back to Mexico. They probably made her sleep on a pile of straw.

I wasn't so sure. To me, it seemed more a question of energy. I'd seen Guadalupe operate, and I was developing a theory that she was hyperactive. I explained this to Eve and she got very excited. "My ultimate fantasy!" she exclaimed. "A hyperactive maid!"

Because Guadalupe certainly didn't *seem* exploited. On the contrary, she was about the merriest person I'd ever come across. Every time she saw me, she smiled and waved, whether she was airing pillows on the balcony, or washing windows, or hanging out laundry in back. Conversation, though, was a different story. Whenever I began to talk to her in my high school Spanish, she would start to giggle. Sometimes she had to bite her apron she was giggling so hard. There's nothing like a Mexican maid laughing hysterically every time you open your mouth to make you feel like a real fool. Eve and I ruled out Spanish lessons, at least for the time being.

Around eleven, the postman would show up and leave everyone's mail in a communal box. I made a point of getting there first. The old lady usually got something, but it was run-of-the-mill stuff for the elderly: inspirational magazines, small boxes from vitamin manufacturers, mail order catalogs, sweepstakes from Publishers' Clearing House, an occasional government check. The only piece that looked promising—a squarish letter post-marked Dayton, Ohio—was in an envelope so thick its contents remained undecipherable even when held up to a hundred-watt bulb.

Even though Jonica was off in Torrance, she continued to receive mail at home. Her name was on a lot of mailing lists, mostly stuff about the Equal Rights Amendment and Tai Chi Chuan lessons. A personal letter would come every now and then—usually a pastel envelope addressed in curly feminine handwriting. Once a week or so, a postcard would arrive from Europe, signed "B." These were apparently the work of a compulsive comedian on some kind of tour. Let me quote a typical example. This is from Paris; it shows the outdoor art market along the Seine. All the paintings are in the style of Keene, the guy who paints the kids with the big, sad eyes:

Cherie—

Ah, l'Art, c'est wonderful! They said Europe was full of old masters but I never expected this! That's me in the check coat.

[You turn it over to see a tiny French tot in a checked coat picking his nose in the corner.]

People here are so tall!! Tomorrow we go to see where Marie Antoinette lost her head. You would too if you had to pay these prices—cinq dollars for a bowl of soup. (no joke)

Love

B.

P.S. Guess what—I met the Coneheads!!

The people writing Jonica showed an odd disagreement as to exactly what her name was. Some letters were addressed to "Jonica Hupper," others to "Jonica Fetchko," and still others to "Mrs. Vernon Fetchko." Mr. Vernon Fetchko, whoever he was, received nothing all summer save a series of intimidating-looking letters from a law firm in Long Beach.

But it was Guadalupe, strangely, who got the most mail. Every day there was at least one blue tissue-paper Aerograma for her. Most were from Rogelio Cruz Ramos, who had a typewriter he must have been quite proud of; he typed the address in red caps and underlined "Estados Unidos" with stars.

Around noon there was a lull in the activity, during which Guadalupe presumably read her mail. At 1 p.m. on Tuesdays and Fridays, I would see her trot down the driveway in a pink pants suit and let herself out of the gate. Two hours later she would return in a cab filled with groceries and cleaning supplies. And once a week, on Thursdays, an old Japanese man would show up in an ancient but well-cared-for pickup truck and spend several hours doing whatever was necessary to keep the foliage from engulfing the house completely. Like most Orientals, he kept to himself, spurning my offers of iced tea by pretending he didn't speak English.

Afternoons I had pretty much to myself. I tried to get out of the house at least once a day; otherwise the tedium would drive you hooey. Pool-house fever I believe it's called out here. I got in the habit of driving over to the Howard Johnson's Motel in North Hollywood for a swim. I thought I was the only one who snuck in. Then it dawned on me after a couple of weeks that the group of shifty-eyed people hanging around the pool hadn't changed one bit. Nevertheless, the level of paranoia was so high that we never acknowledged each other. You could tell the real guests: they were the ones who didn't bury their face in a magazine every time a bellboy walked by.

Sometimes I'd drive over to UCLA and use the Research Library. Their collection of Hardingiana was small but interesting. Harding had died in San Francisco, so the local papers had given it pretty good coverage. But the parking was so bad, I'd have to walk about two miles.

I always made it a point to be home by five thirty to continue my observations of the house. I had a hunch that if Jonica was going to drop by at all, it would be during dinnertime. But she never did. Not once. I looked at a map. It wasn't *that* far from Torrance. The thought of all that mail piling up bothered me.

Not much happened at night. The light in the old lady's bedroom would stay on until either 8:58 or 9:58. This puzzled me until I realized she must be watching television. If there was nothing to her liking on at nine, she would turn the set off and go to bed. By checking the TV listings I was able to get a pretty fair, if conjectural, idea of her taste. She hated cop shows, but if there was a medical program or a family drama on, she wouldn't miss it. The only time she ever stayed up past ten was to see the ending of "Songbird," the mini-series based on the life of Kate Smith that won so many Emmys.

Sundays were the only days to offer a significant change of pace. Guadalupe would slip out around eight thirty in the morning, dressed for church. She returned around three, always accompanied by two middle-aged Mexican women dressed in bright polyester outfits. The trio would stroll up the driveway, chattering in Spanish, and disappear into the servant's quarters over the garage. For the next several hours, the sound of mariachi music could be heard drifting through the open windows. I once snuck around back to see what was going on; and from my hiding place in the bushes, I could see Guadalupe and one of her friends bounce by the window, doing the rhumba. At dusk, the women would leave, via a circuitous route that kept them out of sight of the main house, burdened with shopping bags bulging with most of the groceries Guadalupe had purchased earlier in the week, plus lemons from the tree in the backyard, and once with what looked like a set of sheets.

But what about the old lady? What did she do? I only knew what she *didn't* do. She never sat on the porch, she never wheeled herself out on the balcony, she never even peeked out the window. I never saw her.

Except, that is, once a week, and then under the strangest circumstances. Every Wednesday at precisely 1:45 p.m., a yellow van of the type used to haul around the handicapped would show up and park by the front door. A bearded, blue-jeaned young man would hop out and, assisted by Guadalupe, would wheel the old lady into the van via a complicated series of ramps. Then they would drive off, only to return two hours later, when the procedure was reversed.

Two or three other old people were visible in the back, staring impassively from their clamped and anchored wheelchairs. Where on earth were they going? I tried to follow them one day, but the driver recognized me and tooted a greeting—I had opened the gate for him—so my cover was blown. Since Mrs. Kinney always wore a green eyeshade on these outings, I began to fantasize that this was some sort of courtesy bus provided by a nearby gambling den.

But the fact remained that I was getting nowhere. Short of going up and banging on the door, I had no idea what to do next. All the logical solutions to my problem—the granddaughter, the servants—had proven dead ends. A note left under the door (suggested by Eve) describing my plumbing problems was answered in kind with a phone number of a plumber. A second note blatantly requesting a meeting—purpose unspecified—went unanswered.

My money was disappearing. I hated the hot weather. I hated the smog. It hadn't rained since I arrived. Los Angeles was beginning to turn my stomach. I missed Pam. I missed Morris dancing.

In short, I was getting discouraged. I needed to quit or come up with a new plan. This one wasn't working.

Then, exactly thirty-three days after I moved in, I came home late one night to find the main house all lit up—as the locals would say—like a used-car lot in El Monte.

4

The situation Rebekah Kinney found herself in during the spring of 1919 surpassed even the melodrama of the silent films which she now had to abandon after such a promising start. She was a newcomer in a fickle town. She had no real friends or confidantes. She was carrying the child of a prominent US senator, a national political figure known for his probity and moral conservatism. And he was three thousand miles away. Panicky and confused for the first time in her life, she boarded a train for Washington.

The trip across country was agonizing. Rumors had already filtered back to her that Harding had a new "friend," the famous Hungry Helen. An eighteen-year-old secretary with the Farm Bureau, Helen Swedbord acquired her nickname after local wags noticed she and the senator often dined at a restaurant known for its "All-you-can-eat" specials. Had she replaced Rebekah in the senator's affections? That question, which had seemed so trivial in California, grew more terrifying with each passing mile.

Rebekah wired Harding that she must see him immediately. He met her at her hotel looking "clammy" and suspecting what was up. After a "startled exclamation, followed by a rather odd moaning sound, almost a whisper," he appeared to accept the news calmly.

> He walked over to me, a little unsteadily at first, and kissed me on the forehead. Then he sat down on the sofa next to me and gently took my hand.
>
> "Rebekah, dearest," he said comfortingly, "I don't want you to worry for a minute. I know exactly what must be done."

It did not take Rebekah long to find out what Harding meant. In less than an hour he was back with a small bottle of Dr. Morse's

Indian Root Pills. He instructed her to swallow fifteen pills along with a quart and a half of tepid tap water.

Rebekah protested but soon saw that Harding meant business. Exhausted by her journey and cowed by his take-charge attitude, she acquiesced. But not completely. She took only half his recommended dosage; the rest she flushed down the toilet.

Nevertheless, the pills she did take were enough to cause severe nausea and hives. Harding left around six, pleading a dinner engagement (Hungry Helen? she wondered, despondent and retching). He checked in every hour or so like a better with a large sum at stake. She lay in her bed, miserable.

For the readers of *The Price of Love*, though, all remained sweetness and light. She awoke early the next morning, feeling better than she had in weeks and still pregnant. Harding took the day off. He and his chauffeuse went for a drive through the chilly Virginia countryside. She tells us they pledged their eternal love; what really went on in the car, we can only imagine. Rebekah departed Washington the next day. "I needed time to think."

Thus began one of the strangest episodes in Rebekah's career: an obsessive, nomadic journey to the off-season resorts of the Eastern Seaboard. She traveled from one spa to another, sometimes spending only a day or two; sometimes as long as three weeks. She would check into the best hotel, always under a different name, and devote her days to long walks along the deserted beach and her nights to writing poetry in the solitude of her room. She spoke to no one save waiters and hotel personnel, but her mind was constantly busy. She realized it was the watershed of her life. The wrong decision (and she feared she might already have made it) would condemn her to a life of what she feared most: failure, mediocrity, and most of all, anonymity. But the right decision—the possibility made her shiver with excitement.

There were letters. To Benay Bamer she wrote: "Do you think Metro would make me another offer? Have I been away too long? How is Edmund? I miss him—and you!! Everything here is so damp." And to Emily Frobisher: "Time is passing so slowly I think I might go mad. My life is so unsettled. I must act!"

Circumstances made her decision for her. Harding had been writing her daily—gentle, encouraging letters, but ones which always led up to his point: an "operation" must be performed immediately. In May, a political meeting brought him to Kennebunkport, Maine, where Rebekah had been staying. She was at the end of her emotional rope, and he was not much better off himself. The way Rebekah had been acting terrified him. Her distraught letters, pleading for "A name for my baby" and threatening "double suicide—myself and our love child" told him something must be done. During a clandestine meeting in an amusement park, he offered her $10,000 if she would have an abortion. He loved her more than ever, he said. When Mrs. Harding (who was five years older than he was and in notoriously poor health) passed away, he would make her his bride.

The money and the proposal had a soothing effect on Rebekah. She immediately departed for Norfolk, Virginia, where Harding had made arrangements with a certain doctor. "Air out my room," she wrote Benay Bamer. "I'll be back next week."

Rebekah's experiences in Norfolk, which constitute chapter 18 of *The Price of Love*, are largely responsible for the book's lurid reputation and the main reason it was banned in many communities until well into the 1930s. Although mild by today's standards, this was the first time such a graphic description of an abortion mill had appeared in print.

Her account, complete with street corner meetings, a filthy "clinic" over a wholesale poultry business, and an unkempt doctor whose "bloodshot eyes sent daggers of terror through my heart," makes riveting reading. She should have come much sooner, she was told after a cursory examination. It might well be too late, but the doctor said he was willing to "give it a try." "What do you mean, too late?" Rebekah demanded, but she was jabbed with a needle by a "foul-smelling foreign nurse" and left by herself in a tiny cubicle with blood splattered on the wainscoting. A woman screamed in the room next door.

Rebekah decided she had had enough. Nothing was worth this. She slipped out the window in the brand-new nightgown she had bought just for the occasion and crawled down the back stairs. For the next hour or so, she wandered through the lowest black slum of Norfolk, fighting off unconsciousness and terrifying passers-by, until a trolley conductor took pity on her and returned her to her hotel.

When she awoke from the effects of the sedative, she found a bouquet of roses waiting, with a card signed "W.G.H." He hoped that all had gone well "under the knife."

This unfortunate bit of phrasing was the last straw. There was no turning back now. She would go ahead and have the baby.

They had terrible arguments. Where should Rebekah spend her "confinement"? Harding tried to talk her into a "Christian Home," but she recoiled from this idea so strongly that she locked herself in a closet until the senator promised her it would not come to pass. He next suggested she move to Vancouver, where neither of them knew a soul; but Rebekah, grasping at straws, said she couldn't leave the country "so soon after a major war."

They finally settled on Santa Barbara, California, some fifty miles up the coast from Los Angeles. Rebekah had visited the peaceful old mission town during her West Coast sojourn and found it "picturesque and charming, yet with sufficient opportunities for entertainment."

A financial arrangement was made. We do not know the details, but subsequent events proved it could not have been very large— certainly not the $10,000 Rebekah would have received if she had gone through with the abortion. All evidence points to some kind of reconciliation between the two lovers: a recognition that they were both in this together, for better or worse. Somehow they would muddle through.

In keeping with this new spirit, Harding presented her with a diamond and amethyst band. Rebekah had suggested that a ring might make her feel more comfortable in public. After an emotional farewell dinner in a hotel suite, the mother-to-be set out westward, stopping in Indianapolis to visit her sister. The girls cried in each other's arms for hours and then went out for Chinese food and thought up names for the baby.

Upon arrival in Santa Barbara, Rebekah stayed at the Biltmore but soon found it "impersonal." It was also expensive. After making inquiries, she moved in with a Mrs. Webster, who accommodated the sickly in her rambling home up in the hills.

Rebekah, who had a fondness, if not a talent, for intrigue, passed herself off as the wife of a South American diplomat. She invented elaborate schemes involving pseudonyms and mail delivery designed to throw any Nosy Parkers off the track. She also contrived to have the baby's birth registered under the last name of Bamer, an homage her friend the film star did not appreciate and which led to a permanent breach between the two women.

The later months of her pregnancy saw a strange burst of unchanneled energy. Her poetry continued; several examples extolling the sunset and other natural phenomena were published the local paper. Her most curious undertaking was the invention of an expandable corset for expectant mothers. She was all set to go into business with her brother-in-law on this item until Harding, approached for capital, put an end to the project.

Blanche Marie was born 10 November, 1919. She weighed a little over seven pounds at birth and surprised her mother with a head of thick, black hair that soon fell out to be replaced by soft, blond fuzz. "She has the sweetest disposition," Rebekah wrote the father, "and she smiles whenever I come near her." But what delighted the mother most were her looks: by the time she was two months old, she was a dead ringer for Warren Harding.

5

I had been to dinner at Eve's. Her housekeeper had a bursitis attack, so we ate franks and beans in the breakfast room. She was in a bad mood—Pete (whom I had yet to meet) had just left for Munich, and there was no telling how long he would be gone.

Nothing I said seemed to interest her. For once, my tales of Guadalupe and the house, which she usually found so riotous, fell on deaf ears. This was a particular shame because tonight I had a plan to propose.

The plan involved Eve's pool boy, Osvaldo, a muscular young Mexican who lived for motorcycles. His dream in life was to move to Tucson and open a Yamaha repair shop. He couldn't leave yet, though, because he was still on probation.

Eve had a secret crush on him. Sometimes, she confided, she would go up to her bedroom and lie on the window seat with a bag of Hershey's Kisses and peer at him through the curtains while he added chemicals and vacuumed scum. She could stay there all afternoon. Sometimes her friend Betty Schwinn, who lived down the block, would join her.

Osvaldo wasn't a very good pool boy. Two of Betty's kids came down with salmonella after swimming in the pool. But Eve wouldn't have fired him for the world. I saw him one day. He was wearing blue jeans and a red bandanna tied around his head. No shirt. A tattoo of the Virgin on one arm, an eagle on the other. When he got a haircut, it was all Eve could talk about for days.

After dinner, I pushed my plate back and began to explain my plan. I was unaccountably nervous. I wanted Eve to like it, to be enthusiastic. But the way she was acting tonight . . .

What would happen was this: Osvaldo would drop by my place,

ostensibly to check out the pool and see if we could get it back in working order. Guadalupe would, no doubt, be hanging around and he would strike up a conversation with her. Next thing she knows he would ask her out on a date—

"And who stays with the old lady?" Eve wanted to know. "Or does she go on the date too?"

She had a good point, but I brushed her aside and went back to the plan. I would pay all the expenses. They would go to some restaurant and order drinks. He would take his time. At first, they would probably discuss topics of mutual interest, like what part of Mexico they were from, or what type of immigration papers they had. (As if either of them had papers.) The food would come. Osvaldo would order another round of drinks. Then slowly but surely he would ask her about the old lady . . .

Eve began to giggle.

"I'm serious, goddamn it," I said.

"I know," she said. "That's what's so funny." Then she broke down completely, laughing so hard the table shook.

"Oh, dear," she said, wiping tears from her eyes. "I'm sorry. I think it's beginning to get to me."

"That's okay," I said and waited for her to compose herself.

"What restaurant are they going to?" she asked. "Chasen's?" And she collapsed in laughter again.

By the time I left, around ten, *I* was the one who was depressed. She was now as jolly as a guest host on the Carson show. I was beginning to despise her.

I was so upset, I did something I never do—I stopped off at a bar.

It was the Cattle Call on Santa Monica. I had heard about it somewhere: a hangout for actors and actresses supposedly. A little handwritten sign in the window said "Piña Colada."

All the actors and actresses must have been somewhere else that night. Maybe they were busy acting. At any rate, I took one look and I knew this was strictly a neighborhood crowd. If you can call seven people a crowd.

I sat on a stool and ordered a Lite beer. To be perfectly honest, I can't tell the difference between it and real beer. Everyone rants and raves about Coors, the local favorite, but Pam had told me they were on the wrong side of some labor dispute she felt strongly about, so I'd promised I wouldn't drink any if humanly possible. Anyway, I tasted some once at a barbecue in Westhampton, and, to tell the truth, I wasn't too impressed.

I was well into my second beer and feeling a lot better when a woman walked into the place. Everybody turned to look at her, first, because they were so bored, and second, because she was wearing such an odd hat. It was purple, with pink plumes that looked like insect antennae. They jiggled frantically with each step she took. I immediately thought of the hats my grandmother used to wear. She was crazy about hats—literally. When she died, she had seventy-three. I remember the number because I had to take them to the Salvation Army and get a receipt.

I sized up the lady in a minute: around sixty, dyed red hair. Like most old broads, her nose was failing her and you could smell her perfume across the room. She was about eight drinks ahead of everybody else. A classic bar type and one that I can do without. I had an awful feeling she was going to sit down next to me, and I was right.

She ordered a Black Russian and looked around. Although I did everything in my power to avoid it, she caught my eye. "And now," she said like* she was continuing an interrupted conversation, "where is your homeland?"

* Bruce Pinsky's secretary, Dee Goode, who typed this manuscript during slow hours at work, has pointed out that I "seem to be confused" about some grammatical point concerning the use of "like" and "as if." Ms. Goode may be an accomplished typist, yet try as she might, she has failed to explain adequately exactly what I am doing wrong, and I went to Harvard, as you know. The issue, when taken to Bruce Pinsky for arbitration, was settled in my favor, I am glad to say. But I am indeed sorry that Ms. Goode chose to take the whole thing so personally. She is currently working for another partner at the same firm, I would nevertheless like to thank her publicly for her labors on my behalf.

I had noticed this before. People in California tend to think I'm foreign, usually French or Dutch. I think it has something to do with my glasses. Tonight, though, I just didn't feel like getting into it.

"Flatbush," I said and went back to my beer.

She thought about this a moment and turned to me again.

"What do you know about kamikaze pilots?"

"Absolutely nothing."

She seemed satisfied, as if I'd given the correct answer. She polished off her drink and ordered another. I made a point of looking at my watch.

She turned to me again, thinking very hard. I waited while she formulated her thoughts.

"I like raw fish," she finally announced.

The man next to me, who had been watching our exchange, fascinated, said, "Somehow, lady, I knew you would."

She then began to tell us a long story about how she was in Hawaii in 1956 and became ill at a luau. She was so sick they almost had to fly her back to the mainland on a special hospital plane they kept for such emergencies.

The story in its own way was rather interesting, particularly the part about how they had to carry her to the hospital in a makeshift sedan chair because there was a taxi strike going on. The man next to me moved his stool a little closer. He was tall and thin, with a lie-down crew cut and a beaten look. He was wearing a leisure suit, a raspberry plaid, with some peculiar stains on the front. Axle grease, they looked like. I got the feeling he was out on a day pass from somewhere.

"And you know what?" the woman asked.

"What?" we both said.

"That plane, that very same plane, originally belonged to Henry J. Kaiser. He fixed it up and donated it to the Hawaiian people."

"That's one for the books," I said.

"I remember those little cars he used to make," the man said. "What were they called?"

"Henry J's."

"That's right! They had little fins. Didn't they have little fins? Little tiny fins?"

By the time I left, I was merry and inebriated. The lady had convinced me to switch to Black Russians, and the man gave us each his business card. It said "Ray Lewis" and in each corner it listed a different occupation: "Telephone Switching Engineer," "Christian Lay Preacher,'" "Rosecrans Memorial Foundation, Public Relations," and "International Executive, IESC."

"My goodness, you're an international executive," the lady said.

I thought, not in that suit, he isn't. But in an odd way, I was stimulated by their company. Let's face it: after a month with nobody but Eve to talk to, even those clowns were okay. I was beginning to wonder about all her fancy friends, anyway. I'd certainly never met any of them. She kept saying she'd take me to lunch with Joan Didion, but that had yet to materialize. In her favor, though, I will say she did introduce me to Joan Didion's nephew, who dropped by the house once while I was there to borrow a tape recorder. Eve had told me that his side of the family was famous around Beverly Hills for being the recipients of a series of bungled nose jobs, but his nose looked fine to me.

Anyway, Ray Lewis and the lady set my mind to working. I was coming up with all sorts of ideas and couldn't wait to get home to jot them down. Eve's withering behavior notwithstanding, I wasn't licked yet.

Driving home was difficult. I kept misjudging where to stop for the red lights. It finally got so bad I pulled into a supermarket parking lot, where a sudden wave of nausea overcame me and I vomited twice, once out the door and once more by the ice machine.

It was almost one in the morning by the time I turned off Beachwood on to Casino. Something had been bothering me all the way up Beachwood—things just didn't *look* right. The hillside looming ahead of me, sprinkled here and there with lights—I knew it by heart. And something was off.

With a shock that sobered me to my shoes it hit me: all the lights were on at the Kinney house.

"She's had a heart attack!" was my first reaction. I stepped on the accelerator and raced home, the Mustang fishtailing around the curves. Thank God the road was deserted.

My heart was beating so fast I thought I might be having an attack myself. I sped through the gate, which I had left open, and screeched to a halt by my kitchen door. I jumped out and ran into the pool house.

The view through my shutters was frustratingly serene. The big house was perfectly still. Nothing seemed out of place—only the lights that blazed the length of the second floor.

I calmed down a little and tried to get my bearings. Had they taken her to the hospital? She certainly couldn't be asleep, not with all those lights. Maybe they were still waiting for the ambulance.

I got a Coke from the refrigerator—I had a terrible taste in my mouth—and paced around in the dark. I had to find out what was going on.

But how? I couldn't very well go up and ring the doorbell just because some lights were on. I cursed myself. Why hadn't I been there when it happened, whatever it was? The irony of it—the one night I hadn't been sitting home with my binoculars, the one night I was out carousing with some down-and-out barflies ...

Too bad I didn't have a dog. That would be perfect. I could take him out for a stroll, all the time edging closer and closer to the house ...

Then an idea seized me which, if not perfect, I knew immediately would serve my purposes.

I would take the garbage out.

Now, I had already taken the garbage out once that day. So I was forced to improvise some new garbage. I got a brown paper bag out from under the sink and stuffed it with whatever I could find: an empty cookie box, last Sunday's *New York Times* (minus the cross-word puzzle, which I was still working on), some oranges that had turned rotten, a jar of pickles I had bought on impulse and hated, a shirt the laundry had ruined, and a pornographic magazine I had found in a phone booth at UCLA and had been meaning to throw out for weeks. I added some wadded-up paper towels as fillers.

It looked very authentic. I put in the empty Coke bottle at the top (the perfect touch) and set out through the kitchen door, trying to appear nonchalant by whistling some tune. I think it was "I Won't Dance, Don't Ask Me."

Exactly what I was going to do remained a little unclear. You have to remember that I'd hoisted a few and my mind, while it had flashes of brilliance, was not at its analytical best. I guess what I hoped would happen was that someone in the big house would notice me and enlist my help in whatever emergency was going on. Failing that, I figured I could always just get real close and eavesdrop.

I admit it: I was drunk and shameless. A bad combination anytime. Mix in a little stupidity and you've got serious career trouble, or worse. I can laugh about it now. But it's hard to laugh when you hear a police siren and you know they're looking for you.

But I'm getting ahead of myself. The garbage was supposed to go around back, by the garage. I had plenty of time to take in the front of the house. The blinds were drawn in the old lady's sitting room. As for the newly lit-up rooms, I couldn't tell much about them. They seemed to be empty.

I rounded the corner of the house and saw something that caused the tune to die on my lips and my feet to stop in their tracks.

There, parked in front of the garage, was Jonica's little red Datsun.

So that was the solution. It had never even occurred to me.

Jonica had finally come back.

I stood there in the dark, clutching the garbage and pondering the implications of this latest turn of events. On the whole, it seemed very much in my favor. Aside from a little initial queasiness, Jonica seemed to like me. I'd even detected signs of an incipient crush. Even if she were only back temporarily—

A sound broke into my thoughts. It can best be described as a muffled snort. The kind you use to add emphasis during an argument. As in "Hah! That's what you think!" As far as I could tell, it had come from the house.

I crept further around the back, avoiding a collision with a lawn chair by sheer luck. The sound seemed to have come from a second-floor room at the other end of the house; it was the only one lit up on this side. I had noticed it before. It had a Moorish porch from which a rickety wooden stairway led down to an abandoned rose garden.

It was a mild night and the door to the porch was open. As I got closer, I could hear voices drift out. Or rather, *a* voice. It had to be Jonica.

By now, I was at the bottom of the stairway. I strained to listen. But the acoustics of the Hollywood Hills are notorious for their unpredictability. A case in point: Sharon Tate, et al. According to experts, they really put up a racket while being slaughtered, but the vegetation ate it all up.

I could only make out a few words and phrases. But they were tantalizing. "One thousand dollars," "How do you know?" and either "Vernon has a system" or "Vernon has a sister" or possibly "Vernon has a cistern."

I looked up at the white curtain—nylon, I guess—that covered the door. It occurred to me that no one in the room could see out.

I tiptoed up the first three steps. Jonica's voice said, "I don't know and I don't want to know. That's his business." A thrill ran through my entire body. This was it. I was about to learn something.

I couldn't make out the muffled reply. Then Jonica shouted, "Would you leave him alone? This just happens to be the twentieth century in case you haven't heard."

I figured if I got just a little bit closer, I could hear the other person. I crept up three more steps and paused. Not quite. One more should do it.

It did it all right. As I placed my foot on the seventh step, I heard a funny cracking sound. Before I knew what was happening, my right leg shot toward the ground, throwing me against the wooden railing, which also collapsed. I hit the dirt with such force all the wind was knocked out of me. I think I must have passed out for a second. Then the shrieks from upstairs revived me.

My first—what am I saying, my *only*—thought was to get out of there. Don't ask me how I made it back to the pool house. It's all a blur. The only thing I remember was turning the corner and looking back over my shoulder. There was Jonica, standing on the balcony in an orange nightgown that made her look like an overweight Buddhist monk, pointing at me and emitting shrill little yelps of terror and outrage.

The first thing I did was lock the door. Then I ran into the ladies' dressing room. I generally use the men's, but the ladies' had better mirrors. I switched on the light. Then it was my turn to shriek.

I was literally covered with blood. My beard, my chin, my shirt, my hands. The sight was so frightening, I collapsed on a bench; anybody who lost that much blood shouldn't be on his feet. Then I began the dreaded but necessary search for my wounds.

Fortunately, all the blood seemed to be coming from my nose. I have a history of nosebleeds, probably aggravated by the fact that as a three-year-old I stuffed an entire bottle of aspirin up my nostrils (just the aspirin, not the bottle). God knows what was on my mind.

Only when I got up to go over to the sink did I discover my ankle was sprained, or, God forbid, broken. I never want to relive that feeling. It was one of the worst nights of my life.

I'll say this for the Los Angeles police—they are very prompt. Less than five minutes later, a squad car pulled through the gates. Guadalupe ran down to direct them. She looked very dramatic: barefoot, wrapped in a blanket, and carrying—I guess for self-defense—a rake. At first, the police thought she was the victim and began to question her; but she gestured frantically toward the main house and they sped up the driveway, leaving her to trail behind, like the villagers chasing Frankenstein.

Jonica was waiting by the front door. She had thrown on a kimono and was beside herself with excitement. Her breasts heaved, she clasped and unclasped her hands. "In here, in here!" she yelled at the cops before their car had even stopped.

Now I realized I was in a tricky spot. I figured I had three options. First, I could get in my car and take off. I had rejected this from the start. Too risky. The folks in the main house were undoubtedly running around, peering out windows, etc. A car pulling away would be the first thing they'd notice.

Second, I could make a qualified admission of guilt. Some unusual, but believable, chain of circumstances that would put me on the stairway. As if there were one. Try as I might, I couldn't come up with any explanation that would explain all my actions, particularly my panic-stricken flight.

So I was forced to use my third option. When the knock came— as I knew it surely would—I was ready.

I took my time answering the door, calling out phrases like "Just a minute" and "I'm coming, I'm coming." By the time I finally did open up, Jonica and the cops were presented with the sight of a sleepy, pajama-clad academic type, sniffling into a wad of Kleenex because of a summer cold. I let my eyelids droop convincingly and kept my jaw slack, not just for appearances, but because I had to breathe through my mouth.

"Yes?" I said, trying to convey with that one word the divergent moods the situation called for—exhaustion, annoyance, curiosity, a desire to help, and above all, total ignorance.

"We had a prowler," Jonica blurted out before the policemen could open their mouths. "Did you see anybody?"

"A prowler!" I said, the very picture of astonishment. "Did he get anything?"

"No," said one of the cops. "But he left this." He held up my garbage.

My God. My God. I had forgotten all about the garbage.

I stared at the bag like it was a bomb ready to go off.

"Do you know anything about this?" the other cop asked.

Somehow I found my voice. "Like what?"

"Is it your garbage?"

I looked at the bag uncertainly. "I ... don't know."

He started to reach in the bag.

"Wait a minute. I think it is my garbage."

I grabbed the bag and began to rummage around.

"Yes, it is my garbage. In fact, I'm certain of it."

"Where did you leave it?"

"Outside my kitchen door."

"You're supposed to take it out back," Jonica said.

"I was going to in the morning."

The cop reached out for the bag and my heart stopped. I gave it to him—what was I going to do, have a tug-of-war?—and then watched in dumb horror as he began picking things out and examining them.

"Is this your shirt?"

"Yes." I could hardly get the word out.

"How come you're throwing away a perfectly good shirt?"

I had an answer ready but it wasn't necessary.

"What's this?"

He pulled out the copy of *Bound and Gagged*. On the cover was a blonde woman tied to a dentist chair. She was wearing a garter belt and black stockings and a nurse's cap. Another woman, similarly clad, was threatening her with a whip. A blurb promised "Swinger Ads and Pix Inside."

The policeman opened the magazine.

"Jesus."

He shut it and handed it back to me.

"I found it in a phone booth."

"Sure."

I don't remember much about the rest of the interview. They asked questions—what time had I gone to bed? had I heard anything?—and somehow I was able to answer. But horrible thoughts kept going through my head. Were they going to add me to some secret list of sex offenders? Was I going to get rounded up every time a youngster disappeared? I remember back when I was a kid in Mt. Lebanon. There was a guy who ran the local candy store named Murray the Homo. He had orange hair and was suspected of plucking his eyebrows. Now I knew how he must have felt. Poor Jonica was so embarrassed; she just stared at the ground and played with her kimono sash.

Finally they left. After a short conference at the squad car, the police gave Jonica some forms. Then they pulled out of the driveway. She locked the gate and walked back up to the house, glancing nervously now and then at the shrubbery.

Her hysteria was gone. She seemed tired, even thoughtful. She paused for a moment at the front door and looked back at the pool house. Then, abruptly, she went inside and closed the door. It was almost as if she knew I had been staring at her.

6

I spent the next three days recuperating at Eve's. Her doctor said the ankle wasn't broken, just keep off it for a while. That was fine with me—a trip across her Country French guest room to the bathroom would trigger off such waves of pain that Eve started giving me codeine pills to shut me up. She said she couldn't stand to see me in such agony.

Of course, half of it was mental. Three days in bed gave me plenty of time to reflect on my stupidity. There's no doubt in my mind that I would have gone back to New York right then and there if I'd been able to travel. I didn't care if those girls from Texas were still in my apartment. I could stay at Pam's.

I told Eve what had happened, of course. But I left out the part about *Bound and Gagged*. That was one episode I was planning to take to my grave.

"If only" ... I kept thinking. If only I hadn't stopped off at the goddamn Cattle Call. If only I hadn't climbed the goddamn staircase. And the biggest "if only" of all—stuffing the goddamn magazine in the goddamn garbage.

What on earth had been going on in my mind? My God, the care, the preparation, the *skill* with which I usually discard pornography— the people who design nuclear power plants could get pointers from me. Backup system after backup system. Nothing left to chance. What I do is this: with a pair of sturdy kitchen scissors, I cut the stuff into one-inch squares, mixing in something totally innocuous, like *People* magazine. Then I dump this mixture into a shopping bag and set out, after dark, pausing at every litter basket I pass and tossing in a handful. I keep going until the shopping bag is empty, and then I take a bus home. Once I made it all the way to Grand Central.

Eve wasn't being much help. On the surface she was bright and perky, but it was that mindless chatter that you'd use to comfort somebody whose family was wiped out in a flood. The third morning she bounced into my room dressed in a bright yellow outfit with little white daisies all over it. She sat down on the edge of my bed and smoothed out her skirt.

"I'm going to a funeral," she announced. It was a "business funeral"—Pete's accountant had met his Maker during a head-on collision on the Pacific Coast Highway. She showed me the article in the LA Times—FOUR THOUSAND OAKS RESIDENTS KILLED IN AUTO CRASH.

I may have been full of codeine but I was stunned. "Four thousand people were killed in an automobile accident?" This was it. I'm getting out of here. Call the airport.

"No, no. Thousand Oaks is a *place*. It's near Tarzana."

"Oh."

"And then I have an appointment at the museum. They want something of ours for a show. I'm excited to death but it's still very hush-hush."

"You mean I have to stay here all by myself?" I hated being left alone in the mood I was in.

"The dogs will keep you company. And Osvaldo comes today. You can go in my room and watch him."

"Ha, ha, very funny."

A word about the Biersdorfs' twelve-room, $1,150,000 house in one of the better sections of Beverly Hills: it had the common touch. No elegant parquet floors for them. Oh, no. Everything was beige wall-to-wall carpeting. Even on the stairways and in the powder room. The Louis XV chairs in the living room were upholstered in a Scotchgard chocolate plaid. On the circular marble coffee table were stacks of sophisticated magazines, like *Sunset* and *Arizona Highways*. Not to mention a silver dish full of lemon sourballs, each wrapped in a little piece of cellophane, and Eve's extensive collection of three English snuffboxes.

Bert and LaBelle Lance could have moved in with just their toothbrushes.

Bert would have loved Pete's den. Here, the decorator had truly let his imagination run wild. He had created a Bavarian fantasy, a perfect little *Bierstube* complete with all sorts of *Gemütlich* touches: rows and rows of beer steins, a stuffed rabbit over the mantel, and some leather furniture so masculine I was surprised to hear there was a decorator involved. It was here, Eve told me, Pete loved to sit and read scripts, listening to some *Studentenfest* music on the stereo in the company of his German shepherds, Heidi and Panzer. This canine duo was so vicious they had to be locked in the cellar before anybody was allowed to answer the door.

And LaBelle would flip out over the master bedroom, done, Eve told me, "in eleven different shades of blue." She went on: "It was my idea to dye the bed canopy the same color as a pack of Gauloise cigarettes. It looks unusual, don't you think?" I did. But not as unusual as the practically empty bookcases that lined one wall. They seemed like a good idea at the time, but neither of the Biersdorfs was a big reader. All they contained were some novels by Harold Robbins and a complete set of books about that person named Seth.

And the kitchen, where I soon found myself soft-boiling an egg. It was so neat and well organized. Banks of ovens, microwave and regular. All sorts of little energy-guzzling gadgets. Racks and racks of spices, all arranged alphabetically. I was doing my own cooking because Freda, the German (surprise!) housekeeper, spent all day up in her room watching soap operas. Eve was terrified to ask her to do anything because of rumors that she had survived Auschwitz. And *not* as an inmate, if you get my drift.

But Eve loved the house. She grew up over a butcher shop in South Chicago. And now look at her—living in "the high-rent district" and collecting English snuffboxes. "Shelley Winters gave me those snuffboxes—all of them. Somewhere she got the idea that I collect them. I think she has me confused with Leo Jaffe's wife. Every time she sees me, she says, '"How's the snuffbox collection?"' What can you do? You can't tell Shelley Winters she isn't playing with a full bag of jacks."

Anyway, I took my egg and some after-dinner mints I found in the pantry and hobbled out by the pool for several hours of sun and fun. Osvaldo showed up uncharacteristically early. As soon as he found out Eve wasn't home, he lit up a joint, pulled up another chaise longue, took off his boots and socks, brushed his hair out of his face, turned on his enormous portable radio, and joined the percussion section, beating out the rhythm on the little metal table that sat between us.

My watch was on that table. I eyed it nervously.

"How's it going?" he asked.

"Fine." I figured I could last about another minute.

"Hey, what's this shit?"

"Those are after-dinner mints. You want some?"

"I don't eat candy, man, I eat pussy."

"Gee, I'm fresh out of pussy."

Osvaldo found this remark so hilarious he laughed for several minutes, repeating it out loud and then doubling over again. "I sure gotta remember that one," he said.

I decided to stick it out a little longer. He certainly was an appreciative audience. I started racking my brain for pussy jokes.

It wasn't necessary. Osvaldo was off and running. First I heard all about his girlfriend, a waitress in Santa Monica named Sharon: "Blonde hair, man, down to her fucking ass and zoomers as big as your head." Sharon still lived with her folks—in fact, Sharon was still in "fucking high school"—but that didn't stop her from satisfying Osvaldo's "needs."

I listened spellbound. He had some very unusual needs. Most of them involved his motorcycle. He liked to tie Sharon to the handlebars and then have his way with her. They would do this in the parking lot behind Sambo's, the place she worked, after it closed at midnight.

"Have you ever been caught?" I asked, wide-eyed.

"Fuck, no. Those cops, they come and watch, man. They come and watch."

"*In Santa Monica?*"

"And you know what I yell at them? Whenever Sharon screams— she screams all the time, man—I yell, 'You hear that, you fucking cops? You know what that sound is? That's me fucking your mother!'" He ate a mint. "You got a girlfriend?"

I was so mesmerized by Osvaldo's adventures that I wondered if Pam would even qualify under his definition of the term. God knows we never pulled any parking lot stunts. Neither of us even had a car. Although I do remember once we were going at it on the terrace of her aunt's apartment on Central Park West. However, I rolled over on a brick and scraped my shoulder, so we had to call it quits. And a good thing, too, since her aunt got home about five minutes later and went *right to the terrace* to see if the bird feeder needed refilling. Imagine doing something like that at one in the morning. It really threw us for a loop.

"Huh?" Osvaldo said.

"Yeah, I got a girlfriend." In a gesture of masculine camaraderie, I pulled out my wallet and showed him a picture of Pam taken at a swimming party given by some mutual friends in Bedford Hills.

He whistled as I handed him the picture. He examined it so closely that for a minute I thought he was going to start sniffing it.

"Hey, you give her that bruise?" he cackled.

"What bruise?"

He pointed to a discoloration on her thigh.

"That's a birth defect," I said rather stiffly.

"Yeah, well it looks real hot."

God, what style! What finesse! Osvaldo wouldn't go to pieces over *Bound and Gagged*. No way. "Yeah, that's my fucking magazine and that's me on page forty-four with the electric cattle prod. You wanna make something out of it?"

I took a hit of Osvaldo's grass. Funny, I never realized how effective peasant wisdom can be. There were many lessons to learn from this man. God—with his attitude and my brains . . .

Osvaldo got up and began to do a little cha-cha. "*Tiburón, tiburón, tiburón.*" He turned smartly on his heels. "*Hepa, hepa,*" he yelled.

The song ended. He did a hilarious imitation of Eve paying him—all fluttering eyelids, seductive glances, pelvic maneuverings. I laughed till tears came. Then he sat back down next to me. His manner became confidential.

"Hey, man, how is she?"

"Eve?" I wiped my eyes.

"Yeah."

"She's fine."

"No, man, how *is* she?"

Then it dawned on me: *He thinks I'm Eve's lover!* He thinks I'm some gigolo who's moved in while Pete's out of town!

I never felt so flattered in my life.

When Eve got home she found me lying on the kitchen floor. Osvaldo and I had somehow started lobbing eggs at each other and the place was a mess. After he left, I'd started to clean up, but then, don't ask me how, I fell asleep.

Eve started screaming. But when she realized nothing was seriously wrong, she was so relieved she didn't even get mad. I told her I often took naps on the floor.

The truth was, I woke up very excited. My mind had been spinning all afternoon. And out of nowhere had come an idea. I finally had the whole thing all figured out.

I was going to have a party.

7

Eve was skeptical about the party idea, but at least she didn't laugh. She kept saying, "But I don't see the point," in this whiny voice that I was starting to find very annoying. The point was so obvious—to make friends with Jonica—that I knew this couldn't be her objection. She was just miffed because she hadn't thought of it first.

"What's it going to be?" she asked when she realized I meant business. "A little cookout?"

"No, it's going to be a full-scale dinner party, and I need your help."

Time was of the essence. I had no idea how much longer Jonica would be around. Her car was still parked out back when I returned from Eve's, thank God. I was so relieved I ran to the phone and dialed her number before I could chicken out.

She certainly didn't play hard to get. Her reaction was everything I could have hoped for—almost. "I'd *love* to come," she said over and over again. She offered to bring food, potato salad, wine, extra chairs, you name it. It was a little embarrassing.

"There is one thing you could bring," I said.

"*Any*thing."

"Your grandmother."

There was an abrupt pause. I realized I had made a mistake. Here she was, all excited about what she thought was going to be this glamorous party, and I'd asked her to bring her *grandmother.*

Okay, I decided then and there, if she wants a glamorous party, that's what she'll get.

Fortunately, I like to entertain. Pam and I often would have small dinner parties for from four to eight people. I do the cooking, though; Pam's idea of party food is pot roast, mashed potatoes, and a can of LeSueur peas.

Over the years, I've developed some rules about giving a party. I call these the three P's: Planning, People, and Props.

Planning: allow two weeks. Make sure you're not competing with some major drawing card, like *Traviata* in the Park or the TV special of some hot young comic. The food *cannot* be too special. *Always* serve a first course. You can throw together a salmon mousse in a matter of minutes with a food processor. As for the entrée—make it just a little bit out of the ordinary. Like homemade noodles with the veal (yes, I make my own noodles). And for dessert, experiment with the unexpected. How about homemade raspberry ice cream? Now, there's a conversation piece.

People: every party needs a "star." Stars can be the most unlikely people. Once it was my Aunt Fran from Albuquerque. She kept us laughing all night with her anecdotes of volunteer work among the Navajo Indians. But make sure you don't invite *two* life-of-the-party types. Nobody wants a rerun of *Star Wars* on their hands.

Props: fresh flowers—very important. Twenty dollars' worth, and scatter them around the house. Little dishes of nuts are a nice touch. Music can make or break a party. Put on something bouncy as the guests arrive—it gets them in a good mood—then switch to, say, Roberta Flack for dinner. Afterwards, I like to play my tapes of the old Big Bands, or perhaps a show album, or maybe even a comedy album.

After dinner? Games can be fun—*if* it's the right crowd. Proceed with caution here. And, of course, there's nothing wrong with going somewhere else—a late show at the Thalia or to some club to catch a new act you've read about (make sure everybody brought money before you try this). The point is—*do something!* Don't just sit around the living room watching everyone fall asleep.

Who to invite was a bigger problem than you might think, since I knew only seven people in Southern California, including infants and illegal aliens.

So I decided to keep it simple. Me and Jonica, Eve and a date.

"What do you mean, a date?" she asked nervously.

"Some attractive person who'll keep the conversation going."

She looked worried. "Like who?"

"Eve, use your own judgment. I've got a million things to do and I've only got two days."

So I guess I have no one to blame but myself when she showed up a half hour late, drunk, on the arm of a man so offensive, so obnoxious, so pathetically seeking attention, that after five minutes we had declared war.

He was wearing tight blue jeans and a plaid shirt. The sleeves were rolled up to reveal a pair of pneumatic-looking biceps. His hair was short. So were his beard and moustache. His teeth glared in the light whenever he smiled, which he did with unnecessary frequency.

Hmpf, I thought. Her latest orphan from the storm.

I immediately suspected he was homosexual. A certain type—Christopher Street is full of them, working in those boutiques that sell overpriced accessories for the bath, designer candles, and manacles.

Then he turned around.

Just in case there might be a misunderstanding, just in case anyone had the slightest lingering doubt, just, by *chance*, in case some drunk or blind person might wonder what side of the fence he was on, he had *keys* hanging from his belt and a *red bandanna in his rear pocket*.

"I love your kitchen," he gushed, sweeping around the room. "It's almost as big as mine." He came to a choreographed stop in front of the sink. "Can I give you a little hint? You don't mind, do you?"

"Of course not."

"You should always have the chicken breasts boned by the butcher. If you do it yourself, you'll rip the meat. See what I mean?"

He held up the breast I'd been working on.

Eve rushed over before I could slug him. "Just tell us what to do," she said. "We're at your command."

"Ooohh, command," he said, rubbing his hands together.

I sent the faggot out to start the charcoal and put Eve to work on the salad dressing. That is, until I remembered I had once seen her prepare tuna fish salad with Miracle Whip (and not even apologize or say, "Gee, all I seem to have is Miracle Whip," which leads me to believe she makes it that way *all the time*). I took her off food preparation altogether.

She was crushing ice for the margaritas when the faggot wandered back in (total elapsed time = 30 seconds) and said he was thirsty. Now at this point, I was still giving him the benefit of the doubt. I hadn't decided if he was an asshole or merely someone I didn't "get." So I dropped everything and made the margaritas. After all, he was the guest.

Eve took advantage of her break to move over by the refrigerator with the faggot. There, laughing gaily and ignoring me completely, the two of them talked about what kind of tennis shoes he should buy and wolfed down all the good cheese.

It was a depressing moment. I could see the pattern of the evening emerging. The faggot was going to hog the spotlight. Jonica would be completely intimidated and would clam up. Worse, she'd go home thinking what creepy friends I had.

I looked at them. She would be right. Sometimes Eve was a fancy producer's wife, but other times, like tonight for instance, she seemed well on her way down a road that led to one place and one place only: the Cattle Call. I could picture her during her declining years, hanging out with Ray Lewis and wearing a funny hat. Only in her case, it would probably be that ugly caftan she had on tonight.

And as for the faggot ...

We took our drinks and moved into the living room. I braced myself for some oohhs and aahs. The place had been completely transformed. It was hard work, but it had turned out so good that every time I looked at it my heart started beating faster.

The green carpet was gone. The floor was waxed and shining. The walls were all freshly painted a flat white.

A fire was burning, casting a warm glow on the bamboo chairs I had rescued from the boiler room. They were grouped on a quite passable rya rug I'd picked up at a garage sale. At the other end of the room, by the window, was my bed. It was covered with a simple white polished cotton spread and lots of green pillows in different shapes and sizes. Very inviting. Out the window twinkled the lights of LA. Big bunches of rhododendron leaves, massed in big vases, cast shadows against the wall.

"Looks like somebody's been reading *Apartment Life*," said the faggot.

Luckily Jonica arrived at that moment and prevented a murder. She tapped so gently at the door we were wondering what that sound was. I let her in and she walked in shyly. The first thing she did was present me with a box of date cookies. I thought she was giving me a bribe for inviting her to the party. I appreciated the thought, but let's face it: *date cookies?*

Eve and the faggot were spellbound. They hadn't run up against her fashion sense yet. Tonight she was wearing white painter's pants, a lilac T-shirt with a silver scarf around her throat, a white tuxedo jacket, and blue plastic sandals. Somehow it all worked. But she reminded you of a big Christmas tree: not so much dressed as decorated.

I jumped into action. Never in the history of hospitality had a guest been made to feel more welcome. She got the best chair—I made the faggot move—and an extra large 'rita.

For better or worse, the party had officially begun.

Now, Eve and I had spent a lot of time on the phone discussing strategy for the evening. Our goals were numerous and complex, but reduced to their crudest terms, what we planned to do was to get Jonica drunk and make her tell us everything. "We'll focus the whole evening on her," we agreed. With this end in mind, we decided that one of us would always be at her side.

Eve took the first shift.

We had moved out to the terrace. I was busy at the managed to overhear most of the conversation.

"So Elliot tells me you moved to Torrance."

73

"Ugh, Torrance. Spare me."

Jonica was nervous. She was trying to project the image of a bored sophisticate.

"So you miss Hollywood?"

"Is the Pope Catholic?"

Eve smiled politely. "What do you miss most?"

"Oh, everything."

Eve leaned back in her chair and took a long swig of her drink. She looked at me. She wanted me to know how hard she was trying. If the whole thing failed, it wasn't going to be *her* fault.

"Elliot tells me you have the most adorable baby," she said, trying a new approach.

"Yes, he's a cutie all right."

Inspiration seized Eve. She shot up in her seat. "Can we *see* him?" she asked breathlessly.

If Jonica didn't want her grandmother tagging along, she certainly didn't want her baby either. "He's asleep," she said, and that was that. Eve sank back down in her chair.

They continued this lethargic conversation for several minutes till it bogged down completely. Jonica seemed determined to make a good impression and not monopolize the conversation. And Eve was just as determined to pry information out of her, with a crowbar if necessary. The faggot got so bored he wandered off. I saw him over by the driveway, picking up leaves and examining them.

By the time we started to eat, I had just about given up any hope of sparkling conversation. All I wanted to do now was somehow get through the evening. It had gotten so bad, we were sitting around eyeing each other nervously and sighing a great deal. So I admitted defeat. I did the only thing I could, under the circumstances. I let the faggot take over.

We dined al fresco. Jonica was sprawled out on one of those aluminum lounge chairs with the plastic webbing. She would have been more comfortable in an iron lung. Eve looked at the cushion

I'd put out for her, and then went inside and dragged out a chair. The faggot made a big point of sitting right on the ground. So starved for conversation were we that we discussed for about ten minutes whether he would get his pants wet.

I ate standing up. There was so much to fetch.

First we had cold squash soup—my own recipe.* Eve, apparently hoping to salvage the evening, proposed a toast: "To our host."

"Hear, hear," said the faggot.

I winced. When the guests start acting like this you know you've got a real turkey on your hands.

With exaggerated gusto everyone attacked his soup. The women had some trouble balancing the bowls on their knees.

"Gee," said the faggot. "You hardly ever see soup at a buffet."

Eve rushed to my defense. "Break the rules, that's Eliot," she said merrily, taking a sip right from the bowl.

The chicken à la ginger, although overdone, proved easier to eat.

"Ah, finger food," said the faggot, and he began to tell us all about himself, as I knew that, sooner or later, he would.

Don't ask me why, but in five minutes, the women were completely under his spell. They sat there stuffing food in their mouths and hanging on his every word. I don't know what it was, his cheap, greasy good looks or the way he flattered them outrageously. He reminded me of the starlet who said, "But enough about me. Let's talk about you for a while. What do *you* think of my tits?"

His story was simple enough. He was *not*, he informed us at

---

* My agent has insisted that I include the recipe because "people like those things." Frankly, I think he's nuts, but here goes:

COLD SQUASH SOUP

6 scallion bulbs	Cut scallion bulbs into thin slices and saute in
2 tbsp. oil	oil. In a saucepan, cook sliced yellow squash
4 yellow squash	in chicken broth until tender. Add scallions.
1 cup chicken broth	Put mixture through food mill or blender.
Salt and pepper	Chill. Add salt, pepper, double cream. Serve
1 cup double cream	very cold with cut scallion tops as garnish.

the very start, an actor or a model like everyone thought. Then he launched into this long description of his acting and modeling career. I was getting a little confused, not that I cared that much. Then it turned out that he wasn't an actor or a model *any more*. Now he was a writer.

"What kind of things do you write?" Jonica asked.

"He writes puppet shows," Eve said.

He shot her a withering look. "Not any more, I don't," he said, marshaling all his dignity. "I only did that for the money." As if we might think he did it for kicks.

Now he was on the verge of a big development deal for a movie based on an original idea of his. He wasn't at liberty to give us any of the details; all he could say was that it was about the wife of a Frank Sinatra-type entertainer whose plane gets hijacked when she's on her way to Israel to plant rose bushes. Then he proceeds to tell us every possible detail, some of them twice.

Even the women were a little stunned at how bad the plot was. There was an uncomfortable silence after he finished.

"I met Frank Sinatra once," Eve said.

"Do you ever still model?" Jonica asked tactfully.

The faggot gave a long-suffering sigh. "I'm through with all that. But I still get offers. Just yesterday this guy stopped me in the supermarket and asked me if I was interested in playing Tarzan. Can you believe that? A person like me, swinging from a vine?"

Personally I would have loved to see him swinging from a vine— preferably by the neck. But after several more tales of stalled movie deals and "problems with my agent"—who, Eve told me later, operates out of a phone booth at the Hamburger Habit on Santa Monica—I started to feel a little sorry for the guy. Here was a classic case of somebody who could make a perfectly good living posing for cigarette ads but he wouldn't do it. He felt he was above it. He wanted Art. It was pathetic.

But that doesn't forgive what he did after dinner. It might explain it, but it doesn't forgive it.

What happened was this: the Santa Anas were blowing that night. The Santa Anas are this strange West Coast phenomenon, these hot, dry winds that blow out of the Mojave Desert. They're part of the local folklore: evil and dangerous. Children go out after dinner, hang out till all hours, pulling pranks and refusing to go to bed. The crime wave goes up. People are famous for freaking out. Maybe that's what happened to the faggot.

We remained on the terrace after dinner, listening to him talk about himself and watching the wind swoosh through the trees. It was hypnotic. But the candles kept blowing out no matter what we did, so I started taking stuff into the kitchen. Jonica offered to help. I was surprised and so was the faggot. "Put out" might be a better term. Now his audience was down to one, and she was starting to doze off. Ten thirty was past Eve's bedtime.

I was starting to like Jonica now that the pressure was off. She was brighter than she seemed. "Definitely a C student," Eve had whispered to me, but I was beginning to wonder.

In her favor: beautiful skin, flaming red hair, big green eyes. The big drawback, of course, was what Eve and I had come to refer to as her "weight problem."

Now the inevitable question: How fat was she? I would guess that she tipped the scales at around two hundred pounds. She was *fat*. She was what you mean by *a fat person*. She was so fat you wondered how she found pants in that size. She was so fat you'd hold your breath if you saw her attempt a subway turnstile. She was so fat ... well, you get the picture.

Wait, I've got another one. She was so fat she ate the leftovers off the plates! I watched her out of the corner of my eye. It was riveting. I kept losing my train of thought. Before she scraped them into the garbage, she picked them clean! Oh, she'd leave a token shred of lettuce and the chicken bones, but otherwise, her fingers would dart out and jam everything in her mouth—but only when she thought no one was looking

"Where do you want the garbage?" she asked.

So traumatic was her mention of the word "garbage" that I forgot all about her eating habits. A spasm of terror clutched at my stomach and raced down my legs.

"I'll take it out," I said, hoping my knees wouldn't buckle.

"No, no, allow me."

The last thing on earth I wanted was a fuss over the garbage. "Okay, just put it on the back porch."

As Jonica and the you-know-what disappeared out the back door, the faggot strolled in. Eve had conked out for good and he had to "split." He got up every morning at seven to work on his screenplay. I marveled out loud at his dedication.

Dinner was delicious, he told me. One more bite and he'd turn into a blimp. "And speaking of blimps, where is Miss Goodyear?"

Jonica chose that moment to appear in the doorway.

It was awful. She seemed not to have heard, but her face turned red; she continued into the room and busied herself at a counter, not looking at either of us.

I thought the poor faggot might have a coronary. He looked at Jonica, then at me, then back at Jonica in speechless embarrassment. She ignored him; I glared at him. He opened his mouth but thought better of it. With a final, very guilty look at Jonica, he slunk from the room.

Jonica and I remained silent for quite a while. Your heart went out to her. What a sad, lonely life she must have. I was surprised at how strongly I was affected by all this—it was bringing out my most maudlin qualities. There was something about the situation that had the same feeling as those books for Young Adults about sensitive-misfit adolescents who are made fun of in high school. For a short, intense period, they were my favorite reading.

What should I do now? Pretend nothing had happened? Or bring it out in the open? What did they do in those books? It seems to me there was always a best-friend character who gave bitter, yet brave, advice and came to a sad end. This somehow gave the hero/heroine (and the reader) hope. Later on, I learned at Harvard this was the essence of tragedy.

I looked at Jonica for clues about what to do. She was dealing with the situation by piling sugar cubes on top of each other with the utmost concentration. Only her fingers moved; her back was ramrod straight.

"How about a cup of coffee?" I asked.

She looked at me. Or rather looked my way. Then she burst out crying.

We sat in the kitchen until one thirty. She poured out her heart and soul to me—all her hopes and fears, her feelings of inadequacy, what it's like to be made fun of all the time. It was all very interesting. But it wasn't about Warren Harding.

I kept pressing her for *facts*. *When* did her mother die? *Where* did she grow up? This kind of stuff meant nothing to her. She brushed it aside. What mattered was *why*. *Why* was she afraid of people? *Why* was she so insecure? She had many theories. She explained them all in the greatest detail.

Fine. I was willing to listen. In fact, never in her life, I'm sure, had she had such a sympathetic ear. But to my great disappointment, these details were rooted not in childhood trauma but in present psychological absurdities. "I have to trust. I have to feel," she told me.

I have to go to bed, I thought. Never had I heard such tripe. But I sat there and listened to it. Her goal was to become whole. I could make a nasty crack here but I won't.

Anyway, I did pry this much out of her: her parents were divorced when she was five and her mother died several years later. Since then, she's been raised by her grandmother. Two years ago, she married a hillbilly songwriter and had little Warren. Now the marriage was falling apart. It did sound ghastly: he would stay away for days at a time and had traded her brand-new color TV for a half-ounce of marijuana and a puppy. She was a woman at her wits' end. That's why she was trying to become whole.

"Tell me about your grandmother," I kept begging.

Jonica reflected for a while on their relationship. She felt it was complex and Freudian. I found it boring and predictable. Here were two women who had lived together for twenty years. Of course they got on each other's nerves. So what.

"I don't know if I'll ever get away from her," Jonica said. "She doesn't miss a trick. She knows everything that goes on." She paused. "She even knows all about you."

My blood ran cold.

"What about me?"

"That you're writing something, that your mother comes to visit all the time—I think she means Eve—and that you're using the bamboo chairs. She's trying to figure out a way to get them back so she can sell them."

"Anything else?"

Jonica laughed. "Yes. She thought you were the prowler."

I held my breath.

"What made her think that?"

She shrugged. "Who knows? Who knows what you're thinking when you're that old?"

Eve walked in yawning and apologizing for falling asleep. Ordinarily I would have been furious, but tonight I was so caught up in Jonica it was all I could think about.

I lay in bed all night going over what had happened. Did this mean we were friends? Or would she wake up so embarrassed that she would never speak to me again?

I found out early the next morning. There was a note under my door. It was written on old-fashioned notepaper, the kind that folds over and is engraved on the front. This particular one was yellowed with age.

Dear Elliot,
    These belonged to my great dead aunt. Or rather my dead great aunt. At any rate, my aunt is dead. I also got a pair of little pink booties you wear in bed. My grandmother got the real "booty" (all the IBM stock). I feel they are an appropprite thank you for such a wonderful party. You are a truly mangificent chef. Please have another one (minus you-know-who on the guest list) so I can write you another thank you note. I've got a lot of them left.

Seriously, I had a wonderful time. Thank you again.

Sincerely,

Jonica

That's sweet, I thought. Although I sensed an unconscious irony in the phrase "appropprite thank you." Where did she get this ratty old thing? I turned it over to look at the name on the front.

"Mrs. Edward Beale McLean."

Jesus Christ, I knew that name. Anybody who knew anything about Harding knew that name. But she certainly wasn't Jonica's great-aunt.

It didn't make any sense.

8

Evalyn Walsh McLean was the Lee Radziwill of the 1920s. She was no great beauty but always the height of chic. In her life, she went through several fortunes, none of which she earned. She was in her element in the innermost circles of political power but cared nothing for politics. She was never out of the news for long, but her fame rested on one quality: her foolishness.

"The one continuing problem in my life has always had the shape of just one question," Evalyn once wrote. "What amusing thing can I do next?"

She began looking for the answer when she was ten. Her father, Tom Walsh, an Irish immigrant, dragged his family from one western mining town to another. It was an unsettled childhood but an exciting one; Dad was full of stories about Jesse James and other famous desperadoes he'd crossed paths with. The Walshes were far from poor; Tom's wheelings and dealings placed them in the upper brackets of Colorado society, such as it was. They were helped along by the ambitions of Mrs. Walsh, the perennial social climber. Wherever they might find themselves, she established an Episcopal congregation and once went as far as changing the name of one of her husband's camps from Sowbelly Gulch to St. Kevin's.

In 1896 Walsh's claim trading finally paid off. He acquired control of an abandoned silver mine. The silver had all been played out and the mine was considered worthless. Only Tom realized that the grayish quartz which everyone thought was silver-lead carbonates was actually gold in a tellurium form. Overnight the Walshes were rich on a ducal scale. They had more money than they could ever spend in Colorado, so they moved back east to Washington, D.C.

The reasoning behind this choice of a new home is a little obscure, but it turned out to be an ideal one. The word got around that

Tom Walsh was a man with "money to burn." Furthermore, he was an attractive, rakish, and rather romantic figure. Soon he was serving on political committees for President McKinley and refusing congressional nominations. He never ran for anything and never held political office; he realized, quite rightly, that his real power lay in money. By 1902, he was an institution in the capital. President Theodore Roosevelt dropped him a note: "When I was riding yesterday in the Park, I waved to you." Tom Walsh hadn't noticed.

Evalyn adored her father (her autobiography is entitled, revealingly, *Father Struck It Rich*). And for his part, he doted on her. No whim was ignored, no present too expensive. Soon she and her brother, Vinson, had turned into perfect brats. She was expelled from the Masters School in Dobbs Ferry, New York, for wearing too much jewelry to class. "You disgrace this school," old Miss Masters told her, seething with contempt. Upon arrival in Paris, Evalyn tried to dye her hair red but it came out green and yellow; someone was sent to fetch her.

She and Vin continued such antics until one August in Newport when, coming back from lunch at Mrs. Clement Moore's, Evalyn's red Mercedes had a blowout and Vin, at the wheel, lost control. The car went off a bridge; Vin was killed and Evalyn's leg was shattered. Her recovery was slow and painful. The experience left her a morphine addict (a recurring problem), but at least she was able to suffer in style. When more surgery was needed (the injured leg healed an inch too short), her bathroom was set up as an operating room to save her the inconvenience of a hospital stay. That it was more than adequate reflects the size of the Walsh mansion at 2020 Massachusetts Avenue.

Perhaps the accident told Evalyn it was time to settle down. At any rate, she eloped with another Washington rich kid, Edward Beale McLean ("Ned'), who was, if possible, even more spoiled than Evalyn. He was handsome but vacuous, a well-known boob whom everyone was nice to since his father owned the *Washington Post* and the *Cincinnati Enquirer*.

Ned seemed to possess every flaw found in the wealthy: he was an alcoholic, a compulsive gambler, a crybaby, an intellectual moron and, later in his life, a lunatic.

Evalyn had her doubts about the marriage, but that didn't prevent her from enjoying the honeymoon. The newlyweds sailed for Europe and the Near East and managed to spend their entire wedding present of $200,000. Everybody wanted to meet them, and they had all sorts of adventures, including a visit to a sultan's harem ("Just a lot of fatties, except for two or three who wore Worth gowns," Evalyn reports). Sightseeing was fine, but it couldn't compare to spending money. While examining the Pyramids, Evalyn became "impatient to get out before it was too late, and buy something I might want."

Back home the newlyweds set up housekeeping in Washington and soon Evalyn gave birth to Vinson McLean, whom the press dubbed "the hundred-million-dollar baby." Vinson slept in a gold crib, a present from his godfather, King Leopold of Belgium. His parents were so terrified he might be kidnapped he was constantly surrounded by nurses and detectives.

One day when he was five, his father had one of his rare insights; he realized Vin might become spoiled. "Last year we provided him with a private showing of the circus," he told his wife. "My plan is to change things a lot. Let's find him a Negro boy to play with. When he grows up the Negro boy can be his valet."

Why not, thought Evalyn. They found a suitable candidate, five-year-old Julian Winship, and the appropriate papers were drawn up, giving the McLeans custody of Julian for ten years. Julian loved the arrangement, though the Pullman porters on the train to Palm Beach were scandalized. Evalyn had nothing against the child, but she was vaguely disturbed that so much time and effort was spent cleaning and dressing him. But it was Vin who decided things. He hated Julian so much he finally beaned him with a watering can they were fighting over. Julian was sent back to his family. Evalyn felt she had learned a lesson even though she wasn't quite sure what it was.*

---

* Vinson's favorite playmate then became Shirley Burden, father of New York politician Carter Burden.

About this time, Evalyn embarked on her most notorious folly: she bought the Hope Diamond. One of the world's most famous jewels, it had graced the crown of Marie Antoinette. After the French Revolution, it was stolen and slightly recut, but its midnight-blue color was unique and unmistakable. It passed through a succession of owners of various nationalities. They all had one thing in common: terrible things happened to them after they bought the stone. They were shipwrecked, they lost their fortunes, their relatives died strange and horrible deaths. By the time the diamond came into the hands of Paris jeweler Pierre Cartier, it was a mythic talisman of misfortune.

The Hope Diamond was considered unsellable, but Cartier took a chance with Mrs. McLean. Evalyn leapt at the opportunity and paid the asking price—$154,000. Her mother had a fit when she found out and made Evalyn return it at once. Cartier sent it right back, saying a deal was a deal. A month later, her mother was dead.

In her grief, Evalyn became readdicted to morphine. Then Vinson, aged nine, managed to elude the servants and slip out the front gate for a second. He dashed onto Massachusetts Avenue and was struck by a car. At first, he appeared no more than badly shaken. But later that day, he went into a coma, and by 6 p.m. he was dead. Evalyn, rushing home by private train from the Kentucky Derby, was distraught. It was the tragedy of her life.

But by now, there were two other sons and a daughter. Life had to go on. The family moved to an estate called Friendship, near Georgetown. It had once been a monastery, but the McLeans totally renovated the place, spending $50,000 on rose bushes alone, and putting in a private golf course. It soon became the social center of official Washington. As the *New York Times* noted in Evalyn's front-page obituary, "The McLeans were such social arbiters that they never went out—they only received."

As Evalyn entered middle age, she matured somewhat and her better qualities began to show. She loved people and she loved to entertain. Her grasp of politics was nil unless she could smell a party: "The President and the Secretary of War had just astonished everybody by proposing to destroy battleships and limit future naval building in the interests of peace," she wrote with a straight face. "It seemed to me that was sufficient excuse for an entertainment."

She was a Washington institution by the end of World War I, the only competition being her good friend Alice Roosevelt Longworth. Evalyn was much more ingenuous than the caustic "Princess Alice"; one can picture Mrs. Longworth's reaction when Evalyn forced her to accompany her one snowy evening on a journey through Washington's parks, looking for homeless people Evalyn could bring back to Friendship and offer shelter. She had heard the parks were full of such people and was puzzled to find only one, an elderly woman huddled in a ladies' room, who insisted she already had a home and a family and that they were coming to pick her up.

Shortly after she bought the Hope Diamond, Evalyn and Ned went over to the Longworths' for an evening of poker. Among the guests were a couple new to Washington: Warren Gamaliel Harding, the newly elected senator from Ohio, and his wife, Florence.

Evalyn was intrigued. The senator was a charmer—"A stunning man." He chewed tobacco and wore suspenders and seemed delighted with his new status.

But Evalyn, the confidante of kings and presidents, was most fascinated by Mrs. Harding. She remembered their first meeting vividly: the Duchess, freshening drinks, but not touching the cards, "Her chin lifted haughtily each time she scented a challenge." Both couples were in the newspaper business, but aside from that, they had nothing in common. The Hardings were self-made and the rough edges were painfully apparent. But to Evalyn, there was something in the meshing of their two personalities—he with his charm and commanding presence, she with her business sense and ambition—that made them irresistible.

The evening was such a success that another was immediately planned. But the Hardings didn't show up. Alice told Evalyn the Duchess had been taken ill and was dying.

Shocked, Evalyn rushed over to find out firsthand what was going on. Up in Mrs. Harding's cluttered bedroom, with a rack of neckties hanging from the chandelier, Evalyn listened, rapt, as the Duchess, flat on her back and her complexion blue, poured out the story of her life: her autocratic father, her worthless first husband, their divorce, her only son—who followed his father to alcohol and an early grave—her marriage to the handsome young editor and how they built up the paper together, with her running the business end and even scrubbing floors when necessary. And finally, their local prominence, which forced a reconciliation with her father.

Maybe something in the story touched a chord in Evalyn. Perhaps she saw elements in her own life. At any rate, that day, the two women formed a friendship that was intense, lasting, and complete. They were to remain best friends until the Duchess's death. An unlikely pair, certainly; but in a way, they were well suited to each other. Evalyn was above the conventions of Washington society, and the Duchess didn't even know what they were.

The intimacy between the two women certainly helped the Hardings socially. And in 1920, when Harding won the Republican presidential nomination, the McLeans were able to help out politically as well. The *Cincinnati Enquirer*, one of the bastions of the Ohio Democratic Party, broke all tradition by printing story after story favorable to Harding. And when the rumor surfaced during the campaign of "colored blood" in the Harding family, the McLeans used all the power they had to make sure there was no mention of it in the press. They even temporarily kidnapped Harding's sister Carrie, to prevent the well-intentioned but naive ex-missionary from addressing a meeting of "colored people" at the height of the crisis.

With the election came the rewards. Harding couldn't quite figure out what post to offer Ned; it is an indication of Ned's reputation that no one ever suggested he should be given anything important. He was finally put in charge of the inaugural festivities.

Ned took his new job with all the seriousness of an idiot stringing beads. He envisioned a mammoth celebration involving fireworks, battleships sailing up the Potomac, etc. Then Congress got wind

of the cost and the whole thing was canceled. Undaunted, the Mc-
Leans threw their own party. Evalyn sat next to Calvin Coolidge, the
new Vice President, who complained all night of a stomach ache.

For the next three years, the couples were virtually inseparable.
They vacationed together (usually on a yacht the McLeans would
charter), and Friendship became a second White House, only more
elaborate and glittering than the original.

The summer of 1923 brought the Voyage of Understanding, a
two-month presidential journey through the western states and
Alaska. The McLeans were planning to go, but at the last moment,
Evalyn's doctor told her she needed an immediate operation for her
goiter. Disconsolate, they saw the Hardings off at Union Station.

Halfway through the trip, Harding was dead in San Francisco.

The nation was shocked. None of the scandals was out in the
open yet. He was hailed as a great and good man, a martyr to his
country, struck down by overwork and the inhumane demands of
the presidency. The Duchess, heavily veiled, accompanied the body
back to Washington, where Evalyn met her and drove with her to
the White House.

She never cried, Evalyn reports. The first night, the two women
went down to the East Room, where the body was lying in state. A
chair was placed next to the coffin. The Duchess talked to her dead
husband for an hour and a half.

"No one can hurt you now, Warren," she said. Evalyn shivered.
The cloying scent of the flowers was making her ill.

With the President dead, the Duchess lost her will to live. She became reclusive and moved into a sanatorium back in Marion. Evalyn
went to visit, and they had dinner in her private railroad car. As the
Duchess left, she bade her friend good-bye. "Evalyn, this is the end."
And it was. Within a month, she was dead.

Evalyn's life quieted down after both the Hardings were gone.
She and Ned were not that close to the Coolidges. Once the Teapot
Dome Scandal broke and Ned was implicated as a high-level errand
boy, they found that they didn't have as many friends as they used

to. Ned testified under oath; everyone agreed it was a pathetic performance. But everyone also agreed he was much too stupid and childlike to have taken any important role in the fraud. He was never indicted.

Nevertheless, the strain finally broke their marriage, and they separated in 1929. Evalyn was uncooperative about a divorce after Ned decided he was in love with Marion Davies's sister, Rose. She forced him to go to Riga, Latvia, to obtain a decree of questionable validity. Ned never got a chance to marry Rose, though. He was adjudged insane in 1934 and spent the rest of his life (he died in 1941) in an expensive Maryland insane asylum. A fellow inmate, Zelda Fitzgerald, wrote to her husband, "Guess who they checked into Ward 4 the other day—the infamous Ned McLean. We danced at social night—he *made* me dance—the Hokey Pokey. But he throws a tantrum if you call him by his real name, so we call him Mr. Orlo, or *l'enfant terrible* when he's not around."

It was a wonder the *Washington Post* survived as long as it did under the McLeans' management. In 1933, it was sold at the auction block,* and Evalyn began making secret trips to New York to pawn her jewels. Her final brush with notoriety involved the Lindbergh kidnapping. She was bilked out of $104,000 by a con artist who convinced her he was in contact with the abductors.

World War II brought out the best in Evalyn. Her financial picture improved once the Depression was over; she began a strenuous schedule of volunteer work. Her parties at Friendship for wounded GIs and their girlfriends became legendary. The best food and champagne were served, and afterwards there was dancing, with the soldiers trying out their new artificial limbs on the highly polished floor of her ballroom. Evalyn was everywhere, cheering them up and letting the girls try on the Hope Diamond.

Evalyn Junior carried on the family tradition of Washington marriages by becoming the fifth wife of Senator Robert Reynolds of

* To Eugene Meyer, father of subsequent owner Katharine Graham.

North Carolina and heir to the tobacco fortune. But in 1947, while staying with her mother at Friendship, she died of an overdose of sleeping pills. The parties stopped. Evalyn never quite recovered. In a year she was dead. She was sixty years old.

Harry Winston purchased her jewels from her estate, with plans to resell them. But he knew he could never sell the Hope Diamond. He could never find another Evalyn Walsh McLean. He donated the stone to the Smithsonian Institution.

9

Suddenly everything was different. It was like I had become a member of the household. Guadalupe began hosing down my car every morning, the same way she did Jonica's. Neighborly gifts—ant spray, shopping coupons, a first-aid kit—appeared on my back porch. Even the gardener sensed the change. He pruned the bougainvillea that was blocking my kitchen window, and—while I watched in astonishment—cleaned all the leaves out of the pool.

And *then*, to top things off, the old lady called. She offered me a space in the garage. "Now don't worry, I won't charge you extra," she said, sounding exactly like an old lady in a TV skit. If you had told me two months ago that a phone call from an eighty-four-year-old with a free parking space would cause me to enter into a euphoric state unequaled since the day I received an unexpected tax refund of $1,400, I would have thought it highly unlikely.

I had them eating out of the palm of my hand. It was just a matter of time before I could call up Yale University Press and begin contract negotiations.

And Jonica! Jonica was my best friend. Every afternoon we would meet out by the empty (though now clean) pool and kill a couple of hours in sunbathing and self-analysis. Now, in theory, these meetings were accidental; we both just *happened* to want to sunbathe that afternoon. In reality, of course, it was about as impromptu as D-day. I wouldn't have missed it for the world, and I later found out that Jonica canceled a dentist appointment so she'd be there.

To add to the illusion that what we were doing was casual, Jonica would bring her work out there. She had a job decoupaging ice buckets for a store in Laguna Beach.

"That's one good thing about this job," she said. "You can do it anywhere." Of course, if you do it outside, all the whisky labels blow away and you get dust particles in your polyurethane. I think she got about three ice buckets done the whole time.

Considering the size of her crush on me, these afternoons were surprisingly decorous. I remember one day we spent the whole time discussing the pros and cons of capital punishment. The intensity of that night in the kitchen did not reappear. Instead, we carried on the same kind of casual conversation you might have with people at the office. Which only seems appropriate. After all, we were both working.

I let Jonica choose the subject matter. My plan was to let her take me gradually into her confidence. So we'd talk about whatever she wanted to talk about. Since she was one of those people who are very easily influenced, she loved to talk about what was influencing her at the moment. This was usually her friends.

I was to find out all about them. Their lives were appallingly banal, but I feigned such convincing interest that soon I was hearing the most minute details of their attempts to find themselves.

Only one sounded like she had anything on the ball. This was "B," the clever postcard writer. Though cards continued to trickle in, she had already gotten back from her six-week tour of Europe with a feminist theater troupe called Live Nude Girls.

"B" stood for Barrie, and her last name was Shostack. She was Jonica's best friend and had been ever since seventh grade at a fancy private school in Brentwood, before financial difficulties forced Jonica to transfer to Hollywood High.

Barrie was Jonica's Svengali. Not a move was made without consulting her. "So you can imagine what it was like all summer. I didn't know whether to do this or to do that or to do *what*."

What made Barrie so special?

Jonica had a ready answer for this. "She is the only person I've ever met who is truly psychologically arrived."

I wasn't so sure. It sounded to me like she was still on the platform, waiting for the train.

Barrie, it seems, was the product of a particular type of Hollywood union—that of the star marrying her psychiatrist. The star in this case was Alice Amber, always referred to in *TV Guide* as "the rubber-faced comedienne." After the inevitable divorce, Barrie was shuffled around, as they say, with her father moving back to New York and a lucrative practice on Riverside Drive and her mother going through a series of poorly thought-out career choices and a descent into alcoholism.

According to Jonica, Barrie and her mother had finally reached a level of understanding notable for its warmth and maturity. This came to pass after many difficult years of scheming to get control of each other's money and/or forcing the other to submit to some sort of bizarre therapy, usually under court order. To illustrate her point, Jonica dashed into the house and returned with an old movie magazine containing a photo of Barrie, aged sixteen or so, wrapped in a towel. She was being handed over to her distraught mother by the Beverly Hills police following a raid on a pool party where marijuana had been smoked. The caption hinted darkly that this was not Barrie's first brush with the law: "Another heartbreak for Alice Amber—wasn't daughter Barrie's conviction last year for shoplifting bad enough?"

"I was at that party," Jonica said, the thrill of the whole experience still evident in her voice.

"Did you get arrested?"

"No," she said sadly. "I had to leave early."

It would be hard to overstate the influence this glamorous criminal had on Jonica. Barrie had, among other things, chosen her college (UCLA), told her which movements to get interested in, introduced her to her future husband, Vernon, and convinced her to have a child. Or rather, talked her out of an abortion.

"It's not that I didn't want to have a baby or anything," she explained. "It was Vernon."

"He didn't want to have a baby?"

"Oh, he was dying to have a baby."

I looked at little Warren over in his playpen. He was flailing a Raggedy Ann doll against the railing.

"So?"

She hedged a moment. "I thought he was too young. We *all* thought he was too young."

"How young was he?"

"At the time he was eighteen."

Eighteen! No wonder he wanted to have a baby—so he could play with the toys.

When I found out, as I did very shortly, that Barrie was opening in a new play on Thursday, I saw my chance and jumped in: "Hey, why don't we go together?"

At first, she made a pathetic attempt at nonchalance. "Oh, fine," she said. "That might be fun." Might be fun! I could just see her little brain calculating how fast she could get to a phone and call Barrie and shriek, "He asked me out! He asked me out!"

For suddenly she was full of nervous energy, like she'd been hit in the butt with a hypodermic of adrenaline. "I can't wait for you two to meet," she said, and raced on and on about how much we would like each other. But underneath all this gushiness, I sensed there was something left unsaid.

Then it came out. "I have to tell you something that nobody else knows."

"What?"

"It's about Barrie."

I waited while she had second thoughts. She frowned and gritted her teeth. "No, I can't tell you," she blurted. "Forget I even mentioned it."

"Tell me," I commanded. "Tell me or I'll tell Barrie."

She made an agonized sound. "You're forcing me," she wailed. Then she glanced around at the bushes and pulled her chair closer.

"It just so happens that Barrie is Donna."

"Huh?"

"*She's Donna.*"

I didn't get it. "Donna?"

"Yes. You know—'*Hi, gang, it's Donna.*'"

Now, anyone who has been in Los Angeles for more than twenty minutes knows who Donna is. Every time you turn on the radio, there she is, demanding in rhymed couplets and the heaviest Brooklyn accent you ever heard, that you drop everything and dash over to the nearest branch of Just Jeans and buy some pants. As a commercial, it's famous for its tackiness, inanity, and just plain unbelievable badness. But it sure must sell pants. The recurring opening line—"Hi, gang, it's Donna"—had become the buzz line of a hundred local jokes. Disc jockeys delight in telling Donna to shut up or where she can stuff her Just Jeans. One radio station had a Donna-Sound-Alike Contest. First prize was a weekend in Bakersfield. Second prize was two weekends in Bakersfield. You get the picture.

I received the news with a detached interest that obviously disappointed Jonica. I couldn't figure out what the big deal was. Eve soon set me straight.

She was so excited when I told her the news that night that she wanted to drop everything and call up her friend who was managing editor of *People* magazine. She had alerted him once to an earlier story, about how Betty Ford always washes out plastic bags and saves them (and teaches her children to do the same), which they managed to use in an article to prove some point or other. I forget what. Ever since then, she has fancied herself an investigative reporter.

I told her if she got near the phone there was going to be a murder.

"You don't understand," she pleaded. "Everybody thinks Donna is the daughter of the guy who owns Just Jeans. She's a Jewish princess who wants to be a radio star. That's the gimmick. That's why she's so bad. Now if people—or *People*—find out this legend is really a professional actress just pretending to be bad *and* Alice Amber's daughter to boot—"

We argued all night. You'd think I had stumbled across the news of the century. Jesus, what people in California think is important. If only she'd gotten this excited about Harding, I'd have a book published by now.

By the time I left, I'd sworn her to secrecy against her will. I was beginning to think that maybe Eve didn't have to know *everything*.

I have one rule in life: never think about anything important while lying in bed in the morning. If you do, chances are you'll never get up. There's something about a prone position that brings out the Joan Kennedy in everyone.

So the morning of the play, I waited until I had gotten up and had two cups of coffee before I started worrying. I'm one of those people who tend to get very nervous if something is about to happen. It doesn't have to be earth shattering; I'm incapacitated waiting for the carpet installers to come over. So you can imagine how I felt anticipating my date with Jonica.

Now "date" is a strange word. I find it most peculiar when used as a verb—as in "Do you date?" or "I plan to start dating again." It implies a certain specific physical activity, like crocheting. A certain amount of skill is involved, and if you get really proficient at it, people will refer to you as "A good date."

A date itself covers a wide territory, but it can perhaps best be defined as an occasion when two people, usually of the opposite sex, agree to a formal meeting for the purpose of social intercourse. I have been to a lot of these meetings in my life, and at times, more than I care to remember. "Coke dates" with acne-faced girl editors of high school literary magazines back in Mt. Lebanon. "Study dates" with intense Radcliffe English majors. "Business dates" with homely heiresses who might be persuaded to fork over a healthy sum earmarked toward zoo maintenance in return for an expense-account dinner and a stroll up Fifth Avenue. And what lessons have I learned from this lifelong frenzy of dating?

Many, but two stand out. Number One: Play Hard to Get. Be charming, congenial, witty—but keep your distance. It drives women crazy. Number Two: Dress Up. Nice clothes have a strange way of bringing out the poet in you. This also drives women crazy. And what is the ideal net result, if not to drive women crazy?

Since I already knew I was breaking Rule Number One—I was playing about as hard to get as a Big Mac—Rule Number Two was becoming more and more important. I looked through my wardrobe. Formality seemed inappropriate for a feminist theater opening, but still I didn't want to blend in with a bunch of grubby leftists. My eye caught the silk shirt Pam had given me for Christmas. Perfect! Elegant but casual. My way of acknowledging the importance of the avant-garde.

But there were problems, mostly having to do with sweat. Knowing me, I was going to get very nervous, what with meeting Barrie/ Donna for the first time, not to mention her mother, a longtime favorite of mine who Jonica told me might very well show up. The shirt was a shade of purple I never would have chosen for myself. It did not look its best with dark half-moons of perspiration emanating from the armpits. I had already learned my lesson at a party at the Museum of Modern Art, and I swore it would never happen again.

But what could I do? The more I tried not to perspire, the more I would, and pretty soon everybody, including Alice Amber, would be staring at my armpits instead of the play. And as for anti-perspirants, forget it. One application and it's Niagara Falls.

So I was about to pass, reluctantly, on the silk shirt when an idea struck me. I remembered that Pam occasionally wore these devices—I believe they are called dress shields—which attach to her brassiere and cover her underarm area with little pads that soak up all the perspiration. Why couldn't I wear something like that? Who would ever know?

Twenty minutes later I was down at Woolworth's, surreptitiously examining a box of dress shields and trying to figure out a way to attach them without the aid of a brassiere. It seemed I had two choices: I could rig something with rubber bands or I could use tape.

To cover all my bases, I bought the dress shields, rubber bands, *and* adhesive tape; and then rushed home to try them out. The rubber bands were out of the question; they slipped right off whenever you lifted up your arms even an inch. The adhesive tape was a little more practical but the dress shields had no flexibility—you could tape them on but then you'd have to walk around like a robot all night, unable to move your arms. In addition, they were surprisingly small, and I could just picture excess perspiration pouring over the edges.

I tried on the silk with an undershirt, but that looked terrible. I was about ready to forget the whole thing when inspiration struck. What I needed was something pliable *and* absorbent. *Like Pampers!* I'd seen those ads—"Baby stays drier even after he's wet."

So I rushed back to Woolworth's, bought a box of Newborn Pampers, and rushed home. It took about forty-five minutes of cutting up the Pampers into various sizes and experimenting (and those things are hard to cut, let me tell you), but finally I came up with a workable solution: they covered the whole area, were virtually undetectable, and allowed me to move my arms in practically any direction except bending over and touching my toes.

I showed up around seven fifteen. Guadalupe, at least, was pleased with the shirt. "*Qué guapo,*" she cooed, and for a moment I was afraid she would reach out and finger the material. Her enthusiasm didn't cheer me up, though; it just confirmed my worse fears. I didn't look elegant, I looked like a fool. All this time and effort, and I end up looking like Sonny Bono.

While she bounded up the stairs two at a time to announce my arrival, I wandered around the entrance hall trying to figure out how I could sneak home and change. In the harsh light of the chandelier, the shirt really did look ugly. I moved over by the living room, where the light was a little dimmer. Maybe that was the answer: I could hide in the shadows all night. Then I noticed something.

The living room rug was missing.

"Yoo hoo," a voice behind me called out. I turned to see Jonica descending the stairs. She was dressed like a little English boy: a vest, knickers, a little tweed cap. Well, there was one problem solved. With her in that getup, nobody would give me a second glance. Besides, I couldn't change to my tweed jacket now. We'd look like father and son.

"Nice shirt," she said.

"Where's your rug?" I demanded.

She looked guilty. "We sold it."

"When?" I couldn't believe they had carted the rug out under my very nose. I was slipping.

"Last week."

"Why?"

"Well, we got two thousand dollars," she said a little huffily. "Anyway, it looks better without it."

Something at the top of the stairs caught my eye. The old lady was sitting there in her wheelchair, a hideous purple afghan covering her lap.

"Hello," I yelled, a little too loudly.

"Hello to you too," she yelled back when the echo died down. "We had a robbery."

"So I heard."

"Jonica scared them off. They didn't get the family jewels."

"I'm glad."

"You have any trouble?"

"None whatsoever."

"Oh, look," Jonica broke in. "You two are wearing the same color."

The theater was located on a sleazy stretch of Hollywood Boulevard near Western. Jonica was confused about the address ("I know it's around here *some*where . . .") and we almost entered a massage parlour, mistaking the crowd of pimps and winos hanging around outside for theater patrons.

But the LA Women's Theatre proved to be across the street, next door to a Thai restaurant with a bullet hole in the window. It was my least favorite kind of theater in that it didn't use to be a theater. It used to be a bar and grill. You know what that means: a bad case of TB ("Tired Butt").

A card table had been set up in the lobby and behind it sat a nervous, tight-lipped woman with frizzy hair who looked like she should be on David Susskind discussing something like single parenting. "We have comps," Jonica informed her proudly, and the woman rifled through some slips of paper, chanting Jonica's name and looking perplexed.

"Maybe we should just pay for the tickets," I said after a while, but Jonica wouldn't hear of it. "Barrie said there'd be comps," she insisted.

"You're friends of Barrie's?" the woman said, perking up. She immediately handed us two tickets and then forced us to put down our names on the mailing list.

I had suggested we arrive early to avoid the crowd. Clearly my plan was a success; we were the only people there. To pass the time, we wandered around the lobby examining photographs from past productions (*The Sins of the Fathers, Women's Ward,* and a modern-dress, all-female *The Resistible Rise of Arturo Ui*). That accomplished, we read notes tacked to a bulletin board. Debbie lost her leg warmers. Allison L. was starting an improv group. Anybody interested?

From behind the closed doors leading inside we could hear occasional feminine outbursts concerning some last-minute lighting problems. They became more and more intense, with the emphasis shifting from technical matters to issues of personal betrayal.

Jonica and I glanced at each other uncomfortably and then at the ticket seller. She winced as another outburst began.

"We had our electricity turned off," she said by way of explanation. "They just turned it back on this morning. It's not easy rehearsing in the dark."

By now it had dawned on me that this was no Broadway production we were about to see. I was just hoping we wouldn't have to see it alone—at five minutes before curtain time, we still had the place to ourselves. The ticket seller was starting to look very worried. She kept sticking her head out the door and peering up and down the street.

Then, all of a sudden, people started streaming in like they'd just got off a bus. Women mostly, with severe haircuts and aviator glasses. It hit me what an important moment in feminist fashion it was when Gloria Steinem dropped by her optician's and said, "I'll take *those*."

It seemed that all these newcomers had free tickets awaiting them. A hush fell over the crowd when the critic from a local TV station made an entrance. In addition to his ticket, he was asked if he wanted a cup of coffee. I took this as a bad omen.

Around five after eight, a thin girl in overalls rushed in and began passing out mimeographed programs. The ink was still wet, so there was much blowing on them and fanning them in the air. I looked at the title of the play we were about to see: *All My Sisters Slept in Dirt: A Choral Poem*.

The doors were thrown open and the crowd filed in.

The theater itself turned out to be tiny—so small that at first I thought we were in another waiting room. The only seating was what I feared, folding wooden chairs. I can't imagine who set them up—Helen Keller maybe. There was much switching around of seats until everyone realized that *all* the seats were bad. Then they calmed down and shot envious glances at the people in the front row. Jonica spotted a pillow lying in a corner. For a while, we debated the possibilities of using it as a cushion, but finally decided it was too dirty.

By eight twenty, the play still had not begun and the audience was growing restless. One group near us ostentatiously started playing cards. Then the ticket seller entered, followed by a weary-looking female with grey hair. I took her to be the cleaning woman.

Jonica nudged me. "That's Barrie's mother."

That's Barrie's mother? That old hag? That bag lady in the dirty raincoat? That's my childhood heroine? My fantasy mother-figure, so devil-may-care, so wacky, yet so glamorous?

When I was a kid around ten or so, while all the other kids would play baseball after school, I would run home and watch reruns of *Dear Alice.* Alice Amber played an advice-giving newspaper columnist, like Ann Landers, who could solve everybody's problems but her own family's. Husband Dudley, a prominent lawyer, was a pompous jerk (his toupee was a running joke); teenage daughter Marcia was boy crazy; and the twins, Jimmy and Janie, were cunning monsters who belonged in a reformatory. Only Alice's younger brother, Bill, a marine who came to visit every now and then while on leave, had any sense. My favorite episode, which I still remember vividly, was when Bill took Alice and the kids on a camping trip, and a freak snowstorm forced them to take shelter in what they *thought* was an abandoned cabin, with hilarious results. As far as I was concerned, nothing, not *I Love Lucy,* not *I Married Joan,* not *My Little Margie,* could hold a candle to *Dear Alice.*

"After the show went off the air, she started drinking," Jonica whispered. "Then Barrie's little brother died of a brain tumor. It was in all the papers how she took him to see the Pope so he could get blessed. But he died anyway. After that is when they stuck her in the bin."

She had made a comeback of sorts in the late sixties, playing the wisecracking mother-in-law on *Figueroa.* Today she made a comfortable living touring state fairs every summer.

"I saw her act once in Oxnard," Jonica went on. "She talks about how good the Lord has been to her and then makes everybody sing hymns."

With much resentment, a place was found for Barrie's mother in the front row. She smiled condescendingly at her detractors, fished in her bag, and pulled out a pack of cigarettes.

"No smoking!" a woman hissed and suddenly the lights went out.

Jonica clutched my arm. "I'm so nervous. If you don't like it I'm going to die."

The lights came up to reveal eight young women staring belligerently at the audience.

"Which one is Barrie?" I whispered.

"Second from the left," Jonica whispered back, just as the actresses began to chant a prose poem about what it's like to be a woman in contemporary America.

"Right on, sisters," said a voice from the third row.

Barrie must have taken after her father. She was short and dark, muscular and Jewish-looking. A wild growth of hair flowed down to her shoulders, like lava. It gave the appearance of having been left to its own devices for several months, but maybe she just fixed it that way for the play. Her nose was sturdy and her jaw wide, but her most remarkable feature was her eyes. All of the actresses seemed to be attempting to outdo each other in intensity of facial expression, but Barrie was far and away the best. When she focused on me with a line about how contemptuous she was of television advertising, I had to look away, she was so overpowering.

I knew right away I wasn't going to like the play. No plot, no jokes, and God knows, no stars. Just eight ugly girls whining about rejection. Well, I'll say this for them—they looked like experts on the subject.

Things picked up a little when the actresses left the stage and came out in the audience. Uh-oh, I thought, audience participation time. Get me out of here. But what happened was this: each actress went to a different part of the theater so that she could address, directly, a small group of six or eight people. Then they all described, simultaneously, a sexual experience they had had recently.

"This is the part Barrie told me about," Jonica said, breathless with anticipation. We got a redheaded girl with braids who told us how the photographer who took her passport picture for the European tour exposed himself to her right when he was taking the picture. I guess this was supposed to prove what beasts men are. At any rate, to prove her point, she pulled her passport out of her pocket so we could examine it ourselves. Needless to say, we nearly killed each other trying to get at it first. It did show a rather peculiar expression on her face, like somebody had just stepped on her toe. Now this was all very interesting, but what I wanted to hear was the sexual experience of the black amazon two rows in front of us. From what drifted back our way, she seemed to be describing, in the most graphic terms, group sex in a coed prison. I looked around for Barrie. She was on the other side of the room, holding her own little group enthralled.

The actresses went back on the stage. Something told me we had just witnessed the high point of the evening. I searched the program for mention of an intermission, but the producers, wisely for them, had decided not to include one. So I spent the rest of the performance shifting position and deciding what research I had to get accomplished next week. I borrowed a pen from Jonica and made notes on the back of the program. She thought I was taking notes on the play and was thrilled.

I get a lot of thinking done during boring plays. And I certainly had plenty to think about tonight. Number One: What did Jonica know about all this? Did she have any idea who her grandfather was? Strange as it seems, I was beginning to think she didn't; I would have heard about it by now. If she would use her friend's radio commercial to impress me, then chances are she would have figured out a way to let me know her grandfather had been President of the United States.

Number Two: How on earth was I going to broach the subject? I already knew the answer to that: Very, very carefully. But when? And where? And how on earth did Evalyn Walsh McLean fit into the picture? What should be the angle of my book? Should it have pictures? If so, where would I get the pictures? Should it have a picture of me on the back? Should Pam's brother take the picture? Would he get his feelings hurt if I didn't ask him? Who pays for that anyway, the writer or the publisher?

Enmeshed in such thoughts, I had no problem passing the time; the evening seemed to fly by. During a brightly lit scene, I pretended to scratch my head and was able to make a surreptitious pit check. Everything was under control. The action on stage had become a blur. The actresses recited poems and monologues, sang little songs, pounded on the floor, and gave each other meaningful looks. I couldn't follow a thing.

Just when I'd had enough and was starting to doze off, the company joined hands, sang a song about how to share love, and performed a Sufi dance. Suddenly the play was over. The audience, whether through enthusiasm or relief, cheered wildly. After three curtain calls, the cast members came out into the audience again, this time to kiss people at random in a gesture of sisterhood.

As soon as all the actresses had disappeared backstage, the audience rose en masse and followed them, for it appeared that everyone had a friend or a relative to congratulate. The critic struggled against the tide; his eyes met mine for a second—we were practically the only men there—and from the face he made, I could already hear the review.

Jonica and I were propelled along with the crowd back into the dressing room, which used to be the kitchen. The girls stood around makeshift dressing tables, kissing and hugging each other and their friends.

Barrie shrieked when she saw us approaching. "I thought you were coming *tomorrow!*" she cried out, acting as if our presence were the most remarkable event of the evening. Alice Amber, who had been congratulating her daughter, seemed a little upstaged by our entrance. She shot me a very cool look.

Jonica performed the introductions. I told Barrie I enjoyed her performance.

A sour look came over her face. "I was awful tonight," she said. "You'll have to come back and see it again next week."

I pretended to take this ridiculous suggestion seriously and then turned to her mother. Up close she looked much better, I was relieved to note. More wrinkles, maybe, but also more character. And you could tell where Barrie got her eyes. For a moment, I was transported back to those afternoons in the rec room in Mt. Lebanon.

"Alice Amber," I said, taking her hand. "I'm your biggest fan."

"How sweet!" she said, delighted to be in the spotlight again.

"Honey"—she turned to Jonica—"you can bring this guy around any time."

Jonica blushed. "You look wonderful," Alice Amber went on. "Lose some weight?"

"A little," Jonica said, looking around uncomfortably.

I was flabbergasted. You mean she used to be fatter?

"And how's the baby?" Alice continued, determined not to relinquish the floor.

"Enormous." A bad choice of words.

"And Vernon?"

"We're separated."

"Ai yi yi," said Alice Amber, and she gravely embraced Jonica.

It was decided that we would all go to Alice Amber's house for an impromptu celebration. The cast and their friends were also invited; Barrie stood on top of the stove to make this announcement, which was greeted with a roar. She then gave directions, which she insisted everybody write down.

I was beginning to realize that Barrie liked to take charge of things. She decided, for instance, that she would ride with me; her mother and Jonica would go in the other car and "catch up on things."

The little group of theatergoers, in a carnival mood by this time, traipsed back through the theater and out into the street. Alice Amber had long been forgiven—something to do with the offer of free food, I suspect—and one girl who knew more about *Dear Alice* than even I did began to explain how it was an early feminist show. "Bullshit," said Alice Amber, and this won the crowd over even more, don't ask me why.

Barrie and I piled into the Mustang. She had changed from her costume (jeans and a sweat shirt) into jeans and a sweat shirt.

"Jonica was right," she said as we pulled away from the curb.

"Right about what?"

"She said you were real cute."

I laughed. "That's not a very feminist remark." There was a pause. "I've heard all about you, too."

"Yeah, I can imagine."

Somewhere around Crescent Heights we ran into a traffic jam caused by a head-on collision. In the next car were some girls from the play. They rolled down their window and passed us a joint. I took a puff and gave it to Barrie.

"Where's my mother?" she said, craning her neck.

"Isn't that her?" She was about two cars ahead, deep in conversation with Jonica.

Barrie took a hit. "Good dope," she said, holding it in and then exploding in a coughing fit. "Jesus, I'm stoned already."

The traffic started to move and we drove slowly past the wreck. "You see that car?" Barrie asked, pointing to one of the smashed vehicles. "I was going to get a car just like that, only blue. But just think—then that would be *me* in the accident!" She paused. "I am *sooooo* stoned."

By the time we got to La Cienaga, she was turning kittenish, brushing imaginary crumbs off her chest, and moving her shoulders around to some music only she was hearing.

"You know what?" she asked, her eyes glinting like some demented elf.

"What?"

"That's what!" she screamed and collapsed in hysterics. Christ, I thought, get me out of here.

She pulled herself together by slapping her cheeks and rolling the window down. "I'm *sooooo* stoned," she yelled, her face in the breeze. Then she settled back in her seat, her hands folded in her lap.

"I have something very important to tell you," she said.

"What?" It was like humoring a drunk.

She looked at me. "Jonica really likes you."

"And I like her too."

She let out an exasperated sigh. "No, you don't understand. She *really, really* likes you."

Now I understood.

"You know what she does?"

"What?"

"She collects pictures of models in magazines that look like you. And she writes down all your jokes."

"And then what?"

"She shows them to me."

"What jokes?"

Barrie thought a minute. "The one about the Puerto Rican airline. And the one about the British TV show."

"She told you *that* joke?"

"Like I say, *she wrote it down*. She has a *shoe box* full of them. All she can talk about is your taste in clothes"—she eyed my shirt but didn't comment—"And what you all did today, and how well you and little Warren get along."

This was news to me. Every time I tried to tickle him or interest him in a toy, he would start howling for his mother. "Children can see right through you," Pam said once after an awful weekend we spent with her nieces.

"And you know what else?" Barrie went on.

"What?" I said, fearing the worst.

"She just bought a divorce-yourself kit for ninety-nine dollars."

I could just feel the sweat trickling down my arms. Jesus, thank God for the Pampers. This was getting a little heavier than I'd bargained for. It was like overhearing gossip about yourself: agonizing, but you wouldn't leave even if the house were on fire.

"So when's the divorce?" I asked

"Well, it turns out she can't use the kit, which we're both furious about since I lent her the ninety-nine dollars. It's something about whether it's uncontested or not. And since Vernon got wind of what's going on with the house, I guess he smells money if he sticks around. The bastard."

"What do you mean, what's going on with the house?"

"Oh, haven't you heard? They just sold it."

Alice Amber lived on a cul-de-sac in Brentwood, right near where Marilyn Monroe swallowed her last Seconal. Her house was a long, low structure, with cantilevered roofs and many different wings. Inside it looked like a museum of 1950s furniture. The place had been decorated within an inch of its life circa 1955 and had remained untouched ever since.

I ran into the living room looking for Jonica. Some girls from the play stood by the record player, a Magnavox console, searching for something newer than Ella Fitzgerald. But Jonica was nowhere in sight.

Intuition told me to look in the kitchen. Sure enough, there she was, preparing a dip. She looked up and licked some sour cream off her fingers.

"Why didn't you tell me you sold the house?" I shouted.

Her smile froze. "Who told you that?"

"Barrie."

She looked out toward the hall. "Where is she? I'll kill her."

"Why didn't you tell me?" I demanded.

She didn't have an answer. A nervous hand went up to her face. I thought she might start crying. "We were trying to figure out how to tell you," she said at last.

"Sure, and cheat me out of a month's rent."

"No—" she began but thought better of it.

"Who bought it?"

"I don't know," she said miserably. "Some people from Phoenix."

Now it all made sense! The gardener, the bougainvillea, the pool—they were sprucing the place up! And those gifts— house-cleaning! Packing up! God, what a dumb fool I had been!

"Maybe you won't have to move ..."

"Of course I'll have to move," I snapped. Then: "Where are you moving?"

The question seemed to relieve her. At least this she had an answer for. She explained their plans. She and Warren were moving in with Barrie. The old lady would enter a Methodist home in Santa Barbara. And Guadalupe was returning to Mexico to marry her fiancé, an engineering student.

"When?" I barked. "When is your grandmother going in the home?"

"As soon as they have an opening. She's at the top of the waiting list."

I shook my head. "Great. Just great."

She seemed to shrink against the counter. "We had to do it," she said in a plaintive voice. "We're broke. We've been living on what you're paying us."

"So I'll keep on paying."

"But it's not enough," she said.

Barrie stumbled into the kitchen. "Have you seen my mother?" She clung dramatically to the refrigerator. "I'm *sooooo* stoned."

"Barrie, you're *tooooo* stoned," Jonica said and flung a radish at her.

I beat it back to the living room, leaving them to battle it out. "Don't blame me, sweetheart," I could hear Barrie yell out sarcastically.

I needed to talk to somebody. I looked around for a phone. People were trickling in and standing around uncertainly, impressed at being in a star's home. I found an empty room and shut the door. The walls were covered with plaques and photographs of Alice Amber kissing crippled children.

I dialed Eve's number. There was no answer.

I began to pace around.

Twenty minutes later I walked back into the living room. The party was in full swing. The girls had turned the radio on to a New Wave station and were bouncing around to the music in groups of threes and fours.

Those who weren't dancing were eating. Some were dancing *and* eating. That's one thing I've noticed about parties that are mostly female—they take their food very seriously. It looked like the entire contents of Alice Amber's refrigerator had been emptied out on the dining room table. There was potato salad, cheese, a plate of raw vegetables, Fritos, a Sara Lee cake (*that* went fast), some Pepperidge Farm cookies, a frozen pizza, crackers, three dips, some fruit, and, to wash it all down, Tab.

Alice Amber, though, preferred the stronger stuff. She wandered around with a glass of vodka in one hand and a Kool in the other, grinning like a loon and already smashed out of her mind. At one point she joined in the dancing, bumping and grinding her pelvis in a burlesque of what the others were doing. Everyone cheered. Jonica was nowhere in sight. I looked toward the kitchen.

Make her wait, I decided.

Someone shouted that it was time for the late news. A TV was hauled out and placed on the coffee table. Everyone gathered around. Still no Jonica. Christ, what if she'd left?

People continued talking during the weather report; then, after a commercial, the critic suddenly appeared—right in the same tie he'd been wearing earlier that evening—and there was an abrupt silence.

"*All My Sisters Slept in Dirt* is a strange title for a strange play," he began, the girls hanging on every word. "When it's good, it's very, very good. And when it's bad, it's not bad." Applause and cheers, quickly hushed. He went on to compliment the "refreshingly natural company" and state that the script and the direction were "cogent and lucid." "There's a sex scene—eight of them actually—that will knock your socks off. And I can only hope that for their next production, the company will live up to its name: Live Nude Girls."

"Hiss, boo," shouted the girls, and "chauvinist pig," but in general the review provoked mass rejoicing. Exactly how this critic, who was obviously on the take, could steer people toward *All My Sisters Slept in Dirt* with the promise of a good time, much less sexual stimulation, and not be rebuked by the FCC was beyond me. "Broadway, here we come!" Barrie yelled. Alice Amber staggered up to her daughter and planted a wet kiss on her cheek. Tears flowed from her eyes. "I'm so proud of you I could plotz," she croaked and then, twirling around unsteadily, collided with an end table and went sprawling on the couch, landing on the black amazon, who was preparing some cocaine. The drug spilled on the carpet and all the girls dived down on their hands and knees, trying to snort it up and laughing hysterically.

Somehow I couldn't get into it. I had too much on my mind. It was time to do what I had to do.

I went back into the kitchen. Jonica was in the exact same place I'd left her, eating mayonnaise with a spoon and looking guilty about it.

"Where have you been all night?" I asked.

"Here," she whimpered.

"Why don't you come out in the living room?"

She went over to the sink and washed off the spoon. "You hate me. We sell the house because it's either that or go on food stamps and now you hate me." She threw the spoon in the silverware drawer.

I stared at her until she became self-conscious. "Come here," I said.

"Why?" she said warily.

I shrugged. "Because I think we should dance."

She didn't move. "You don't want to dance with me," she said, staring down at the floor. "You hate me."

I walked over to her and put my arms around her. "I don't hate you," I whispered. "I like you too much to hate you."

I could feel her heart race. She stood there awkwardly, her arms at her sides. It was like embracing an armoire.

"Now I want you to say good night to Barrie and then I want you to get in the car and come home with me. Okay?"

She swallowed.

"Okay."

It was around one when we pulled into the driveway. I parked by the garage and we sat there for a while — one of those incredibly awkward moments masquerading as relaxed intimacy. Finally Jonica asked if I wanted to smoke a joint. I said, yeah, let's go over to my house.

Once inside, I lit a fire and we smoked the grass. I lay down on the rug. I hated the role of seducer and was postponing it as long as possible.

After a while, she came over and began to stroke my hair. Then my back.

"Elliot want a back rub?"

"Um, sounds good," I murmured, my eyes closed, the picture of bliss, but terrified she was going to climb aboard and straddle me. But she massaged me, thank God, from the side and it was only when her hands got up near my shoulders and she said, "What's this?" that I realized I was in trouble. Let's face it, it doesn't look too cool to climb into bed with somebody when you have Pampers taped to your armpits.

I excused myself and ran into the bathroom, where I ripped them off, plus most of my flesh, and flushed them down the toilet.

When I got back, she was still lying on the rug, looking up at me.

What can I say? You can guess what happened next.

As for her body, I won't go into details but I will say this: she had a lot of dimples. Everywhere.

10

Most women, Pam included (what am I saying—Pam *in particular*), need time to themselves. God knowns what for. To meditate on the state of their wardrobe, maybe, or jot down feminine insights into a hardbound notebook from Pier One Imports. "Private space" I believe is what Dr. Joyce Brothers and others of her ilk call this phenomenon.

Well, count Jonica out. Once we had done the deed, she was mine completely. I have no doubt she would have spent twenty-four hours a day dry-cleaning the carpet with her tongue if I'd asked her to. It didn't take me too long to realize this. I began to smell trouble when she called the next morning at eight fifteen for absolutely no reason at all, billing and cooing at me while she gave little Warren his bottle. I finally hung up claiming stomach cramps.

That was just the beginning. Poor Jonica. She was so ordinary. Her mind was unsullied by any original thought. Later on, I told Vernon that maybe he could have her declared legally dead on the basis of zero brain activity.

Some loophole in the state educational system had gotten her into UCLA where she spent four years working on her tan in the sculpture garden and majoring in something called "Art." I don't know what they meant by this—she had never heard of Mantegna *or* David Hockney. Still, on the basis of graduation from this diploma mill, she considered herself a very well-educated person, even a little exhausted by the intellectual rigors they'd put her through. "If you want to *buy* the degree," she sniffed, "you go to Pepperdine."

Her college days had been the happiest ones of her life, and judging from the short time I had spent at UCLA, I could understand why: never had I seen a school with so many places to eat. And they all had themes, like they were planned by some tourist commission. There was the Gypsy Wagon, which drew the Jewish hippie crowd, all sandals and kinky hair; Potlatch in the Business School, which looked like the cocktail lounge of a Marriott hotel; the Bomb Shelter, all futuristic and semi-underground, full of math majors with calculators clipped to their belts; and so on and so on and so on, all the way to the main dining room in Ackerman, which reminded me of a Puerto Rican social club, only brighter and more garish.

Now if she'd spent a little more time hitting the books and a little less on carbo intake, she might have learned to read and write. This girl had no idea how to spell. "Youth" came out "yowth" and as far as she was concerned, the month after May was "Juen." She wore "pance." With anything over one syllable, she went completely to pieces. I remember seeing a shopping list reminding her to pick up "6 avocolorados." But how was she going to learn the finer points of the English language? She never read anything. Peer pressure forced her to lug around one of Virginia Woolf's weightier tomes, but the only book I ever saw her nose buried in was something called *Animal Babies*, and Warren kept screaming until she gave it back.

Nevertheless, everybody felt she was "Artistic." This gave her an excuse to put on those bizarre clothes. Everything was a possibility. I once saw her pull a tank top out of a trash can on Hollywood Boulevard. "This is a nice shirt," she said. "Yeah, but its got vomit all over it." "That's just pizza sauce," she said, actually sniffing the thing and then stuffing it into her purse. "It'll wash out."

"She never met a dress she didn't like," Barrie said. The two of them were always running off to Eagle Rock or Long Beach on thrift-shopping expeditions. Barrie favored military gear, long-sleeved undershirts, and boots that laced. Jonica bought anything that reflected light.

She had antique clothes, she had old lady dresses with shoulder pads, she had a rack full of bowling shirts with things like "Miller's Funeral Home" stitched on the back, she had bus driver uniforms, she had meter maid blouses, she had complete greaser outfits from the fifties, she had mini-dresses from the sixties that she wore as shirts, she had white dinner jackets and black dinner jackets (these she wore around the house like sweaters), she had drawers full of scarves and funny socks and plastic jewelry, not to mention rhinestone clips and tin bug pins and little ice cream cone pins and palm tree pins, etc. I'd guess she had about four thousand T-shirts, all *from* someplace, like Eddy Martin's Show Place of the World in Asbury Park, New Jersey, or the Downtown Minneapolis YMCA, or the Marin County '74 Folk Festival. She had plastic sandals, she had jap flaps, she had huaraches with old Firestone tires for soles, she had sneakers, she had yellow rubber desert boots you wear fishing, she had Enna Jetticks, she had Clark desert boots, she had nurses' shoes painted green. She had an alligator purse (the kind where the head folds over and becomes the snap) she hauled around everywhere, plus a tote from Hughes AirWest for the stuff that wouldn't fit in the purse, like extra makeup, several changes of clothes should the whim seize her, about seventeen address books, new additions to her swizzle stick collection that hadn't been cataloged yet, some Sweet 'n Low packets, a year's supply of gum, an assortment of combs and hairbrushes, an Archie comic book, a broken Timex watch, and some Vaseline to keep her lips from getting chapped.

So great was her reputation as a tastemaker that she decided to redecorate the pool house. Without even asking me, I guess she figured no mere male could understand the ABCs of design. To her, that understated elegance that I worked so hard to achieve was a "just-moved-in" look. She decided it needed a woman's touch.

If I could play God and eliminate one art form from the face of the earth, it would be that California homegrown favorite, macramé. Why anybody would sit around and braid that fuzzy twine is beyond me. So when Dorothy Draper showed up with a pair of sickly spider plants she intended to hang in my window on a set of matching macramé plant holders ("the good kind," she said, the implication being that those rocks, seashells, and bits of driftwood embedded amongst the scratchy tendrils were supposed to be some sort of *plus*), I put my foot down with such a thud it could be felt in Burbank. I liked things just the way they were, I informed her, and *no*, I did not think it needed "warming up." She sulked for a while, but then I gave her a bag of marshmallows and all was forgiven.

Food! My God, I could do about seven hours on her eating habits alone. This was one weight problem that had nothing to do with glands, except maybe the salivary ones. As far as gluttony went, this was the Big Time. The major leagues. God forbid she should miss a meal—General Foods stock would plummet.

My food bills shot up to three digits after she started coming over. I learned I had to have snacks around; otherwise, she would attack the staples. An example—late one night, we're both a little bit stoned:

"What do you have to eat?"

"Nothing."

"Nothing? You must have *something*."

"I haven't been to the store."

"Think."

"I tell you, I don't have anything."

Pause on her part.

"Are the olives all gone?"

"Yes."

"What about those Froot Loops?"

"I threw them out."

"You *what*?"

"I had to. They were full of ants."

"Rats ... What's in the freezer?"

"Just part of that deer Eve's husband ran over."

She seriously considers this for a while but rejects it. "Deers are a whole other world to me."

We watch a commercial for a set of cookware that can do all sorts of amazing and unbelievable things, like be cleaned by peripheral vision.

"You must have *something*."

"I have some bouillon."

"Chicken or beef?"

"Beef."

"Cubes or little packets?"

"Little packets."

"Well, why didn't you *say* so?"

She lumbers out of bed like a grizzly bear. I expect her to return with a steaming cup; instead, she comes back with three packets plus a can of Mai Tai mix that came with the house and then proceeds to *down them* all right there in front of me. This woman eats *bouillon raw*! And she doesn't even have the decency to do it in private! I could hardly watch I was so repulsed. And, of course, the bouillon made her so thirsty she downed several gallons of ice water and then sloshed around every time she shifted her weight.

Lunch in a restaurant was embarrassing. She belonged to the Clean Plate Club—not just hers, everybody's in reach. After putting away her meal in record time, her little eyes would fidget around and focus on yours. "Do you want your pickle?" "Are you going to finish your rice pudding?" Pretty soon she threw caution to the winds. I had to stab her wrist with my fork when she tried to make away with a half-eaten baked potato. She apologized, truly embarrassed, so embarrassed she even let a crust of bread be cleared away without snatching it first.

"It's like alcoholism," Barrie told me. "She gets a high from all that sugar and loses control."

"Do you ever talk to her about it?"

"I talk but I don't preach. That's the worst mistake you can make with a lardo."

"What does she say?"

"She says, that's easy for you to say, you wear a size seven."

She had tried diets, Barrie said. Sometimes she'd lose a couple of pounds but just let one little thing go wrong, like she'd get a parking ticket or her new steam-mist curlers would break before she even sent in the warranty, and it was back to the icebox. We compared notes on some of the things we had seen her down. On Barrie's list, new to me, were a whole bottle of Green Goddess salad dressing, uncooked bacon, and a banana some ants had started a colony in. "She just brushed 'em away."

When she wasn't eating, or in between bites, she liked to watch TV. She wasn't what you'd call a discriminating viewer. She'd watch anything that moved across the screen. She'd watch Saturday morning cartoons (she'd never *miss* Saturday morning cartoons). She and Guadalupe would watch *Disco Fiebre* on Channel 41. Then they'd practice the steps. This was something to see. Sometimes when she got stoned, she would talk back to the set. She'd argue with the newscasters and offer them her views (really Barrie's, I'm sure) on nuclear weapons and the energy crisis. It was all a plot by Mobil and Exxon against the world's animals, flowers, and children, the usual bleeding heart rhetoric. She hated beautiful women on TV. "Blow it out your shorts, Kelly," she'd yell at the weather girl. Or "So your little plan isn't working, Greer," she kept sneering while we watched *Random Harvest.*

Sex with Jonica was a trial. She kept affecting these impish little ways that were unbecoming to one of her bulk. Her favorite was to surprise me with a drawing of a butterfly or some such thing on her abdomen. I'd pretend to be delighted and try to keep from blowing lunch; she'd flutter her eyes and act seductive. God, what a sight.

One night I pretended to turn into a monster and just about scared her to death. She ran into the ladies' dressing room and locked herself in the stall. I followed her and switched off the lights and just stood there, not saying anything, while she went nuts, begging me to say something or turn on the lights. She thought she'd got mixed up with the Hillside Strangler. She made all kinds of outrageous promises if I'd just say something. She offered to write me a check for all the money she had in the bank (only $178, it turned out). She said she'd give me her new stereo that she'd bought from a teamster Barrie's mother knew. Finally, I took pity on her and turned the lights on and apologized. She heaved a sigh of relief; I led her back to bed, smothering her with kisses. She kept fanning herself and rolling her eyes. "Holy Jesus," she kept saying.

We crawled under the covers.

"Elliot, promise me you'll never do that again."

No answer.

"Elliot?"

She ran shrieking, this time to the kitchen, where she grabbed a bottle of Karo syrup and threatened to pour it into my toaster unless I, right then and there, put it in writing that if I ever turned into a monster again, or even did anything that could be *interpreted* as turning into a monster, I would pay her $30. What could I do? I prepared the statement.

She was a strange girl.

Now, since the old lady suffered from heart trouble and was still recovering from the shock of Jonica's entanglement with Vernon Fetchko, part-time aspiring songwriter and full-time fortune hunter, we had to pretend that nothing was going on between us. That was fine with me; the more sub rosa the better. I have no particular scruples against an affair with a married woman, but I didn't care to be squiring the world's largest fashion plate around Hollywood. The looks we'd gotten during lunch at Tiny Naylor's were bad enough, not to mention ice cream cones at Swensen's, where the staff knew Jonica by name, or sundaes at C. C. Brown's, where Jonica held some sort of indoor world's record, I didn't care to learn for what.

We were "cheaters." The relish with which Jonica took on this role was something to watch. I don't know what it is, something in the genes I guess, but an illicit love affair brought out an astonishing amount of cunning in the Kinney women. If they could only channel this energy into something more practical, they could wind up like those women I read about in *Fortune* magazine recently, the ones with their own cosmetic and baked goods companies, plus lavish homes and a satisfactory, though hectic, family life.

Jonica laid down many rules. Foremost among them; we could

never spend the entire night together. She got no argument from me on this score. What she would do was kiss her grandmother good night and then retire to her room. There she would make phone calls (usually to me), sort out her laundry, give her hair a henna treatment, and check on the baby. Long ago, she had conned Guadalupe into sleeping in the nursery whenever she and Warren were at home. Since Guadalupe was the oldest of twelve children, this seemed logical to her. She probably could have handled another eight or nine infants without any undue hardship.

Around eleven thirty, Jonica would sneak downstairs and out the back door, take the long way around through the bushes, and let herself into my kitchen. First she would make sure all the shutters were closed. Around 2 p.m., she would sneak back. I wasn't getting much sleep.

But it finally paid off. One night she mentioned a family album. Suddenly, I was all ears. Why didn't she bring it over one evening— like tomorrow, for instance? She was thrilled at my interest.

We rearranged the lamps so as not to strain our eyes and opened the leatherette portfolio. I was instantly disappointed: it started with Jonica's birth. Uh-oh, I thought. Limited historical value. No vintage photographs. Mostly out-of-focus Brownie shots and some early Polaroids with streaks from improperly applied fixer, Oh, well . . .

On page one, Jonica arrived home from the hospital—a blanket-wrapped salami as far as I could tell—in her grinning mother's arms. But wait a minute—there was something about that grin. Then it hit me: pure Warren G. Harding. I perked up.

Next we saw shots of Jonica in every conceivable pose you can get a baby into, short of painful contortions. She crawled across the famous Chinese rug in diapers. She got swung over her daddy's bald head. He, by the way, was a pudgy man with glasses and bad dental work. She played naked at the beach, waving a tin shovel at the camera while an old lady in a housedress—"Aunt Irma"—hovered over her lest a freak wave should wash her away. And my favorite, sharing her grandmother's surprisingly svelte lap with a one-eyed teddy bear named Woger, after her father's favorite Yankee, Roger Maris.

They lived in a pleasant stucco house in Mar Vista, where Mr. Hupper did something—Jonica had no idea what—at a local savings and loan. Their life-style was the middle of the middle class. They had a screened-in back porch, a portable barbecue, and a brand-new Plymouth that they managed to include in just about every shot. I never saw so many photographs of people grouped around a car. One day they drove it over to Gramma's and photographed it there with Aunt Irma behind the steering wheel, a mad grin on her face.

The contrast between sedate, conventional Mar Vista and Gramma's tropical mansion was startling. The big house was in much better shape in those days. In one photo, water gushed from the ceramic frog while Jonica and her father posed in bathing suits. Dad looked a little uncomfortable. "He never got along very well with my grandmother," Jonica explained.

We next saw pictures of Mom and Dad's well-documented cruise to Havana, some deal they got through the savings and loan. It was just after the revolution and you couldn't *give* trips to Cuba away. Consequently, anybody who happened in the country was given VIP treatment by the Cuban Tourist Commission and forced to tour rum factories and agricultural campuses. It looked pretty dismal: umpteen pictures of them posed under welcoming banners, surrounded by Cuban Youth and being handed free samples. One night, January 25, 1960, to be exact, they went to the famous Tropicana nightclub. They got a cha-cha lesson, a complimentary cocktail, and five pesos' worth of gambling chips. Mom's ankle was in an Ace bandage, the result of tripping over some loose masonry at Morro Castle; so Dad did most of his dancing with a weak-chinned blonde in a Debbie Reynolds hairdo.

The blonde showed up again on the next page, sitting next to Dad at the captain's farewell dinner on board their ship, some Liberian firetrap. I immediately smelled trouble. Her name was Olivia Pratt, Jonica informed me, and in less than six months, she was destined to become the second Mrs. Hupper!

"I still have a very emotional reaction to this," Jonica fumed.

"That's her husband. He was a retired veterinarian."

Judging from his photograph, I could hardly blame Olive. Jonica's father may have been no Errol Flynn, but he was in a lot better shape than old Dr. Pratt, who kept a walker parked next to his chair and had such bad liver spots he looked like a Dalmatian. But the one I felt sorry for was Jonica's mom. There she was, her foot all taped up (by Dr. P? I wondered), wearing a Nina Khrushchev cast-off evening gown, looking miserable but trying a feeble smile as she put out a cigarette in the remains of her baked Alaska.

The divorce, Jonica said, was messy. Dad felt so guilty, he gave up all rights to Jonica and moved with Olive to Chicago, to start a new life in the upholstery and slipcover business, a skill he learned, believe it or not, in the army.

"Do you keep in touch?" I asked.

"Keep in touch?" she screeched. "After what he did to my mother?"

She turned the page, evidently to show me exactly what he did do. As far as I could figure out, he caused her to gain a lot of weight and go around in ugly clothes. Maybe this is where Jonica picked up her eating habits.

At any rate, Mom was starting to slim down by the time of Aunt Irma's funeral.

"Looks like she's pulling out of it," I said.

"Pulling out of it?" Jonica snorted. "She has cancer."

She went quick. The next picture was her last, a hospital room party for Jonica's ninth birthday. Mom was unrecognizable at a hundred pounds. Her frazzled hair and bewildered expression plainly stated that she was not long for this world. Jonica stood to one side kissing her forehead, Rebekah Kinney stood on the other, the saddest expression on her face. Two weeks later, Mom was dead. They buried her next to Aunt Irma. Jonica began to sniffle. I tactfully turned the page.

"I can hardly bear to look at that picture," she said. "After an experience like that, you want to throw the camera out."

They almost did. There were a few school pictures and some snapshots from Girl Scout camp, but precious little else. Jonica's teenage years were entirely missing. I could understand this, though. My sister, who was also a junior chubbette until paratyphoid, contracted on an American Youth Hostel tour of Greece, whittled her down to ninety-seven pounds, also used to run at the sight of a camera.

I did find some pictures stuffed in the back, unmounted. Jonica's class picture from Hollywood High (mostly industrious Asians in the cleanest clothes you ever saw. Everyone else looked very high. Jonica was discreetly tucked in the back row). Jonica and Barrie in charro hats and a frame that said "Recuerdo de Tijuana." *And* Jonica's wedding picture, taken seconds after the ceremony at one of those quickie chapels in Las Vegas. Vernon was what they call a "tough customer." He had homemade tattoos on the back of his hands, swastikas mostly ("Nazi signs," Jonica called them), and a narcissistic scowl on his face. Jonica looked happy and terrified at the same time, like she expected to get killed on the honeymoon but had decided it was worth it.

I closed the album.

"Who's Aunt Irma?" I asked. There was no Irma in the Kinney family that I knew of.

"My aunt. Or my great-aunt."

"You mean your grandmother's sister?"

Jonica—no Alex Haley she—pondered this for a while.

"I don't think they were actually sisters. In fact, I know for certain they weren't sisters."

"Then who was she?"

Jonica thought some more.

"You know, that's a very good question."

"Well, how about your other aunt?"

"What other aunt?"

"The one with the note cards. Mrs. McLean."

"Oh, her. She died before I was born. I don't think she was really my aunt either. She was a friend of Aunt Irma's."

Great, just great, I thought. Here I am dealing with some space cadet who doesn't know the meaning of the word "aunt."

"Well, tell me about your grandfather then," I blurted out impulsively.

This didn't faze her a bit. "My grandfather," she began. "He was somehow mixed up in oil."

"What was his name?"

"Warren."

"Warren what?"

She shrugged. "Kinney, I guess. Little Warren's named after him."

"Was that your idea?"

"Are you kidding? I wanted to name him Lyle."

"So?"

She smiled ironically. "So my grandmother gave us five thousand dollars to change our minds."

I digested this. "Does you grandmother ever talk about your grandfather?"

"Not to me."

"To who, then?"

"God knows, herself, I guess." She paused and her face softened. "She must have been nuts about him, though."

I held my breath and let her go on.

"She still reads his letters."

I thought my heart might stop.

"His letters?"

"Yes. Every night before she goes to bed, she reads his letters."

"You mean, the same letters? Over and over?"

"I guess so. He's not writing her any new ones."

I looked down at the album and tried to compose myself.

"Are there a lot of them?"

She laughed. "A lot of them? Only about seven trunkfuls, that's all."

I got no sleep that night. I questioned Jonica about the letters until a cleverer woman would have become suspicious. There were not just letters, she told me: there were photographs, postcards, some things that looked like legal documents, jewelry he had given her, some of his shirts, God knows what else. The seven trunks were an exaggeration, she confessed, but there was one, and it was big, and packed full of stuff. It stayed in the old lady's bedroom and no one was allowed near it, not even Guadalupe.

As a small child, Jonica had snooped through it when her grandmother wasn't home. For a while, its contents fascinated her; then she became interested in something else and the trunk lost its appeal. She hadn't been in it in years.

But she still remembered where the key was. In the drawer of the night table, right next to the bed.

11

About ten days after my affair with Jonica began, I got a second phone call from the old lady. Thank God, because I was about to turn into a total nut case.

During this period, I spent most of my day avoiding Jonica. Seeing her every night was enough of a strain; being dragged over to Barrie's house for the afternoon was unbearable. So I invented a thesis that had to be finished immediately. I need time to work, alone, I told her. In reality, I'd lie on my bed and read magazines.

The more time that passed, the more paralyzed I became. How did it all get so crazy? Had I lost my mind? Jesus, what I was doing was probably against the law.

And it wasn't even getting me anywhere. There was this major historical find about fifty yards away. I could look out my window and practically *see* it. But I couldn't figure out a way to get my hands on it. My affair with Jonica—what a joke. She knew less about what was in the trunk than I did. I doubt if she'd ever even *heard* of Warren Harding. And they could haul the old lady off at any minute . . .

The phone rang. Jonica knew better than to call me when I was working, so I figured it must be Eve. I immediately felt guilty. She had her feelings hurt because I was neglecting her. But I couldn't bring myself to confide in her, to tell her what was really going on. Somehow I knew that underneath that flip exterior she would be severely shocked.

"Eve?" I said, picking up the phone.

A strange silence told me that whoever it was, it wasn't Eve.

"Hello?" said a little voice. "Mr. Weiner?" It was the old lady. I sat bolt upright.

"Yes?" I said, playing it cool.

"This is Jonica's grandmother." God, what a revealing turn of phrase.

She wanted me to come over for dinner tomorrow night. Could I make it?

I said I thought I could.

"Fine and dandy," she said. "I have something I want to show you. Is seven too late?"

I said it would be fine. "Well, good-bye," she said and hung up.

I sat there staring at the phone. Had that just really happened? It was over so fast, I wasn't sure. Then I remembered the conspiratorial tone of her voice.

"She's up to no good," Jonica said. She was convinced it had something to do with her. Some horrible fact would be revealed and then I would never speak to her again. Ever since she'd heard about her grandmother's invitation, she'd been hysterical with dread. Now we were up in the old lady's sitting room, waiting ...

"Where is she?" I asked. Jonica was sitting on the daybed. She was much more nervous than I. In fact, the more nervous she became, the more I calmed down. The end was in sight. I *knew* that whatever the old lady had to say, no matter how awful or humiliating, it would free me from the corner I'd backed myself into. Because I couldn't take it much longer.

"Getting dressed," she answered, staring at the TV. She seemed to be drifting in and out of a coma.

I sat down next to her. Some quiz show was on, one of those with celebrity guests who get paired up with ordinary people from the audience.

"Barrie's mother used to be on this show," she said after a while. I didn't answer.

"She got Barrie on as a contestant, even though it's against all the rules."

I was sick of hearing about Barrie. Here this dumb girl's life is practically at stake, and all she can do is name drop ...

"She didn't win much, though. Just an island stove. She was pissed."

I put my hand on her knee. Maybe she'd get the hint and change the subject.

"Don't!" she hissed and flung it back in my lap. "She might come in at any moment."

Hating her as much as I've hated anybody in my life, I leaned back stiffly and glared at the TV. The guest celebrity, a tennis pro with show biz aspirations, had to give hints for seven things in thirty seconds. The category was "Those Were the Days." She was stuck on "Tin Lizzie." The seconds ticked away.

"Where's the bathroom?" I asked.

"Shhh!" Jonica said, and leaned forward to see if she would make it.

That did it. Something snapped. She had pushed me too far. I just blew up.

"Who the hell do you think you are?" I said, savagely turning on her. "Do you think you're some beauty queen? Do you think you're Miss Los Angeles County? Is that who you think you are? Huh? 'Cause I got news for you. You know who you are? You are Miss Fat City, that's who you are."

She looked at me, her face frozen in terror. She lifted her hand as if to fend off what I was saying. I swatted at it, then grabbed it and twisted.

"How dare you tell me to shut up! How dare you shush me, you fat pig! How dare you!"

She cried out in pain.

"I don't know why I've put up with you as long as I have. All you do is stuff that fat face of yours. It's sickening. I want to vomit every time I watch you eat. You fat pig slut."

I heard the squeaking of her grandmother's wheelchair out in the hall. I threw her hand down and looked at the door. I couldn't believe how hard I was shaking.

The old lady entered and pushed herself to the center of the room.

"Why, hello, Mr. Weiner," she said. "Making yourself at home?"

"Oh, absolutely," I said idiotically. I shot a glance at Jonica. She was clearly in some sort of shock.

"Fine and dandy," the old lady said. "Fine and dandy."

She wheeled over to where she could see the TV.

"Is this Ann-Margret?" she asked, looking around for her glasses.

"No, I don't believe so."

"I thought Ann-Margret was on."

"Maybe she's on later." I looked at Jonica again. She was staring at me with an expression that I had never seen before and couldn't interpret.

"Is Ann-Margret on later?" I asked her.

She refused to answer.

I looked back at the old lady. "Could you please tell me where the bathroom is?" She could; and after she did, I got up and walked out, giving Jonica a haughty look. Fuck her if she won't even talk to me.

I shut the bathroom door and leaned against it, still shaking. What the hell had gotten into me? Holy Christ, I'd actually twisted her arm till she screamed.

I splashed some water on my face. Then I looked in the medicine chest. Nothing but an old rubber sink stopper and a safety pin. I sat down on the edge of the tub for a minute to compose myself. Then I went over to the toilet.

Although I was lost in thought, I distinctly heard the door open. I jerked my head around.

There was Jonica.

She was kneeling on the floor. Tears were streaming down her face. Mucus was streaming out of her nose. She opened her mouth. This cawing sound came out. Then she started crawling toward me, the way peasants approach the Virgin.

I, meanwhile, am peeing on the shower curtain.

I got my fly zipped up, and she grabbed my hands. She began to kiss them and to rub them against her wet cheeks. It appeared to me that she was trying to say something, but all I could make out were unintelligible sobs.

So, Elliot, the moment of truth. What on earth did you expect would happen if not this? Are you happy now? Here you take this forty-watt product of the California school system, this emotional basket case, then you lavish attention on her, wine her and dine her, treat her like she was Liv Ullmann—my God, the poor girl must have been terrified the whole time. Your interest in her didn't make any sense. She was dumb, but she wasn't *that* dumb. She was just waiting for the balloon to burst. And it finally had.

I looked down at her, huddled on the bathmat like a beached whale, her thrift-shop skirt hiked up around her thighs. What am I going to do now? What in God's name am I going to do now?

"It's okay, Jonica, it's okay."

I bent over and patted her.

"Now get yourself together. Get cleaned up. Take your time. Don't worry. It's going to be okay."

She looked up at me. "Why do you hate me?" she sobbed.

"I don't hate you, Jonica. Now get cleaned up."

Dinner was a nightmare. We ate in front of the TV on little trays that Guadalupe brought up—boiled chicken, carrots, and Mexicorn. A sit-com about a black family droned on—where was their cousin from Buffalo going to sleep during his visit? The old lady never took her eyes off the screen except to examine her food. She had reached the age where eating requires a great deal of concentration. She bit down tentatively, like she was afraid of finding bones.

This gave me plenty of time to study Jonica's face. It was not a pretty sight. She had come back from the bathroom with an expression so blank, it had me worried. It made me think that maybe she should be wrapped in a blanket. She'd stopped crying, but her eyes remained swollen and red. They just stared ahead. Every now and then she sniffled.

For once she was off her food. She took some mechanical bites of her vegetables and chewed very slowly. She paused before swallowing, as if her throat were sore. I don't think she touched her chicken at all.

Conversation was nil. Everyone's eyes were on the TV. At one point, the old lady said, "Oh, look, there's Robert Young." It wasn't Robert Young, but I let her go on thinking it was. Jonica didn't seem to have noticed. Dessert arrived: chocolate pudding.

The old lady looked at it unhappily. "Oh, dear," she said and turned to Jonica. "Here, take mine."

Jonica looked at the pudding like she was trying to figure out what it was.

"Go on," the old lady said, waving it at her.

"No," she said uninterestedly, and looked back at the TV.

"Well!" the old lady exclaimed, plainly flabbergasted. "Maybe Mr. Weiner wants it."

The awful meal finally ended. Jonica got to her feet. "I have to check on Warren," she announced and began to walk out of the room. She was in such a hurry she banged against the desk while trying to avoid her grandmother's wheelchair.

Guadalupe arrived with some instant coffee. I looked at Mrs. Kinney. She had a self-satisfied expression on her face. Her dinner party was obviously a big success as far as she was concerned.

I waited for her to speak. Take all your cues from her, I'd told myself earlier. Although now I was sure that whatever bomb she had to drop would be an anticlimax after what had happened. Just how much of an anticlimax stunned even me.

"Is it true," she asked, her eyes all lit up, "that you teach English?"

To be perfectly honest, I couldn't recall what I'd said I taught. But I said yes, it was true.

"And what do you know about poetry?"

"Ah, poetry." My tone implied that she had stumbled upon my life's passion.

She beamed. "I thought you looked like a fellow poet."

"Only poets know the truth," I parried, quoting the motto of the prep school I attended (and a very inappropriate motto it was, I might add).

"What sort of poems do you write?" she asked.

I froze for just the slightest second. "Nature poems," I said.

"Do you use rhyme?"

"I often use rhyme."

"I *always* use rhyme. It's what makes a poem a poem."

I pretended to think about this.

"Do you *teach* poetry?" she went on.

"Oh, no," I blurted out but caught myself. "Not this semester, no. Not this year at all."

"But you have taught poetry?"

"Yes."

She paused. "Would you do me a big favor?"

"Of course."

"Read my poems. Just read them. Tell me what you think."

I said I would be delighted.

"Fine and dandy," she cackled. She held up her coffee cup in a little toast. Like an idiot, I toasted back.

"Tell me," she said, her mood shifting to the more serious. "Have you ever heard of Howard Kesselbaum?"

Howard Kesselbaum. Who the hell was Howard Kesselbaum? Was he somebody who was mixed up with Harding? Was she about to tell me something? Was this the *real* reason I was invited?

"That name sounds familiar."

"He's my teacher down at the Senior Citizens' Center," she went on. "He's a published poet. He thinks I'm good enough to get in magazines."

So *that's* where she went every Wednesday afternoon. Of course.

"Well, you must be very, very good then," I said.

The same thought had occurred to her. "I want a second opinion, though," she said, "before I start sending them around."

It was decided that I would return in a day or so to have tea and to read her work. I made a big point of writing down the appointment in my book. She became so excited her leg began jiggling. I looked at it out of the corner of my eye: was I going to have to call Guadalupe? Then it began to subside.

"And I expect you to reciprocate," she said as I rose and shook her withered hand.

"Reciprocate?"

"You have to show me your poems too."

I stared at her.

"It's only fair . . ." she began, backing down a little.

"I never show them to anybody."

"Aha," she said, holding up a finger. "Howard Kesselbaum says that's the first sign of a bad poet."

Fuck Howard Kesselbaum. "Well, we'll see."

It was inexplicably chilly that evening, and houses in Los Angeles are not built for cold weather. Still, even the flimsiest of them have some sort of heating mechanism, usually an unvented gas gizmo that is always being blamed for the holiday deaths of a family of four. I was shocked to discover the pool house lacked even this safety hazard.

So I pulled on a pair of pajama bottoms that used to belong to Pam. They were gathered at the ankles with elastic: I believe this is referred to as the "harem" style. Which is strange because they were a hearty Scotch plaid. Anyway, they were the ugliest things you ever saw. But they were warm. I also had on a sweat shirt and a pair of argyle socks.

I huddled in front of the fireplace, burning old copies of the *Los Angeles Times*, page by page. You know how it is when you're doing something like that—you keep getting engrossed in the articles you haven't read. I came across a piece about the San Diego Zoo. God, what a nice, simple little business, the zoo business. I'd never realized exactly how nice and simple it really was. It had attractions I never fully appreciated until now. I wondered if they would take me back.

I heard a knock at the door.

I had been expecting something. How perfect, I thought, that she should knock. And at the front door yet. She loved a shallow, dramatic gesture. This was, no doubt, her way of heralding a change in our relationship. I could just picture her on the other side of the door, her face a mask of noble suffering, like Melina Mercouri in those movies she's always winning European Oscars for.

But it wasn't Jonica.

Barrie stood there, engulfed in a big green military coat, a grim expression on her face.

"I have to talk to you," she announced and marched into the room. It was like Napoleon had dropped by.

"I was just going to bed," I said, more to explain my getup than anything else.

"Tough titty."

She had never been in my house before. She glanced around and made a face, as if her worst suspicions had just been confirmed.

"How is she?" I asked.

"How is she?" Barrie mimicked. "Just threatening to kill herself, that's all. Just your average, run-of-the-mill suicide. How's that going to feel on your conscience, asshole?"

I kept my mouth shut and stared at the floor. Let her talk it out, I figured. Curiously, I found myself unmoved by the insults she was flinging at me. On the contrary, the more she went on, the more buoyant I became. *I have all these people fooled*, it started to dawn on me for the very first time. In my own crazy, insane way, I am doing a spectacular job. In fact, my only problem came from fooling them *too* well. That, and taking everything that happened so personally.

It was an electrifying realization. I started to see all sorts of possibilities.

Barrie went over and sat in one of the bamboo chairs. She shook her head sadly and stared at the fireplace. "How many times?" she murmured. "How many times?"

"How many times what?"

She looked at me sharply. I'd picked up my cue a little too quickly.

"How many times will Jonica keep getting mixed up with the wrong men?"

I guess this was to make me feel guilty. I tried my best to look that way, at any rate.

"I can't let this happen to her again. I *won't* let it happen."

"Let what happen?"

She couldn't seem to explain it. "Oh, you know," she said, and buried her face in her hands. I waited. After a moment, she looked back at me. "Jonica has a pathological history of getting hooked up with men who are no good."

She saw me bristle.

"Now I'm not saying you're no good," she went on quickly. "I'm just begging you. Please, please don't hurt her."

"What makes you think I'm planning to hurt her?"

She sighed. "Because I've seen the pattern before." She thought about this and gave a short laugh. "God Almighty, have I seen the pattern . . . She sets herself up so she gets hurt. Did she ever tell you the David Winickie story?"

I shook my head.

"He was tall and skinny and had sloping shoulders. He was famous for his acne. He was the standard by which all acne was judged. No matter how bad yours was, you always had the consolation of knowing his was worse. And it wasn't just acne. His voice didn't change till senior year. He was the only boy who took home ec. Always had the lead in the class play. You know the type."

I felt my face redden. One of the triumphs of my prep school days was the Gene Kelly role in *Brigadoon*. I still knew all the songs.

Barrie didn't notice. She continued her story: "David and Jonica had this big quote romance unquote. They were always going to Bullock's after school, or to the movies in Westwood. These other girls used to hang out with them too. Real losers. I remember one, Isabel Titus, she had these strange hands. The thumbs were enormous. They looked like lobster claws." She shivered. "Thank God I never went to that school. Anyway, just before graduation, David Winickie got arrested for groping a vice cop down at Pepino's Adult

Theatre on Hollywood Boulevard. That was the same place the deputy mayor got caught. Do you remember that?"

I said that it must have been before my time.

"It was a big mess. They weren't going to let him graduate. Jonica tried to get a petition going. Nobody would sign it except for the other fat girls and the music teacher, who spent most of his spare time down at Pepino's anyway."

I wasn't quite sure I saw the point of the story.

"So what happened to David?"

"Oh, they sent him to a psychiatrist and then he tried to commit suicide ... Finally he had the common decency to move to San Francisco and disappear."

There was a moment's silence. "And Jonica?"

Barrie paused before answering. "I think Jonica was too naive to understand what was really going on. But I'll say this for her. She stood by him till the end. She's very loyal. Once she loves you, she'll do anything for you."

Food for thought. So much food, in fact, that I thought quite a long time.

Barrie must have felt she'd lost her audience. She lit a cigarette—an old actor's trick—and then scared the shit out of me by reading my mind.

"What do you want from Jonica?" she asked. For a crazy second, I actually considered telling her. It wouldn't be so bad having her on my side: she was a bigger schemer than I was; and all that Donna business proved she could really keep her trap shut. But I backed off immediately. I didn't have her figured out yet, and until I figure people out I never trust them.

"What do you mean?" I said, playing for time. Make her define her terms.

"At first, I thought you were after the money," she said with a faint smile. "Vernon was after the money. Then he found out the hard way there wasn't any money. But you already know that. So I'm back where I started."

I shook my head and tried to look resigned. But my heart was beating uncontrollably. Change the subject! I screamed to myself.

"What can I say?" I shrugged. "Maybe all I want to do is make her happy."

Barrie looked at me and her expression softened. "Maybe you do," she said. "Maybe you do."

The occasion seemed to call for a truce. I went into the kitchen and foraged around for snacks. God knows I had enough food. I also found a bottle of Scotch. Barrie, who had been to wilderness camp as a teenager and learned survival skills, made a credible little fire. The room actually became cozy.

"Well, well, well," she said, taking a bite of a Triscuit. "Maybe we'll become friends after all."

"What do you mean, after all?"

"I was a little put off you at first," she confessed. "I thought: snobola time. It was something about the way you looked."

"How do I look?"

She folded her arms, leaned back, and squinted at me.

"You want to see my profile?"

"Please."

I turned my head.

"You have a beautiful nose."

My nose is usually regarded as my best feature, with my eyebrows and cheekbones as close runners-up. The most obvious flaw—a not very strong chin—is pretty well camouflaged by a neatly trimmed beard, and a slightly receding hairline is hardly ever noticeable except when it is very windy, and let's face it, that's something you have to learn to live with. None of those products do a bit of good. Actually, if you want to know, the thing that's wrong with me is that my legs are two inches too short for my body. But as long as I avoid low-slung pants, it's no problem. My younger brother, who got the looks in the family, was voted "Best-Looking Senior" in his class at Shady Side Academy. (My year, I got "Out of the Ordinary"—you figure it out, I never could.) Anyway, this led to an offer for him to do a Scope mouthwash commercial; but he turned them down because he'd have to play somebody with bad breath and he felt it was beneath him. The dumb shit. He could have made $12,000. And he didn't have bad breath at the *end* of the commercial.

I thanked Barrie for her compliment and poured us both another drink. The conversation became easier: a discussion of art, time, and space, such as one has over Scotch at two in the morning. We had strayed so far from our original topic—Jonica—that when she appeared in the doorway, a pathetic little smile on her face, we looked up as guiltily as if we'd been caught flirting.

"Hi," she said in a raspy little voice. She coughed and dug a Kleenex out of her pocket.

We jumped to our feet. Barrie ran over and took her hand.

"How do you feel?" she asked in concerned tones.

"I've felt better," Jonica said.

She'd looked better, too. Her eyes were so sore from crying it hurt her to dab at them. And the raincoat she was wearing. It was buttoned the wrong way and made her look like an enormous nursery-schooler.

"Do you need anything?"

"I don't need anything."

Barrie said she had to go. She put on her coat and embraced Jonica. "You know I love ya, hon," she said and kissed her cheek. Then she hugged her again and left. She didn't so much as look my way.

So. Alone at last. I guided Jonica over to the chair Barrie had just vacated. She was so stiff and remote it was like moving furniture. The fire had died out. The room was chilly and it seemed inappropriate, even perverse, to ask her to remove her coat.

I sat her down. The second heavily garbed woman to sit there tonight. Only this one was twice as big as the last. That is what it must be like to be a psychiatrist. One problem after another, but the chair remains the same.

Jonica was scared to death. No wonder, she probably thought I was going to slug her.

But I was the picture of compassion. I made her comfortable; I fixed her a drink; I sat down next to her and took her hand. And then, starting very slowly, I did something that surprised even me.

I told her who I really was. I told her who she really was. I told her what I wanted.

I told her the truth.

12

I don't know what I thought her reaction was going to be.
Actually I did. I pictured it going one of two ways:
—She gets very excited, realizes she's famous in her own pathetic little way, starts making plans to go on *Donahue*, and generally makes a fool out of herself (this because I knew Jonica).

OR

—She has a nervous breakdown; the knowledge of her family's tawdry background pushes her over the edge on which she has been teetering since about age two. Now she can never, never be a "normal person" (this because I knew myself).

Let me try to explain what I mean. I may have rejected many of the values of the Pittsburgh haute bourgeoisie of which I am a product, but I still have certain standards I cling to. I don't regret, for instance, that everyone in my family has seen fit to get married before they reproduce themselves or that their choice of partners are people who are attractive, well educated, and not likely to be made fun of at the country club. Not that I would be caught dead at the country club. But still and all. My sister's unfortunate first marriage to an Italian who designed stickpins which he sold himself from a makeshift table in front of the J. C. Penney Building on Sixth Avenue was a horrible experience for the whole family. "Susie's solution for now," my mother kept stoically referring to it. After about six months, she finally came to her senses and is now married to a wheeler-dealer in Cleveland who owns six Fotomats and is also an attorney. This left me to inherit the title of family ne'er-do-well. I've always had a love/hate relationship with Pittsburgh. I think I'm too emotional or too driven or too *something* for that grey city on the banks of the Monongahela. "The Medea of Mt. Lebanon" Pam once called me.

So it was with a great deal of trepidation that I began my confession. Was I playing with fire? Was I making a big mistake? Maybe I should consult first with Pam's psychiatrist, Dr. Munsterberger, via long distance. He was a well-known comforter of neurotic females. But once I started, I couldn't stop. It all came pouring out.

As many times as I'd played the scenario for this moment over in my mind, nothing prepared me for what really happened.

Jonica, quite simply, couldn't have cared less.

I laid out the whole story—practically the whole story anyway—and what does she do?

She looks at me with those big cow eyes and says, "Elliot, you hurt me."

At first I thought she meant I had inflicted psychic pain. Then she looked down at the wrist I had twisted.

"You hurt me. No matter what you think about another person you should never hurt them. Even Vernon never hurt me. Physically."

Now, I knew she had been listening. Her eyes had been open during the whole story. She had even nodded at several points.

I got up and walked over to the window. The lights of the city were blinking furiously. I had to turn away. They were giving me a headache.

"I'm sorry I hurt you," I said.

"It scared me," she said sullenly.

I went over to her. "It scared me too," I said, in a lighter tone. She looked up, a flicker of hope in her eyes. "You can't understand the pressure I've been under," I went on.

"Oh, I can understand," she said eagerly. "I can understand."

I looked at her for a long time. "Jonica, what do you think about what I've just told you? About your grandfather?"

A panicky look crossed her face, as if there were a correct answer to my question but she had no idea what it was.

"I think . . . it's fine."

"But how do you *feel* about it?"

She appeared to concentrate on this, mostly, I'm sure, to appease me. Then something struck home.

"Elliot," she began urgently.

"What?"

She fumbled for words. "Did you ... do what you did ... with me ... because ... of my grandfather?"

So here it was at last. The moment everything hinged on. My head was pounding.

"Of course not."

"Then why?"

"Because of you."

The room was so still I could hear the faucet dripping in the kitchen. Jonica stared at the wall. She could have been facing a firing squad.

"Do you love me?" she asked like it was the hardest thing in the world to do.

"Yes," I said, and she burst into tears.

She cried for about five minutes. I went over and held her, just letting her cry it out. I looked at my watch. It was two thirty in the morning.

After a while she became more coherent. "I love you so much, Elliot. Sometimes I want to die, I love you so much. I never dreamed anybody like you would fall in love with me. I still can't believe it. I just can't believe it! When you yelled at me I nearly killed myself. I actually got a knife—"

"Shhhh," I said, rocking her. "Everything is different now. Now we're really together. We're really a team." She sobbed some more. How was I going to steer her back on the subject? "You're going to be famous now, you know."

She pulled back a little and looked at me, her nose running.

"What do you mean?"

"Your grandfather. Don't you see?"

She looked surprised. "You think so?"

"You're like Julie Nixon."

Her eyes began to gleam as she saw the connection. She dug a Kleenex out of her pocket.

"Of course," I said, "it all hinges on the papers."

She looked at me. "Papers? What papers?"

My headache was getting worse. "The papers in your grandmother's trunk."

"Oh, *those* papers," she said and blew her nose. "Well, I don't think there's anything we can do about those. She's going to burn them."

"*When?*"

"Oh, before she goes to the home. She doesn't want a lot of nurses going through them." Jonica's mind had wandered off somewhere. Then she noticed the way I looked. "Are they that important? People will believe who I am without the papers, won't they?"

"Jonica, those papers are irreplaceable. They're historical documents."

"My grandmother's papers?"

I tried another tack. "And they're worth a fortune."

She nibbled her thumbnail. "A fortune? How much?"

I waved my hand in the air. "Depends. Thousands."

She pursed her lips for a moment. "I don't care about the money," she said grandly, her mind made up. "My grandmother wants to burn them and that's that." She noticed this wasn't sitting very well with me. "Elliot, she *is* my grandmother."

I took her hand and looked her in the eye. "And who am I, Jonica, who am I?"

She got my point real quick. "Oh, Elliot, please, I'm sorry, I'm sorry. I'll get them for you, I'll get them for you, I promise, oh, honey..."

She left around three, repeating her new favorite expression. "This feels so *right*." She elaborated. "Us, I mean. It's totally crazy but it feels so *right*. You know what I mean?"

I said that I certainly did. Then, as soon as she left, I took three aspirins and collapsed.

The next day we went shopping. Thrift shopping. We had reached that awful phase in a relationship when you feel you have to spend all your time together or else it means something is wrong. As a phase, it usually doesn't last very long. With me and Pam, it lasted about five minutes. But with Jonica . . . I had visions of its going on and on.

Much hand holding accompanies this phase. Jonica and I did most of our squeezing in the car. I learned always to keep my hands in my pockets when in public. I never liked holding hands very much anyway—it's so sweaty.

Ann Landers once said a love affair is not a love affair until it has survived a major fight. Well, we had just survived physical violence; so you can imagine how intently Jonica was taking the whole thing at this point. It seems she had an almost legal definition of the word "love." Once you said it, you were placed under all sorts of contractual obligations. You couldn't make plans without asking the other person. You always had to tell the truth. You always had to be there.

In my own way, I had rather got to like Jonica—the old Jonica, that is. I was occasionally fascinated by her long analysis of why Vikki Carr's career is on the skids or her rundown of all the women Marlon Brando ever dated, just to name two of her favorite subjects.

But the new Jonica—ugh. She had become serious. She only wanted to talk about Us. She did this in the most solemn tones, like somebody about to break some bad news.

Occasionally she would loosen up and try something she no doubt felt was cute. For instance, she spent most of one morning trying to guess my middle name. What the dumb idiot didn't realize is that she already *knew* my middle name—it's Elliot. She should have been trying to guess my *first* name (it's Rodney). No wonder she couldn't get it.

Overnight she had developed an irresistible urge to take care of me. "Give me your dirty laundry," she said. "I'll make Guadalupe do it." No thanks," I said. I wouldn't trust Guadalupe with my sweat socks, much less my good shirts. She'd probably go out and beat them against rocks.

All the way to Pasadena I kept glancing at her out of the corner of my eye. She always seemed to be staring at me, a faint, dopey smile on her face. I smiled back.

Now, I know dumb people can fall in love too. I just didn't realize that they did it so completely and so dramatically. Maybe that's what makes them dumb—they get into something they don't have the brains to handle.

(Interestingly, I had a long discussion on this subject with my psychiatrist once. He said it could never happen to me. My problem was that I was "too concerned and too analytical." I would see all the difficulties, why something *wouldn't* work rather than why it *would*. Then I would get discouraged and not do anything. Hah. He should see me now.)

(By the way, you read that right. I was in therapy—Pam's idea. *But only for three weeks.* Then one day the doctor brought out a large teddy bear dressed in little overalls and told me to talk to it, pretending it was my father. Now, I was a little taken aback—stunned might be a better word. I was paying $70 an hour and somehow talking to a teddy bear didn't seem to be the height of psychiatric sophistication. Then the doctor, sensing my discomfort, got up and *manipulated* the teddy bear's arms so that he waved hello, and tried to put me at ease. After that session, it was so long, Dr. Rosenbaum.)

So we went to Pasadena. Now this was not just *any* thrift-shopping expedition, you understand. This one had a purpose. We had to get outfits for our yachting trip tomorrow.

"What yachting trip tomorrow?" I asked.

It seems Barrie had invited us on her mother's new boyfriend's yacht. He was a Texas millionaire. This fact fascinated Barrie. Sometimes she pretended to be repulsed by the idea, in her pseudo-leftist way. Other times, she was condescending and sarcastic, like when she referred to his condominium in Marina Del Rey as "the north forty."

But she hardly knew the man, and that's why she wanted us along for company. She usually hated her mother's boyfriends; the last one had been arrested for being drunk and disorderly in the lobby of the Montecito Hotel and a week later at the Hi-Hat on Robertson. ("He hits all the classy spots," she sneered.) So now she assumed that any man who wanted to go out with her mother was an A-Number-One creep until proven otherwise.

Quite frankly, I was thrilled by the invitation. Eve listened spellbound while I told her about it. I could just picture her hanging up the phone and seething with jealousy. The fact that I pulled off such a social coup as the yachting trip without her help was driving her crazy.

But yachting outfits I didn't need. I had a pair of Topsiders and that was enough. Jonica wanted something special "though not necessarily nautical," which was a relief since I had been afraid she might show up looking like a cast member of *H.M.S. Pinafore.*

She had a little routine whenever she went to Pasadena. "First I go to the Salvation Army, then Corodin's, then Disabled Vets." I don't know why the stores had to be visited in this order, like the stations of the cross, but she confided that it made her uneasy to go to Disabled Vets first. "It's a purely emotional thing," she explained.

"Why not?" I said, But I thought: What is with this woman? She goes to pieces if she goes to the wrong thrift shop first?

"Oh, goody, goody," she said, pointing to a sign in the Salvation Army window: ALL BINS HALF PRICE.

I pushed the door open. Jonica entered and dashed toward the bins. She certainly knew her way around a thrift shop, I'll say that for her. She could pick up an article, give it the once-over, check for stains and rips, look at the label for fiber content, and toss it back in two seconds flat, and *then* be able to relocate it again ten minutes later. I was mesmerized.

But I had work to get done.

"Jonica," I asked, "how much time do we have?"

"Time? Time for what?" she asked, not breaking her rhythm.

"Till your grandmother goes in the home."

"They said it would probably be the fifteenth."

I entered into some calculations. "So that gives us two weeks."

"Huh?"

"I said that gives us two weeks. To get the papers."

"Oh." Then she noticed something on the other side of Housewares and ran over. I followed behind. She had the attention span of a hamster.

"Look, look," she squealed. It was an enormous hand-knitted sweater, bright green, with an LA Dodgers pennant sewn on the back. It was the ugliest thing I've ever seen.

"Jonica, you can't wear that on a yacht."

"I was thinking of it for you."

I let out a short, unpleasant laugh and went right on. "Jonica, how do you *know* she's planning to burn the papers?"

She sheepishly put the sweater back.

"Huh?" I prodded her.

"She told me."

"What did she say? What were her exact words?"

Jonica tried to think. She was devastated that I hadn't liked the sweater, and had trouble concentrating. "We were sorting everything out ... ah ... trying to decide what to do with it. I asked her about the trunk. She said she was burning all that stuff."

"Where?"

"In the fireplace, I guess. There's a fireplace in her room. It works. You have to remember to open the damper." Out of the corner of her eye she was watching an old woman go through a bin she hadn't worked over yet. It was making her very nervous.

"What would happen if the papers disappeared before she burned them?"

"Disappeared? How?"

"Never mind how."

"She'd call the fucking police."

I wandered around the store for a while. Absurd plans filled my head. I tried to figure out a way for Jonica to sneak them out one by one, then I would Xerox them, then Jonica would sneak them back. Plans like that.

I was browsing through the book section when I remembered something—poetry class. Every Wednesday afternoon the trunk was sitting there unguarded.

I ran over to Jonica. She was in front of the mirror, trying on a dress over her clothes. Some other thrift shoppers stood to the side, waiting a little impatiently. Usually two people can look in the mirror at the same time, but Jonica took up the whole thing.

"Jonica, Jonica," I said. "I think I have it figured out."

"What?" Jonica said. She was pulling the dress over her head and it was stuck. "Gimme a hand."

I tugged at the dress. It was some African dashiki. I couldn't believe she was seriously interested in it.

The other people started shifting their weight and rolling their eyes, one woman in particular. She had a cigarette dangling from the very center of her mouth. She flicked it on the linoleum floor. "Take your time," she called out.

She was making me so nervous I yanked at the dress harder and we all heard a big rip. Jonica and I slunk away and when nobody was looking, we stuffed the dress in a bin. Then we got out of there.

So it was all set. We would go through the trunk on Wednesday. I promised Jonica I wasn't going to take anything and I meant it. First, I just wanted to look. Then I would decide what to do.

For the first time since renting the pool house I was excited. I could finally see the light at the end of the tunnel. Once I knew exactly what was in the trunk, I could make plans. After all, what to do next depended entirely on what was there. That only made sense. And, as for Jonica ... well, I would think of something. Emotional problems have always been the least of my worries, at least when compared to career problems.

That night I was lying in bed. I was too exhilarated to sleep, so I was writing postcards. (Jonica was with little Warren—I had shamed her into spending more time with him.) All the messages were more or less the same: "Having a wonderful time in LA. Blah, blah, blah, see you soon, Elliot," and then the clincher: "P.S. Going yachting with Alice Amber tomorrow." I decided to write the postcards *before* the trip, just in case it didn't pan out.

I'd just finished the one to the Stratford Morris Men when the phone rang. It was Pam with the worst possible news.

13

Our conversation went something like this:
"Hi, honey, it's me."
"Hi, honey, how are you?"
"I'm in Vancouver."
"That's nice. What are you doing in Vancouver?"
"I'm at that conference I told you about."
"What conference is that?"
"Arts and old farts."
"Huh?"
"Arts and the Senior Citizen."
"Pam, have you been drinking?"
"Well, I am in the hospitality suite. You know what John Weiss just called it?"
"Who's John Weiss?"
"He called it the hostility suite."

She collapsed in laughter. I lay there patiently, phone in hand, listening to the party noises and her snorting convulsions. These young professional types are horrible drunks. Strictly amateur night.

I began another postcard. This looked like it might be a long conversation.

"Guess what?" she said after she had finally pulled herself together.

"What?" I asked, writing down my sister's address.

"I'm coming to visit."

A spasm seized me. The postcards slid to the floor.

"When?"

"Tomorrow."

I tried everything. I told her there wasn't enough room. She said she would stay at a hotel. I told her the timing was inconvenient. I told her the timing was *impossible.* I was busy every minute. She said she wouldn't be any trouble. She would go to museums when I was busy.

"Pam, they don't *have* museums here."

"Yes they do," she said, and named about ten. Finally I told her point-blank I didn't want her to come right now. But you try reasoning with a drunk Ford Foundation official. They live like movie stars when they're on the road, these people. They know no law, almost. There was no stopping her.

The next morning, bleary from worry and lack of sleep, I kept my poetry appointment with the old lady. She was watching television when I walked in, some religious program. For a moment I was afraid she didn't remember who I was, but then she grinned and reached over to turn off the TV. The trouble was she tried to turn it off with the color tint knob. And she kept trying. The screen turned from pink to green to black. I didn't know whether I should offer to help or not, but after five minutes, it was becoming ridiculous.

"Let's try this knob," I said brightly.

"Oh," she said, staring at the knob, mystified.

The old lady's poetry was not the best. Her work had a strong religious flavor. Some of the recurring themes were forgiveness, charity work, the afterlife, and how to prepare for Judgment Day. Love your neighbor, she counsels, but rely on the Lord. On the other hand, don't rely too much—"we are allotted only what we earn." In general, she took a cautionary tone.

As for the Kesselbaum technique she had been mastering all these many months, it consisted of stringing together a series of clichés and giving them a snappy, one-word title which would telegraph the metaphor she was planning to massacre. For instance: "Carousel," "Autumn," "Tidewater." And my favorite, "Freeway."

Since to my knowledge there are no copies extant of the oeuvre, it is difficult to convey some of the subtle nuances she managed to express. But one couplet from "Symphony" is forever graven on my brain. Notice, if you will, its unusual, yet innovative, use of rhyme, not to mention a tricky triple metaphor combining science, music and divinity:

> *The incandescence which Thou art*
> *Rivals that of Edison and Mozart.*

"I'm impressed," was my official verdict.

"You are? Really?"

"Absolutely. You have your own style."

"Do you think I could get them published?"

"Where?"

With trembling hands, she gave me something called the *Lantern*. I thumbed through it: PR from some Catholic missionary group, plus several photographs of lepers making sandals.

"I shouldn't think you'd have any trouble whatsoever."

The old lady's eyes beamed maliciously. "That'll show Miriam Feit. She said they were stupid."

I didn't ask who Miriam Feit was. I didn't want to know. One thing I didn't want to get involved in was rivalries down at the Senior Citizens' Center. I had enough on my mind, and it was all about Pam.

Pam is a wonderful person, brilliant in her own way, attractive, full of quirky, intellectual interests like jazz, modern art, and philosophy. Hegel is her hero. I know nothing about Hegel, never having formally studied philosophy (it never seemed to be offered the right term), but many are the nights I've listened to Pam talk about his dialectics while she chain-smoked and drank bourbon. In college, she wrote a little play called *Hegel Goes Hawaiian*, in which Hegel was portrayed by a Lawrence Welk-type character and Absolute Spirit was a chorus girl. It sounds hilarious.

But for all her good qualities, she has a few flaws. Not flaws, really, but things which drive me hooey. Two immediately jump to mind. One, she has slob tendencies, and two, she always says exactly what's on her mind.

An example: once we were invited to a fancy dinner party given by a trustee of the Jewish Museum, a woman named Mrs. Supowitz. Now, Mrs. Supowitz grew very excited when she found out Pam had something to do with the Temple of Dendur, just installed at the Metropolitan Museum and, that week anyway, the talk of the town. Pam's connection was incredibly slight (she helped arrange a grant from the Ford Foundation), but still and all, she knew the history of the Temple, etc., and all the inside machinations that went into getting it to New York. So after dinner, we are all sitting around the living room of Mrs. Supowitz's Fifth Avenue co-op, and she shushes everybody and says, "Now, Pam, you must tell us all about the Temple of Denver."

Pam rolls her eyes, puts down her coffee cup, and says, "Well, first of all, it's the Temple of Den*dur*, not Denver, and second of all, it's such a piece of junk it's not even worth crossing the street to take a look at." There was a short, profoundly awkward silence, then everyone began talking at once, about all sorts of topics.

We had a terrible fight in the cab going home. Pam refused to admit she had said anything wrong. Furthermore, she insisted that the Temple of Dendur was a well-known piece of shit, was in the US due to politics, and should be exposed as such. I said that all may very well be true, but you never, *never* take that tone with a funding source. "La di da," said Pam, "I *am* a funding source."

She was due in at five forty-five that afternoon, an hour etched in the membrane of my stomach lining. I was busy choreographing the weekend so that under no circumstances would her path cross Jonica's. So far it looked like it actually might work.

Anyway, to get back to the old lady's poetry. There she was, fantasizing how she was going to get rich sending this junk off to *The Lantern*, and I was having doubts about her ability to fold it and get it in an envelope.

"How much do they pay?" I asked, just to make conversation.

"Twenty-five dollars a poem," she reported. Then she flashed me a grin. "Interested?"

I found myself actually considering it. Selling a couple of these a month would pay the phone bill. And they looked so easy to write.

"You want to write down their address?"

I wrestled with my conscience. I couldn't deprive all these old ladies of their livelihood via unfair Harvard-bred competition. Or could I?

"Let me see your poetry," the old lady said. "I'll tell you if they'd like it."

I didn't like the way the tables had been turned, but I was prepared for this. I reached in my pocket and pulled out a particularly obscure verse by Robert Frost that I had scribbled on a piece of paper. The old lady took it, spent a while trying to figure out which end was right side up, and held it about an inch away from her glasses. "I have trouble unless it's large print," she explained.

She took her time reading it and then looked up at me. "This doesn't sound Christian," she said.

For some reason, this remark profoundly depressed me.

"I didn't write it for the magazine," I pointed out.

"Oh," she said and examined it again. She went over each word. She obviously didn't understand a thing.

"What does this line mean?" she asked at last.

"Which line?"

She read it phonetically. "The flower blooms to find its majesty alone."

Damned if I knew what it meant. But don't forget, she was dealing with someone who, back at Shady Side Academy, had written a book report on a nonexistent book (*The Third Reich: Collusion or Calamity?* by Major Ernest de Barr) and not only had got an A on it but had ended up winning the Senior History Prize as well. So I muttered some mumbo jumbo about imagery and universality that left her overwhelmed.

"It's a beautiful poem," she said, completely convinced. "And you know what?"

"What?"

"I'm going to show it to Howard Kesselbaum."

"No!"

She shrank back. "Why not?"

Why not indeed, Elliot, you idiot? "Because it's my only copy."

She looked down at the scrap of paper. I could see her thinking: *This* is his only copy? This tattered remnant? This Dead Sea Scroll?

"Perhaps I could copy it over," she suggested.

Then I got an idea.

"Take it, please," I said. "It's yours. My gift to you."

It was a brilliant move, I saw that right away. I had given her my poem. One poet to another. For a moment, I thought she might cry.

She did even better. She took a sip of tea and started talking about herself.

"I know what you're all thinking," she said. "An old folks' home. Everybody feels sorry for me."

I murmured something sympathetic.

"Well, don't," she said. The Adelaide Home, she prophesied, would mark the beginning of a new chapter in her life. It wasn't what everybody feared. "They have card rooms so you can play bridge and canasta. They have TV rooms. They have rooms for everything under the sun. And I hear the food is decent—special diets on request. No salt for me. It's the silent killer. I already met my nurse. She's a colored girl and her name is Stephanie. I gave her a carton of cigarettes to get off on the right track."

Sure, she was sad to leave the old house, but it needed a new roof and those fools from Phoenix were paying $495,000.

"$495,000," I said, astounded.

"They say it's one of the most valuable pieces of property left in Hollywood."

"Holy cow."

"And we sure need the money. I figure I got two, maybe three years left, and I don't want to spend it living on Campbell's soup." We chuckled. "After that it all goes to Jonica."

We silently pondered the implications of this statement. There were all sorts of hidden subtexts swimming about, waiting to be fished out and brought to the surface. I held my breath.

"I just hope she settles down with somebody honest," the old lady said, and I felt my ears turn red. "That was the trouble with Vernon. He wasn't such a bad boy, but he was such a fibber. He was always fibbing about where he was going, where he was getting money."

I picked up a piece of cinnamon toast and started nibbling at it. "That's a problem," I said. I had a horrible feeling what was coming next.

"What she needs is some young professional man, some—"

She broke off as Jonica flew into the room. "Vibrant" I believe is the best word to describe her. She flounced around the room, smelling the African violets, inhaling air from the window, giving her grandmother a peck on the cheek.

"What a great day to go sailing!" she exclaimed. Her yachting ensemble: black corduroy slacks, a pair of backless high heels, a velour pullover, a silk scarf at her throat and a lot of gold jewelry. Her hair was done in a peculiar style, all off to one side. It was very Beverly Hills and very out of character. I wondered what in the world had gotten into her.

"Well, aren't we the glamour puss," the old lady said.

Jonica seemed embarrassed. "Well, this guy *is* a Texas millionaire."

I got up to leave.

"'Bye, Gramma," Jonica said, pausing in the doorway. "Don't forget to take your nap. And don't try to go to the bathroom by yourself. You call Guadalupe, okay?"

"What?"

"I said, call Guadalupe if you want to go to the bathroom."

"Oh, I don't want to go to the bathroom."

"But if you do. Now 'bye." She waved and I waved and we left.

It was the last time they ever saw each other.

14

We drove over to pick up Barrie. She had bought a house in a part of Los Angeles called Palms with her Donna money. That struck me as a funny name for a town. Just Palms. Not *The* Palms, or Palms City. Just Palms. "I don't think it's so strange," Jonica said, when I commented on it to her. "Look at New York. They have a place called Queens. Just Queens."

Actually Palms and Queens have a lot in common. They are both very middle-class and unfashionable. Jonica had lived in this area when she was very small. She pointed out some of the landmarks as we drove past: the municipal swimming pool, where she cut her foot (she still had the scar); Dox Drugs, where her mother had worked briefly selling cosmetics; the International House of Pancakes (I don't know what happened there and I don't want to know). All the sights.

We turned on to National Boulevard. "Uh-oh," she said. "Look. Billboards in Spanish."

Los Angeles is home to millions of Mexican-Americans, but the only place you ever see them is waiting for the bus or shopping at Zodys. Easterners think they are like Puerto Ricans, but let me tell you, there is no comparison. Mexicans tend to be polite, short of stature, barrel-chested, and sentimental. They dote on children but kick dogs and cats. They don't understand the concept of pets. Puerto Ricans, on the other hand, are aggressive and vindictive, and they have this strange habit of rolling up the cuffs on their trousers. Why on earth do they do that? What's their problem? Hot ankles?

I ought to know. An enormous Puerto Rican family moved in on the third floor of my building. The other tenants took one look at the plastic-covered couches being hauled out of the truck that said

MUDANZAS LOCAL O AL CARIBE on the side and went into a panic. "Let's get a petition!" they screamed, wobbling through the halls with their walkers and aluminum canes. I told them to calm down. Live and let live, I said. It could be worse. At least these were the kind of Puerto Ricans who wore designer jeans.

One of the things we noticed coming out of the truck was an enormous Mediterranean-style "entertainment center." Isn't that nice, I thought. Music lovers. Hah. What a fool I was. That very night it started. Eddie Palmieri records wafting up through the air shaft. My bathroom sounded like a dance hall in Mayagüez. Toward the end of the week I happened to look down the air shaft and you know what I saw? Milk cartons! They were tossing their garbage down the air shaft! After that, it was war. That's why I joined the Y: karate classes.

But enough about Puerto Ricans. I could go on and on. I only bring it up to point out the contrast. For it seems there was one Mexican family on Barrie's block—right next door to her, in fact. They were the most mild-mannered people you could imagine. They operated their own bakery business, supplying Mexican specialties all over town. They were especially busy when the Day of the Dead rolled around each year. The whole family worked overtime at the factory, making those little sugar skulls with the names of dead relatives written on them: 'Chela," "Horacio," etc. Try to picture a Puerto Rican family staying up all night doing that.

Considering they had made their fortune in sugar skulls, the Mexicans' home was remarkably restrained. No garish statues of the Virgin in the front yard. Just a yellow stucco façade, with aluminum frame windows that didn't open. Next to their little temple of middle-class values, Barrie's house looked like where the eccentric recluse with the thirty cats lives. She had the only overgrown lawn on the block, the place badly needed a coat of paint, and a piece of shirt cardboard had been taped to the broken living room window. To make matters worse, she was always getting confused and taking out the garbage on the wrong day. Then she'd figure it was too much trouble to take it back, so she'd leave it sitting there on the curb. There was something about that garbage. It didn't tip over or anything, but you could just see the neighbors staring out their windows at it, arms folded, fuming.

The Mexicans had just put in an in-ground pool. It was the first one in the neighborhood, and they were so proud of it they used it night and day. We could see them from Barrie's kitchen. They all made the sign of the cross before they jumped in. (Not *every* time they jumped in, just at the beginning of each session.) The kids were at that stage where they loved cannonball dives. On weekends, their cousins came over.

There was much talk about "us" getting to know them so that we could use the pool. But it was felt that they didn't like "us" or "our friends" very much, particularly after one of "our friends'" dogs went over and left a neenie on their front lawn.

"Our friends"—what can I say about this collection of human dreck, this pathetic crew of lame-os, this flock of no-talent would-be actors, screenwriters, etc., who hung around Barrie's house the way winos hang around Washington Square. There was the feminist theater troupe, of course, but they were the Royal Shakespeare Company compared to the real hard-core losers, the ones who sat around the living room all day smoking cigarettes and whining about their bad luck. Lou Montezinos, the handsome actor/wife beater. Janice "I'm More than a Waitress" Malone. The Sinclair brothers from Texas, who started a food stamp scam down at the Unattached Men's Assistance Center and kept their VW camper up on blocks in the driveway all summer. Howie Linowitz, the forty-two-year-old head of the Young Socialist Media Corps. Kirk Somebody who was arrested for breaking into a house in Santa Monica and stealing brassieres. Jill Rainey and Tony Rumpp, who sold Fiesta Ware at swap meets with their mother. God, what a crew.

It was so depressing I couldn't stand being there for more than ten minutes at a time. You never knew what awful thing was going to happen next. One of their favorite kicks was to get the cat stoned, which I thought was perverse. They would blow marijuana smoke in the poor creature's face and he would stagger around slack-jawed and do all sorts of humiliating things. "Our friends" thought it was hilarious. "He probably loves to get stoned" was their theory. I kept my mouth shut.

The most depressing thing about it was that Jonica fit in so well with this crowd. In her own loony way, she was a fundamentally decent human being. She deserved better than this. Given a normal family life and taught a little self-discipline, I got the feeling she would have turned out a lot different.

That was the trouble with these people—they were raised so poorly. I don't even think they were raised; they were just allowed to grow up. One of the Sinclair brothers told me his parents never taught him he was supposed to brush his teeth every day. He had to figure that out all by himself.

It had nothing to do with money. These people were from middle- and upper-middle-class backgrounds, just like myself. I guess the difference is that I come from the kind of upper-middle class they must have had in Sparta. We were taught *values*. No Cadillacs for us, even though my father could easily afford one. A Buick was fine, and one of the cheaper models at that.

My father has a morbid fear of being thought ostentatious. I think it stems from our name: Weiner is one of those names that can go either way. German or Jewish. All his life he has been terrified people will think he's Jewish. This is no idle worry—it's happened plenty of times. There was the hotel in Bermuda that refused reservations. I've never seen him so upset; he kept talking about legal action. Personally, I don't get the least bit upset about it, because I know I'll get the last laugh when they find out the truth.

But what can you say about somebody like Barrie? Her grasp of reality is bound to be tenuous. How could it be otherwise, when your mother is world famous for her facial contortions? She thrived in this atmosphere. She was the Queen Bee.

It was into this loony bin that Jonica and little Warren were moving in two weeks' time. I shuddered every time I thought about it.

When we showed up around twelve thirty, only one of the walking wounded was there, thank God, and he was leaving—a guy named Ward, who had so little on the ball that he tried even Barrie's patience. She called him Wart behind his back. He had a job for the afternoon testing stunts for a new quiz show at some warehouse over in Culver City. He was getting paid $40 off the books—"Perfect, 'cause now I can get my car painted." He showed us a color chart, and we discussed the pros and cons of various colors.

"Make sure you get all the bird doo-doo off before they paint it," Jonica advised. "Otherwise it bakes right on."

We all trooped out to examine his car for bird doo-doo. I kept looking at my watch. Jonica actually found some; she chipped it off with a nail file. Ward thanked her extravagantly. Then he remembered he wasn't getting the car painted until Tuesday, so he would have to check it for bird doo-doo all over again.

Finally he drove off, staring at some directions Barrie had given him. It turned out it was she who lined up the job, through her mother's connections. "I just hope he has insurance," she said, waving good-bye. I looked at my watch again.

But Barrie wasn't quite ready to leave. She dragged us into the kitchen to test out some radios she had found in the box the night before.

Now there is one important character trait I must explain about Barrie before we go any further. She was without a doubt the cheapest person I have ever met in my entire life. When you went somewhere with her in her beat-up Chevrolet, she charged you for gas. We went to the movies one night and she made us each pay fifty cents. "I'm only doing this because I own a guzzler" was her excuse.

But this is nothing compared to the story of the box. It seems that at the end of her street was a supermarket, and in the supermarket parking lot was a box, actually a small, tin hut with a swinging door, where you deposit donations for the Goodwill. Every evening at eight, when the supermarket closed and the parking lot was deserted, Barrie would sneak up with her flashlight and go through the day's haul. Then she would lug whatever she wanted home in a shopping cart she stole from the supermarket.

She furnished the entire house from the box: lamps, curtains, appliances, sheets, pillows, the entire contents of her kitchen, the clown paintings in the hall, the luggage she took to Europe, electric fans, books, you name it. *Literally everything in that house came out of the box.* Sometimes, if people have something too big to fit in the box they leave it alongside. Hence, the living room sofa (no cushions, unfortunately), the mismatched dining room chairs, the driftwood coffee table, the Barcalounger that wouldn't recline, the trundle bed in the guest room.

And the clothes! The box had provided the backbone of Barrie's wardrobe, and the contributions it made to Jonica's extensive designer collection should not be underestimated. I still have a football jersey and some Fruit of the Loom T-shirts that got passed my way. For if Barrie didn't have an immediate use for whatever she came up with, it went on to somebody else. Another way of holding the troops in line. What the Goodwill thought about all this is a good question. Weren't they getting a little suspicious? The box hadn't supplied a usable item in the past year and a half.

At any rate, we watched Barrie test the radios. "This one is completely kaput," she said and tossed it in the garbage. "Let's try this one." She plugged it in and fiddled around with the knobs. "I think these kind need a minute to warm up." It was a big old green Zenith; my grandmother used to have one just like it. I can remember sitting in her kitchen listening to *Mr. Keene, Tracer of Lost Persons.*

We heard some static. Barrie and Jonica gave a little cheer. Then a traffic report came on, and then:

> *Hi gang, it's Donna!*
> *Schooltime's here*
> *And you know what that means*
> *It's time to buy*
> *Some new blue jeans*
> *Or green jeans, red jeans, orange jeans, yellow*
> *jeans to please that special fellow —*

Barrie clicked it off. Jonica and I looked at each other, caught off guard, the guiltiest expressions on our faces.

"You told him!" Barrie screamed and began pummeling Jonica. "You rat! Just for that you don't get the radio."

"I don't want your dumb radio," Jonica said, fending off the blows. "You already gave me about eleven. All I do is give them to Guadalupe."

Barrie's face was quivering with rage. She turned to me, her eyes narrowed to little slits.

"If you tell . . ." she said darkly.

She seethed all the way out to the car. I could tell it wasn't just the radio. The real problem was, Jonica and I had turned into a couple and she felt left out. Now it was Jonica and I who had the secrets, not Barrie and Jonica.

She climbed into the backseat of the Mustang and huddled silently in a corner. Every once in a while I would glance in the rearview mirror and catch her watching Jonica, a wary expression on her face.

Any fool could tell Jonica was madly in love. She had been hovering around me all day like a puppy hoping to be petted. I could do no wrong. Even Pam's visit didn't ruffle her. Of course I could have the night off to have dinner with my old friend from the zoo, the middle-aged spinster who lived alone and attended chamber music concerts and collected antique quilts and who would be in Los Angeles only for one day, maybe two tops. Jonica understood.

No, the trouble I smelled was not with Jonica. It was with Barrie. Her little matchmaking venture had worked too well.

So I asked about her mother's new boyfriend.

"What do you want to know?" she asked suspiciously.

"How did they meet?"

It was too good a story for anyone of Barrie's temperament to keep feigning indifference. After thirty seconds, the Liz Smith in her had completely taken over.

They met, she reported, at a Christian Crusade in Lubbock. "He's a publisher. He's the second largest publisher in the world, after the people up in Chicago who print all the phone books. Mostly he publishes books about Loretta Lynn and Elvis Presley. He sells them mail order. He published a book by Elvis's barber and another by Elvis's cousin. It was a cookbook. It was called *Foods Elvis Loved.*"

"He published that?" Jonica exclaimed. "I know that book."

I figured she might.

"Oh, really?" said Barrie politely, and then she raced on. She didn't want anybody spoiling her story. "He's nuts about my mother. He thinks she's some big star."

In unison, the two girls gave a snort, the same one they always gave whenever Barrie's mother was referred to as a big star. I was starting to pick up the habit myself, not even knowing why. "The same day he met her, he was so smitten he gave her a fully let-out chinchilla car coat."

"Such an awkward length," commented Jonica.

"Not if you're in a wheelchair," Barrie went on. "It belonged to his dead wife. She suffered in agony for twenty years with multiple sclerosis."

"Eeech," said Jonica. "Who'd want that coat?"

"My mother, that's who. She wears it around the house to save money on heat." Barrie leaned a little closer to the front seat. "My mother's going crazy. She doesn't know whether to marry the guy or not. She keeps calling, asking my advice, wanting to spend time with me, I can't get her out of my hair ... Just yesterday she called and said, "Barrie, here you are twenty-five years old and you've never had me over to your house for dinner." '

"Serve fish," Jonica suggested. "She hates that."

By the time we found a parking place, Barrie was in a much better mood. She had vague directions—some slip number where we would find the yacht—but it was clear we were going to need help. Marina Del Rey was an enormous place: pleasure craft as far as the eye could see, ringed by fancy apartment complexes with names like Balboa Reef.

We must have presented quite a sight to the suntanned swinging singles who were sipping Ramos Fizzes on their rear decks: Jonica tripping around in her high heels, me in my pink Brooks Brothers shirt and khaki slacks, and Barrie sweltering in a pea coat ("It might get cold out there') and looking like she was in the market for a tugboat. We finally found an employee, a dour old man in a hurry to get somewhere.

"Where is Mr. Kentner's boat?" Barrie asked, running alongside him.

"Other side of the alfred," he said, picking up his stride.

"What the hell's an alfred?" Barried asked me as we watched his disappearing back.

"I thought *you* knew."

It turned out the *Alfred* was a boat and, sure enough, right next to it was the *Columbine*, with Alice Amber and Claude Kentner, the Texas millionaire, sitting there doing a crossword puzzle.

"I thought I said one o'clock," Alice Amber said, and I immediately wished I were somewhere else. Her tone was ominous enough, but what really made me uncomfortable was Claude Kentner. One look and I could tell he was a nervous wreck. Clearly he wanted everything to go according to plan and be "nice." And clearly, it just wasn't. I could feel it in my bones.

"So shoot us," Barrie said, and we climbed aboard. Two little white poodles appeared from nowhere and began barking at us. "Oh, God, the dogs," Barrie said.

Jonica and I were introduced to Claude Kentner. He may have been a Texas millionaire, but he was far from perfect. I think the problem was Parkinson's disease. At any rate, he drooled. The first thing we learned that afternoon was not to stand downwind of him.

"Welcome aboard, fellows and girls," he said, shaking our hands vigorously. I was fascinated with his hair. It was done up like Johnny Cash's, long in back and over the ears, with an elaborate pompadour roll in front. So much hair spray was holding it together it glinted in the sun like a silver football helmet. He seemed tremendously glad to see us; I got the feeling Alice Amber had been giving him a bad time.

"Well," he said, looking around uncertainly, "I guess we're all set." Nobody moved. "I guess we can cast off now."

Something told me he didn't have the sea in his blood.

"We should have cast off an hour ago," Alice Amber said.

Claude Kentner climbed up a ladder to the bridge. As he did so, everyone's attention fell on his shoes. They were white patent leather with stacked heels. Cuban heels, I believe they're called. Suddenly I realized who he looked just like—Louis XIV.

The shoes were a shock to everyone and they took a moment to digest. I felt particularly sorry for Alice Amber. He was *her* boyfriend. We were all too embarrassed to look her in the eye.

Claude Kentner had hired a high school student to crew the boat. We watched nervously as the kid hot-rodded the thirty-four-foot cabin cruiser out of the slip and into the channel.

"Slow down, Dennis!" we heard Claude Kentner plead, with no discernible effect.

I peeked inside. The *Columbine* was a big disappointment glamourwise, obviously some secondhand bargain built circa 1952. It smelled like the men's room on disinfectant day. Everything was plaid: the little drapes covering the portholes, the cushions on the built-in couch, the carpeting, the owner's pants.

Claude Kentner climbed back down the ladder. Alice Amber had fixed some brunch snacks,* unfortunately chilled by this time. We

---

* What she *should* have served, I casually mentioned to my agent while we were reviewing the manuscript, was something more like Pam's Grandmother's Sour Cream Coffee Cake. My subsequent attempts to locate this recipe have given rise to all sorts of misunderstandings among my friends, mostly having to do with the ridiculous rumor that for the past year and a half I have been working on a cookbook. It is a pleasure finally to set the record straight.

SOUR CREAM COFFEE CAKE

2 cups flour	Take flour, sugar, butter, baking powder, rub to-
1 cup sugar	gether as for a pie crust. Add vanilla, eggs, sour
½ cup butter	cream. Beat for 5 minutes. Put in a loaf tin. Sprin-
2 tsp. baking powder	kle with sugar, cinnamon, and nuts. Bake at 350
1–2 tsp. vanilla	degrees for one hour.
2 eggs	
½ pint sour cream	

sat in director's chairs on the aft deck and tried to eat them while the boat lurched. The poodles ran about, yelping in terror.

"Make him slow down," Alice Amber said.

"Sugar, he knows what he's doing."

"I can't pour the coffee."

"It'll be smoother when we get out in the channel."

"I said, make him slow down. It's your boat, for Christ's sake."

Once again all eyes went to Claude Kentner's shoes as he climbed back up the ladder and took Dennis aside. I don't know what he said but this time it worked: the *Columbine* slowed down to a sarcastically slow pace. Claude Kentner climbed back down the ladder, teetered over to his chair, and plopped down. No one spoke for a while. We were drained.

We sailed out the channel, past Venice on our right. By this time, we were moving so slowly we were holding up traffic. It was a beautiful day and the concrete embankment was crowded with strollers and roller skaters ogling the boats sailing by.

So here you are, Elliot—on a Texas millionaire's yacht, in the company of a big Hollywood star (snort) and the granddaughter of a President of the United States. Enjoy it while you can.

"Oh, gross," said Barrie, and I looked up. One of the poodles was vomiting on her sneakers.

By the time we reached open ocean, factions had developed. Barrie was particularly miserable; she kept muttering about her shoes. Alice Amber put them to soaking in the little sink in the galley. Finally Barrie peeled off her pea coat and went up to the foredeck to sun herself. "Go with her," I whispered to Jonica. "We should be nice to her."

Claude Kentner felt the girls were rejecting him. "Do you think they're having a good time?" he kept asking me. I thought it highly unlikely. There wasn't a thing to do on the yacht except sit there and roll with the waves. I've had more fun waiting for a subway train.

"You know women," I told him. "Girl talk."

He frowned. "Maybe they need to wet their whistle." In a moment he was back with plastic tumblers of Coke for everybody.

"Do you think Dennis wants a Coke?" he asked me and Alice Amber.

"Why don't you ask him?" said Alice Amber in a tone of deadly boredom.

Soon he returned, still eyeing the girls uneasily. "Maybe I should go and talk to them."

"Go ahead," said Alice Amber.

He started forward and then hesitated, sniffing the air. "What's that smell? Gas? Is that a gas leak?"

Alice Amber and I sniffed. The odor of marijuana was drifting down from the bridge.

"Claude," she snapped, "go talk to the girls."

He ran off. She rested her face in her hand for a moment. "Ai yi yi yi yi," she said. Then she looked at me. A glint came into her eye. She scooted her chair closer. "How about a drink?" she whispered. "Claude doesn't allow booze on the boat, but fuck him."

I followed her inside. From a drawer under the couch she pulled out a bottle of Chivas Regal, wrapped in a blanket. "It just kills me to put this good Scotch in Coca-Cola," she told me with a sigh and then filled up both tumblers to the brim. She wrapped up the bottle, replaced it, and we went back outside.

We sat in silence for a while. Alice Amber put away half her glass with the measured precision of a serious drinker. I studied her face in the blinding sunlight. It was lined but pleasantly so; all those facial contortions over the years had taken their toll. Her hair was greyish blonde and worn rather long for a woman who must be sixty. Her eyes, which didn't come across at all on TV, were her best feature — pale blue and sad. She wore a plain white blouse, grey slacks, and a pair of large, square-cut aquamarine earrings. Aside from a plain gold watch, they were her only jewelry. She was a chain smoker, and even though the breeze was constant, she knew all these tricks of getting a cigarette lit.

It was strange sitting there next to an icon from your childhood. I had trouble putting the two of them together—was she Alice Amber on Channel 5 in black and white or was she Barrie's mother? Okay, so the yacht was tacky, so she was a washed-up alcoholic— still, I was thrilled.

From the foredeck we could hear merry peals of laughter. Claude Kentner's campaign was going well.

"I had the strangest dream last night," Alice Amber said suddenly. "It was me and Shelley Winters. For some reason we decided to file a joint income tax return."

"Oh, Shelley Winters," I said.

She looked at me. "You know Shelley?"

"She's a friend of a friend," I replied lamely.

"Who?"

"Eve Biersdorf."

"Eve Biersdorf," Alice Amber repeated, trying to place the name. "Is she Pete Biersdorf's new wife?"

"Not that new. They've been married three years."

"Oh." She took a swig of her drink. "Well, I hear she's a real yo-yo." I stiffened. "I wouldn't call her a yo-yo," I said loyally.

She looked at me and realized her gaffe. Her eyes widened, full of concern. "I'm sorry," she said and took my hand. "Can you forgive me, please? Jesus, I'm a great one to talk about yo-yos." She tossed her head in Claude Kentner's direction.

We both laughed and for the first time since I'd been in LA, I felt a rush of complete trust and friendship.

"He has this fancy apartment in Dallas," she said, a wonderfully malicious quality in her voice, "with *nothing in it*. Just a roll-away cot with some dust balls underneath."

"I bet you'll soon fix that."

"You bet your fucking boots."

"And speaking of boots—"

"I know, I know. I nearly died when I saw those things. A year ago I would never have married a man who wore shoes like that. But, like Sophie Tucker used to tell me—'I've been rich and I've been poor, and believe me, Alice, rich is better.'"

Oh, I was in love. I listened raptly while she went on about her problems with Claude Kentner. Should she marry him? Was he that awful?

"I love talking to you!" she exclaimed.

"I love listening."

"Somebody with a brain. I'm so glad Jonica brought you. Will you be my new best friend?"

Would I! Imagine hanging out with Alice Amber—showing up at Hollywood parties with her on my arm, everybody wondering who I was, maybe even masterminding her comeback . . .

"Let's get another drink," she whispered, and we snuck back inside. "Fuck all that sunshine." We sat on the plaid couch and had a long, intense conversation about life, the details of which I seem to have forgotten.

"So there you are!" Claude Kentner exclaimed as he entered the cabin, dragging Barrie after him. By dragging I mean exactly that— he had a tight grip on her forearm and she was struggling to get away. For an awful second Alice Amber and I had the same thought—the clown has finally gone berserk and is going to murder us all.

But it was all in fun. They were horsing around. Jonica stood bouncing up and down in the doorway behind them, her eyes bright with excitement.

"You know what I'm going to do?" Claude Kentner asked us.

"No, what?" Alice Amber replied, trying to pretend she wasn't holding a tumbler full of straight Scotch.

Claude Kentner was much too taken with himself to notice. He had come upon the perfect way to liven up the party.

"I'm going to toss her to the sharks!" he exclaimed.

Barrie shrieked. "Oh, no, Claude! Anything but that!"

Alice Amber and I accepted this news calmly. We were both very drunk and determined not to give ourselves away.

"I'm going to make her walk the plank!" he bellowed to us.

We grinned inanely. "What fun," Alice Amber said.

"Claude, don't you dare!" Barrie screamed.

"Come on, Elliot boy, you gotta give me a hand."

I looked round, startled. Was he talking to me?

"Elliot, I'll murder you!" Barrie warned.

I got up unsteadily. The poodles had reappeared, very agitated. My stomach felt queasy.

"Grab her other arm," Claude Kentner instructed me. We dragged her over the hump of the doorway and out on to the deck. She may have been screaming and kicking, but she was in heaven. Anything to be in the spotlight.

Jonica ran alongside of us. "Oh, God, you're not really going to do it!" she screamed. "Oh, God, just don't throw *me* in!" Nobody was paying the slightest bit of attention to her, except the poodles. They were trying to keep from being stepped on.

"I'm going to wet my pants!" Barrie screamed.

It never occurred to me that Claude Kentner was actually planning to throw Barrie overboard. I don't think it occurred to him either. But once the prank started, it was hard to figure out where to stop it.

"What's it going to be?" Claude Kentner asked me. "Hands and feet?" We were at the railing.

"Yeah, hands and feet."

Claude Kentner grabbed Barrie by her wrists and I grabbed her ankles. It wasn't easy because she was kicking pretty hard. We hoisted her up and laid her on her back on the railing.

"My watch!" she screamed. Claude Kentner took it off her wrist and put it in his pocket.

I looked around to see if any other boats were watching us. None were, thank God. We were anchored all by ourselves about three miles from shore. My eye caught Dennis watching us languidly from the bridge. Never had I felt more like a fool.

Barrie sensed the end was near. "Mother!" she screamed. Alice

Amber was the only one who could save her now. But Alice Amber was still inside.

"Just don't throw *me* in!" Jonica yelled.

Claude Kentner and I lifted Barrie from the railing and dangled her over the side. She was perhaps six feet above the water. It was dark blue and looked very cold.

"Ah one . . ." said Claude Kentner. We swung her out. "Ah two . . . ah threeee!" Barrie flew away from the boat with surprising grace and landed ass first in the water.

There was a moment of silence. We stared at the spot where she disappeared. My God, I thought. What have we done?

Suddenly her head popped up, water spouting from her mouth in an arc. I breathed a sigh of relief. It was okay. It was fine.

"You bastards!" she shouted, a big smile on her face. Her hair was plastered all over her head like overcooked spinach.

I looked at Claude Kentner. He was beaming. "I sure bet this here is one boat ride you're gonna remember for a long time," he yelled down at her.

"Like hell I will," she yelled back, splashing water up at us.

"Oh God!" shrieked Jonica to no one in particular. "Just don't throw *me* in!"

Claude Kentner got the hint. "Okey doke," he said. "Who's next?"

Jonica let out a scream so piercing the poodles fled toward the cabin, colliding with Alice Amber, who appeared in the doorway with a camera. "Sure sounds like fun," she said, trying her best to get in the spirit of things, though she looked like she would have preferred a nap.

Claude Kentner and I approached Jonica, both of us thinking the same thing—how on earth were we going to get *her* overboard? She outweighed both of us. Barrie's 130 pounds were bad enough; I felt I'd strained my lower back.

But Claude Kentner, who could have made a good living torturing prisoners for North Korea, immediately hit upon a solution: we would use intimidation rather than force.

"Hey, Jonica," he said like he was talking to a cat. "You wanna jump in the water, don't you?"

"Oh, God," wailed Jonica as she realized what was happening. "Please don't make me jump."

He grabbed her by the arm and led her over to the railing. "I'm not gonna make you do anything, pumpkin. You're gonna do it all by yourself."

"Oh, no," she moaned.

"Let me get a shot of this," Alice Amber said.

"Put your foot over. That's right. Now the other one."

I looked up at Dennis. He was reading a comic book.

Jonica's leap was a little anticlimactic, but she made a bigger splash. Alice Amber took some pictures of the girls playing around in the water, and then some of me and Claude Kentner. He was so proud of himself, he began posing in these body-builder positions. For a moment, I was afraid he might try and top things off by tossing me in the water, but by then the girls were complaining so loudly of the cold it was obvious the joke was over.

"How do we get back on the boat?" Barrie yelled up.

"I'll get the ladder," Claude Kentner said.

But the ladder wasn't where it was supposed to be, and a search failed to produce it. It wasn't in any of the logical places it might have ended up. Dennis couldn't recall the last time he had seen it.

"Hurry up," Barrie yelled. "I think I just saw a fin."

We held a conference on the after deck. Dennis, who knew a lot about knots, figured he'd rig up a harness with some nylon cord. That should do the trick.

While Dennis prepared the harness, we leaned over the railing to joke with the girls. They were turning cranky, particularly after Barrie realized she had her latest Donna residual check in her hip pocket. The thought of sailing home in their wet clothes wasn't appealing to them.

"I'll make some coffee," Alice Amber said, shooting Claude Kentner an "I hope you're happy now" look.

Claude Kentner was anything but happy. His self-confidence was vanishing by the second. He avoided watching the girls and spent his time nagging Dennis to hurry up.

Finally the harness was ready. We lowered it to Barrie, who, following Dennis's instructions, slipped it over her arms up to her shoulders. Then we began hauling her aboard.

There were many false starts. The angle of the hull proved to be an insurmountable problem; so we moved around to the stern of the boat, which hit the water perpendicularly.

Dennis and Claude Kentner pulled; Alice Amber and I reached down to grab Barrie's arms, and she managed to walk herself up the side of the boat. We pulled her over the railing, and she plopped down on the deck, frozen and exhausted but mostly relieved. We all were. There had been a few nasty moments when it seemed we would never get the girls back on the *Columbine*. Claude Kentner shook Dennis's hand and congratulated him.

But our relief was a little premature. The system didn't seem to work for Jonica. The harness was too small, but even after it was adjusted, there were problems. Some law of physics was at work involving mass, density, and angles; we couldn't seem to pull her far enough out of the water to grab her arms. Barrie suggested she peel down to her underwear so there would be less bulk, but without a shirt on, the nylon cord chafed her arms so badly she screamed out in pain. We told her to try pulling herself up the rope, but she couldn't get more than six inches out of the water.

"Try harder, Jonica," we called down. "All you have to do is put one hand over the other and pull yourself up."

"I *am* trying." She was starting to cry. Her pants had sunk from view and her velour top was floating out to sea.

An atmosphere of crisis gripped the yacht. We shouted encouragement to Jonica, but away from the railing, everyone was panicky and bitter. Alice Amber wasn't speaking to Claude Kentner. "I don't want to aggravate the situation," she whispered to me. He was afraid even to look at her. Barrie was taken up by the melodrama of the situation; she ran around the boat tearing at her damp hair and proposing bizarre rescue schemes. Dennis told her why they wouldn't work; finally he became ominously silent. It seemed no one was in charge.

I suggested that I enter the water and try to figure out something from that point of view. Everyone leapt at the idea, particularly Barrie, who wanted to do it herself. But her mother forbade it; the girl was even more hysterical than Jonica. Alice Amber wrapped her in the blanket from the Chivas Regal and gave her a cup of coffee.

I followed Claude Kentner into the master stateroom and he found me a pair of swimming trunks. A daze had settled over him. He had trouble opening drawers and his drooling, unattended for the past half hour, hung in long streams down his chin.

"We're counting on you," he kept telling me. "You can do it." I was afraid he might start to cry.

As soon as I jumped in the water, I saw it was hopeless. From Jonica's perspective, the situation was even more terrifying than it was from the boat. The *Columbine* loomed up like some floating skyscraper. And the water was freezing. It hit you with a stab that took your breath away and left you gasping.

Jonica clung to me. Her whole body was shaking and she had developed the hiccups. "Elliot," she sobbed, "don't leave me here."

I could make out the buildings on the palisades in Santa Monica, glittering in the afternoon sun. They seemed as far away as Mars.

I tried. I really did. But there was nothing I could do. I got underneath her and tried to push her up but all that happened was that I sunk deeper in the water. The farther down you got, the colder it was.

They pulled me back on board, and we held another conference. Jonica was turning blue, she was hysterical, and we had no way to get her back on the boat. We needed help.

Claude Kentner told Dennis to call the Coast Guard.

15

Looking back on it now, probably the most amazing thing about that whole crazy afternoon was that I met Pam's plane, and right on time, too.

Since she was coming from Canada, her flight was scheduled to disembark at the International Arrivals Building, a minor structure compared to its counterpart at JFK, catering mainly to obscure airlines plying once-weekly routes to the South Pacific. Some years ago, a mad Yugoslav known as the Alphabet Bomber did his best to destroy the place; this is why the tile around the baggage lockers doesn't match that in the rest of the building. I sat on a bench, munching a candy bar, and tried to figure out which tile was before the bomb and which was after.

At the risk of sounding abnormal and perverse, I must confess that I am one of those people who find airports totally absorbing. I can sit there and watch the people for hours. "Book me through Atlanta," I tell the startled reservations clerks; two or three hours between planes is my idea of heaven. I get my shoes shined, I buy plastic combs from the vending machine in the men's room, I hang out at the newsstand, checking out what tripe travellers are reading these days, I drop by the souvenir stand and order a dozen football decal highball glasses to be shipped back to my "Home-town," I watch the hand luggage being x-rayed, and I even allow myself to be corralled by those Moonies, or whoever the cretins are wandering around selling records in accordance with their First Amendment rights.

So it was no effort for me to sit there and watch the passengers from the plane ahead of Pam's file out of customs. I played my favorite game, Where Are They From?, even though this crowd was pathetically easy: tall, blond, one even carried a pair of skis—obviously

Scandinavian. A bunch of them ran over to the sliding glass doors and, jabbering excitedly in Swedish or Danish or whatever (*that* good I'm not), they pointed at something out in the parking lot.

I twisted around to see what was the source of all this excitement—Big American Cars, no doubt—but it was an eighty-foot palm tree, rising in majestic splendour from a glass-covered traffic median. That did it. One look at the palm tree and reality came flooding back to me in a sickening rush. I feared I might faint. If only I were someplace else, I thought. Anyplace else. My life is over. I'll never be happy again.

"You look awful."

Pam suddenly appeared before me, toting a plastic shopping bag of duty-free liquor and looking like she needed a shampoo.

An involuntary cry emerged from my throat and I jumped to my feet. There was something about the sight of her standing there, in her fifteen-year-old London Fog, with that yellowish-green pallor in her cheeks that comes only from years of difficult subway commuting—an island of sanity, a glittering diamondlike point of logic in the morass of Southern California. There *is* life outside of that pool house on Casino Drive. Remember Bloomingdale's? Remember rain? Remember Dannon Yogurt? Remember Zabar's? Remember the bodega on the corner that was open all night? Remember *civilization*? I could get out of here. I could—dare I even think it?—pack up and go back to New York. Right now. With Pam.

"I've never been so glad to see anybody in my whole life," I said, hugging her till she started to grunt.

"What's wrong? You need a loan?" And her wisecracks! That's another thing I'd forgotten about. When was the last time I heard a wisecrack?

I started to laugh. Then I noticed I was crying.

"Elliot, what's wrong? What's the matter?"

I couldn't answer. The words wouldn't form.

"I knew you'd be glad to see me, but this is ridiculous."

All her thwarted maternal instincts came into play, and she led me, sobbing into a used Kleenex she found in her pocket, into a gloomy bar (she had a sixth sense for locating airport bars) and sat me down in the darkest corner, where you could barely see your hand in front of your face. In a second she was back with a double Scotch for me and a double bourbon for herself—she fancied herself a hard-drinking, gutsy-type woman—and a stack of cocktail napkins for, clearly, the Kleenex was proving to be inadequate. I took one look at my drink, thought of Alice Amber, and broke down again.

"Take your time, take your time," she said, patting the back of my hand.

"Do you have any Valium?" I managed to burble.

She did indeed—is the Pope Catholic, as Jonica would say—and I swallowed it and closed my eyes for a moment.

Then I began to tell her the story.

The Coast Guard had arrived within twenty minutes, bearing down on us, sirens blaring, the sailors (I'm calling them sailors here—"coastguardsmen" is such an unwieldy word) lining the front of the cutter, obviously intrigued by the purpose of their mission. After all, how many times a day do you get to rescue a fat girl who can't climb back on the boat? A holiday atmosphere is how I'd describe it.

Then they saw Jonica.

She was treading water at the stern of the *Columbine*, clutching on to one of the chrome exhaust pipes. All her pride had long since left her and she was in fear of her life. As Chazal once said, "Extreme terror gives us back the gestures of our childhood," and indeed, she did remind me of nothing so much as a giant, rotund infant, her mouth twisted out of shape by her sobbing and her brow knit in a permanent expression of hysteria. I could hardly bear to look at her.

The cutter glided to an expert stop thirty or so feet away from us and the sailors sprang into action, lowering a length of rope webbing into the water. The officer in charge, a kindly-looking soul with an accent frighteningly like Claude Kentner's, stood by the railing with a battery-powered megaphone. We watched him fiddle with the switch. Suddenly, his voice came bellowing out of the water, asking Jonica if she knew how to swim. She managed a nod.

"Just you paddle over here, little lady," he said, without any trace of irony. "We just put on some coffee brewing and we got a mug with your name on it."

Alice Amber clutched my arm. "God, he's great. Isn't he great?"

A giddy feeling of relief spread over the *Columbine*, that wonderful sensation that comes when you are no longer in charge. God, how resilient we all were. "How are they going to get her back here?" Barrie wanted to know, and she mourned the loss of Jonica's pants and pullover as the biggest tragedy of the afternoon. Alice Amber felt we should get the Coast Guard a gift; she asked for suggestions. "Gift!" pooh-poohed Claude Kentner. "I'm going to give every mother's son of 'em ten bucks!" He had the air of a man whose death sentence had just been overturned by the Supreme Court. I alone, it seems (in my role as Sensitive Intellectual), pondered the bigger issues: What would *this* humiliation do to Jonica's psyche? Would this be the moment of truth that would finally cause her to go down to Pickwick's for a copy of the Scarsdale Diet, or get on the phone to Dr. Echeverria down in Tijuana and make an appointment for a gastric bypass?

Even when it appeared that Jonica was too exhausted, too spent from flailing around in the water, to get herself up the rope ladder we weren't too worried. After all, this was the US Coast Guard we were dealing with. Surely they had all sorts of ways of getting people out of the water.

"No problem," the officer called out. "We'll bring you up in style."

"Style" meant that they rotated out a winch with a canvas seat attached. This was the same type of winch they used to load bananas in Honduras. The seat was lowered till it hit the waterline, then given a little more slack. Jonica, following the officer's instructions, maneuvered herself into it.

"All set?"

She nodded.

"Let's do it!"

She rose slowly out of the water, twirling around in a random circle. Her hands clenched the ropes, and the seawater dripped from her big, glistening body. The sailors stared, spellbound. The tan on her arms and legs had faded to a pasty, yellowish color, but her midriff, between her panties and her big pink bra, was milky white. The fat hung over in folds.

With infinite care, they hoisted her over the railing of the cutter, and she poised there for a moment like a circus performer. The winch continued to swing around until she was safely over the deck. The sailors burst into a cheer; they slapped each other's hands and pumped clenched fists into the air.

On the *Columbine*, we clung to each other, delirious with relief. So delirious, in fact, that we didn't even hear the rip. Or see her fall. I was hugging Alice Amber (and thinking, holy moly, I'm hugging Alice Amber. Wait till the Morris dancers hear about this!) when it happened, when the canvas seat split and dropped her to the deck of the cutter. It wasn't a long distance—eight or ten feet at the most. She had time for only the shortest scream.

We looked over at the cutter—it seemed close enough to touch—and I closed my eyes when I saw her, for her legs were bent back underneath her in the most unnatural way. When I opened them again, I only had time for a quick glimpse of her face before the sailors closed in and surrounded her. She looked puzzled.

"Did they try and move her?" Pam asks, as if first-aid techniques were the point of the story.

I tell her I can't remember. In fact, I can hardly remember anything about the trip back. I do remember that we were all calm and dry-eyed and composed—in other words, truly terrified this time. No one said an unnecessary word. We just followed the cutter as fast as we could, but it was always so far ahead, ready to disappear, almost. They wouldn't tell us anything over the radio. Claude Kentner huddled over it, pleading with them. "Keep this channel open," they kept saying.

Poor Jonica was being transferred to an ambulance when we pulled up to the Coast Guard pier. The sight of those flashing lights goosed us back into action; we leapt off the boat—such daredevils—before it was even tied up. "Take care of the poodles," Claude Kentner called back to Dennis over his shoulder—he didn't want the blood of dead or missing poodles on his hands too—and we ran, tripped, and staggered (for we still had our "sea legs") toward the ambulance. It pulled away just as we got within hailing distance, like a Third Avenue bus, giving Barrie and her mother an opportunity to do their banshee imitations.

At the hospital they told us to go to, everything was in chaos. We ran in like a team of comic bank robbers, colliding with each other and all talking at once. People stopped in their tracks to stare at us. They seemed particularly taken with Barrie's outfit. She had changed from her wet clothes to some things of Claude Kentner's that just happened to be on the yacht: a pair of baggy Bermudas and a V-neck undershirt. For some reason, she was still clutching the blanket the Chivas Regal had been wrapped in.

A woman with glasses cornered Alice Amber. "Are you really Alice Amber?" she asked, wild with anticipation.

"Yes," barked Alice Amber, grabbing her sleeve. "Do you work here?"

"No," said the woman, "I work at LTV and I want your autograph."

"Turn blue!" said Alice Amber.

"Alice!" said Claude Kentner.

"And you shut up!"

A nurse came out of the emergency room and Alice Amber placed herself directly in her path.

"I'm Alice Amber," she said, "And I need your help."

"Alice who?"

"Alice Amber!" she screamed.

"I don't care who you are," the nurse said. "Kindly get out of my way." She walked majestically on.

"Good for you!" the rebuffed autograph-seeker called out.

Thoroughly defeated, we retreated to a Naugahyde couch to regroup. "This is ridiculous," Alice Amber said, gritting her teeth. "I'm going to go pull some strings." And with that, she got up and barged through the swinging doors. I fully expected to see her tossed back out, like in a western, and I think everyone else did too; they all kept staring at the doors until they gradually stopped swinging.

"I guess she made it," Claude Kentner said in a tone of awe.

We were still staring at the swinging doors five minutes later when Alice Amber returned, deep in conversation with a white-coated doctor. She—rather ostentatiously, I felt—made him continue their conference smack in the middle of the waiting room, where everybody, particularly the autograph hound (there with her accident-prone elderly mother), could see them and be impressed. Phrases like "Do you have your own orthopedist?" "*Naturally* a private room!" drifted our way, but we were much too intimidated to break in on this little scene. When they finally parted (indeed, when it seemed she would have to hold on to him to keep him there any longer), she gravely shook his hand—twice.

"She's in X-ray" was the total sum of information she had gleaned. "He says we just have to sit and wait."

So sit and wait we did, staring at the clock and sipping the coffee Alice Amber made Claude Kentner go and fetch. Five minutes passed. Then another five minutes. The supporting cast changed, then changed again. A child was brought in with a bloody towel wrapped around his head. Announcements and chimes flowed over the loudspeaker. An old man was rushed in on a stretcher. A pair of candy stripers came in for a cigarette break and made eyes at me. Before we knew it, an hour was gone. I looked at the clock again: four forty-five.

I became vaguely aware of something important I hadn't done. Then I remembered: Pam. Oh, well, I thought. I can't leave now. She'll figure it out. She can take a cab.

"But you're here," Pam says. "What happened?"

"Wait," I say.

Just when we thought we could take it no longer, when we *had* to get some news, no matter how bad it was, just when Alice Amber was going to go and pull some more strings, who should amble into the waiting room with the casual air of a trucker killing time at an all-night road stop but—

Vernon!

Barrie shrieked when she saw him. "What are *you* doing here?" she demanded.

He stared her down coolly. To say I sensed a long and uneasy history between the two of them would be putting it mildly.

"How's Jonica?"

"*What are you doing here?*" Barrie repeated. Once again the entire waiting room was riveted to the saga of the people on the couch.

"The Coast Guard called me," he said, pulling out a pack of Marlboros. His glance traveled down the couch, giving us each the once-over and then dismissing us. "How's Jonica?" he asked again.

Alice Amber squirmed in her seat. "We don't know," she said. "They won't tell us anything."

"Who's he?" Claude Kentner whispered.

So, I thought. I finally get to meet the famous Mr. Fetchko. It was the last thing on earth I ever planned or expected, and quite frankly, my first reaction was one of terror. What did he know about me? Was I going to be gunned down at the beginning of a promising career by a hillbilly avenging his honor? He was an NRA member if I ever saw one.

"I know why you're here," Barrie said, her voice rising. "You smell the insurance money!"

A nurse came out and politely told us to shut up, we were disturbing the other visitors. "Not until you stop giving us the runaround," Alice Amber replied; but she seemed suddenly drained of her combative spirit. Vernon's arrival had clearly unsettled her. In a moment, another nurse came out; she shot furtive glances at the other people in the room and then whispered to us that it had been "arranged" that we could wait in a private office.

We looked around hesitantly, not at all sure this was a wise idea; we had seen enough pain and mutilation for one day, but Alice Amber took the initiative and got up. We followed the nurse past the cashier, out into the lobby, and down a fiercely illuminated hallway to a windowless eight-by-ten cubicle furnished in cast-off metal office furniture that was clearly not what was conjured up in any of our minds by the grandiose phrase "private office." There followed a game of musical chairs, everybody waiting to see where everybody else would sit before they would commit themselves.

Once we became settled, a silence, infinitely more nerve-racking than the din we had been causing in the waiting room, descended over the group. The cumulative effect of the day's misfortunes was beginning to take its toll. Alice Amber rested her face in her hands, occasionally rubbing her eyes and sighing deeply. Claude Kentner stared at the floor, his elbows on his knees like he was sitting on the john. Barrie, who ended up in the chair behind the desk, toyed with a Rolodex.

As for me, I had but one thought: to get out of there. I tried to gauge how long I could last before I bolted and ran screaming down the corridor. Another five minutes? I doubted it very much.

Vernon was looking at me. Holy Christ! I looked the other way and swallowed hard. Those eyes—he may have been twenty years old (a fact I just couldn't seem to get over), but he had a look of deadly experience. What on earth had he and Jonica been like together? I tried to imagine them in bed together (though very gingerly, afraid I might be struck down by lightning, so intense were the vibes), but drew a complete blank. One thing was sure—I bet she didn't draw any butterflies on her stomach for *him*.

Barrie discovered a phone on the desk, and after some experimenting, she found she could get an outside line by dialing "9." She began calling "our friends" and informing them of the accident. It's too bad a talent scout wasn't there. The calls were of such dramatic intensity that any of them could have got her a five-year contract with Universal. By the third call, she was reporting that Jonica was "paralyzed, probably."

The doctor in the white coat walked in. Barrie dropped the phone like she'd been caught stealing cookies.

He scratched his forehead and then put his hands in his pockets, rocking back and forth slightly in his sturdy cordovan oxfords.

"She has a spinal injury," he announced solemnly.

I already knew *that,* so I was rather relieved. At least she was still alive. But Barrie and Alice Amber took the news like Greek peasant women. Custodial personnel peeked in to see who was wailing so loud.

Claude Kentner asked the inevitable "How bad is it, Doc?"

"It's possibly severe," he said, whatever that meant. "I have to get her medical history. Who's next of kin?"

Everyone looked blank. "Vernon, I guess," Alice Amber said.

"Vernon?" the doctor said, looking at me.

I pointed toward the corner where Vernon sat, as far away from the rest of us as he could get. He had his chair tilted against the wall; slowly, the personification of boredom and indifference, he leaned forward till all four legs rested on the ground.

The doctor rattled off a list of unlikely diseases. Had Jonica ever had any of them? Vernon shrugged.

"Hmmmmm," the doctor said, and he decided to try another approach.

"Does she smoke?"

This was too much for Barrie. She flung up her hands. "Jonica has a broken back and you want to know if she smokes? I don't believe this."

"Barrie—" her mother said in a tone of warning.

"No, she doesn't smoke," Barrie said sulkily. "Except grass."

Claude Kentner looked stricken.

"Does she use birth control pills?" the doctor asked.

Everyone looked at me for an instant, then their eyes shot up to the ceiling to examine the acoustical tiles.

"Er ... yes," I said.

"No," called out Barrie at exactly the same time.

The doctor turned to Vernon. "Mr. Fetchko?"

"I dunno."

By the time the doctor left, mopping his brow and none the wiser, Jonica's reputation was in shreds and I was plotting my retreat. I saw my chance when Barrie and her mother started to pin the blame.

The way they figured it, it was everybody's fault but theirs. Claude Kentner, of course, was the chief culprit. He was the one who forced her overboard. He was the one who was sailing around the Pacific Ocean without a ladder. He was the one who had the party. He was the one who bought the boat. And as for Dennis ...

"Dennis never should have let us do anything like that," Barrie said, shaking her head. "After all, he's the big sailor."

Her mother couldn't agree more. "I saw him sitting up on that bridge all afternoon just getting completely—" She stopped suddenly.

"Getting completely what?" Claude Kentner inquired.

She saw the difficulties her observation might cause.

"Just getting completely crazy," she said at last.

"*Dennis?*" said Claude Kentner.

"Forget it."

There was a strange silence. Alice Amber shifted her weight and lit a cigarette.

"Let's face it," she said. "I hate to say it, but it's Jonica's own fault. When you let yourself get that fat ..."

Her analysis proved very popular. Barrie and Claude Kentner nodded sagely, and Barrie was able to carry it one step further. She turned to me. "You know, if you hadn't yelled at her about how fat she was the other night, this never would have happened."

"Huh?" I said, even though I knew exactly what she meant. A light went on in my brain. I adopted the hurt, yet somewhat noble, expression of the unjustly accused.

Alice Amber, I saw at once, was taken in. "Oh, come on, dear," she said to her daughter.

"It's true!" Barrie insisted, her evil little eyes flashing. "He humiliated her so much she hasn't had a bite to eat since then. Not a bite! I swear to God."

She sensed we weren't making the connection.

"That's why she couldn't pull herself back up. *She was too weak!*"

I made a point of getting slowly to my feet. "Barrie," I began, in what I hope was an infuriatingly calm and reasoned tone, "if you're

187

looking for someone to blame perhaps you should think about your own relationship with Jonica."

Sure enough, she began screaming, hurling invective at me, giving me the perfect excuse to walk to the door. "Don't you dare leave!" she shrieked when she realized my plan. "Not after what you did!"

I paused in the doorway, unable to resist the perfect setup for my exit line. "No, Barrie," I said, sadly. "After what *you* did."

I could hear the screams follow me down the corridor, but as many times happens in such cases, my mind was focused on the most trivial thing: the tattoo on Vernon's forearm which I had been staring at out of the corner of my eye. A comical little devil holding a spear, with the legend "Born to Lose." I'd heard about those tattoos. Not too many Morris dancers seemed to have them, though.

I've finally met somebody who does.

I find myself in a nightmarish situation, so nightmarish, in fact, that I realize it is exactly that—a nightmare. Not just any old nightmare, you understand, but a particularly vivid and detailed one, beautifully plotted, the kind you can get only with too much Valium and too much booze.

Claude Kentner and I, hoping to do a good deed, have put the two poodles into a dryer over at Barrie's house. At the end of the cycle, we discover, much to our horror, that one has disappeared completely and the other has lost the use of his hind legs, forcing him to go around on little wheels. The worst part is that Alice Amber is coming over at any minute, and she will kill us when she finds out what we have done. We hide in the kitchen, peering out the window for her car. Vernon drops by and sells us, for $10,000 apiece, some wigs he found in the box. She'll never recognize you in these, he tells us, but I have my doubts. We hear a noise and see her pull up in a large boat. She starts up the little brick path to the front door, dressed in a fitted grey suit, white gloves, and a hat—everything in shades of black and white. Claude Kentner and I clutch each other in terror. Just when I think I can stand it no longer, just when she gets to the front porch and rings the doorbell—I wake up.

Or at least I think I wake up. Then I'm not so sure. I am lying in a strange bed, in a strange room, staring at a strange pillow in a beige pillow case, not at all like the checked Bill Blass ones I got at the May Co.; off in the distance, I distinctly hear the unmistakable voice of Angie Dickinson. I strain to hear. She seems to be discussing cocaine traffic with some Negroes.

Hmmmmm, I think. Another dream. Get with it, Elliot. I close my eyes.

But something is wrong. Angie Dickinson stops talking and a man comes on. "Has this ever happened to you?" he asks and then some woman finds spots on her glasses before a big party. I open my eyes and turn over.

Of course! I'm in Pam's room at the Century Plaza. It all comes back to me: the drive from the airport with Pam at the wheel ("Gee, would you believe I haven't driven a car in four years?"), cheating death each time we switch lanes, with me clawing in her purse for another Valium; the long, long walk down the carpeted hall, following Mario the bellhop, a cheerful near-midget who tries to talk us into a studio tour, and finally, the glorious sight of a bed, on which I thought "I might lie down for a minute . . ."

I squint—where are my glasses?—and make out Pam perched on a chair and glued to the TV. She is eating a chicken salad sandwich with both hands. I glance at the window. Night seems to have fallen.

Boy, Pam sure has changed in the past two months. Something about her hair—it's not that it's so dirty (nor, on the other hand, is it so clean); it's just that it's so . . . grey. So much greyer than I remember its being. She now has what you would officially call "grey hair."

Holy Christ! I'm going out with a grey-haired woman.

Lately, I've started to get these flashes that last a second or so, when I realize that I am no longer young. "No longer young"—what am I talking about—according to certain statistical ways of looking at it, I am middle-aged! Sometimes, with increasing frequency, I can't even remember how old I really am; the years are turning into one big blur. Back when I was twelve, it seemed like it was five years between birthdays. Now, it's down to two or three weeks. And the worst part is, what do I have to show for it? *Harvard Magazine* sends shivers up and down my spine. It used to be that I'd turn to the very last page to catch up on my classmates; now I turn to the middle. And it seems that everybody who isn't president of a bank has just won the Pulitzer Prize or sold that health food business they started in Vermont during their hippie period for $3 million to some conglomerate. Well, at least I no longer have to face the humiliation of reading, as I once did with bone-chilling horror: "Steve Roth reports that while squiring lovely daughters Tracy, 5, and Melissa, 3, through the monkey house at the Zoo, who should he bump into but Elliot Weiner, who works there." *Who works there!* At least they could say I was Director of Development. They make it sound like I'm some janitor sweeping up orangutan droppings. I was suicidal for weeks. And this was in *Harvard Magazine!*

Anyway, back to Pam's hair. Looking at it, I get another one of these flashes. One of the worst yet.

Not saying anything, I watch her eat her sandwich. I realize when people are alone, they tend to throw their table manners to the winds. Far be it from me to cast the first stone: I drink milk right out of the carton. But Pam ... there was something in the way she was attacking that sandwich that reminded me of Jonica. Particularly the way she licked the mayonnaise off the edge: she held it up over her head and lowered it down to her mouth, like she was eating a bunch of grapes at a Roman orgy.

For as long as I've known Pam (seven years), I've never quite been able to figure her out. She's brilliant at her job. I've seen her in action, joking with the secretaries, calling the boss by his first name. But to hear her talk about it, you'd think it was some stop-gap measure, like waitressing. She's always getting offers from other not-for-profit organizations (women get all the good job offers these days, you might have noticed), but she never takes them. She hems and haws, gives away about $5,000 worth of free management advice during follow-up interviews (a fact that infuriates me), discusses the situation with Dr. Munsterberger and her best friend, Helene, and then always says no. For the simple fact that her one ambition in life is not a job, not a career: what she really wants to do is push her own three-year-old around the block in a stroller.

For somebody—a woman!—pulling down $35,000 a year, she is miserable. She has a dark, depressing apartment in a blah non-neighborhood in the East Twenties. It faces the back of a Merit Farms and always smells like fried chicken: "I know I should move, but it's so *expensive*." She's had the same $4,000 in the bank for ten years and professes to have no idea where her income goes. If she kept better records, she might realize she almost single-handedly paid for Dr. Munsterberger's new beach house in East Hampton.

Pam has a lot of friends, but they are all in the business end of the "arts" or in one of the "helping professions" i.e., social work—and to be brutally honest, they are a pretty dreary bunch of people. Overeducated, bitter about their take-home pay, trapped in Manhattan without cars, deprived of the profit motive in their dull but harried jobs, too timid to take charge of their lives but too intelligent to be satisfied with the little they have—I should know, I was one of them, until I decided it was now or never and went back to school. I didn't want to wake up one morning, forty-five years old and still be working for a zoo, for Christ's sake. My idea of a good time was no longer a wine and cheese party on 110th Street.

I knew it was going to be tough and it was. My father was no help. He's a lawyer for Gulf Oil, famous around Pittsburgh for his "slick" handling of labor negotiations, but when it came to a request for a loan, he suddenly claimed poverty on account of the stock market. This meant I had to sign my life away to something called Student Life Funding, a Shylock-type operation out of Boulder, Colorado, which sends me, like clockwork, a letter that starts out "Dear Young Professional" every time my check is a day late.

Columbia seemed glad to get me—almost *too* glad—and after I got there, I figured out why: what a bunch of scholastic turkeys were my fifty or so fellow graduate students in History. Only one of them appeared to be any kind of threat, a sickly Jew from Chicago known as the Nose, who had won a famous scholarship for developing computer models to predict the future course of historical events. His theory was that all you had to do was identify all the variables: economic, political, religious, all the way down to changes in the weather and the availability of contraceptives, and presto! you could tell what was going to happen whenever a foreign crisis reared its head. The simplest model, proven to have an astonishing eighty-seven percent rate of accuracy, has over five thousand variables. This system is called Proto-History and it's extremely controversial. Fortunately for me, this poor visionary was nearly always in the infirmary.

Twenty-five or so of the other students combined a childlike enthusiasm with an untiring industry. They worked to the point of exhaustion without learning very much. Two or three of them were probably quite intelligent. But they had been so poorly educated at the undergraduate level that they were unable to think for themselves.

The rest were just plain stupid.

And not just stupid. The men all seemed to favor drip-dry shirts covered with dandruff; they had long, stringy hair and wispy beards and wire-rim glasses. The women tended to be chunky little creatures with prominent teeth. The main concern of these future female historians seemed to be that the older male faculty members didn't make any sexist remarks. Holy moly, I thought—what have I got myself into? Pam's friends looked like rock stars compared to this School for Dorks.

But I turned it to my advantage. I was, for the first time in my life, the Big Man on Campus. Word soon got out how I had single-handedly turned the zoo's fundraising picture around, about how I had made decisions involving millions of dollars, about how I had "hired and fired" (a phrase that thrilled these soon to be chronically unemployed job-seekers), *and then* thrown away all this glory to return to the groves of academe. All they had ever done was graduate from Podunk U with some senior thesis about the Massacre of Glencoe, and they were pathetically easy to impress. Pam and I had them over around Christmastime; we served French champagne and made Pam's brother show up later in the evening with his old girlfriend, who had once checked coats at Studio 54. They all thought it was the most sophisticated evening they had ever spent, and from then on, I could do no wrong.

It was Pam, now that I recall it, who first got me interested in Warren Harding. She was browsing through an antique store in Newfane, Vermont, looking for Depression glass, which her sister collects, when she came across a copy of *The Price of Love*. Since it was only a quarter and since she needed something to read on the bus ride back home, she bought it. She read it straight through and then rushed over to my house. "There's something here," she said. "I don't know what it is, but there's something here."

I could immediately see her point. The problem was, what? The next day, I dropped by Low Library to see what else I could find out about our twenty-ninth president. The literature in the card catalog was indeed curious. The titles said it all: *Ohio Romeo* by Ellis Mc-Cawber, *The President's Mistress* by Angela Mae Watkins, *The Strange Death of President Harding* by Gaston B. Means, *The Truth about Teapot Dome* by Alfred Voles, *Behind the Harding Tragedy* by E. J. Ingalls, and so on and so on. Virtually everything written about the poor guy was scandal and gossip of the most malicious sort, radically different from the dull, reverential tones that most Presidents inspire.

Since I had a big paper due at the end of the week that I hadn't even started, I collected all these tales, these memoirs of ex-mistresses, these muckraking exposes, these prison-penned confessions of ex-cabinet members, these fabrications of literary con artists, and put them together under the title: "Anything for a Buck: Warren Harding and the Beginning of Modern Political Gossip." The paper created a small sensation around the History Department. It was passed from professor to professor, all of them starved for a good chuckle, till I had to make another copy, it was so smudged with countless thumb-prints. Then one of them, the student favorite (thought to be hip because he wore bell-bottom jeans to class), suggested I try and get it published. Why not? I thought.

It came out in the *North American Historical Review*, Spring 1977, and was a tremendous success. My thesis was that Warren Harding was inadvertently responsible for a whole genre of American literature that continues today unabated. Just look at *My Story* by Judith Campbell Exner, or *Past Forgetting* by Kay Summersby Morgan, or *The Last Kennedy* by Edward Chappell. I even got on a talk show. Granted, it was in Camden, New Jersey, and it was on a Sunday morning, but it was a talk show.

Predictably, Paterson Decker had a fit. "Of interest only to serious collectors of trivia," he called it, in print. But what did I care? I was thrilled. Here I throw together this paper at the last minute to beat a deadline, and all of a sudden I'm a minor—very minor—celebrity in the world of academic history. Better yet, I'm an antiestablishment maverick, the spokesman (if not the creator) of the brand-new "History as gossip" school of thought. I made it a point never to take any of this too seriously, though. After all, when all is said and done, two thousand years from now, the history of the US presidency is not going to be told through wives and mistresses.

But (and it is an important "but"): there is one exception to this rule and that is Warren Harding. His wife and his mistress *were* his presidency. They created it, they shaped it, they gave it its texture and its importance. And they ended it.

To be more specific:

In a later article (*North American Historical Review*, Winter 1978), entitled "The Power Behind the Throne" (adapted from my doctoral thesis), I attempt, and I believe succeed in that attempt, to prove an important point: the presidency of Warren Harding was the deliberate and brilliant accomplishment of his wife, Florence. A scheming, ambitious woman with no outlet in the Ohio of the early twentieth century for her incredible drive, she realized her only chance for real power and glory lay in her husband. Granted, he was only a small-town politician of limited intelligence, but he gave wonderful speeches, was well liked by all, and better yet, he "looked like a President."

It was "the Duchess" who guided Harding to the US Senate. Membership in "the most exclusive club in the world" dazzled Harding. He was certain he had reached the pinnacle of his career; even the Duchess was astonished they had got this far. The social life in Washington, her friendship with Evalyn Walsh McLean—it seemed like a dream come true.

Harding's name was being bandied about for the Republican presidential nomination in 1919, but even Florence knew it was a shot in the dark. There were half a dozen contenders ahead of him—men of real experience and political savvy, like General Leonard Wood, Teddy Roosevelt's protégé, or Frank Lowden, the brilliant reform governor of Illinois, or arch-conservative Hiram Johnson, the Ronald Reagan of his day, or the enormously popular Herbert Hoover. Even to see his name on such a list was enough of a thrill; she made scrapbook after scrapbook.

Then, one day when Evalyn canceled out on a shopping expedition, Florence accepted a last-minute invitation from some other Senate wives to go and visit the famous Madame Marcia. A Brooklyn-born ex-chorus girl, Madame Marcia was a Washington institution—the town's leading clairvoyant and a figure of considerable power. "President-Maker and President-Ruler," she billed herself. Her predictions, helped out by an insider's knowledge of Washington gossip, turned out to be uncannily accurate.

That rainy February afternoon proved to be a fateful one in US history. Florence Harding listened raptly as Madame Marcia pronounced her horoscope for someone born 2 November 1865, at 2 p.m.—Warren's birthday: "If he runs for President, there is no one alive who can stop his nomination and election."

The prediction turned Florence's life around. The obsession grew: if "Wurr'n" sought the nomination, he would become president. It was that simple. It was written in the stars. There was no doubt in her mind.

Only in May, at another session (they were weekly occurrences by now), did she hear the rest of Madame Marcia's prediction: "But he will not live through his term ... Following the splendid climax in the House of Preferment, I see the Sun and the Moon in conjunction in the eighth house of the zodiac. And this is the House of Death—sudden, violent, or peculiar death."

Heavy stuff. But if the Duchess had second thoughts, it was too late now. She had set a series of wheels in motion that would culminate in the nomination next month, in a "smoke-filled room," of the classic dark horse, Warren Harding. It was a coup, part luck, part genius, part circumstance, that remains unparalleled in American politics. If she had faltered at any step of the way, if she had shown the slightest doubt, the candidacy would have collapsed like a house of cards. But she didn't. For as Madame Marcia kept telling her, she had her own drama to live out now. She had a star on her forehead. She was Destiny's Child.

"Look at this!" Pam exclaims when she realizes I am awake. "They have *Policewoman* on Channel Thirteen here."

"What time is it?"

"Around nine. How do you feel?"

I think about it for a moment, searching for signs of a headache or extreme muscular fatigue, but strangely enough, I feel fine. I don't tell Pam this, though; heaven knows what demands, sight-seeing or other, she'll make. "About the same," I murmur, settling back on the pillow.

Assured there is nothing she can do to make me more comfortable, she returns, fascinated, to the television. She is one of those people who insist they never watch TV, except for election returns, the Oscars, and Miss America. She doesn't even own a set, she tells people proudly. But put her in a hotel room or a Holiday Inn and she plunks herself down on the edge of the bed and stays hunched over the thing for hours on end, devouring every show and saying things like "Gee, *The Price Is Right*! Is *that* still on?"

"So where do they have all the stuff they usually have on Channel Thirteen?" she asks.

I've never been able to figure that one out myself, but suddenly I have more important things on my mind. Feeling very guilty and knowing I'll never get back to sleep until I know what's going on, I call the hospital. After much switching around of extensions, I finally get through to Alice Amber.

She sounds exhausted. "We're all going home to collapse." No mention of my dramatic exit.

Yes, there has been a diagnosis. One, possibly two, herniated discs.

"What on earth is a herniated disc?" I ask.

"It's when the vertebrae have little hernias, from the impact. Spinal fluid or something."

"Is it serious?"

"*Very* serious. She could be flat on her back till Christmas."

I find myself strangely elated by the news.

"But she'll be okay?" I ask, poker-faced. "She'll walk again?"

Alice Amber sighs. "That's what they say."

There is no point in returning to the hospital, she tells me (even though suddenly no sacrifice is too great to make). Jonica is full of Demerol and out like a light. They just went in to take a peek at her.

"How did she look?" I ask, full of concern.

Alice Amber searches for the right words. "Sweaty. They have a tube up her nose." Vernon is staying in case something should happen. "He's turning out to be a piece of the rock."

"Has anyone told the old lady?"

"No ... Do you want to?"

The one sacrifice too great to make. "Gee, I'm not home now ..."

I hear a muffled conference. Alice Amber comes back on. "Barrie says she'll do it. She's going over there right now."

I tried to think of other loose ends.

"How is Claude?"

A very pregnant pause. Then: "He's in big trouble."

I promise I'll be at the hospital in the morning.

"Was that really Alice Amber?" Pam asks after I hang up.

"Yes, that was really Alice Amber," I say, lying back on the bed and staring at the ceiling.

Pam watches me for a long time. "Can I make a suggestion?"

"What?"

"Come back to New York with me and forget about all this nonsense."

I look at her sadly. "Pam, I might have to do just that," I say with the grave and sorrowful air that is so becoming to people when an unexpected stroke of luck extricates them from a living hell.

16

Early the next morning, we meet as planned in the hospital coffee shop, and over a breakfast of tepid scrambled eggs and what purport to be "golden hash browns," we discuss what Alice Amber has begun to refer to, not without a certain smug satisfaction, as "this Disaster with a capital D." Barrie is there, of course, but otherwise our group is considerably diminished. Claude Kentner, they report, remains under self-imposed arrest at his condominium back at the Marina, where he is "packing and praying." And as for Vernon, "He might show up any minute, so let's hurry."

News of Alice Amber's tantrum yesterday has spread through the hospital like a plague virus; a constant stream of faces, a veritable UN of Third World types, comes to peer at us through the kitchen doors. But none of these curiosity seekers dares ask for an autograph today. No sir, we are given a wide berth, which is fine with us, since, if truth be told, we are not looking our best. Alice Amber, one of those women who must "put on her face" each morning, has been negligent about this chore today; she got as far as her eyes and then abandoned the task altogether, hoping, no doubt, that no one would notice. But notice they do; how could it be otherwise when, at twenty paces, she resembles nothing so much as a wizened racoon. As for myself, well, I have come directly from the Century Plaza and am still wearing the same outfit I had on yesterday, a point that is certainly noticed, but not remarked upon, by the two women.

"Jesus," says Alice Amber, pouring herself a third cup of coffee from a carafe commandeered from a frightened Filipino. "I haven't been up this early in a long time."

Barrie seems subdued. Officially she attributes this to shock, but I suspect it is really the prospect of endless months of hospital visits that has her down in the dumps. The fun part is over. She sits there making spitballs out of a paper napkin. "You know how much parking costs in this place? One dollar!"

I seem to be the only one in a good mood. There are problems, of course; Jonica has my address in New York (a foolish oversight on my part; she was updating one of her numerous address books and sentimentally wanted me in it). But who knows what shape she'll be in when she comes to? Personally, I am praying for brain damage.

Only now, in this vinyl and Formica booth in Santa Monica, in what passes for the coldest and clearest light California has to offer, do I realize I have been playing a fool's game. Only now do I realize that I am in the middle of a story that has no happy ending. And only now do I realize that I have mercifully been given a way out. It is enough, I decide, to make you believe in God.

I am about to excuse myself, ostensibly to visit the men's room, but in reality to drop into one of those pay phones I noticed out in the lobby and call TWA, when who should show up but an unexpected (for me, anyway) guest: a well-groomed young man named Bruce Pinsky, whom Alice Amber introduces as "my lawyer *and* a hell of a nice guy," as if the two categories were mutually exclusive. Mr. Pinsky is all dolled up in a severely cut Cardin suit and Gucci shoes—"Jewish clothes," my mother calls them—and he cleans off the seat with a napkin before sitting down. I figure I can wait another five minutes.

Mr. Pinsky does not seem particularly happy to be joining us.

"For Christ's sake, Alice, I'm an entertainment lawyer, not an ambulance chaser."

She fixes her beady eyes on him. "Do you want me to help you get into production or not?"

"Oh, ho, ho," he sneers. "The star turns mean."

"Bruce," she cries. "*Help us.* Just tell us what to do."

For it seems that she and Barrie have not been sitting idly by, worrying about Jonica. Oh, no. They have been developing a plan. It is simplicity itself. What they are going to do is file lawsuits against Claude Kentner, the US Coast Guard, and everybody else they can think of. For a shaky moment or two, I fear that I also may be on the hit list, but it seems they need a sympathetic witness more than another settlement.

Of course Jonica is to be beneficiary of all this largesse. They're just getting the ball rolling for *her* sake. But, just out of curiosity and to get out of the way right now, they want a complete legal definition of "mental anguish" to see if what they went through just might qualify. Bruce Pinsky doesn't seem to think it would ("Are you out of your minds?") and the Famous Rubber Face, and Rubber Face, Junior, make some very put-out expressions.

"Be that as it may," says Barrie, moving on to the next point, "the most important thing is that Vernon can't get his hands on a penny."

"Who's this Vernon?" Bruce Pinsky asks.

"Her husband," we all chime in.

He whistles. "That's going to be tough."

Alice Amber stares moodily across the room, dividing up the millions in her head. "The grandmother will have to get some, I imagine. And let's see. Some for little what's-his-name."

Little what's-his-name! We all come to attention in a rattle of coffee cups. *Who's taking care of the baby?* Have arrangements been made? If so, what arrangements? Has he been fed? Has he been changed?

"Guadalupe's there," Barrie says, a little lamely.

"Guadalupe!" snorts Alice Amber. "We must get this settled at once."

For some reason, she decides that the first step toward settling it is to go up and look at Jonica. I have been dreading this inevitability all morning; indeed, my latest fantasy is to slip out of town without ever seeing her again. We stride purposefully down the corridor toward Intensive Care. My pulse rate increases and my palms become damp. Will I feel guilty? Will the sight of her suffering overcome me and force me to stay? Will she suddenly come out of her coma and grab my wrist, like that scene in *Scream of the Mutilated* that so terrified me back in fifth grade?

We enter her cubicle noiselessly, almost reverently. They have her strapped to a board, surrounded by monitoring devices on which, I note, there is very little activity. A nurse explains things, rather like a museum guide. The board is standard operating procedure in certain back-injury cases. This way the angle of the body can be changed to reduce pressure, etc., and so on.

"How interesting," I mumble. Any interest I have in the medical intricacies of the case is vastly overwhelmed by my relief, however. For I feel absolutely no remorse whatsoever. Not one pang. In fact, an inward giddiness overtakes me. "So long, fatso," I chant to myself.

So compelling are these sacrilegious impulses that I force myself to stare mournfully at Jonica to try to get into the spirit of things. She certainly looks awful enough. Her face is a pale grey, her hair a tangled rat's nest, her lips puffy and cracked. Even her *eyebrows* look like they've been through hell. As we watch, the nurse jabs a needle-tipped tube of glucose into the back of her wrist. Her eyes remain closed and unflinching, although Bruce Pinsky gags slightly and jumps to the side as some blood spurts out and lands on the hospital-blue sheets.

I have visions of him rolling her into a courtroom like this, still co-matose, for the trials which will undoubtedly occupy the remainder of the twentieth century. Exhibit A, Your Honor. A horrible thought crosses my mind: Can they make me come back to testify? I will have to check on this point with Pam's uncle, a *real* ambulance chaser.

A squeal from Barrie breaks into these and the other solemn thoughts that all of us, gathered around Jonica's board, seem to be thinking. Vernon is standing in the doorway. He is carrying a black guitar case. What does he have in mind? I wonder. A serenade?

"Vernon!" Alice Amber exclaims in a tone so cordial he immediately suspects a trap. "We were hoping you'd be here."

"How come?"

She laughs and then becomes very serious, as befits the subject she is about to bring up. "We have to decide what we are going to do about the baby."

Vernon lifts his eyebrows. "'We?'" he says. Touché. From that point on, I am completely on his side.

An awkward silence. Bruce Pinsky examines his immaculately manicured fingernails.

"Excuse *me*, *you* have to decide. Of course." She smiles as graciously as she knows how.

"I've already decided," Vernon says, his eyes fixed on Bruce Pinsky, whose eyes are fixed on the floor. What bad manners these people have, I think. Nobody ever introduces anybody. At least not to Vernon.

"Oh?" Now it's Alice Amber's eyebrows' turn to do their stuff.

"I'll take care of him."

We all think about this. While I have no sentimental attachment to little Warren—they can boil him in oil, as far as I'm concerned—does this seem wise? What if Jonica never comes out of her coma? What if she remains a cripple? Is that any way for a kid to grow up? He'll probably spend his childhood riding shotgun in some truck between here and El Paso.

Alice Amber also senses some flaws in his plan.

"Are you sure you have room?" she asks tactfully.

"I'm gonna stay at Jonica's gramma's for a while," he says. "It'll be less hassle."

"Yes, I suppose so," Alice Amber says. Then: "Have you checked with her?"

The faintest smile crosses his hillbilly lips, and for the first time, I notice one of his front teeth is chipped. For some reason, at that moment, it makes him strangely attractive.

"I went over there this morning," he says. "She don't know if she's coming or going."

Suddenly I realize what it is about Vernon: he is, quite simply, a throwback to the darkest fears of your childhood. He is the sinister Big Kid you're not allowed to play with (not that he'd ever deign to play with *you*) (not that he ever *plays*; he's too busy beating kids up). He's the one your mother calls "that juvenile delinquent." But she doesn't know the half of it: how he hangs out with older kids, Italians, who smoke; how you had to spend all afternoon hiding in the garage because Robby Leach said he was "after you" (not that he has any idea who you are); and finally, how, as scandalized rumor around the swings has it, he took Cathy Condon out in the woods and put sticks up her fanny.

Now that I have a PhD and can afford to be nonjudgmental, I find I rather like him. In fact, I am so engrossed trying to psych him out that five minutes later, riding down in the elevator, it occurs to me that I have forgotten to give Jonica one last look of farewell.

I figure I can live without it.

Bruce Pinsky asks when Barrie and I can come in and talk to him about the accident.

"Gee, I don't know," I say, scratching my head. "I have to go to New York."

All heads turn.

"What?" says Barrie.

"When?" says Alice Amber.

"Tomorrow."

"For how long?" demands Barrie in that strident, Donna-like tone I plan never to hear again.

"Oh, just for a couple of days," I say, jauntily stepping from the elevator into the underground garage. "Then I'll be back. Now, what level are you all on?"

There was so much to do that afternoon. I called the airline and got what they told me was the last seat on Pam's flight; I called the car-leasing place about returning the Mustang; I called the phone company about getting the phone disconnected; I ran down to the library to return some books; then I went to Lido Cleaners and demanded my garments, ready or not, from an easygoing black woman who was so accommodating she threw in a couple of shirts that didn't even belong to me; then I dashed across the street to the Triangle Market and raided the dumpster out in their parking lot for cartons. It was so exhilarating driving around with the radio blaring that I tried to invent more errands, but time was growing short so I went back to the pool house to rejoin Pam, who had already started the packing.

She hadn't made much headway. She spent most of her time staring out the window at the big house, fascinated. "Aren't you even going to say good-bye?" she asked.

Good-bye to who? A religious fanatic who's losing her marbles? A beaner maid who can't parlay voo? Little what's-his-name?

In my mind I was already back at 151 West 80th Street, Apartment 5D. My sublettees, the girls from Texas (spending a "summurh" in New York for obscure reasons involving a "trainin' program fer inshurnz"—not that I believed *that* for a second), wouldn't be out for another three weeks. Three weeks is a long time in Pam's apartment. I stayed there once for three days while my place was being painted, with the result that we canceled our planned vacation to St. Croix, even though it meant forfeiting the deposit. It was the closest we ever came to breaking up.

Pam had been going over to my apartment every Saturday to pick up the mail and she reported that they were keeping it "reasonably clean" (I knew her standards and I suppressed a shudder). She seemed to remember that they had taken my almost priceless Kandinsky lithographs down and replaced them with some personality posters of Robert Redford and a centerfold from *Playgirl* magazine of some construction worker photographed in the unlikely circumstance of operating a lathe in his underwear, but other than that ... "Oh, and guess what?" she adds as afterthought, while tossing my mattress cover onto the Salvation Army pile.

"What?"

"Guess who Joanne is going out with?"

"Which one is Joanne? The redhead with the Farrah Fawcett hairdo?"

"No, that's Shelby. Joanne is the short blonde with the Farrah Fawcett hairdo. Not to be confused with Linda, the tall blonde with the Farrah Fawcett hairdo. Joanne is the one with the cat who looks just like Morris the Cat. And you know what she named him?"

"No, what?"

"Morris the Cat."

"Wait a minute, what cat? They have a cat?"

"Yes, didn't you know?"

Two beers later, after I had calmed down a little, Pam makes me continue the guessing game—Who is Joanne Going Out With? Pam loves these little games: Guess Who I Saw at the Theatre Last Night? Guess Who Helene is Renting a House with This Summer? She has the ability to make them last for hours. I steel myself. This is one side of her I seem to have forgotten, or at least not dwelt upon, during the romantic musings of our separation.

"Is it somebody I know?"

"Not really."

"I take it he's male?"

"Yes."

"Is it somebody famous?"

"Hardly."

"Is it somebody I've seen?"

"Yes."

"Is this person under thirty?"

"I think so."

"Is this person in analysis?"

A sharp laugh tells me the answer is a probable no.

"Have I ever shaken hands with this person?"

"It's highly unlikely."

"Does this person live in the neighborhood?"

"Yes."

"Does this person live on Riverside Drive?"

"No."

"Does this person live on my block?"

"Yes."

"Is this person a medical student?"

"No."

"Is it the French body-builder?"

"No."

"Is it the Cowboy?"

"No."

"Is it the guy who gave Helene gonorrhea?"

"No."

"Is it the ex-priest with the basset hound?"

"No."

I'm stumped, though intrigued. That about covers all the local characters, the ones Pam and I point out to each other and gossip about (the straight men, anyway) ... unless—I get a horrible feeling in the pit of my stomach.

"Pam, does this person live in my building?"

"Yes."

"Does this person live on the third floor and have a Spanish accent?"

"You got it, bub."

Feeling considerably less elated, I clear up the only other loose end I can think of: Eve. By some fortuitous coincidence, Pam and I have been invited over for dinner that very evening. I speculate, in my increasingly fatalistic mood, at the symmetrical way in which my West Coast sojourn is drawing to a close. What does it all mean? What lessons have I learned, if any?

Eve has invited us, of course, to find out firsthand what Pam is like. I, in my naivete, saw no reason they wouldn't get along: both are well-educated name droppers, sentimental to the core, with an infinite tolerance for things not quite going their way. But immediately I sense a certain lack of communication, a failing of nuance if you will, between the two. For example, Pam and I arrive. The two women greet each other with the enthusiasm of beauty pageant finalists. So far so good. Eve ushers us into the living room, fusses over some drinks, brings out the hors d'oeuvres she's spent all afternoon making, puts on a Modern Country record to alert Pam to the fact that she's hip, and then says, with the laid-back irony that only a resident of Beverly Hills can carry off, "So, Pam, how do you like the land of the smog and the freeways?"

Pam can be forgiven if she misreads this statement and detects in it a kindred spirit. For she has already formed strong opinions on the subject which she is anxious to share. "I can't believe it," she begins in a tone that makes me reach for my drink. "My hotel is on a street called—are you ready for this—Avenue of the Stars. Now, at first, I thought they meant regular stars, you know, like Orion and the Crab nebulae. Which is bad enough. *Then* it dawns on me they mean *movie stars*! They have actually named a street after movie stars! I'm staying on *Movie Star Street!*"

Eve looks at her blankly. She reaches for a canape. She takes a bite, chews, and swallows. "So you must be at the Century Plaza," she says, brushing some crumbs from her lap. "I hear it's very nice." She turns to me. "So tell me, how was the big yachting trip?"

Of course, once Eve is brought up to date, any other subject matter pales next to the drama of the past two days. She sits there wide-eyed, taking it all in, and when I jovially get to the bottom line ("So. I'm leaving. Tomorrow"), she is near tears and I am rather touched.

"But you can't leave!" she wails.

"Try and stop me."

"But what about all your research? What about Warren Harding?"

"Warren who?"

Once she realizes I really mean it, nostalgia overtakes the poor woman. Pete's wine cellar is raided for a bottle of Piper-Heidsieck, and the evening degenerates into an evening of reminiscences between me and Eve ("Remember your sprained ankle?" "Remember that awful dinner party you had?") while Pam fiddles with the salt shaker and squints at the chandelier.

"A farewell toast," Eve says, lifting her glass, and then, in mid-swallow, an inspiration seizes her and she dashes from the room. Pam smiles tolerantly at me. "This time tomorrow . . ." she begins.

In a second Eve is back, clutching a large vellum envelope. "You have to come, both of you," she insists. "I'll call them up right now.

I was going to invite you anyway, but ..."

She pulls an invitation out of the envelope and by candlelight we examine it:

The GreenGals
and
The President and Trustees
of the
Los Angeles County Museum of Art
Cordially Invite You to Attend
the Opening of
ONLY ON SUNDAY:
THE AMATEUR PAINTER
Dress: Sunday Best

Also enclosed is what is known in the fundraising trade as a "freebie"—in this case, a poster. Eve deftly unfolds it, as if after hours of practice, and thrusts it under our noses. "What do you think of *that?*" she demands.

A garish painting, in a sort of pointillist style, of an abandoned and forlorn carousel. Or wait a minute—is it a birthday cake? No, it's a carousel, it's got horses. Or are they Doberman pinschers? At any rate, our eyes go to the right-hand corner. It seems to be the work of one "Ginger Rogers."

"Is *she* going to be there?" Pam asks, suddenly starry-eyed. I must admit, I feel a tingle of excitement crawl down my spine: a real Hollywood party. The perfect send-off. I look at Pam. "Do you want to go?"

"Are you kidding?" she says. "I'd kill to go."

We laugh and all is forgiven. Funny what the prospect of ogling a few celebrities will do. Pam even begs Eve for the poster. It will look great, she says, on her office wall, right next to *Monet: The Years at Giverny.*

Another secret confession: I love to go to parties. In New York, I'm considered an inveterate partygoer. Show me two or more people and a bottle of booze, and I'm in heaven.

I've never understood why partygoing is thought to be such a shallow practice. "Lounge Lizard," "Sycophant," "Free-Food Weiner" —I've been called them all, and I don't care. I love to be out there "mingling" (my favorite word), eyeing the crowd, munching those tiny little hot dogs baked in the pastry shells. There's something about the drone of conversation I just can't explain. It's music to my ears.

My favorite parties are movie premieres. In addition to all the glitterati on view, you can usually count on a T-shirt and sometimes a record album. (But watch out! They punch a hole in the cover, or cut a corner off, which means you can't exchange it at Sam Goody's for something more to your liking. Take it from one who's learned the hard way.)

My pet peeves are political events. They tend to skimp on the liquor and are past masters at the art of making you feel guilty if you don't contribute. I usually give a dollar just to get them off my back, sometimes two if the candidate is opposed to busing.

New York is, of course, the big time as far as parties go. I'll never forget one night last year, just before Christmas, when I hit six consecutive parties in a row, thus breaking my old record of five set the previous Halloween when I was running all over town dressed up as "Elliot Mess" in a gangster outfit you wouldn't believe. The record-breaking evening: first I met Pam at the Christmas party at the Ford Foundation (el snoro, if truth be told), then we ran over to Beverly Sills's "do" for the staff of the New York City Opera (Pam knows the lead percussionist and La Sills sang!—just some stuff in Hebrew, but quite a thrill nevertheless), then a quick drink at Pam's aunt's (mostly family but I'm counting it anyway), followed by dinner with some Morris dancers I feel close to, then off to the Infirmary Ball at the Pierre, where our dinner host's cousin was making her debut ("The Infirmary Ball?" I cracked. "What are they going to do, dance in wheelchairs?"). Finally, I soloed downtown (Pam was too pooped) to boogie at the loft of a guy I know from Harvard who hangs out on the fringes of the art world. It was quite a night.

The GreenGals. How can I explain the GreenGals? On the way over in the car, Eve fills us in: they are an ultra-exclusive group of eighty or so Beverly Hills matrons, all with last names like Sinatra, Martin, and Davis, Jr. They raise $6 million a year for Mexican orphans—the sicker, the better—through various extortion schemes, particularly the sale of a day-by-day calendar in which everyone in "the Industry" must buy an ad or else they're washed up off the Malibu pier wearing a pair of cement shoes. Single-handed, they support a children's hospital near Acapulco complete with body scanner.

Eve's voice grows hushed and reverent when she speaks of them; it is quite clear she spends a major portion of her day fantasizing about being asked to join. Each year they have a "giant gala," usually a variety show down at the Music Centre with Johnny Carson as emcee. The gimmick is that the GreenGals get to perform right along with the stars, doing Rockette-type numbers and generally having a ball. This year, though, they're trying something new: a full-scale art exhibit, but not just any old masters, you understand. No, Hollywood's *own* have been asked to participate; any star, director, producer, or major agent who has ever committed a straight line to a piece of paper is donating something, plus special loaned stuff by really famous amateurs, like Eisenhower and Churchill. When Eve found out about this several months ago, she was beside herself. Because, you see, Pete paints! "He started after his heart attack. He got all those Walter Thomas books about how to paint sunsets and landscapes and the human figure and went to it. *Somehow*, the GreenGals found this out ..."

A nasty surprise is waiting for us in front of the museum, the reason, I'm sure, we were "going to be invited but ..." The faggot is standing there, at the edge of a crowd of ragged curiosity seekers, peering into the night with the uneasy look of someone who fears he has been stood up. As we approach, he continues to squint; I add myopia to his ever-lengthening list of loathsome traits.

He is wearing a curious outfit, or, more correctly, he is wearing an outfit curiously: a dinner jacket, with the collar turned up as if to protect his throat from arctic gusts, yet at the same time, his sleeves are pushed up all the way to his elbows, treating the spectator to a view of his bare forearms. Some latest fashion, no doubt. I stifle an impulse to vomit into the spotless California gutter.

"How's the script going?" I ask as we shake hands.

"Huh?" he says. The idiot is so excited he's going to a fancy Hollywood party, his mind has gone blank. He has forgotten he's ever met me, much less come over to my house for dinner. All his attention is focused at the top of the stairs, from which party sounds of the most glamorous sort are floating down. Pam and I look up. It's like the first act in *Tannhäuser*, she says, when you can hear Grace Bumbry and the nymphs cavorting in Venusberg but you can't see them yet.

After an argument with a beefy security man over which list we are on, the four of us start slowly up the stairs. No one says a word. A tremendous feeling of anticipation overtakes us. This is the Real Thing. The faggot pushes his sleeves an inch higher and licks his lips. Eve appears to be doing some sort of facial calisthenics to relax her cheek muscles. Even Pam smooths her hair. The sounds grow louder. We are almost there.

At the top of the stairs, we are rewarded beyond our wildest dreams. A stunning blonde, a dead ringer for Candice Bergen, is the first thing to meet our eyes. She is dressed in black silk pants and a short jacket made of blue feathers.

"Hi!" she says, so perky and friendly we say hi right back, grinning like a group of retarded people on an outing. She runs over to a man who looks like Jack Lemmon, only shorter and older.

"Jack!" she squeals and kisses his cheek.

"Candy!" he squeals back, and, stumbling uncertainly in a box-step pattern (for he is very drunk), he allows Candy to lead him off.

"Get me to a phone, girls!" the faggot exclaims, clutching his chest.

It is quite a sight. An unbroken expanse of celebrities stands before us as far as the eye can see. The women are shimmering in satin and silk, their necks and wrists glittering with diamonds, and the men are resplendent in black tuxedos, none, I notice, with their sleeves pushed up. Although I know not a soul, it seems like I do; they all look so familiar, like old friends. They buzz around, talking celebrity talk to each other and laughing loud, raucous laughs.

I look back at my companions. They appear to have lost their motor skills. All they can do is stand and gape. The faggot is surreptitiously trying to get his sleeves down. But the one I feel sorry for is Pam. It's not that she's out of place, but ... let me put it this way: she's the only woman there in a chocolate-brown polyester pants suit.

I suggest we try to find the bar. Thoroughly dazed, everyone consents, and we set off through the crowd, me in the lead, like native bearers heading into the bush.

The GreenGals have taken over the entire museum. The paintings are in the Armand Hammer Wing, where the general public can start viewing them tomorrow for an additional charge, and the museum itself, a giant, cubelike space, has been turned into a disco. On the terrace in between, round tables have been set up, each one covered with a green tablecloth and an arrangement of baby's breath and yellow irises. All the ladies receive a package of Revlon products (a tacky touch, Pam and I think), but the men get sterling silver key chains in the shape of a four-leaf clover, with the date engraved and an emerald chip in the center. As soon as the word gets out that they are *real* emerald chips, one quickly learns not to leave one's keychain sitting with one's date's Revlon products, or it will disappear as soon as one's back is turned.

We stand by the bar and survey the crowd. We don't have much to say; small talk seems inappropriate during such an intense experience. Eve warns us when a particularly famous person is walking by by making a sound I find hard to describe, a sort of frantic keening noise similar to what my parents' dog does when she has been forbidden to bark but nevertheless remains extremely agitated.

And there is so much to watch. Two beautiful young women, starlets most likely, frisk around a sculpture trying to attract Robert

Mitchum's attention. Bob Hope walks by, looking rather glum ("Still mourning der Bingle," theorizes the faggot). Desi Arnaz kisses Lucille Ball and then bums a cigarette from her new husband. Carol Burnett looks our way; she waves at Eve. Eve has both hands full; by the time she shoves her drink and deviled egg into the faggot's hands to wave back, Carol Burnett has turned away.

By this time, it has dawned on me that there are two types of people at the party: the glamorous celebrities and the four of us. Greetings from Carol Burnett notwithstanding, Eve's real place on the Beverly Hills social ladder has become blindingly clear. It is down toward the bottom and slightly off to the side. The obsequious way she defers to Eydie Gormé at the crudité bowl clinches things.

"Show us Pete's painting," I say when I feel I can stand it no longer. Me, the original celebrity hound. Eve is more than a little reluctant to give up such an excellent vantage point, but something in my tone of voice tells her I mean business.

We enter the Armand Hammer Wing and I know I want to go home.

"Just look at this shit," Pam whispers.

Home, I think. I don't even have a home.

Pam's judgment, however accurate, can't begin to convey the quality of the work displayed before us. We wander past the never-ending parade of still-lifes, the all-too-numerous *Flowers in a Vase*, the countless street scenes—Montmartre, Taxco, Bel-Aire—each with its own laws of perspective, the sunsets, sunrises, cloud formations and seascapes with colors not found in nature, the Grandma Moses rip-offs, the cross-eyed portraits (*Mrs. Melvin Franks; Kim, Aged 5*), the Balinese dancers and native markets laboriously copied from vacation snapshots, the random puddles of color labeled *Abstract*, the attempts at surrealism that are indistinguishable from the attempts at realism—oh, I could go on and on. An inexplicable watercolor of a plate of fried chicken, a work called *Little Angels* that should have been banned on racist as well as aesthetic grounds— well, enough is enough.

Pete's work was right at home here. I guess you could say he belonged to the mannerist school. There was more than a hint of El Greco in his portrait of an old fisherman mending his nets. The somber colors, the elongated shapes, the blurry outlines.

"It was either this or a picture of the dogs," Eve tells us. "But he has such trouble with fur and the curator liked this one much better."

Pam looks stunned. "There was a *curator* for this show?"

"It's lovely," I say real quick. "Just lovely."

"Just look at those nets," marvels the faggot. "They must have taken *ages.*"

"The nets were the easy part," Eve says. "Look at that tiny village on the mountainside."

The faggot gets closer. "Oh, that's a *village.* I thought it was part of the wall."

"No, see, that's a window there, and out the window is a village."

"Well, I'll be."

"Wow."

"And see how each house is painted separately?"

"That's amazing."

"Hey, look! A tiny donkey!"

The faggot and I examine the painting until our necks begin to ache. Eve turns to Pam.

"What do you think, dear? I'm dying to get the opinion of the New York art world."

Pam studies the painting critically. I become so nervous I can't bear to watch.

"I want to move it up," she says at last.

Eve knits her brow. "Move it up?"

"Yes, move it up. About three inches."

"The whole painting? You mean, rehang it?"

"No, just the composition. See, the figure should be up *here*, not down *there.*"

We stare at the painting, trying to imagine the fisherman three inches higher.

"But then you wouldn't see the *village*," moans the faggot.

"That's the point," Pam says.

"Let's dance," I say.

Why do I feel like I've suddenly been plunged into this cosmic despair? Is it the paintings? Is it Pam, the social time bomb? Is it the fact that I'm going to have to de-Puerto Ricanize my apartment? Change my six-month-old Medeco lock? What?

Dancing, anyway, was not the answer.

An attempt has been made to turn the central hall of the museum—an enormous atrium-like space five stories high—into a disco. Flashing lights have been attached to the balconies, but the scale is all wrong and the place ends up looking like a construction site. A handful of couples bounce to the music in this forbidding ambience, but the cavernous floor is just not attracting crowds. For the first time in my life, I truly understand the meaning of the phrase "lots of room to dance."

Not that any of this deters Pam. Oh, no, quite the contrary. As soon as we get near, she grabs me and drags me to the center of the floor.

I remember too late what a horrible dancer Pam is, what a truly egregious spectacle she presents out on the dance floor. She is one of those people who "abandon" themselves to the beat, clapping their hands over their heads and emitting little yelps. To make matters worse, she studied modern dance in college and thus considers herself a Movement Expert. The things she does—I can only describe them as Martha Graham routines. Her arms fly out into space, she makes sudden turns, then she half-squats, her head flung back in ecstasy.

Now these gyrations always attract a certain amount of attention. Other dancers, quite understandably, stare at this performance going on next to them; occasionally they go as far as to form a circle. I find this mortifying. A prayer comes to my lips. "Dear God, please don't let them form a circle. Not here, not at this party. I don't care if they stare, I'm resigned to that, but *please* don't let them form a circle."

Well, to make a long story short, they not only form a circle, they start *clapping along*! There may have been only ten people on that floor, but they drop whatever they are doing and run right over. I am ruined socially in Beverly Hills. I will never forgive Pam. Never. I look at her face, her features distorted by the orgasmic convulsions she's going through, and I want to slug her.

Thank God for the faggot. True to his heritage, all it takes is the sound of Grace Jones coming from a loudspeaker to propel him out on the floor. He elbows his way through the onlookers and joins us in a *pas de trois*.

His arrival allows me to fade into the background, and I join Eve, seated on a bench in front of a Giacometti. She is having a ball, under the impression that Pam and the faggot are the life of the party.

They stay out on the dance floor for a long time. It gets more crowded and they are no longer the center of attention, but this only makes them dance all the more frantically, hoping, no doubt, to regain their former status. Eve begins to confide in me; she pours out her hopes and plans for becoming a GreenGal. Not a word about my departure. I listen to her drone on, a reflective expression on my face, Pam's Revlon products in my lap, and morbid thoughts about the futility of human existence in my head.

Going home in the car, Pam and I have the inevitable fight. In a way, it is a microcosm of our whole relationship.

It starts out, as these fights always do, with a silence on my part. That's all—just a silence. Pam, famous for her "maturity" and "level-headedness," is really a twelve-year-old when it comes to her emotions. Any pattern of behavior that does not fit into the easygoing, comic bickering that Katharine Hepburn and Spencer Tracy made millions from (needless to say, they are Pam's "ideal" couple), or the pseudo-psychoanalytical jargon of a "serious" discussion (i.e., She: "I sense all this hostility in you." He: "It's not hostility, it's anger because you burned the pork chops." She: "I only burned the pork chops because I wanted you to pay attention to me." etc.), is an unaccountable mystery to her. She panics when she sees it. And then she accuses me of what she and her overanalyzed friends consider the cardinal sin of the twentieth century: "withdrawing."

The trouble begins when I do not respond enthusiastically enough to her cliché-ridden observations about the GreenGals' party. Normally we would laugh about something like that for weeks. Nothing makes us feel more superior than philistine vulgarity, particularly when it's masquerading as culture. But tonight I answer with a wan, enigmatic smile or, even more frustrating, *defend* them. "It's not what you think, Pam." "What is it then?" I shrug, maddeningly. "You have to live here to understand."

After this puzzling exchange, all her emotional antennae are on the alert. She stares out of the window plotting her next move. To my surprise, it seems to be a capitulation.

"Do you think there's anything good on TV?" she asks.

"What time is it?"

"A little after one."

"There's nothing on at one in the morning except fucking *Baretta*."

Still she ploughs ahead, determined to be cheerful: "I thought you liked *Baretta*."

"I hate *Baretta*."

"You liked the one where the people were trying to smuggle the butterfly collection."

Actually I did, but would I admit it now? Never. Instead, I say in a tone fraught with all sorts of meaning (but meaning nothing at all), "I have nothing but contempt for ''Baretta.'"

Pam mulls this over for a while and comes to the conclusion that things must be brought out in the open. "Do you have contempt for me?" she asks softly.

I wait a long time before answering. Too long. "No, I don't have contempt for you."

"What do you have then? You sure have something."

At this point comes the famous silence. A *long* famous silence. One of my *longer* famous silences. We pass two freeway exits and it still goes on. (Jonica, moron that she was, remained completely unintimidated by these silences. I finally had to give them up.) I honestly try to find some way to express myself, but nothing comes to mind. I can't very well say "I don't like the way you dance." It just doesn't sound right.

"Well?" she says.

Still my mind is a blank. The green glow from the dashboard seems to have me hypnotized.

"Is it because I danced with that guy all night?"

God, what fools women are. What self-centered little fools. Not only is she 100 per cent wrong, she is handing me on a silver platter the perfect opportunity to become a martyr. Which, of course, I jump at. The quality of my silence at last finds a definition: deep, profound hurt.

"Honey, I'm sorry," she says and attempts to take my hand. I pretend it's needed on the steering wheel.

Pam is no dope, though, and by the time we have turned on to Avenue of the Stars, she realizes that (knowing me) there must be more to it than that. She becomes rattled and defensive. Why didn't I say anything if I didn't want her dancing with that clown, who, "by the way, doesn't like you either." She would have gladly kept me company, talking to Eve all night, except she was afraid she might fall asleep and "that would have been so embarrassing."

By the time we get in sight of the hotel, it all comes pouring out: "Never in my life have I met somebody who is more out of touch with his feelings than you are. You have no idea who you really are or what you really want out of life. Look at the pattern: the zoo, a seven-year waste. Then Columbia, because the only thing you were ever good at in your life was being a college student. Then Warren Harding, this obsession you have with the shallowest president in history, trying to find all sorts of metaphorical significance where it doesn't exist ... And, of course, now that this hasn't worked out, you'll go on to something else, thinking, well, maybe this time ..."

We pull into the hotel driveway.

"You have no passions!" she blabbers on. "Wait, I take that back.

You do have one passion. You want to become famous. You desperately want to become famous. But the only way you're ever going to become famous is to sell your soul to the devil, just like the people back at that party!"

I come to a stop in front of the hotel entrance. "There are worse fates than winding up like Carol Burnett," I gently remind her.

She tugs her lips to the side in disgust. Then she notices something. "Hey, aren't you going to put the car in the garage?"

I look at her and sigh. "Pam, I think I'd rather be by myself tonight."

For the first time all evening, a look of pure, unplanned emotion comes over her face. "But you're coming back with me? Tomorrow? Right?"

"Yes, I'm going back with you. I just want to be by myself for a while."

Since the line "be by myself for a while" is one that has figured prominently in our relationship over the years, she puts up no further argument. She smiles sadly, gives me a kiss, and slips out of the car. I watch her plod into the hotel. From the back she looks like Barrie.

By the time I got back to Casino Drive it was after two thirty in the morning and I was so tired I was starting to hallucinate. All the fire hydrants on Beachwood were trying to flag me down, like little munchkins. Bed, I kept thinking. I'll pick up the pieces of my shattered life in the morning. Even so, I still parked the Mustang around back, just like I promised I always would. That's Elliot—the Perfect Tenant.

The walk back to the pool house felt like it took about half an hour. A full moon was out (somehow I wasn't surprised), giving the big house a sort of radium glow, like it was lethal to the touch. Gee, I thought, it's so bright you could read a newspaper. Not that I was tempted.

I entered the pool house through the kitchen door and staggered the last thirty feet into the living room toward my bed. Where a nasty surprise awaited me. The bed was stripped. We had packed the sheets.

Cursing rather loudly, I rummaged around for the box they were in. The mattress was foam rubber and its—what's the word, ticking?—had ripped one evening when Jonica, overexcited while watching *Family Feud*, had bounced once too often. It needed some kind of covering; otherwise you might as well be sleeping on scrambled eggs.

As luck would have it the box the sheets were in was all taped and sealed, ready to take down to the post office in the morning. So I threw an old tablecloth from the Salvation Army pile down on the bed and collapsed, expecting to pass out within thirty seconds.

Ten minutes later I was still lying there. I was so wide awake my eyes weren't even closed.

Problem Number One: Was I about to make a major mistake? Was I letting my emotions get the better of me? When you really stopped to think about it, I was *this close* to getting my hands on the papers. Today was Monday (actually Tuesday morning). The old lady had her poetry class on Wednesday (tomorrow!).

Problem Number Two: It looked like Pam and I had come to the end of our mutual road. I'm sorry, but the way she danced was just the last straw. Let's face it, that's *not* what I'm looking for in a woman ... Yes, the more I thought about it the more I realized that it was all over. My mind focused on the necessary arrangements that would have to be made. She could keep the Rolling Stones records but I really wanted Pachelbel's Canon back, plus my navy sweater. Her juicer was a thorny problem: how had it ever ended up at my house? Of course, it was *her* juicer but I *knew* she was never going to use it. Her aunt gave it to her.

It isn't easy, lying on a slightly soiled tablecloth in the Hollywood Hills and watching a seven-year relationship go down the tubes. The thing that really frightened me was *how little I cared*. It was like I just couldn't be bothered.

Of course there was stuff I would miss. Our Saturday afternoon strolls up Madison Avenue. The way she got along so well with all the Stratford Morris Men. Talking to her on the phone five times a day, just to check in.

On the other hand there were things I wouldn't miss at all. Her unbelievably sloppy housekeeping habits. Her hairs in my drains. The way she left the bathroom floor sopping wet every time she took a shower. Her whining about her dental problems. Her loudmouth family. Dinner with them was like attending a labor negotiating session.

If I went back to New York I didn't have to stay with her. I could move in with one of the Morris Men for a while. Or I could check into the Collingwood or the Seville Hotel. I still had some fellowship money left—

Jesus, the fellowship money. Would they make me give it back? The Reed Foundation must be expecting *something* for their $7,500.

I think you're beginning to see why sleep was not coming easily. Maybe if I had something to eat. Then at least my stomach juices would stop attacking my incipient ulcer.

There was plenty of food left. Cupboards full, all these beads and trinkets I'd bought to bribe Jonica with. I was planning to give them to Guadalupe just before I left so she could distribute them amongst the poor.

I opened a jar of artichoke hearts and went over to the sink to drain them. As I did so I happened to glance out the window—just a casual glance—and what I saw made my knees turn to jelly. At first I had no idea what it was so I ran back to get my glasses. Then I peered out the living room window, my heart thumping so badly I had to take deep breaths.

It was a ghost. I was seeing a ghost. Great.

It moved.

Maybe it wasn't a ghost.

A tiny figure on the terrace of the big house, standing there, like it was lost. It was short and almost roly-poly. A horrible thought seized me. Was it one of the Manson family? Squeaky Fromme? This settles it, I'm leaving, my mind has just been made up.

Then it moved and the moonlight caught its face.

It was the old lady.

She took a halting step in the direction of the pool and then stopped again and looked around, like she was straining to hear something.

I pulled on my pants and ran out the door, past the pool, up to the terrace. She didn't see me coming. She was off in her own world.

"Mrs. Kinney?" I called out, for I feared that she might keel over at any second, she looked so unsteady. I had never seen her on her feet before. I didn't even know she could stand. The sight was unnerving. What on earth does she have on? I wondered. It seemed like she was wearing her entire wardrobe, like she'd started to get dressed and just kept putting on sweater after sweater.

She looked around at me, the strangest look.

"Mrs. Kinney?" I repeated, breathless. "Are you all right?"

She stared at me, bewildered.

"Where's Warren?" she asked, grabbing my hand.

"He's in the nursery," I told her.

"The nursery?"

And then I realized she didn't mean little Warren at all. I felt my skin crawl.

"Help me to find Warren," she said.

She began to cry. Her grip on my arm was so strong.

"I will, I will," I said.

Suddenly Guadalupe appeared from nowhere, scolding in Spanish. She took Mrs. Kinney from me, thanking me profusely, and guided her through the front door, that massive front door that somehow she managed to get open. They were gone and I was left standing there on the terrace.

At seven in the morning I called Pam and told her that I wasn't going back to New York, that I couldn't leave. Not now. Then I went back to sleep.

I slept late that morning. It was the first time in weeks. Usually I was wide awake at 6 a.m., wondering how on earth *birds* could make so much noise. I would actually lie there chewing my fingernails. But today I didn't even stir again until ten thirty. And let me tell you, it was heaven.

I love to sleep late. Pam has a theory that I quit my job at the zoo so I could sleep late. She's partially right. What happened was this.

First of all, let me explain that I am no clock-puncher. I believe in doing the work you are paid to do, *but* in your own time and according to your best judgment. What's the point of sitting there rearranging your desk until five thirty rolls around? Leave a little early, mix yourself a drink, watch the news, and in the long run the zoo will have a more refreshed (and more productive) employee.

I also don't see any point in getting to work at nine just to be there. Have you noticed the people who do? It's not like they're *doing* anything. They just sit there and read the *Times* and drink coffee and eat crullers and answer the phones of the people who aren't there yet. I often wouldn't arrive till eleven or so.

This theory of working hours (I believe Spengler mentions it in *Decline of the West*) did not sit too well with my ex-boss. He was found somewhere by a "search committee." I kept picturing this committee, wild-eyed, disheveled, frantically combing the streets for a new executive director. Under what particularly slimy rock they found this bozo I do not know. Suffice it to say that he had a doctorate in something called "recreation." He called himself a "recreator." He was always going off to places like Houston to attend "recreators' conferences."

When not engaged in "professional development," Mr. Recreator kept himself busy writing memos about coming to work on time. His secretary, a female Nazi from Trinidad, personally checked everybody's time sheets; don't ask me why, they were so easy to fudge. Anyway, what I would do is this: I would sneak (a strong word, but an accurate one in this case) in the basement door and leave my coat and briefcase behind an unused display case in the storeroom. Then I would energetically dash up the stairs in my shirt sleeves, clutching some report, the clear implication being that I had been down discussing some new money-saving idea with Maintenance. Nine times out of ten I would invariably bump into the retard, since he spent his mornings prowling the halls for latecomers. Either that or he stood guard by the Xerox machine, making sure no one was Xeroxing a friend's play.

Then, later in the day, when I was sure he was in a meeting, I would go downstairs and get my stuff. As luck would have it, I eventually got caught one day when he was personally supervising the moving of the display case (he was also a whiz at delegating authority). That was the day I seriously started thinking of graduate school.

But not before I snuck into his office when he wasn't there and got his overcoat, and with a single-edged razor, I very carefully cut half of the stitches holding the sleeve on to the coat, so that when he was wending his way homeward that evening to Co-Op City or whatever little plebeian enclave he called home, he would reach up to grab the subway strap and the sleeve would come off.*

Anyway, where was I? Oh, yes, sleeping late. So I finally forced my leaden body out of bed and down the hall to Pepe's, where I took a long shower. I let the water run over my face for quite a while to remove bags. Then a cup of coffee after which I set out for the hospital. My theory was to get the inevitable visit out of the way and then spend the rest of the day wandering around Westwood. I needed a day off.

But while driving down Beachwood whom should I see but Vernon, standing by the Hollywoodland gates with his thumb sticking out. My first impulse was to floor the accelerator. Who wants one of those awkward conversations with a near stranger? Particularly a

---

* Speaking of work, here is another way to look busy. Sit at your desk with a piece of paper in front of you. Preferably the paper should have a column of figures on it. Stare at the paper, squinting slightly. It looks exactly like you're trying to figure out some important problem, but actually you can sit this way for hours and just let your mind wander. Remember: the secret is in the squint. That's what makes it look authentic. P.S. Some people don't like to squint because they're afraid they'll get crow's-feet. It's up to the individual.

near stranger with whom I shared so much—what is the word the hippies use—karma? But Vernon was staring down everybody that drove by with this thoroughly intimidating sneer, so I decided it was wiser to stop than to risk hatchet murder by a slighted hillbilly. I could just see the headlines—VAGRANT SLAYS COLLEGE PROF. "'He wouldn't give me a lift,' claims troubled youth."

So I screeched to a halt and Vernon saunters over like he's trying to decide if a Mustang is good enough or should he hold out for at least a Monte Carlo. I lean over and open the door and he climbs in languidly, glances my way in an extremely bored fashion, and does a double take. "Hey, hey, hey," he says. "It's Popeye the Sailor Man."

Shit. So he *didn't* recognize me.

"Which way you headed?" I say, under the impression this is the appropriate opening conversational gambit when one is picking up a hitchhiker.

"The hospital," he says, slouching down in his seat.

Guilt is such a powerful emotion. And so universal.

So we set out, the two of us. His first remark: "What's your name, anyway?" This, I must say, turns out to be the extent of his curiosity about me. He seems to have not the slightest desire to figure out how I fit into the picture. Jesus Christ, isn't he wondering who I am, this strange, well-groomed presence always lurking in the background? No, his only concern is that we stop at the Liquor Locker for cigarettes and Kleenex. He suspects he is catching little Warren's cold.

Vernon was white trash, all right, but there was something in his backwoods genes that just *clicked*, the same way it did with Elvis Presley's X's and Y's. His mouth, for instance, was what you might call "sensual"—meaning pouty and cruel at the same time, and his eyes were grey and intense. (Except when they were *pink* and intense, if you know what I mean.) His best feature was his black hair, which was perfect. He was always running his hand through it, but it always fell right back into place. Even the lousy $2.50 haircut from the Peter Pan Barber Shop couldn't ruin it. ("We are Not a School" they had to advertise, their personnel was so inept.) He didn't have what you'd call an extensive wardrobe, though. He always wore a white T-shirt and Levi's. Although I must say it was a *clean* white shirt. He must have had several drawers full. On his feet he wore blue sneakers with white stripes.

Women found him devastating. Definite swoon material, as Helene used to say. The cashier in the Liquor Locker mooned over him the whole time we were in there. When he said, "Thank you, ma'am," I thought her knees would buckle.

Then we got back in the car. If Vernon wasn't interested in *my* story, that didn't prevent him from telling me his. I was amazed at how chatty he was once he became removed from all those women.

Vernon was from one of those large Appalachian families that are always coming down with lower-class diseases involving tumors. I don't know what accounted for this, maybe they were all raised adjacent to a chemical dump. What a sickly bunch of people. They all seemed to live off some sort of mysterious disability insurance. Last year Vernon's father had to sell the diner he operated a block from the Kentucky State Capitol in Frankfort because he was wheezing so much. This gave him plenty of time to stay home and babysit for his grandson, Vernon's nephew, who was born with webbed feet.

Ugh, I thought, get out of my car.

In a very smart move, Vernon left Frankfort and came to Hollywood immediately upon receiving his high school diploma. For you see, ever since he won a speech contest in his junior year he had harbored fiery dreams about becoming an actor.

A week after he got to LA, he got his very first job, playing a flea in this children's show that toured public schools every morning. It was called *Flea Power!* and it sounded extremely left-wing. Barrie was also in the show. She played a dog. Typecasting, I guess.

After six months the Board of Ed got these closet Commies to come up with a new show, mainly because every schoolchild in Los Angeles County had seen the play about ten times and they were getting sick of writing compositions on what *Flea Power!* meant to them. Much to his surprise, Vernon was *not* rehired for the new show. I could understand this decision. The only role model Vernon was well suited for was Juvenile Delinquent. But Vernon was sure it was due to some backstage backstabbing on Barrie's part. He had just started "dating" Jonica and even though Barrie had introduced them with all the alacrity of a waterfront madam, once Vernon saw the house and things started to get "serious," she did a complete about-face.

His male ego ruffled, Vernon laid down the law: Jonica would have to break off her friendship with Barrie. Jonica, desperately in love, agreed. For several months everything was okay. Then Barrie, through an incredibly complicated series of machinations, managed to "bump into" Jonica as she (Jonica) was hauling garbage out of the trailer court. (Vernon and Jonica received a discount in exchange for this chore.) That was the beginning of the end. That was also why Vernon started calling Barrie Garbagewoman.

Jonica's room was painted bright blue and it had yellow curtains. It was designed to be cheerful. There was a television and a bunch of other stuff Barrie had carted over in a shopping bag—a radio that was missing most of its knobs, some toilet articles, a plastic troll holding a sign that read "I Wuv You." She also had brought some flower vases, but so far Jonica had received only two get-well bouquets: a $5.95 special from the Coast Guard, and some spider mums from Claude Kentner, already starting to wilt. As we walked in Barrie was just finishing giving Jonica a Mini-poo. This is a form of dry-shampoo suitable for bed-ridden patients.

Jonica was barely conscious, it seemed. She moved a pair of heavily lidded eyes toward the door. A croak came from her throat.

"Elliot," she said in a most unusual voice—gravelly, but squeaky at the same time. Holy Christ, I thought. Talk about being drugged. The poor girl. It all went right to her tongue.

"They told me you went to New York," she managed to get out.

"What?" I said, moving to her side. "And leave you?" I debated the possibility of clasping her hand but decided, why play with fire, with my luck it would probably be attached to one of the damaged nerves.

"And Vernon," she said, just noticing him. "What a surprise."

"Hi, Jonica," he said.

I rocked back and forth on my feet for a moment, smiling down at her.

"You look great," I said. She still had Mini-poo clinging to her hair.

"Yeah," Vernon said. "You look great."

"I feel awful!"

I felt Barrie's eyes bearing down on us. Ever since we walked in all her attention was riveted to the fact that Vernon and I had walked in together. Her mind was in overdrive. Was it a plot? Was it a coincidence? What did it mean? How should she handle it?

For what seemed like hours Vernon and I answered Jonica's painfully mumbled questions about little Warren and Mrs. Kinney, making it sound like not only had they totally adjusted to Jonica's absence but they were giving each other such strength and support that the *Reader's Digest* was interested in serial rights. This topic finally exhausted, I snuck a peek at my watch. We had been there three minutes.

I looked up to see Jonica staring at me with something I interpreted as an "If only we could be alone" look. I chose that moment to develop a coughing fit.

Barrie suggested we play Alphabet Trivia. This was her favorite game, where you think of celebrities' names to match random sets of initials. You're supposed to use paper and pencil but Barrie figured out a way we could do it in our heads. I wasn't too bad at it, actually (I got "Xavier Cugat" for "X.C."), but Jonica became confused as to which set of initials we were on and Vernon was such a poor fourth he finally refused to play any more. "I gotta find the can," he said and wandered out of the room.

Suddenly, with Vernon gone, the vibes in the room did a dramatic change. Barrie, her jaw set, glared at me.

"Has he asked to borrow money?"

"No," I said.

"He will," she said grimly.

"Well, he's asking the wrong person." I laughed.

She ignored my joke. "A word to the wise," she said. I waited. "Don't ride in the same car with him. That is, if you value your driver's license."

"How come?"

"He always has drugs on him."

"Oh."

"And I wouldn't drop by any 7-Elevens."

"No 7-Elevens?"

"He was arrested in a 7-Eleven."

"In Riverside," Jonica mumbled.

"What for?"

"Armed robbery."

"It wasn't armed," said Jonica.

"Well, it was robbery."

"What happened?"

"Suspended sentence," Jonica whispered.

"They should have given him the chair," Barrie said. "Boy, does that kid have problems."

What could I say? I looked at my knees and began picking at the crease in my pants.

"Of course," Barrie went on, "I could forgive everything—well, *almost* everything—except for what he did to Jonica."

I felt a thrill run down my back. "What did he do to Jonica?"

Barrie looked at me like I wasn't very perceptive. "Well, first of all, he left her alone."

Left her alone! That was disappointingly trivial.

"He left her alone?"

"For days. He left her alone for days."

"He went to Manmouth without telling me."

"Yes," Barrie said, suddenly remembering. "He went to Manmouth without telling her."

"For three days."

"What could she do? I told her to assert herself."

"But it didn't work," Jonica said, to the ceiling.

"How could it?"

"Tell him about Lisa Kemp!"

"Lisa Kemp!" Barrie repeated and both women shuddered.

A moment went by. "Who's Lisa Kemp?" I asked breathlessly.

At this point Vernon sauntered back into the room. It was quite obvious where he had been—Ole Pink Eyes was back, if you catch my meaning. He sat down and picked up the troll. Everybody's attention was on him, it was even coming from the corner of our eyes.

"Lord, Lord, Lord," he said, for no apparent reason.

When we left around one, Vernon asked me if I would drive him over to the trailer in Torrance. He wanted to pick up some of his "shit" since he was going to be staying at Casino Drive for a while.

I said sure.

Vernon didn't have a car. It had been totaled down in Long Beach by two guys who ran into him early one morning while they were scouting carpentry jobs and Vernon was returning from the night job he had at a photo-developing plant. He had only been working there a week and was glad he was forced to quit since he hated the job. But the guys were making his life a living hell. Vernon was technically at fault—this story is getting very long. Suffice it to say that the guys were despicable people, one of them staged convulsions in a State Farm office, and Vernon was becoming bitter. The amount of the lawsuit was $250,000.

Anyway, he didn't have a car.

Which is a shame because he was one of those people who are completely at ease only in a car. I don't know what it was, the breeze in his face, the radio, or what. His whole body seemed to vibrate as we drove along. Come to think of it, it actually *did* vibrate: he was always moving ever so slightly to the music. He knew all the songs by heart. (Also all the commercials.) There was something about the way he flipped open the ashtray. Nonchalant authority is the best way to describe it.

We drove through a pleasant neighborhood of one-family homes, then through a not quite so pleasant neighborhood of two-family homes (some cars were parked on the *lawn*), then through a neighborhood of small apartment buildings that looked like unprosperous motels set perpendicular to the street, and finally to an industrial area on the far edge of which stood Brecker's Mobile Home Park.

We proceeded through a green and white wooden arch, badly nicked (from oversized loads, I imagine), down a rutted dirt road on which some foreign children were chasing each other on tricycles and bopping one another with plastic baseball bats. A surly, liver-lipped woman in shorts and a halter was watching the melee while drinking beer out of the bottle (this at 1.30 p.m., remember). Vernon actually waved at this woman. She grinned, revealing several missing teeth, and lifted her Bud in greeting.

Now, my reaction to all this was curious. One the one hand, I was speechless. This was true tackiness. This was one place you were sure to lock your car. But on the other hand, I must admit to a certain perverse thrill. For you see, when I was a kid I thought nothing could be more glamorous than being poor and living in a trailer. *Those* kids didn't have to go to dancing class. To me that was real liberation. Why, their parents were probably even *divorced.* When I was ten, the most exciting thing I could think of was for your parents to get divorced. This was a kick I never experienced, though, since the idea of my parents' getting divorced was about as likely as the reunification of Korea.

And Vernon's trailer! There it was, at the end of the rutted road, sitting under a eucalyptus tree and backed against a chain-link fence. It was perfection; it was poetry in motion. It was one of those aluminum jobs from the late 1940s. It looked just like a giant toaster.

And the interior! One look and I was hooked. It was beyond my wildest childhood dreams. *Everything* was built in.

There was literally no free-standing article of furniture. Just cupboards and drawers and hampers that tilted out and tables that flipped up and down. The couch in the living room, for instance. It had drawers underneath, and behind it were porthole-type windows, over which were shelves. That type of couch, Vernon informed me, was called a gaucho bed. It was upholstered in this kind of green plush you just don't see any more. There was one drawback, though. Sitting on it was like sitting on a Glad Bag full of tin cans.

Then Vernon showed me the kitchen. It had a tiny stainless steel sink (full of dishes) and green Formica counters (full of empty beer cans). Here the built-ins were even tinier, like a long, narrow drawer just for knives, and a special cabinet with slots to keep your tumblers from banging each other as you rolled along the countryside. But it was the bathroom, just behind the kitchen, that was the true marvel of economic spatial design. "You can shit, shower, and shave, all at the same time," Vernon said. He showed me how the shower worked, something to do with hydraulic pressure that I didn't quite understand.

Vernon remembered he had to make some phone calls so we went back into the living room. I sat on the gaucho bed, leafing through *Stereo Buyer's Guide* and eavesdropping shamelessly.

Call number one went to somebody named Scott. After a while it became clear that Scott was boarding Sparky, the famous dog acquired in the color TV trade. Vernon was behind in his weekly payments. He made some desperate promises. I got the impression that Sparky was severely straining the Vernon-Scott friendship.

Call number two went to somebody with whom Vernon was on such intimate terms that all he said was "Hi, it's me." (Lisa Kemp?!?) He canceled a date they had to go someplace called (unless my ears were playing tricks on me) the Blah-Blah. This was not a popular move. The other person went on at great length about something. Vernon said he would be "Hard to reach for a couple of days." In general his tone was arrogant and a little distant. If I were Lisa Kemp, I would have been furious.

Call number three was to the office of a Mr. Rossi. Mr. Rossi wasn't in and the person answering the phone was unable to clear up a misunderstanding about some demo tapes.

Vernon hung up the phone in a hostile manner. He sat there for a while fuming.

"Bad news?" I asked brightly.

"Suck my dick," he said to the phone.

We got some beer out of the half-sized refrigerator, and Vernon began rummaging around for the stuff he wanted. This put him in a better mood, since he seemed to have the instincts of a pack rat. He pulled a Gordon's Gin box down from a shelf and unloaded the amplifier jacks it contained. Then, into the box he put some clean underwear and socks, a thermos, some Ace bandages, many, many cassettes, a coffee mug Jonica had given him (one of those with ice-skating bears on it), a snake-bite kit, and some books. That's funny, I thought, I didn't have him pegged as a reader. So I looked at the titles. One was called *On Your Own in the Wilderness*. The others were mostly about how to build your own boat, or, once having built it, how to sail around the world on it by yourself.

One of the books was a little different. It was about that plane crash in the Andes where the soccer team eats the dead bodies. Vernon was absolutely fascinated. "I only lack two chapters," he told me, which made me wonder whether he meant he was two chapters from the end or that somebody had ripped two chapters out of the book. Anyway, he thought it was the best book he had ever read.

"Would you eat a dead body to survive?" he asked me.

"In two seconds flat," I said.

"So would I," he said. "Unless it was really gross."

"Well, Vernon," I said, "I wouldn't eat it if it was really gross either."

"No," he agreed. "You gotta draw the line. Would you eat a relative?"

I thought about this. "I would eat my brother, but I just couldn't see eating my sister. Aunt or uncle I would have no qualms about."

"Parents?"

"Ugh, please."

"My sentiments exactly."

It turned out there was a movie made about the plane crash that Scott had actually seen. Vernon had missed it, though. When he showed up at the theater, it had gone away and something starring Sonny Chiba was playing. To this day he cursed that piece of bad luck. He asked me to tell him if I ever heard the movie was playing anywhere and then we could go together because Scott had been very impressed and recommended it very highly even though the snow looked phony.

It was getting hot in the trailer and Vernon was sweating from all his packing so he decided to take a shower. He wedged himself in the tiny bathroom (you had to keep the door shut or you'd flood the hall) and I sat on the gaucho bed till I heard the water start running. Then I decided to do a little exploring.

I headed for the bedroom, where I hadn't been yet. It was mostly just a double bed, with a foot or so on each side. Needless to say, the bed was unmade. The King Tut sheets were so dingy it took me a while to realize they were indeed King Tut sheets. On each side of the bed was a built-in nightstand. One was covered with dusty Pepperidge Farm cookie bags. This must have been Jonica's side. The other one had all sorts of implements for smoking marijuana, an alarm clock, some Vaseline Intensive Care Lotion, and a black notebook which I picked up to examine.

This was Vernon's journal. It didn't seem to have any particular organization, just random jottings and such. One page was a list of family birthdays. Another had odd facts ("There is only one state that begins with the letter A that does not end with the letter A. That state is Arkansas") and quotes. On another, under the heading "Lyrics," were some song lyrics he was working on. To be perfectly honest, I was pretty impressed. In fact they were a revelation. I had no idea he had such a sensitive way of looking at things. One went:

And sometimes when we touch
The honesty's too much
I want to hold you till I die

Till we both break down and cry
I want to hold you
Till the pain in me subsides

And not just sensitivity. I'm talking about craftsmanship. It's very difficult, I imagine, to use the word "subsides" in a love song. I don't recall ever seeing it done before.*

Another interesting entry:

> People are so rude. Yesterday Scott and I nearly broke our necks trying to get to Culver City so that I could cash a personal check I had received from my parents. The bank closed at 3 p.m. and I arrived just when the security guard was locking the doors it was only one minute after three and there were still a lot of people in the bank transacting business. The security guard and the manager of the bank have always been friendly and nice to me until yesterday. I knocked on the door hoping the security guard would be understanding. He came to the door and I explained my problem that I had come all the way from Torrance and barely had enough money to get home and I asked him to kindly let me cash my check since I really needed the money to pay my phone bill the next day. Instead of being nice he was downright cocky. This was only between me and him, right? Wrong! Instead of telling me quietly he screams out for the whole bank to hear, "I can't let you in I turned away eight people already (untrue I'm sure, how could he turn away eight people already when it was only one minute after 3 p.m.). You should have been on time," he says in a goody-goody tone of voice. He was trying to prove something to the whole world. Look at me everybody I'm a good cop who does his job well and sticks to his guns.
>
> Then I asked for the manager explaining my story to him but all I got was a mouthful of sarcasm. His exact words were laugh you should have been here on time!
>
> Understanding? No!
> Inhuman? Yes!

---

* It has since been brought to my attention, by my lawyer among others, that these lyrics are not by Vernon but by Dan Hill and Barry Mann and are from a popular song entitled "Sometimes When We Touch." My face is slightly red.

Stuck in this journal like a bookmark was a snapshot of Vernon and Jonica and little Warren, all dressed up in their Sunday best and standing in front of a restaurant called the Tick Tock Inn. Vernon was wearing one of those six-piece suits from Penney's, with the two pairs of pants and the reversible vest. What on earth was the occasion? I wondered.

I heard the sound of the water stop. I thrust the picture back in the journal and dropped the whole thing back on the nightstand as if it had suddenly burst into flame. Should I dash back into the living room? What if I got caught dashing? That would be even more embarrassing than being caught in the bedroom. Gee, he takes short showers.

In a second Vernon walked into the room drying his hair with a towel. If my presence was a shock, you never would have known it. He sniffed, wiped his nose with the towel, and positioned himself in front of a mirror.

I decided now was as good a time as any to put my plan in motion.

"Vernon," I said, "I'm an antiques dealer." Then I asked him to help me get the trunk in return for some help ($) on the trailer payments.

He listened to all of this and then sat on the edge of the bed and began to dry his toes. He seemed very, very interested.

Once I finally did get the trunk it was so ... so *physically easy* that I felt like a real forty-watt klutz for the way I had been running around like a chicken with its head cut off for the past two months. All that wasted time. All the energy expended.

Not that it was *that* easy. There were a couple of false starts. Ho, ho, ho, were there a couple of false starts.

For you see, the old lady's mental condition, never one of her trump cards, had taken a nose dive since Jonica's accident. Looking back on it now, it's pretty obvious that she had suffered some sort of minor stroke. Like her face, for instance. She looked awful. Her mouth was always hanging open and she wore this perpetually stunned expression, like she'd just been whacked in the solar plexus with a snow shovel. The strangest thing, though, was that she was walking again. Vernon and I figured out that she must not have been crippled all this time, just lazy. And now the old faker's mind was so far on the fritz she forgot to keep her act together.

Excuse me, did I say "walking again"? Is that the simple non-committal little phrase I just scribbled down? "Walking again"? Somehow it just does not seem adequate, does not even come *close* to describing the breadth and extent of her palsied hikes and wanderings. The woman was unable to sit still for longer than five seconds at a time. You would literally turn your head and she would be gone, off to the bathroom (the location of which she couldn't remember no matter how often she went and, believe me, she went often) or on some life-and-death errand, like feeding the chickens ("Gee, I didn't know we had any chickens," Vernon said. "Sure we do," she said. "Well, where do we keep them?" Vernon asked. She looks at him like he's nuts. "In the chicken coop, of course.") Now, don't think that just because she was "walking again" meant she was good at it. Watching her attempt the stairs was an exercise in terror. Would she make it? Could you dash over in time to catch her? Somehow, though, she never seemed to fall over.

So at first we thought the senility would make things a piece of cake. What a stroke of luck. After all, all Vernon had to do was keep her busy and keep her downstairs.

Going home in the car we formulated a plan. It was simplicity itself. Vernon said he would call me when everything was set, so I baked some frozen cookies and watched the news. Anything to keep busy.

The phone call came. I ran over and knocked on the kitchen door.

The entire crew was grouped around the kitchen table, in front of the TV. Mrs. Kinney was dozing quietly for a change. Little Warren was crawling around on the floor, trying his best to get into the cabinet under the sink and drink some bleach. Guadalupe was engrossed in the show. It was the Mexican channel and a buxom woman named Olga Something was performing a production number.

Vernon and I stared at the TV for a while, as per our plan, trading banalities designed to give Guadalupe the impression that I had just dropped by to shoot the breeze. This was not necessary, though. Guadalupe was so taken with Olga her eyes never left the set. Every time Olga came out in a new outfit she fanned herself with excitement.

"Well," said Vernon after a certain amount of time had passed, "why don't we go upstairs and I'll show you that thing I was talking about."

"Oh, yes," "I said. "Let's do that. That would be nice."

The old lady's bedroom was at the end of the hall on the right. Vernon led me in and turned on the overhead light.

Guess what—it was exactly the way I pictured it would be. Exactly. Talk about omens.

It was not very large, twelve by fifteen tops, certainly not the size of the master bedroom (Jonica had that). A double bed in an old-fashioned enamel bedstead stood against one wall. It was covered with a chenille bedspread, faded over the years to a pale rose. Next to it was a maple night table with a lamp, a flashlight, and a pile of religious tracts.

All this I took in later, though, for the first thing my eyes went to was the trunk. It was standing opposite the bed, where you would normally have the TV. My heart started to pound—there it was at last. I had to put my hands in my pockets, they were trembling so bad.

"Try and hurry up 'cause she might wake up at any second," Vernon said, cool as a cucumber. Then he left and I was alone.

I went over to the trunk. It was one of those enormous old steamer trunks, black with brass fittings. The initials R.A.K. were in faded red letters underneath the lock. Pasted on the sides were the remains of steamship and railroad labels. Sitting on the top were two items, a washcloth and a pair of glasses.

Jesus, I thought, do you think she cleans it every day with the washcloth?

I tried the latch but it was locked. Of course I remembered where the key was—in the nightstand drawer, just like Jonica said.

But it wasn't there. A Bible was there, and some nose drops, and a coin bank, and some pictures of Jonica in a Brownie uniform. But no key.

I went back downstairs and stuck my head in the kitchen door. They were all still in front of the TV. Vernon was holding little Warren, clapping his hands in time with the music. Olga had changed into her skimpiest outfit yet—feathers, mostly—and was playing Liszt on the violin. What a strange country Mexico must be, I thought.

The old lady's chin was still resting on her chest.

"Pssst," I said very softly, so as not to wake her up. Naturally, as luck would have it, she woke with such a start you'd think a bomb had exploded in the next room.

"Who's that?" she said, squinting at me.

"That's just Elliot," Vernon said, putting Warren down. "You remember Elliot."

The old lady gave me an unnerving stare.

"Vernon," I hissed through my fixed smile. "Come out in the hall."

"I can't find the key," I told him when we were alone. "It isn't where Jonica said."

Vernon made a face and started to say something but shut up real quick when we saw the old lady come puttering toward us, propped up at the elbow by Guadalupe.

"Where you headed for, Gramma?" he asked in a loud, friendly tone.

"Bed," she said.

"But don't you wanna watch the end of Olga?"

"Nope."

"Get her back in the kitchen," I said under my breath. Vernon ran over and grabbed her by the other elbow and yanked her away from Guadalupe. He steered her in a slow arc away from the stairs. "Let's watch the end of Olga," he said. I followed them and watched as he sat her down in the chair. Olga, in a can-can outfit, was waving good night.

"I want to go to bed," the old lady said.

"You can go to bed in a minute," Vernon told her.

He told Guadalupe to watch her. We ran back upstairs and Vernon took a look at the lock. "All we need," he said, "is a Phillips screwdriver."

He ran back downstairs. A screwdriver, I thought. Was that wise? Wouldn't it ruin the lock? I checked in the drawer again. There was no key, there was no getting around it. But hmmmm ... that Bible looks a little lumpy. I picked it up. A key fell out.

I ran downstairs to tell Vernon but the moment I entered the kitchen I was confronted with such an unusual sight it made all other topics of conversation pall. The old lady—how can I put this?—was attempting to crawl up on the kitchen table.

"Vernon!" I screamed. "What is she doing?"

"I don't know but I think she's planning to stretch out and take a nap."

That did it. That was the last straw. "Vernon," I said. "Forget it. We'll do it later."

He couldn't see the problem. "She'll be okay. She won't fall off. We'll watch her."

"No!"

"Why?"

"Because it's just not right."

Vernon shrugged. "Okay. You're the boss."

So he told Guadalupe to put her to bed and we went back over to my house. We ate all the cookies and I taught Vernon the rudiments of bridge.

I knew something was wrong the minute we walked into Jonica's room at the hospital the next morning, mainly because Jonica wasn't there. All that was left of her was her board and her tubes. My God, I thought, what happened? Dead of complications and we weren't even there.

Barrie and Alice Amber were there, however, and if they'd witnessed the last moments, they seemed remarkably composed. "Well, if it isn't the Doublemint Twins," Barrie said, and then she and her mother went back to discussing a truly earth-shattering subject, "Ethel Mermans" and how to get rid of them. An "Ethel Merman," just in case you don't know, is show biz for that flabby skin that hangs down from the upper part of your arms when you stretch them out while hitting a high note. Alice Amber had them pretty bad.

"I live in mortal fear they're going to stop calling them Ethel Mermans and start calling them Alice Ambers," she said.

"No, they'll probably start calling that stuff on your thighs Alice Ambers," Barrie said.

"Cracks like that I don't need, young lady," Alice Amber said.

I broke in. "Where's Jonica?"

"X-ray," Barrie said. "Purely routine. You know, there was this article in *California Magazine* about this doctor in Artesia or somewhere who was arrested for performing this operation where they actually removed the fat—"

"What issue?" demanded Alice Amber.

Clearly, we were being snubbed. And clearly I had no time for this bullcrap. "Come on, Vernon," I said and we strode from the room.

Because we had a big problem staring us in the face. We'd started talking about it last night and ever since then it kept getting bigger and bigger.

Today was Wednesday. *Should the old lady go to her poetry class?* Pro: it would get her out of the house so I could get in the trunk without risking a heart seizure.

Con: so much could go wrong. Howard Kesselbaum might notice her deterioration (unless of course he's suddenly become deaf, dumb, and blind—then he wouldn't notice a thing). He would probably come over to the house with a team of social workers, have me and Vernon arrested, deport Guadalupe, place Warren in a foster home . . . No, it was just too risky.

"When the van comes we'll tell them she's sick," I said.

"Then how do you get in the trunk?"

How indeed? We had to get the old lady out of the house.

"I've got it!" I shouted. "We'll—you'll—take her to visit Jonica!"

Vernon looked at me like I had taken leave of my senses. "Jonica will *freak out.*"

I saw his point. "Then take her someplace else. Take her anywhere. Take her shopping."

We decided after some discussion that Vernon would take her on a drive through Griffith Park, Los Feliz, and Glendale. Just a casual outing, so she could look at the trees, etc. We were so engrossed in planning the details—like the signal he was to give when he got back—that the station wagon parked in the driveway didn't really register at first. For some reason I thought they were delivering the new phone books. A note in my last phone bill said this would be happening soon, so I'd been sort of half expecting it. Then I saw two middle-aged women standing alongside, watching us drive up. Not only did they not look like phone book deliverers, but I immediately sensed—don't ask me how—that in some way they made their living off the elderly. They just had that air.

At once I saw the whole picture. "Are you from the Adelaide Home?" I asked out the window, my mind furiously rearranging things.

"The where?" said the taller of the two, an Eleanor Roosevelt look-alike.

"The Adelaide Home in Santa Barbara."

"Why, no. We're from the Senior Citizens' Center down on Las Palmas."

That threw me completely. "But ... you're so early. And Mrs. Kinney can't go today. She's sick."

"She is?" said the other woman. "Why, we just said hello and she looks *fine*. Walking and everything. She looks better than she has in *months*. Are you the granddaughter's husband?"

"No, *that's* the granddaughter's husband." I pointed at Vernon, who had left the car and was slinking into the house. "I'm the tenant in the pool house."

"The professor!" they both exclaimed. "We hope you'll come to the poetry reading."

My eyes went to the back of the station wagon. I saw a coffee urn, a stack of folding chairs, and some other meeting-type paraphernalia.

"What poetry reading?"

Eleanor Roosevelt explained that since this was the last class, they were going to have a little celebration, a recital as it were, and all of the seniors were going to read from their work. "We were going to have it down at the center, in the multipurpose room, but then Mrs. Kinney graciously offered us the use of her home."

"When did she do this?"

"Oh, a couple of weeks ago."

"Well, a couple of *days* ago she was taken ill—"

At this moment the old lady all but skipped out of the house, looking so chipper I was afraid she might start attempting acrobatic routines. Was it my imagination or had she put on a special outfit for the occasion—turquoise Capri pants that hung grotesquely on her emaciated figure and a sleeveless orange blouse that showed off an extremely withered pair of Ethel Mermans. The women squealed and ran over to her, asking after her health, the implication being that I was spreading nasty rumors. She replied in ringing tones that she was "fine and dandy" and I decided it was a good time to disappear into the pool house.

I called the main house and told Vernon what was going on. We adjusted the plans to the old lady's going on her outing *after* the poetry reading. Then I peered out the window at the preparations. Eleanor Roosevelt and her friend were making Guadalupe unload the chairs, while the two of them ran in and out of the house looking for electrical outlets. The old lady pranced around getting in everybody's way. They would drag her off and plunk her down in a folding chair and beg her to stay put. She'd promise she would; then the second their backs were turned she'd jump up and set off.

After a while there was a knock on my door. It was Eleanor Roosevelt.

"I don't want to bother you ..." she began apologetically.

"Yes?"

"But I'm worried about Mrs. Kinney."

"Oh?" I said, playing it very cool.

"She just offered me ten dollars to drive her to Washington."

"I told you she's not well."

The woman looked back at the old lady, who was beginning to dismantle the coffee urn. "Bea!" she yelled. "Stop her!" She looked at me, her face a mask of indecision. "Maybe we should go back to the center." She took a step and then stopped. "But everyone knows to come here. We gave them maps."

"Can I make a suggestion?"

She looked at me hoping against hope that I would make the decision for her. Which is exactly what I did. "Go ahead and have it here," I said, for a vision had just come to me in a blinding flash of light: a large group of impartial visitors seeing firsthand the old lady was incompetent, liable to rant and rave, with delusions of persecution ... "In fact, do you need any help?"

"Do we need any help!" she exclaimed. "What do you know about microphones?"

"Microphones? How many people are coming to this, anyway?"
She did some calculations in her head. "Fifty or sixty, not counting staff. But you know seniors. They just don't project."

So the next half hour we ran around like beavers, sweeping up the terrace and hooking up extension cords. Another station wagon arrived with more chairs. We arranged them in a semicircle facing the kitchen table, which Vernon and I dragged out and Bea and Eleanor Roosevelt draped with a paper tablecloth that had "Party Time!" written all over it, plus pictures of tooting whistles and popping champagne corks.

Eleanor Roosevelt eyed the tablecloth nervously. "Do you think it's too much?" she asked.

I thought it was the ugliest thing I'd ever seen. "Why do you need a tablecloth?" I asked.

She hesitated a second. "Because some of the ladies will be wearing skirts."

"So?" I said, dummy that I am.

She cleared her throat. "They'll be sitting facing the audience."

Of course! By all means a tablecloth. "I think this tablecloth is fine," I said. Then a gust of wind blew up the front of the tablecloth. If any ladies in skirts had been sitting there it would have been one of the biggest gross-outs of all time. "Scotch tape!" I said and ran off to get some. We also anchored down the top with potted geraniums, just to be on the safe side.

We were just about finished around one thirty when some of the more mobile seniors began to arrive in their own cars. These they parked all over the driveway until I put Vernon in charge of traffic control, a job he loved. Fifteen minutes later a yellow school bus pulled up and dislodged a braying contingent of the shaky-legged elderly, all of them wanting to know where the nearest bathroom was. And just after that the invalid coach arrived, driven today by a slight, wispy-haired man in ill-fitting mustard-colored slacks. Eleanor Roosevelt dragged me over to meet him. It was Howard Kesselbaum.

He was everything you hate in a poet. Frog-eyed, ill-coordinated, arrogant, with arms and legs as skinny as toothpicks, and brown teeth, no doubt from smoking all those Camels while waiting for the muse to strike. "Is the press here yet?" he kept demanding. "What press?" I asked. He named some handout sheet I'd seen stacked by the door of the supermarket under a sign that said "Help Yourself." "Is Channel Eleven coming? Who set up those chairs? Where do you expect the TV cameras to go? Who put those flowers on the table? Get rid of them, get rid of them."

Who needs this? Vernon and I said to each other, so we headed for the kitchen of the big house and helped ourselves to the tacos Howard Kesselbaum had brought. Tacos! That's how in touch he was with the elderly. Have you ever watched an old person trying to eat a taco? They'd have an easier time landing a DC-10. And this was somebody who works at a senior citizen center!

About ten after two, after much testing of the mike and several false starts during which the hard-of-hearing were tactfully told to shut up, the program got under way. Howard Kesselbaum, hands in his pockets and leaning so close to the mike he looked like he was going to start sipping water from it, made a speech about himself and how successful his program was and why its funding shouldn't be cut off even though the city was totally broke and laying off policemen. I don't know what his theory was, maybe that now the old people could write poems about what it's like to get mugged. At any rate, this met with enthusiastic applause. Then he introduced some Chinaman from the Mayor's Office who presented him with a plaque and then he thanked Mrs. Kinney for the use of her lovely home. The crowd looked around, murmuring their approval, but no doubt thinking, *this* is a lovely home? And poor Mrs. Kinney. She was sitting in the front row looking like *her* funding had just been cut off.

"And now," Howard Kesselbaum said dramatically, like he had Frank Sinatra waiting in the wings, "the *real* reason we are here this afternoon—to honor the indomitable spirit of what the Navajos call *kiowani*—the Wisdom of Age."

First up was the baby of the group, Miriam Feit, a sixty-year-old harridan with flaming red locks. She had this angry aura about her, like her car had just been towed. I could see why she was the old lady's arch nemesis. She strode up to the table and stared out at the crowd. "I don't write pretty poems," she warned, peering out over the top of her glasses.

"Good for you," Vernon said, under his breath.

She clasped the edge of the table and began to read.

> *A plague on this era!*
> *The ERA unpassed.*
> *And why?*
> *An age-old tale*
> *From fear.*
> *Because we're stronger*
> *So they say we should not go to war.*
> *Because we're smarter*
> *So they say we should not share their jobs.*
> *Because inside each of us there is*
> *A flame their sperm can never quench.*
> *I see graffiti on the men's room wall.*
> *It is not poetry; it is rape of my soul.*

"She's right," Vernon said. "It's not poetry." We had retired to the kitchen with a six-pack and were listening through the open window.

Vernon was in one of his life-of-the-party moods, and I must say it took me all of ten seconds to descend right down to his level. There was something about Vernon that brought out the fifth-grader in me. I found everything he did hilarious. He made obscene comments about the old women. One particularly ancient crone teetered by the window. "How much, baby?" he called out. Then he got some shredded lettuce and smeared it with taco sauce and stuffed it up his nostrils. He looked at me completely straight-faced and said, "Frankly, Doctor, I'm a little worried." I guess you had to be there, but I laughed till I was lying on the floor.

I think we both realized we were having too much fun for this particular occasion. I did, anyway. My stomach hurt from laughing and I was suddenly feeling very uneasy about something. I guess Vernon did too, for he finally articulated it. "I guess you know what you should be doing right now," he said, almost apologetically, like he didn't want to bring up a sore subject. Of course he was right. The old lady was sitting outside surrounded by a bunch of elderly poets. From the sound of things she looked like she was going to be there for a long time. Vernon was here to guard the bottom of the stairs. It was the perfect opportunity and I was fighting it every inch of the way. Talk about self-destructive behavior.

"I don't know," I said. "Maybe we should stick to plan B."

"Plan B?"

"The outing."

"Oh. Well," he said, unconvinced. "You're the boss."

Like the hippies say, we were crashing. After a depressing period of absolute silence little Warren crawled into the room. He headed for Vernon, shrieking with laughter, and Vernon tickled him and blew air into his ears. But the more Warren had spasms of ecstasy, the sadder Vernon became. Finally he stopped.

"Fuck her," he said.

I looked at him. "Barrie?"

"Barrie," he snorted. "Garbagewoman." He put Warren down on the floor and crawled over to the garbage pail at the end of the counter. He pressed down the pedal and the lid flew up. "Barrie?" he said. "You in there?" Then he leaned back against the stove.

"I was referring to my wife."

"Jonica?"

"You got it, Sherlock." He sneezed violently. I think it was the taco sauce. "Why is she pulling this stunt? Divorce—gimme a break, man." He flexed his bicep. "Look at this. Pure muscle. She thinks she's gonna do better than this? That junior porker?"

I remained very quiet.

"We're talking pounds here, man," he went on and then paused. "I know Jonica too well. There's something else going on."

"Like what?" I could barely get the words out.

He moved closer. "You know what I think?"

"What?"

"I think Garbagewoman has some Garbageman lined up for Miss Piggy. Some little Garbagefart. You know what I mean?"

I nodded my head. "That's entirely possible." Meanwhile I am dying inside.

"But you know what else?" he said, opening another beer.

"There is going to be no divorcio. No divorcio whatsoever. Dig?"

"Vernon," I said. "Nobody wants a divorce. You don't want a divorce and in all honesty I don't think Jonica wants a divorce. So let's just not think of divorce. Okay?"

Vernon burped. "Okay."

"No divorce, right?"

"No divorce."

"Good." I had to get out of there. I was getting so nervous. "Now, you're right. I'm just sitting here wasting time. I'm going to go upstairs and look in the trunk. Right?"

"Right. Look in that fucking trunk."

"And you'll stand guard down here, right?"

"Right."

"Okay. Here I go. I'm going up to look in the trunk."

I got to my feet.

The old lady's bedroom was cool and dark and quiet. Way off in the background I could hear the drone of some old man reading his poem about the Holocaust; at this distance, through all those walls, it could have been a million miles away.

I looked at the trunk but I didn't feel very jubilant. All I felt was a little drunk and a little sick. Here it was. The moment I had been fantasizing about ever since the Reed fellowship was announced. And all I wanted to do was get it over with.

I've always been a pessimist. I always expect the worst. That way, any little crumbs that are thrown your way are pure gravy. So I told myself, Elliot, that trunk is probably full of junk. Junk that has nothing to do with Harding. You are dealing, my man (I sound like Vernon), with a crazy old lady. You have probably just wasted two months of your life. So cut your losses. Open the trunk, be disappointed, then go out and get drunk (or should I say drunker) with Vernon, find out all about Lisa Kemp, then head back east. It is not the end of the world. So what if the trunk is full of canceled checks or old clothes or broken pottery. Things like this happen all the time.

I opened the drawer to the night table and got the key. I walked over to the trunk and put it in the lock. It turned easily. I undid the latch and pulled the lid open.

"Shit," I said out loud.

The trunk was crammed with stuff. Good stuff. I sat there on my haunches for a moment just staring at it. My emotions did a 180-degree turn. Jesus Christ. I could see black leather diaries, old photo albums, piles of postcards tied with ribbons, a jewel box, letters jammed in all over the place.

And that was just the top layer. I didn't know where to start.

So I started at the beginning. Some latent curatorial instinct took hold of me and I very carefully removed each item and examined it. When I had figured out what it was, I put it on the floor next to the trunk in strict order, so that I would know how to put it back.

God, the things I found. In ten seconds I knew this was a major historical find. In twenty seconds I knew it was not just major but unique: the complete record of the relationship of a President and his mistress. Incredible, mind-boggling things passed through my hands: a picture of Harding spoon-feeding Blanche Marie (everyone had assumed that Harding had never even *met* his daughter), a letter from Florence Harding to Rebekah warning her to keep away from her husband "or else I fear for your safety," Harding's childhood stamp collection, Blanche Marie's report cards, Harding's cuff links, his expired passport, letters he'd received from celebrities that Rebekah must have filched—and some strange stuff like a shaving brush, a pair of pajamas, and even some underwear, all initialed "W.G.H."

But where were the letters, the ones from Harding? There were letters from everybody under the sun (including from Rebekah's mother rebuking her for combing her hair in church), but there I was, almost at the bottom, with nothing but a few noncommittal postcards. I was beginning to get panicky. There *had* to be letters.

Then, under the pajamas and underwear, I found them. They were scattered all over the bottom of the trunk about two inches deep. Some were written on US Senate stationery, some on White House stationery. They were in longhand, either in fountain pen or pencil, and very easy to read. They went on and on. Some were longer than forty pages.

I read one, then another, then a third.

No wonder she kept them under lock and key.

They were filthy.

They were also worth a million dollars.

The first one I picked up was all about somebody named Howard Hardwick and how much he missed "Becky," and then some extremely complex and lengthy statistical data having to do with his size, weight, etc., that made absolutely no sense until I realized "Howard Hardwick" was not a person at all but Harding's nickname for a certain part of his anatomy. In the second letter, he "celebrates" Rebekah's body for thirty pages, fifteen above the waist and fifteen below, but in the third letter it was Howard Hardwick again, this time making some interesting comparisons between himself and a certain donkey that had apparently been quite famous back in Marion—

I heard the door creak open. I looked up. It was the old lady.

She was all alone and she was clinging on to the doorknob, stooped over and staring at me.

I jumped up. I opened my mouth but my throat was paralyzed.

"You . . ." she began in this growl that came from deep down in her throat. "You . . . skunk!" The way she said it was like she was calling me the most obscene name in the world. It was the most terrifying sound I ever heard. She let go of the doorknob and came toward me, her eyes bulging with hatred. Her gnarled hand lashed out at me and grabbed the letter I was holding. She tried to pull it away from me. Her strength was unbelievable.

In a second I realized what a ridiculous position I was in—engaged in a tug-of-war with an eighty-four-year-old woman. So I let go. Too late I realized that though my motives were the best, this was a horrible mistake. She had no warning and it threw her off balance. She took a step backwards, waving her arms in circles. I grabbed for her but it was too late. Her feet shot up in the air and the back of her head came down on the open drawer of the night table. The lamp fell off. She landed on the floor next to the bed.

I was perfectly calm. "There has been an accident," I kept saying to myself over and over. For some reason I stepped around her and pushed the drawer back in. Then I started throwing stuff back in the trunk—just dumping it in. I was so conscious of her lying there. I didn't know if she was dead or unconscious or what. I couldn't tell—I had never seen anybody dead before. Her eyes were almost but not quite closed and her mouth was open.

I've got to get a doctor, I thought. Maybe they have one downstairs.

Then I heard a voice call out "Mrs. Kinney!" It sounded like it was just down the hall and it sounded like it was Howard Kesselbaum. I looked around. Everything was back in the trunk except for the letter she was clutching. I bent over and tried to pull it away from her, but it was still gripped tight in her hand. I would have had to pry her fingers apart to get it.

"Mrs. Kinney?" the voice called out again. It *was* Howard Kesselbaum, and he was getting closer.

What happened next makes no rational sense and I can't explain why I did it. Very calmly I walked through the connecting door into Jonica's room. I went over to the French doors, out on to the balcony, and down the wooden stairway—the same one I had fallen through with the garbage. Then I walked over to the garage and got into my car.

I drove very carefully down the driveway, for the poetry reading was just getting out and there were old people everywhere. I headed down Beachwood and got on the Hollywood Freeway at Gower. It wasn't till Normandie that I got my first attack of panic. But it was bad. Waves of nausea hit me. I thought I might have to pull over to the side. Then all of a sudden I was downtown. I saw a sign for the Santa Ana Freeway and drove straight across three lanes to get on it. I thought it would take me to San Diego, that's how far gone I was. But of course it didn't, it headed east, and so I found myself heading east.

When I was six years old my Aunty Kitty and my Uncle Arn went to Palm Springs for a vacation and sent me a postcard. Since this was the very first postcard I ever received in my life it was a major event. I showed it to everybody. I am afraid that I became somewhat of a bore about it. I took it to regular Show and Tell and then took it to Sunday school Show and Tell (supposedly reserved for religious artifacts like Life of Jesus coloring books, but we had a lenient teacher who let me display it anyway). In fact I think I even slept with it for about six months.

My mother bought me a postcard album since she assumed that I might want to add to my collection. Collection, phooey. I had no time for such nonsense. It was *this* postcard I was obsessed with.

Now wait till you hear what was on this postcard. It showed a large, low-slung desert home, set amid cacti and backed by boulder-strewn mountains. You couldn't see too much of the house, though I wore out my eyes trying; from the vantage point where the picture was taken, it looked like something a not-very-well-to-do Latin American dictator might be buried in. But what we were looking at, the legend across the bottom informed us in early-fifties cursive script, was—are you ready—"The Palm Springs Home of Alice Amber." To lend authenticity to this claim, up in the upper left-hand corner, in a circular black and white insert, was Alice Amber herself, making one of her famous faces, the one with the crossed eyes and the puffed cheeks.

Time marched on. After the initial interest wore off I kept the postcard in an Almond Roca tin; then we moved to a larger home in a slightly better neighborhood and it became misplaced. By this time its importance had diminished considerably, and to be perfectly honest, I had not thought about that postcard in twenty years. Until that evening as I sped past Palm Springs on the freeway around 6 p.m. I was on my way to Orlando, Florida, to begin a new life. I remember reading in an in-flight magazine about how Orlando was an enormous boom town thanks to Disney World, and I figured I would try to get a job as a night clerk in some motel. Why a night clerk? I wondered as I stopped for gas in a town named Banning. Simple, I realized with a shudder. Whenever anybody gets arrested after a manhunt for some bizarre crime, it always says in the paper, "Schmertz had been working as a night clerk at a local motel." Either that or a hospital orderly.

I had exactly $27 in my pocket and a MasterCard. My clothes, thank God, were fresh that morning.

Only when I saw signs for Arizona did I start having second thoughts. Not for a minute did I really think they would have road blocks up. But then, on the other hand, if they were going to have road blocks up anywhere they would have them at the state line.

So I got off the freeway and drove across a bridge and got back on the freeway heading in the opposite direction. So it was to be Palm Springs, after all. In a way I was glad to be going to a town I knew so intimately. Only one line of Aunt Kitty's message was still etched in my mind, but it was memorable and somewhat enticing. "This place is so clean," she wrote, "you could eat off the sidewalk."

Palm Springs is not only clean, it is popular. The Motel Six was full, so was its neighbor the Sage Brush Courts, and so was *its* neighbor, the much-too-opulent-for-me Sheraton Oasis (although the vending machines surrounding the swimming pool took off points). The gentleman behind the counter (no nerdy night clerk he, all decked out in gold chains and flirting with the platinum-blonde switchboard operator) for some reason took pity on me and gave me what he referred to as the "lowdown." It seems a convention of former FBI agents was in town (I clutched the counter to keep from keeling over) and space was "real tight." If I was "seriously" interested in finding a place to stay tonight I had better head down the highway for Desert Hot Springs, a less stylish community. I had heard about Desert Hot Springs. It's always on the TV weather for setting heat records.

I headed down the highway.

Desert Hot Springs was so small I drove right through it, mistaking the three or four blocks of supermarkets and gas stations for outskirts. So I turned around and drove back. I found myself strangely attracted to a red neon sign that said DR POMERANCE'S HEALTH RESORT. The real attraction was that it also said VACANCY. Something about it looked affordable. Also, I couldn't picture it booking too many FBI conventions. So I followed a neon arrow down a sand and gravel road to another neon sign that said OFFICE. After banging on the door for five minutes or so, I managed to arouse a stocky woman with a foreign accent. She told me she was the masseuse, and yes, they did have a vacancy, and even better still, they took Master-Card.

Dr. Pomerance's Health Resort was my home for the next five days. They were without a doubt the worst five days of my entire life. I lost ten pounds. I don't remember too much, which is probably just as well, just random events with long stretches of oblivion in between. I know I must have been doing *something*, but I have no idea what. Curious: the first couple of days I couldn't sleep a wink. The last couple of days all I could do was sleep.

This much I remember: I spent a great deal of time and energy pumping coins into the pay phone in the breezeway between the Social Hall and the Dining Room (where they served only vegetarian stuff like papaya—I had diarrhea the whole time). I called the trailer at regular intervals, but Vernon was never there. I also called the big house at 9 a.m. and then again at 6 and 11 p.m., figuring that was when Vernon was most likely to be there if he was going to be there at all. For the first two days no one answered, which puzzled me greatly, then Guadalupe began to answer, then *Barrie*! Of course I always hung up right after they said hello.

After the 9 a.m. calls I would drive into Palm Springs and buy the LA *Times*. Clean sidewalks aside, it was *not* my kind of town. Everybody played golf and lived in condominium complexes. These condominium complexes looked like Swedish prisons. I would drive back to Dr. Pomerance's, and in the privacy of my room (a concrete cubicle—when I first walked in I thought, Gee, what's that rag doing on the floor, the maid must have left it behind—then I realized it was the *rug*), I would go over every column inch twice. At 4 p.m. I would repeat this process with the *Herald Examiner*. God, did I get sick of newsprint.

Checking out the papers twice a day to see if you're wanted for murder while holed up at some dump in the desert and forced to eat papaya because it comes with the room can be a pretty bleak existence, and Dr. Pomerance's Health Resort was the perfect place to make your depression complete. A collection of little cinder-block buildings scattered over several acres of sand, dotted here and there with dead and dusty plants—I heard a rumor around the pool that the place was originally built during World War II to detain Japs. Concrete sidewalks raised about eight inches off the ground connected one building with another but since they took such circuitous routes they were pretty much ignored by the guests, which meant that the lizards took them for sunning and pushups. Why on earth do lizards do pushups?

I asked this question of the masseuse in an attempt to ingratiate myself and maybe get a blanket out of her, for though it was 110° during the day and I had prickly heat, at night it got so chilly I had to take down the shower curtain and drape it over the bed. She looked at me and said, "Because it builds up the muscles. Hah, hah, hah!" and collapsed in hysteria.

That's when it dawned on me that this woman, whom Dr. Pomerance had put in charge not only of blankets but of extra towels *and* making sure that nobody made off with a second glass of orange juice at the help-yourself continental breakfast, was seriously out of touch with reality. Her perception of the place was that it was a hangout for airline stewardesses who came here to lose weight. *My* perception of the place (perhaps, I'll admit, colored by my own personal predicament) was that the dozen or so off-season guests were all Wanted (or *not* wanted) somewhere else.

I spent a lot of time thinking of ways out. Like suicide. Or a little talk with the DA. Or continuing on to Orlando. Or Corpus Christi, another town that has always struck my fancy. But I rejected them all. *How could I do anything when I didn't even know what was going on?*

One night it got so bad I turned to drugs. The couple next door, a beer-bellied, earringed electrician for Twentieth Century Fox and his Oriental girlfriend, invited me over for some "dynamite hash" and after two tokes their laid-back small talk took on all the aspects of a police grilling. "Where do you live?" and "How long have you been here?" threw me into such a panic that I excused myself and fled back to my room to lie down. But instead of getting better, things got worse. In fact, for the first time, it seems, the total and complete horror of my situation became clear. Just look at the case against me: I had rented the pool house under false pretenses (which proved premeditation), I had hired an accomplice with a bad reputation (conspiracy), what I had been doing when the old lady walked in could easily be interpreted as burglary, and—well, they had a pretty good case for first-degree murder. The trial flashed through my mind. Eve in the witness stand, trying her best to defend me but so badgered by Vincent Bugliosi that she finally bursts into tears. And then the *real* witness for the prosecution, Jonica, testifying from a stretcher, bringing tears to the eyes of the predominantly black and Chicano jury ...

One good laugh I must tell you about, though, definitely the high point of my incarceration. The morning after the drug trip, a little shaky but vastly relieved to wake up in a less paranoid frame of mind, I decided to venture out to Dr. Pomerance's highly touted therapy pool. Because of its name, at first I actually thought this was some sort of "hot tub" where you would be forced to "rap" with fellow guests about emotional problems. But it turned out that the therapy involved was entirely muscular, so I decided to give it a try.

The therapy pool was like a tiny little swimming pool, maybe eight feet square, with a switch that activated a Jacuzzi-like whirlpool effect. The water temperature was about 2,000° and all sorts of warnings were posted about how long you could stay in without risking heart damage (these I read *very* carefully). Two girls were already in the pool, both around twenty or so, and they seemed to be halfheartedly working on a term paper. Every once in a while there was talk about negative models but most of the conversation was a critique of somebody named Didi Barbieri's dating habits, plus information about Didi's relationship with her mother, plus a rehash of what sounded like a famous story about how Didi once did the limbo at a party down in La Jolla while wearing a skirt with no panties.

I had brought out sections of the Sunday paper to keep me company. Now even though I had, of course, gone over the paper in the greatest detail, the Home section I had more or less ignored since I couldn't see mysterious deaths and/or obituaries being reported therein. So you can imagine my surprise when I came across a very long and very elaborate article, with many pictures, of the Green-Gals' party. I must admit I was vain enough to rattle the paper rather noticeably as I read it, hoping one of the term-paper writers would glance over my shoulder and say, "Gee, what a glamorous party," which of course would allow me to give her a bored yawn and say, "Well, I was there and it wasn't so hot."

Any thoughts of bored yawns were quickly stifled, though, when a name caught my eye like a magnet. Time stood still while I read the following:

Eve Biersdorf was justifiably proud of husband Pete's sensitive oil entitled *Winter's Work*. The maverick producer, who made millions with *Don't Shoot, I'm Polish* and even more with *Horace, Morris and Me*, couldn't be there himself. "He's in Munich," Eve reports, getting his next project off the ground, a biopic of Leni Riefenstahl, pioneer filmmaker and (some say) Hitler's mistress.

Any news on casting? "We're talking to Vanessa Redgrave. She's very interested."

Eve is not a painter herself, but she remains one of the busiest girls in town. She is currently collaborating on a biography of Warren Harding and future plans include a book on her favorite subject, Hollywood itself. "I know where all the bodies are buried."

Any tidbits to toss our way? we ask and come up with a real scoop: the famous Donna of those radio commercials you love to hate is none other than Carrie Shostack, actress-daughter of the legendary Alice Amber, now confined to a rest home near Montecito. Let's hope life has another chapter in store for this gallant lady.

Nikki Dantine looked stunning in a Madame Grès which she swore was ten years old . . .

I read it over and over till I had it memorized. It was so brilliant. So many subtle, damning fine points. Like the use of the word "confined," Or "Carrie"—I could see Barrie tearing half her hair out over that alone. My favorite part of course was the rest home. How wonderfully inaccurate. How cunning of Eve's pill-warped little mind to throw that in.

Kudos, Mrs. Biersdorf. You made my day.

But you didn't solve my problem. By the time the fifth day rolled around, I thought I had an answer. I would get on a plane for Pittsburgh and throw myself on the mercy of my parents. I spent a lot of time thinking about this. Every offspring is entitled to one major fuckup. There was my sister's divorce. Actually, her divorce was no problem, it was the marriage. Then there was my brother's motorcycle accident in which he lost a toe.

This would be mine. I was getting so slaphappy by this time it was starting to sound funny. I could just see my folks reel off the major crises of their life together: Susie's divorce. Billy's accident. Elliot's murder rap.

Before I called the airline, though, I called the trailer one more time. Vernon answered.

I was so surprised I forgot what I was going to say.

"Vernon?"

"Hey, it's my man." He sounded like he'd been fast asleep. Now, up until this time I had been planning to murder him. But suddenly, hearing his voice, all was forgiven. I just *knew* from the tone of it that somehow everything was okay.

"You missed all the excitement," he went on. "Where are you, New York?"

"No, I'm in Palm Springs."

"Palm Springs? Where in Palm Springs?"

"Never mind, tell me what happened."

He paused and then exhaled. "The old lady's dead."

"I know. I . . . saw her."

"I thought so," he said and laughed. "Don't worry, the doctor thinks she slipped on the rug. They don't know you beaned her."

"*Vernon*—"

"So what happened, man?"

"*What happened*? You tell me what happened, you jerk-off."

He laughed again. "Sorry about that. I had to take a leak."

There was a pause. I stared out at the therapy pool. A hippie was sitting on the edge, dangling his feet in the water and eating Doritos out of the bag.

"It was an accident, Vernon."

"I never thought otherwise. I swear."

Another pause. Then a question I had to ask, clearly and concisely.

"Am I in any trouble?"

"You're not in any trouble."

"Are you sure?"

"Positive."

"Does anyone even *think* I had anything to do with it?"

A pause. "No, I don't think so."

"What do you mean, you don't think so? Aren't you sure?"

"I'm sure, I'm sure. I cross my heart and hope to die. I swear on a stack of Bibles. Okay?"

"You really mean it? This is very important, Vernon."

He got serious. "I really mean it, Elliot. I was just teasing."

"You promise?"

"I promise."

I felt my knees go weak with relief. What other loose ends?

"What about the funeral?" I asked.

"Howard Whosis sort of took charge of things. They had it at the Methodist Church down on Highland. Warren got to ride in the limo. You should have seen him. He was so excited. I think we got a junior rock star on our hands, man."

"What about Jonica?"

"She's okay. She's still in the hospital. She cried. She cried a lot more 'cause you weren't there. What's this mad passion she has for you, man?"

I tried to ignore this. "So how are you?"

"Me? I'm doing fine. Catching up on my sleep."

"You want to have dinner?"

"Sure."

"I mean tonight."

"Tonight? Why not? I think I can fit it into my busy social schedule."

"Oh, and Vernon?"

"Yeah?"

"What happened to the papers?"

"Papers? You mean all that stuff in the trunk?"

"Yes."

"Oh, it's just sitting there."

I drove back to LA, heading right into the setting sun, breaking all existing speed records, trying to get used to the idea that soon I was going to be rich and famous.

I pulled into the driveway at five past seven and parked around back. The house looked the same, but the vibes were so different—it was like a grammar school during summer vacation. All the mystery and terror were gone. It was just a great big house, sitting there empty. I couldn't believe I had ever been threatened by it.

Loud mariachi music came from the open kitchen windows, for there was no one to care any longer what Guadalupe did; indeed, she answered the door wearing shorts, and then proudly showed me her plane ticket home, on a flight, according to the ticket envelope, with "complimentary French wines" no less. If my arrival surprised her she didn't show it; I sensed that she was long past caring what the crazy Americans were up to (if indeed she had ever cared). After showing polite interest in how clean she was leaving the kitchen for the new owners, I hurried upstairs, my heart beating faster and faster. I had to see for myself.

The old lady's bed had been stripped, and the lamp and night table were gone, but the trunk stood exactly where I had left it five days before. *The key, where is the key?* I thought for an awful moment, but the trunk was unlocked and when I pushed back the lid I could tell that no one had disturbed it. Everything was jumbled around just the way I had tossed it in; the only thing unaccounted for was the letter Mrs. Kinney had grabbed from me and who knows where that had ended up.

It didn't matter. There was plenty left, more than enough. My mind played with the phrases the press would use to describe my discovery. Words like "extensive." No, that wasn't right. "Shocking." It certainly was shocking, but that didn't really begin to convey—how about "mindboggling"? Yes, "mindboggling." Definitely "mindboggling." But would the *New York Times* use a word like "mindboggling" in a headline? Somehow I couldn't see it. "Surprising," maybe. That's about as excited as the *Times* ever gets. Of course they would have to put it on the front page. It would be one of those articles on the bottom half of the front page, with a three-column headline and a picture. Would they use my picture or Harding's? Probably Harding's. Unless I had a real good picture they could use. Wait! How about a picture of me sitting *underneath* a picture of Harding? Like his official White House portrait! Or I could be *holding* a picture of Harding. No, that wasn't right, that's what they do with mothers of POWs. One thing was certain—I was going to invest in a *very expensive* haircut before this picture was taken. No

Peter Pan Barber Shop for me. The *Harvard Magazine* was another problem. I'd give them an interview but first I was going to make them really *beg*—

Footsteps down the hall intruded into this reverie. I jumped to my feet and scanned the room for some innocuous task to be caught performing, but there was nothing, absolutely nothing, so when Vernon walked in, Warren on his hip, he found me doing an indecisive dance behind the trunk.

"Aha!" he said. "Caught in the act."

Strangely, a week of family and funereal business had put some color in his cheeks. In fact, I'd never seen him look better. He was wearing a pair of cutoffs—that's all, just a pair of cutoffs -and he seemed huskier than I remembered. Still and all, he didn't seem particularly glad to see me. Indifferent is the way I'd sum up his mood.

He scowled at the trunk. "What's in there, anyway?"

How could I describe it? Where should I start? He had to know sooner or later.

"And what makes you think Jonica'll let you have it?"

Later, I decided. I'll explain later. But I did say, "Jonica already said I could have it."

"You have a deal with her?"

"Sort of."

He put Warren down and pulled a pack of cigarettes from his hip pocket.

"Is it valuable?"

"You might say that."

He lit a cigarette. "Fuck," he said, exhaling. "Everybody's cashing in on this shit but me." He took another drag. "So I guess you're not gonna pay me. I don't blame you. I sure wouldn't."

"Vernon, is that what you're worried about? Of course I'm going to pay you. In fact I'm going to give you a bonus."

Poor Vernon. Poor, poor Vernon. With my sudden success came a rush of self-confidence—if I could solve my own problems I could certainly solve his, too. What he needed was a man-to-man talk. First step was forget the fancy restaurant I'd been planning. That would only make him feel uncomfortable. Plus he'd look sort of silly at Ma Maison without a shirt on. No, we'd have dinner at the pool house. I had some steaks in the freezer, I seemed to remember, plus Pam's duty-free liquor—I had everything.

The pool house looked like it had just hosted a fraternity party. If there had been a chandelier you would have expected to see underwear hanging from it, it was that bad. Vernon confessed that he had been making the place his own during my absence. "I didn't think you were ever coming back," he explained.

"No problem," I said, stooping over to pick up beer cans.

"You want me to make the bed?"

"Please," I said. Then I looked at the bed. "And could you put on some clean sheets?"

Vernon, never the cook, had inflicted less damage in the kitchen. In no time at all I had a pitcher of margaritas ready, plus some impromptu hors d'oeuvres. We proceeded to get quietly looped watching wrestling on Channel 9 and waiting for the steaks to defrost.

What's going to become of Vernon? I wondered, watching somebody named Relampago Leon pummel Hussein the Butcher with his fists. He kept making mistakes, wrong choices. He was talented, he was certainly presentable once you got him cleaned up, and I was starting to get the feeling that he was very ambitious. An unbeatable combination. Why on earth was he living in a trailer in Torrance?

I went to check on the steaks.

We ate on the floor. I admit the meat was a little on the tough side. Not that Vernon seemed to mind—the booze and the wrestling had put him in a much better mood. Any sort of televised sporting event worked wonders with him. "Way to go!" he kept shouting at the screen. And as for me—well, I can't remember feeling more euphoric. My mind was literally dancing around in my head.

The talk was easy and spontaneous. Our lives—believe it or not, since they were so dissimilar—were full of odd coincidences. We were both eldest sons, with one brother and one sister apiece, we were both born on the twenty-third of the month (he in July, me in

February), and we had both shared a penchant for acting, though I had long ago given up my dreams along those lines. Vernon was still young—a "babe in the woods," I kept chiding him—and his goal was a heady one and youthfully idealistic: performing Shakespeare in some park for scale. In the meantime, though, he indicated he might settle for rock superstardom under the name Brad Stevens. He hated his name. He said it made him sound like a plumber.

"What nationality is Fetchko, anyway?" I asked.

Vernon wasn't sure but guessed it might be Irish.

When it came to wooing the world, Vernon had much to learn. I found myself giving him advice. We discussed his wardrobe and made a date to do some shopping. I suggested that a pair of Topsiders would make a good purchase since they went well with jeans and might wean him away from those awful sneakers that added so little distinction (I had seen his only other pair of shoes; they were black and had *high heels*, after that repellent fashion that has mercifully faded, except among newly arrived Greek waiters and others of that ilk). Vernon accepted my recommendations avidly; it occurred to me that he probably thought I was in some way "cool," and it was only when we got to his accent that I sensed I had gone too far. His accent was like Jonica's weight—you just don't discuss it. It embarrassed him too much. So I asked him to sing one of his songs for me. He found his guitar and sang a ballad called "Brenda, I Love You." I found it full of promise and told him so.

This was not the banter, the male camaraderie, we had always engaged in before. This was more serious and profound. We began to exchange confidences. I told him about my breakup with Pam; it was the first time I had discussed it with anyone, and though I was rather wooly and sentimental about the whole thing, we both agreed it was probably for the best.

The margaritas were gone. We shared a joint. It was getting very late and the pool house was very quiet.

"Vernon," I began and he looked at me. "What's going to happen to you?"

He thought about this for a long time. He seemed to know what I was talking about. "I don't know," he said at last. "I really don't know. Sometimes I fear the worst."

I passed him the joint. "How about you and Jonica?"

He thought about this too. "Remember what I said about no divorce?"

"Yes."

"Well, forget it."

"Oh?"

"After what I've been through this week, man. Garbagewoman. Garbagewoman's mother. Fuck 'em. Fuck 'em all."

I took the last drag of the joint. "I think you're making the right decision."

"I *know* I'm making the right decision. They are fucked up."

I agreed. "There is something sick going on there."

Vernon closed his eyes and leaned his head against the wall.

"Where's the dope?"

"I just put it out."

He laughed. "The dope's over in Palms." He got up and began to wander around the room. He came to a box, one of the ones I still hadn't unpacked, and began to rummage through it. "You got any good tapes?"

"I don't have tapes. I have records."

"You should get tapes. They're the wave of the future."

He went over to the window. "Why me, Lord?" he said, looking out into the night. "It's all so fucking complicated."

"Only if you make it complicated."

"Fuck you, you don't understand."

"Come on, Vernon, don't be like that."

He sighed and kept staring out of the window. "This sure is some view you got here," he said after a while. I couldn't tell if he was being serious or sarcastic.

"Yeah, it's terrific," I said, dismissing the view. Let's be frank: all those twinkling lights made me nervous. Now my view in New York—the back of an apartment building with all sorts of interesting tenants coming and going at all hours—*that* was a view.

Vernon finally turned around. "Any suggestions, Doctor?"

What happened next is very strange. For perhaps the first time in my life I made a totally magnanimous gesture. Out of the blue, yet. God knows what prompted it—guilt, pity, you name it. Maybe it was just because I liked Vernon.

"Come to New York," I said.

"Get serious."

"I am serious."

Vernon turned around and looked at me. "Sure you are."

"Vernon, I am dead serious. Why not?"

"Why?"

"Because you'd love it. It's New York. It's the city that never sleeps." I began to sing. "'You'll want to be part of it, New York, New York.'" I couldn't remember the rest of the words. "Vernon. New York is *it*. LA is a big hick town compared to New York. It's got everything. It's got *life*. You see things there you never *see* here. You see reality. You see couples fighting in the streets, hitting each other—"

Vernon made a face. "I'm going to move there to watch couples hit each other?"

"Not just that. Vernon, I'm talking about the capital of the world."

Vernon was being obstreperous, but I could tell he was interested. There was that gleam in his eye.

"Where would I stay?"

"You could stay with me. I've got plenty of room. I have a whole extra bedroom. That could be entirely yours. We could put the TV in there, I never watch it. I have a stereo, I have a fully equipped kitchen, there are washing machines in the basement, I have every modern convenience."

Vernon started to pace. "But what would I *do*?"

"Exactly what you do here. Only you'd do it right. Because I'd be standing over you, making you. You'd write your songs, you'd get acting jobs. I *know* people, Vernon. I know the creative director of Grey Advertising, I know people in the arts, shit, I know *Beverly Sills*."

He tried to place the name.

"I'll make a deal with you. You can stay with me for three months, rent free, meals included, *plus* I'll give you a little spending money if you need it."

He knit his brows.

"Now *that* is an offer you can't refuse," I prodded.

He scratched his cheek. "Do I have to do the cleaning?"

I raised my eyebrows and looked around the mess of the pool house. "Surely you jest."

"What happens after three months?"

"Who knows? I plan to be rich and famous. How about you?"

I washed the dishes. Vernon dried. What was New York like? he wanted to know. He had a million questions. What about the crime rate? What about the subways? Did I live near Macy's? He had a friend in high school who went to New York once and came back with all sorts of tales about Macy's. "He said the men's department had miles of shirts. As far as the eye could see." And my apartment building? What was it like? Did it have a pool?

The dishes were done and it was after two, but Vernon and I were so wired we smoked some more dope. I showed him some Morris dancing steps, the easier ones, and he picked them up in no time. He can join my Morris dancing group, I thought. "I wanna dance, dance, dance," Vernon said, so he went back to the main house and got Warren out of his crib. He came back and put on the jazz station in Compton. He clutched Warren, who was sound asleep, to his chest, and the two of them danced around the pool house in the dark. "We do all this all the time," he said, and I lay on the bed, floating in space, watching them in the green light from the stereo till I finally dozed off. I guess Vernon finally dozed off too, because when Barrie walked in the next morning she found three of us—me, Vernon, and little Warren—sound asleep on top of the bed.

She was looking for a Magic Marker, I found out later.

I woke up and saw her eyes fixed on the bed. Not on anything in particular, just on the bed. As if she were uncertain of exactly what to focus on.

God knows the possibilities were an embarrassment of riches.

First there was me, groggily sitting up on my elbows one second and then suddenly more awake than I had ever been in my entire life the next. Then there was Vernon, still snoring in his cutoffs, hugging a pillow, one knee against his chest. And little Warren, flat on his back with his mouth open, stretched out between us.

The radio was still on. Very softly.

"Barrie," I said.

She glowered at me. "Well, look who's back."

I swatted a hand in the direction of Vernon's shoulder. "Wake up, Vernon. Barrie's here."

He opened his eyes. "Huh?" he mumbled, looking around and sniffling.

Barrie's gaze began to travel around the bed. "Looks very cozy," she said. Then she turned her head and shouted out over her shoulder, "Hey, guys, look what I found!"

The thought of further company propelled me into action. I jumped off the bed, tugging at my slacks, stuffing my shirt back in, plastering down my hair. I looked around for my watch. It was nowhere in sight but that was the least of my worries. Get out of this room, I kept telling myself. Just get out of this room.

"Jesus," Vernon was saying as he sat up yawning. Little Warren looked like he was dead.

As I stumbled past Barrie, holding the door open with a smirk on her face, I saw to my horror who the "guys" were, the two people I least wanted to see again in my entire life: Number One, Alice Amber, caught in the act of squatting to arrange a small cluster of kitchen appliances, and Number Two, *Jonica*!

She was seated on the low stone wall, looking very stiff, pale, and uncomfortable. She was wearing a pair of pink overalls I don't think I'd ever seen before, and what appeared at first glance to be a particularly ugly turtleneck dickie. At second glance it appeared to be what it really was—a neck brace.

But the thing was, she wasn't fat any more! She must have lost thirty pounds. She looked like a different person. You could see *bones.* She'd crossed the line from "fat" to "voluptuous." I may be exaggerating a little for the sake of effect, but believe me, she looked great.

Not that I had that much time to feast my eyes, however.

"You!" Alice Amber shrieked. "I have a bone to pick with you!" She began to march toward me, still raving. "How did that article get in the paper? What other lies have you told Eve Biersdorf? Do you realize what you've put me through?"

"She's talking to her lawyer," Barrie said.

"And you almost got *her* fired," Alice Amber said, waving a charm-braceleted hand toward her daughter.

"They almost canceled my Donna contract," Barrie chimed in.

For several more minutes I was forced to endure this torture. I defended myself not a whit, just letting them get it off their chests. And get it off they did—I heard in great detail how I had ruined reputations, how job offers had been withdrawn, how multi-million-dollar lawsuits were being mounted by the top legal talent in Beverly Hills.

"And Bruce Pinsky tells me I can win this one," Alice Amber said triumphantly. "They damaged my ability to make a living."

"Your *right* to make a living," Barrie corrected her.

In a way, I was glad of the hysteria that greeted my appearance since its intensity totally overshadowed the possible embarrassments that being discovered in such a circumstance might cause. By now Vernon was up, wandering around with little Warren, who had begun to scream at the top of his lungs. At the sight of her child in distress, Jonica rose awkwardly and began to cross the terrace toward him, moving as stiffly as if she were being conveyed on a handcart.

"Don't pick him up!" Barrie yelled at her.

For a split second I thought she was referring to me.

"Remember what the doctor said—nothing heavier than a sponge."

"I know, I know," Jonica said, patting the baby's hair while he still clung to Vernon's neck, terrified from all the screaming and yelling going on.

"Hi, Jonica," Vernon said.

"Hi."

"Hi, Jonica," I said.

"Hi."

"You look great," I said.

"Va va va voom," Vernon said.

"You know what you're looking at?" Alice Amber asked. "You are looking at a medical miracle!"

Jonica blushed.

"And this time she's going to keep it off," Alice Amber went on. "Right? Aren't you going to keep it off this time?"

Jonica was forced to admit that she was, indeed, going to keep it off this time.

A strange scraping sound mercifully brought an end to this excruciating moment, and we all turned a little too eagerly to see Guadalupe dragging a couch out the front door. Only then did I pause to wonder why the terrace, the front lawn, the top of the driveway— every available space—was strewn with clothes and furniture and bric-a-brac.

"We're having a garage sale," Alice Amber announced rather grandly.

"*Estate* sale," Barrie corrected her—and, as if to prove her point, a middle-aged couple in shorts appeared at the top of the drive, bug-eyed at the spread in front of them.

"No early birds!" Barrie screeched and ran over to shoo them out the gate.

"These early birds," lamented Alice Amber, nervously watching Barrie argue with the woman, who was wearing a coolie hat and insisted they had driven all the way from Bellflower.

"Just a peek," the woman begged to no avail.

There is nothing like a flock of early birds at your gate to put on the pressure. Any bones to be picked were temporarily set aside as Barrie and her mother sprang into action—pricing difficult items, shouting instructions at Guadalupe, setting up Howard Kesselbaum's coffee urn behind a sign demanding a quarter a cup.

I, watching this, am going nuts. Knowing that is only a matter of seconds before I am assigned some chore, and realizing I am in a situation that is going to require some heavy emotional negotiating, I suggest to Jonica that we get some breakfast.

"Where?" she asks in a tone that gives away nothing.

I rack my brain for her favorite restaurant.

"Tiny Naylor's."

We get into my car, not an easy task for her, and as I turn the ignition, Vernon appears at my window, wild-eyed, like one of those people trying to escape the ghouls in *Night of the Living Dead*.

"You ain't leaving me here," he says, lunging at the door handle. What could I do? Punch the button? I had to let him in.

Tiny Naylor's looked pristine in the early morning light, like it had just been hosed down. The asphalt in the parking lot was still wet, so I guess it had. We walked in single file and sat down at a table for four. But the sun was in Jonica's eyes, so we moved to a semicircular booth. I sat in the middle.

"Where is everybody?" Vernon said.

The only other customers were three French tourists. They were poring over a map and grimacing every time they took a sip of coffee.

"Ugh, Frogs," I said.

A mini-skirted waitress arrived with menus. These we studied with exaggerated care.

Vernon turned to me. "You treating?"

"Yes, I'm treating."

"Can I have huevos rancheros?"

"Vernon, you can have anything you want."

"Okay, I'll have huevos rancheros," he told the waitress.

I ordered the eggs Benedict even though I'd had them here before and they weren't very good—powdered Hollandaise.*

"Just coffee," Jonica said.

"Are you sure that's all you want?"

She looked at me. I think it was the first time she had looked me in the eye all morning. "Yes, I'm sure," she said.

After the waitress left, there was a long silence. Finally Vernon said, "I gotta go to the bathroom."

"Vernon, you always have to go to the bathroom," I said, and immediately wished I hadn't. He slid out of the booth. I watched him disappear toward the back of the restaurant.

After a moment I looked at Jonica. She was watching the traffic out on Sunset. I played with my key chain. Then I realized it was the one from the GreenGals' party, so I stuffed it in my pocket. I very badly wanted to brush my teeth.

Suddenly Jonica spoke: "Why didn't you come visit me?"

I looked at her, trying to gauge her mood.

"I'm sorry," I said.

"You just disappeared. Just like that. Can you imagine how I felt? Can you imagine lying there and having you disappear? Can you imagine it?"

"I can imagine it. And I apologize."

"Apologize," she muttered.

---

* If current contract negotiations go through, I will soon be the author of (in addition, of course, to this volume) *The Presidential Cookbook* (working title), which collects the favorite recipes of our Presidents, past and present. Here is one of John Kennedy's favorites, Blender Hollandaise, which in addition to being easier to prepare, is slightly richer, since the eggs don't "cook."

BLENDER HOLLANDAISE

1 stick butter	Melt butter. Put other ingredients in blender.
3 egg yolks	Turn on "High' and pour in butter while motor
2 tbsp. lemon	is running. Once all butter is poured, turn off.
½ tsp. salt	Sauce is ready.
Pinch cayenne	

"Yes, apologize," I said, taking the offensive, which I should have realized from the beginning was the only way to deal with Jonica. "Don't you know that if there was any way I *could* have been there I *would* have been there? Don't you realize the reason I wasn't there had nothing to do with you? Look at me, goddamn it! Now, I *wasn't* there because of *business*. It had absolutely nothing to do with you. I wasn't *avoiding* you. I was not trying to *hurt your feelings*. Now, I'm sorry and I apologize. Okay?"

She was silent for about ten seconds. Then she turned to me, a little shyly. "Business?"

"Yes, business. I happen to lead a very complicated life, Jonica. More complicated than you could imagine."

"Oh," she said. "I knew it was something. I knew you just wouldn't run off." She began to talk faster. "At first I thought it was because you didn't like hospitals. I can understand that. Even Barrie said it was starting to drive her bananas. Just coming in every day like that and staring at a dummy." She laughed. "I knew it was *something*."

I smiled. The waitress brought our coffee. "I knew it was something," Jonica said again. Then she leaned toward me. "Elliot . . ."

"What?"

She seemed unable to put her words together. Here it comes, I thought. Finally, after much sighing, she took my hand and said, "You're still my honey, right?"

I looked away from her, over toward the waitress. She was squeezing oranges for the orange juice.

"Right?"

I cleared my throat. "Jonica . . ."

"What?" She was frozen, motionless.

I'm fucking this up, I thought. I'm fucking this up. My mind was blank. I couldn't think of anything to say.

"Elliot?"

The French people were examining Sweet 'n Low packets, trying to figure out what they were. I guess they don't have those in France, I thought. No wonder they lost the war. No wonder . . .

I saw Vernon coming back from the men's room. I pulled my hand away from Jonica's. She followed my gaze. We both stared at Vernon. He was doing the strangest thing imaginable. He was waving his hands in the air.

"No towels in the bathroom," he said and sat down.

On the way home from this ill-advised breakfast, we saw the first sign. It was tacked on to a palm tree near La Brea and that fact alone made me worry. No sane person would advertise a garage sale in Hollywood this far west.

The first sign was followed by a second, and then by a third, and then by a regular progression. They were the unmistakable handiwork of Barrie. In Day-Glo colors they proclaimed THE ESTATE SALE OF THE CENTURY!!!! For her theme she chose those signs one sees along the highway, counting down the miles to some alligator farm or comparably disgusting extravaganza. As we entered the hills, the signs started to get even cuter, saying things like ALMOST THERE, FOLKS!!! and I feel reasonably certain that there was one a block past the house reading WHOOPS! YOU PASSED IT!!

The signs produced little amusement in my automobile, however. Jonica sat huddled as near to me as circumstances would permit, shooting me pathetic glances I pretended not to catch. Vernon, in the back, was totally unaware of all this emotional turmoil. He babbled away about how he once sunburned the soles of his feet while he had them up on a railing watching a sunset in Panama City, Florida.

By the time we pulled up in front of the house, one thing was clear: Barrie's advertising campaign was a runaway success. Casino Drive was littered with haphazardly parked cars, from which were disembarking what Vernon very aptly referred to as "a whole shitload of people": hordes of anxious bargain hunters who were all but trampling over each other in their efforts to get to the top of the driveway first. Since it was impossible to maneuver the Mustang through this sea of humanity, we were forced to park some distance away and walk—and walk very slowly, it turned out, for Jonica had to stop every ten feet or so to lean against a fender and catch her breath. Vernon, damn him, ran on ahead.

A few people—early birds, no doubt—were already bucking the tide and coming down the driveway with their purchases. The lady in the coolie hat marched by, clutching a hibachi on which rested a pair of maracas and a spice rack. Gee, some people will buy anything, I thought. Then my blood froze. There, being carted away by two shrill young men in tight-fitting pants, were my bamboo chairs. Jesus Christ. *What else might that moron Barrie have offered for sale?*

"Come on, Jonica," I said, grabbing her elbow to hurry her along. She gamely obeyed, trying to cover up the grimace that crossed her face each time she set down her left foot.

Now, I have been to garage sales in my day, but nothing in my past experience quite prepared me for the sight at the top of the driveway. Spread out on the law, the terrace, the pool area, spread out *everywhere*, were what looked like the entire contents of the big house *and* the pool house. And pawing through this half acre of dreck was a frenzied crowd that was obviously bent on some serious shopping. Squeals filled the air. A line had already formed at the folding card table where Barrie sat behind a cashbox. Needless to say, she was in heaven.

"Jonica," I hissed, wanting to kick her in the ankle. "If they've sold anything of mine—"

Then I saw the trunk. I stared at it dumbly for a moment. What on earth was it doing out here—*My God. They're selling the trunk.*

I flung down Jonica's elbow with a jolt that made her scream and dashed through the crowd to the head of the pool, right behind the frog. There was not only the trunk, there was the entire *contents* of the trunk rationed out into little piles, more or less according to theme: a pile of books and the old lady's diaries, a pile of postcards, a pile of clothes …

I searched frantically for a pile of letters. There wasn't one.

I widened the search, going through nearby stacks of junk. Nothing.

I looked at Jonica with murder in my eyes. She had hobbled over to the card table where Barrie had already put her to work bagging purchases. She was wrapping some stemware in newspaper and not daring to look my way.

I sat down on top of the trunk. There must be *something* I could do. Anything. A newspaper advertisement: "Will the person who purchased..." All my ideas were straws in the wind. I felt tears welling up.

Why me? Why did I have such incredibly bad luck? How come the *only* thing missing from the trunk was the one thing I wanted most? Everything else was still there. Why? Why? Was I such an awful person?

That's when I got the idea of looking *inside* the trunk, where, of course, the letters lay scattered all over the bottom, exactly as I had left them.

Relief flowed over me in dizzying waves. I clutched the frog and then sat down on the ground, as I was feeling rather unsteady. But that was just the beginning: relief turned to bliss as the beauty of the situation I was in became stunningly clear. I could *buy* the letters! Then I'd be the rightful owner. Fuck Jonica! I didn't need her any more. The idiot's just dug her own grave.

I waited for my heart to glide back down from its rapturous heights and then walked over to the card table. Barrie and Jonica watched my progress wordlessly.

"How much for that trunk?" I asked Barrie evenly.

"Oh, *take* the trunk!" Jonica pleaded. "Just take it!"

"No, I want to *buy* it," I shot back at her.

"I didn't think you were coming back." She began to cry.

"How much for the trunk?" I repeated to Barrie.

"Oh, just *give* it to him," Jonica sobbed.

A Syrian-looking man ran up excitedly, lugging the old lady's TV. "How much, how much?" he kept saying.

"One hundred dollars," Barrie told him.

"Aiee," he cried, and deposited it very gingerly on the ground. We watched him retreat. I turned to Barrie.

"Now, how much for the trunk?"

She looked at me with a malicious grin. "Sorry, Charley."

"I beg your pardon?"

"You're too late."

"Too late for what?"

"The trunk's been sold."

I gripped the table. "To whom?"

"Him," Barrie said, pointing to a figure bending over to examine a clothes hamper.

Okay, I thought, I'll just go over and buy it from that man. I'll offer him double what he paid. I'll say it was sold by mistake. I'll say it belonged to my grandmother and has great sentimental value. I'll— the figure looked at me as I approached. It was Howard Kesselbaum.

"Holy shit," he said, not a very poetic remark. "Where the hell have you been?"

"Out of town," I stuttered.

Alice wants to have a little talk with you.

"Alice! Now he calls her Alice! What else had happened while I was away?"

"It's all settled," I lied, casting about for some way to get to the point. "Listen, I heard you bought that trunk."

"What?"

"That old trunk," I said, pointing. "With the junk in it."

"Oh, is there anything in it? I didn't even look."

"Just some junk," I said desperately.

"Hey, maybe it's worth something." His eyes lit up and he set out for the trunk. I followed behind, barely able to control my hysteria.

He opened the lid and peered inside. "Shit," he said. He picked up a letter, made a face at it, and threw it disgustedly back. Then he wiped his fingers on his shirt. "I don't even know why I bought this damn thing. How am I going to get it in the car?"

"Hell," I said. "I'll take it off your hands for you—if you really want."

He appeared not to have heard my offer.

"Reaganomics," he muttered, looking around and shaking his

head. "Look at them. It's outrageous." Next to us a young mother was threatening to "smack" her child unless the tot replaced a stuffed koala bear I had once seen adorn Jonica's bed.

"Like I said, I'll be glad to take it off your hands."

"Huh?"

"What did you pay for the trunk?"

He thought about this. "Twenty bucks."

I felt this highly unlikely, but I said, "I'll give you twenty-five."

He looked down at the trunk and tilted his head. "Gee ..."

"Thirty."

He began making tsk-tsk sounds. "What was it Melville said about a trunk? Or was it ... Wallace Stevens? ... Something about—"

"Forty dollars."

"Sold."

He balked somewhat at taking a check, but I sensed this was merely perfunctory. After all, God knows how much he was making on the deal. Besides, the check would provide me with a receipt during any future legal actions. And, just to be on the safe side, I wrote in "Trunk and Contents" (*very* clearly) where it said "Memo."

As soon as Howard Kesselbaum ambled off, whistling to himself and stashing the check in his wallet, I set to work reclaiming the rest of the stuff. Fortunately for me, Harding's underwear had been moving slowly; in fact, *all* the memorabilia seemed to be intact (save for the enameled vanity-table set—Harding's first gift to Rebekah—which I have reason to believe Barrie filched).

We negotiated at the card table. I got her down to $17. Then I located Vernon, who was eyeing the TV, and made him help me carry the trunk into the big house. Taking it to the pool house was impossible—a steady stream of shoppers was traipsing in and out, sent there by Barrie to try on clothes and test small electrical appliances.

Of Jonica there was no sight.

Inside, with the curtains down and the bare floors broom-swept by Guadalupe, the house seemed mercifully cool and quiet. So quiet, in fact, that it reminded me of nothing so much as a sunny, spacious tomb. I peeked into the living room. It was almost unrecognizable. All the furniture was gone, save for a lone chair over by the fireplace, its back toward us.

Almost home, I kept thinking.

Then the sound of someone singing "That's Entertainment" tinctured the air. Vernon and I looked at each other, our brows knit. In a moment Alice Amber appeared in the doorway that led back to the kitchen, a Sony Walkman over her ears and a glass of Scotch in one hand. She was barefoot.

"Keep the front door closed," she snapped as she waddled past us. "I'm sick of signing those fucking autographs." And with that she proceeded into the living room, where she arranged herself in the chair, adjusting her earphones, took a sip, and turned the volume up. One of her fingers began to move like a little metronome to the music that only she could hear. "*The plot may be hot, simply teeming with sex—*" she crooned in a tone that indicated this drink was not the first of the day.

"Maybe we should take the trunk upstairs," I said.

Now that my triumph was more or less complete, I was slightly more conscious of my surroundings again. With any luck I would be back in New York tomorrow. I would carry the letters myself, of course—in fact, I would never again let those letters out of my sight until they were safely locked up in some bank vault. I felt reasonably certain they had special climate-controlled vaults for such valuables. As for the trunk and the rest of the loot, I could send that home via Federal Express or some other reliable thing.

"Vernon, do you know anything about Federal Express?"

He looked at me from the old lady's bed, where he lay engrossed in a *National Geographic*.

"Federal what?"

I sighed. "Never mind."

He returned to the article, his lips moving ever so slightly. It was about supertankers. I know because he read me some captions aloud.

That's what was keeping me from feeling totally euphoric—Vernon. What on earth was I going to do with Vernon? Did he really think he was going to New York with me? What in the world was I going to do with him in the city? Take him to cocktail parties? Openings at the Met?

"Vernon?"

"What?" he said, a little sharply. I sensed that he had arrived at a particularly interesting photograph.

"Never mind," I said.

He reached down the front of his cutoffs and began to scratch himself. I thought, that's going to go over great at the Russian Tea Room. Of course, we could always just hang out on 42nd Street, playing video games and waiting for the Andes plane crash movie to come back to town.

No, Vernon had to go. Breaking the news to him wouldn't be easy. I'd have to figure out the right way. Offer him some appeasement. He could come for a visit maybe. In February. Or I could get Eve to get him a job. Or I could get him a present—

—Like the old lady's TV!

"Vernon?"

"W*hat*?"

"Stay here and watch the trunk for a minute, okay?"

"Okay."

"Promise me you won't leave it alone?"

"I promise."

"You don't have to go to the bathroom or anything?"

He pointedly ignored this last remark.

The TV was still there, thank God, the victim of Barrie's erratic pricing policies. She watched with a smug expression as I wrote out the check.

"Buying a present for your boy friend?"

I looked her in the eye. "What's that supposed to mean?"

She reached for the check. "Don't you want to know where Jonica is?"

I grabbed the TV. "No."

It was heavier than it looked and I had a little trouble getting it through the front door. As I lugged it into the entrance hall, I looked up to see Vernon descending the stairs.

"Vernon!" I started to scream but the look on his face made me stop. There was definitely some panic there.

"It's Jonica," he said, a little breathlessly. "She's like totally freaking out."

"What do you mean?"

"I don't know. All I did was tell her how you were taking me to New York with you—"

"*Vernon!*"

I all but threw the TV down on the floor and took the stairs three at a time. When I got to the top, I noticed a funny smell, something familiar that I couldn't place. Then I could.

It was Jonica's polyurethane.

I ran down the hall and into the bedroom. Jonica was standing behind the open trunk, holding a yellow can. The last long gooey strands of polyurethane were dripping down.

Maybe it hasn't gotten down to the letters yet, I thought. Maybe there's something I could do.

"Jonica," I said as calmly as I could. "What are you doing?"

Her face was contorted. "You fairy!"

"Jonica . . ."

"Barrie warned me about you, you sick person! But I didn't believe her. Well, now I know!"

She flung down the can and grabbed a book of matches resting on a stool next to her.

"Jonica," I said soothingly, for I realized my one and only hope in God's world was to distract her, divert her attention, talk her down. "Oh, *that*. We can talk about that later. The thing is, now why are you doing this?"

"Why am I doing this?" she screamed. "I'm doing this because I happen to believe in God!"

And with that she lit the match. As I lunged toward her, she dropped it in the trunk. There followed a small explosion which took off my eyebrows and left these sort of uninteresting scars on both my hands.

It was quite a morning. By the time the fire department arrived, most of the second floor was in flames and a certain foreign element among the crowd was using the opportunity to loot, causing Barrie to become hysterical and even involved in some violent skirmishes. Guadalupe, with a fierce determination I'd never seen before, made a fireman go to rescue her plane ticket. He couldn't find it, but he did find Alice Amber, very drunk, sitting in the living room with her earphones on and wondering where all that smoke was coming from.

Her entrance, or exit, was something to see. What the hell, I had nothing else to look at.

Thursday Eve drove me out to the airport. It had turned smoggy again, and LA was its usual bumper-to-bumper madhouse. And Eve was her usual talkative self, even more so, maybe because I was so silent. Couldn't I stay another two days? Pete would be back from Munich, contracts in hand, and he would love to meet me.

No, I couldn't.

Oh, and had she told me? The GreenGals had called and asked her to join.

I offered my congratulations.

"I'm sorry about that abominable misquote," she said, looking in the rearview mirror while trying to change lanes. "That Jody Jacobs. She gets everything wrong. She's notorious."

I told her it didn't matter. "Just let me off in front of TWA," I said. But she insisted on putting the car in the parking lot and walking me over.

I checked in.

"Well," Eve said when we got to Security. "I guess this is it."

"Yes, this is it."

She gave me a hug. "What rotten stinking goddamn luck you had."

"Yep."

"Keep in touch, Elliot. I mean it. Hi to your folks."

I kissed her cheek and walked through the metal detector.

Naturally we sat on the plane for an hour and a half before it took off. So long they even passed out free drinks.

"Guess who's up in first class," the woman sitting next to me said after she polished off a Bloody Mary.

"Who?"

"Florence Henderson."

"Oh."

"The stewardess said she has a club date in Massachusetts."

"I see."

"She's real short."

"That's what I've heard."

The woman sucked on an ice cube. "Were you here for a vacation?"

I thought about this. "Business and pleasure."

Her eyes lit up. "Did you make it to the Farmer's Market?"

"I missed the Farmer's Market."

"Marineland?"

"I missed that too."

"Well, don't miss it the next time you're here. It's better than Disneyland." Pause. "You did go to Disneyland?"

"This is very embarrassing, but I didn't go to Disneyland."

She laughed. "I know, Palm Springs."

"You're right, I did go to Palm Springs."

"I missed Palm Springs. I hear it's very chi-chi."

"Very."

The plane took off. We flew directly over the ocean, then turned around and headed east, flying more or less directly above Olympic

Boulevard. I looked out the window and found the Hollywood sign. Underneath it was a tiny black smudge where the house had been. I stared at it for a long time till it disappeared under the wing and I couldn't see it any more.

ROBERT PLUNKET was born in Greenville, Texas in 1945 but raised in Havana and Mexico City. After college he moved to New York and embarked on a successful career as a waiter and office temp, then moved to Sarasota, Florida where he became Mr. Chatterbox, the gossip columnist for *Sarasota Magazine*. Plunket is also the author of the novel *Love Junkie*. He has written for many publications including *Healthy Aging, This Week in Ft. Myers Beach,* and *Sandbars and Sonnets: The Southwest Florida Poetry Review*. He is currently retired and lives in a trailer park in Englewood, FL, where he enjoys collecting old quilts and raising succulents from scratch.

Photograph by Hannah Phillips